W9-CBT-996

DISCARD

Community Library of DeWitt & Jamesville
5110 Jamesville Road
DeWitt, NY 13078

Joe R. Lansdale

This special signed edition is limited to 2500 numbered copies.

This is copy ___2447___.

Fishing
for
Dinosaurs
and Other Stories

Fishing
for
Dinosaurs
and Other Stories

by Joe R. Lansdale

SUBTERRANEAN PRESS 2020

Community Library of DeWitt & Jamesville

Fishing for Dinosaurs and Other Stories
Copyright © 2020 By Bizarre Hands, LLC.
All rights reserved.

Dust jacket illustration
Copyright © 2020 by Timothy Truman.
All rights reserved.

Interior design
Copyright © 2020 by Desert Isle Design, LLC.
All rights reserved.

See page 381 for individual story copyrights.

First Edition

ISBN
978-1-59606-993-0

Subterranean Press
PO Box 190106
Burton, MI 48519

subterraneanpress.com

Manufactured in the United States of America

Table of Contents

Fishing for Stories

BY JOE R. LANSDALE

IT'S NO SECRET that I like to write a variety of stories in a variety of genres, and my favorite of those is the Lansdale genre.

And here you have stories that fit that exactly.

They lean in one direction or another, but their method of attack has what I think of as the Lansdale variation. That is really unimportant in the long run. What is important is that the stories are stories I wanted to write and I hope they engage and entertain you as much as they did me.

Being the sort of writer who does this can be a blessing and a curse. I've experienced a bit of both. One thing is publishers are trying so hard to produce and manufacture a sure hit, it's sometimes difficult to explain that I write what I have to write. Sometimes I know if something is leaning in one direction or another, and sometimes I don't. If I probe my brain too much to see what I plan to do, it's likely the story will die, or become an empty shell.

These days, I try to have stories going that I can turn to and already know that they lean in one direction or another, even if only my subconscious knows where things are going in the end. If I talk about it, write about it, before it's a true story, then I may let all the steam out of my subconscious and it will evaporate like the morning mist when the sun comes up.

These stories are favorites of mine. I have a lot of favorites. But some stand out more for me than others. These are among them. I'm going to discuss them a little, which I can do now that they are finished, but not in a manner that will spoil them for you. I hate the trend these days to tell you the story before you read it. Also, I'm discussing them as I think of them, not in the order they appear in the book.

"Fishing for Dinosaurs" was a surprising Bram Stoker Award recipient. I didn't think of it as horror at all, but more as science fiction or fantasy, and again, Lansdaleian. It is a kind of throwback, and at the same time something modern.

It has many influences. H. Rider Haggard, Edgar Rice Burroughs, Keith Laumer, Jules Verne, H. G. Wells, all manner of adventure writers, as well as stories and characters from the pulps. And then there's me.

When I was a child, my earliest story loves were comics, and then science fiction, fantasy stories, and horror. The furniture of those genres still excites me, and I try to shift them around with more modern attitudes when I have the chance. With this one, I had that chance.

"Black Hat Jack" comes from my love of Westerns and history, both in books and film. I became a Western fan through my dad, who loved Western films. That led me to books and stories about the Old West, and to the history of the Old West.

"Black Hat Jack" was written as my wife and I were driving out to visit George R. R. Martin for an event at his theater, the Jean Cocteau. I forget which event. We went by Adobe Walls on the way out. I had read about the events there, many times, and when I saw the place, I was even more taken with the idea of writing a story about it. I had already started one, in fact. I had several pages on it. Seeing where it had actually taken place was a real inspiration. As we traveled, stopped for the night at motels, I wrote on my laptop, and in the hotel in Santa Fe, which is the city where the Jean Cocteau operates.

I had wanted to write about a character loosely based on Nat Love for years. He was a black cowboy who wrote an autobiography that is as much Dime Novel as it is autobiography. It is a real hoot, and you can see the truth between the Dime Novel events.

Black cowboys, soldiers, marshals, were far more prominent in the West than most people think, due to white washing, literally, of their history in Western films and novels. There were exceptions in the film and novel vein, but they were rare. That's changing. Black Hat Jack is one of the changes.

This was the third time I had written about Nat. I had written two short stories about him, and this novella, before I wrote what I had been wanting to write for years, the novel, *Paradise Sky*, my personal favorite of my novel work to date.

"Black Hat Jack" came fast. I polished it on the way home, and it was very quickly ready to go to Bill Schafer and Subterranean Press.

I'm proud of it. I think it's fun, and though my story is fiction, it does show a lot of the historical elements of the Adobe Walls fight, which is most famous for Billy Dixon's fantastic rifle shot. It was great fun placing Nat at this historical event.

"The Ape Man's Brother" was a love letter to Edgar Rice Burroughs and Philip José Farmer. It is both a pastiche and a commentary. I'll let you decide on what it's commenting about.

I grew up on Edgar Rice Burroughs, and when they became dated, I couldn't let go of the love, and thank goodness, Philip José Farmer was there to pick up the baton that Burroughs had dropped. He brought Burroughs and pulp influence into a modern setting with modern views, and excited me to no end.

Burroughs and Farmer were the reasons this one was written, and it is close to my heart. I have thought about a sequel, but as of yet, I have only started it. Maybe someday.

"Prisoner 489" is my idea of a fun monster story. It would make a cool film, I think. It's influenced by so many things I can't begin to point to all of them, but Frankenstein, and all those fifties monster films certainly were part of it, as well as the unstoppable killer films of the seventies and eighties. I bet E. C. Comics had a hand in it too.

Anyway, nothing profound to say about this one. Enjoy.

"Sixty-Eight Barrels on Treasure Lake" came to me slowly. I wrote part of it, stalled, and then it slowly revealed itself. I finished it on a month-long vacation my wife and I took to Japan and China. Frontier stories, Westerns, and history, as well as myth and legend are the source for this one. I think it's funny that a story about the U.S. in the Western era was written in modern China, finished in Beijing.

As I write this introduction, I am still recovering from that trip, and the astounding things we saw. The Great Wall, Terracotta Warriors, Panda bears. Forbidden City. Chinese operas, to mention a few.

I may for the first time in many years, take some actual time off and rest for a while. I sure need it.

If you're resting, I hope these novellas written over the last few years will cheer you up.

Me, I need a nap.

Introduction to "Black Hat Jack"
What Joe Lansdale Means To Me

by Robin Hobb

I ENCOUNTERED JOE Lansdale by way of his stories long before I met the writer behind them. So I can confidently say that I know him through his works rather than through personal contact. That's the best way to know any writer. Our stories are the parts of ourselves that we want to share with the world. But with an excellent writer, that sharing isn't a pared-down, packaged part created simply to entertain. Instead, readers are offered the bone-deep experiences that can only be conveyed as stories. The writer reserves no privacy, no decorum, no dignity, no false courtesy. The writer puts naked emotional truth on the page.

The Joe Lansdale I know through his stories is a true-hearted friend. He never lies to the reader. His embroideries of the truth only make the truth plainer. He can make the ridiculous sublime. He can poke fun at the most sacred of sacred cows. He doesn't always tell me, the reader, what I want to hear. He tells me hard truths, things I should hear. But somehow he manages to deliver some of those truths when I am laughing so hard that my stomach hurts. Or, as is the case with *Black Hat Jack*, his words deliver stunning sucker punches, but also knife blows so precise the reader doesn't realize how deep the blade went until days later, when some event makes those words stab again. Then he makes me stop and fully consider the ugly things I walk past every day. But amid those hard truths, he will suddenly float a phrase that makes me see that instant of beauty that can occur even during the most savage violence. "Like ink blown in the wind" and that image comes back to me not as words I read but as something I saw while my heart was pumping pure 'I'm going to die' adrenalin.

Joe Lansdale writes diversity. Not in the pre-packaged way where it sometimes feels as if the author were ticking off boxes to be sure one of everything is included. Diversity has always been the rule rather than the exception in every Lansdale story I've ever read. He doesn't shield the readers' eyes so only one sort of character or event is depicted. The full spectrum of life and humanity is in the stories, and with that, the diversity that has always existed.

Black Hat Jack is no exception.

Black Hat Jack is so many things. It's graphically violent, it's nakedly sexual, it's deeply romantic in the old sense of that word. It's a retelling of historical events, including a legendary shot that marksmen still argue about today. It's a pondering of race and violence and the degradation of others based solely on who is the Other. It's a discourse on two kinds of love, and which one might stay with you the longest.

But mostly, it's just an excellent story from a master storyteller. Enjoy.

Black Hat Jack
The True Life Adventures of Deadwood Dick, as told by His Ownself

1

BLACK HAT JACK and me had been riding at night, trying to take in the cooler weather, avoid the sunlight, but mostly avoid being seen. That was almost queered when Jack said he smelled Comanche. I had known Jack a while now, and I had learned that when he said he could smell a bear, a buffalo, a Comanche, or a groundhog fart, then he most likely could.

We got down off our horses, bit their ears and pulled at their necks and they lay down for us. It was a pretty bright night, and that fretted me some, I assure you. Them horses, some fairly tall grass, and tumbleweed and some Texas dirt, was about all that was between us and them. I took off my hat and tossed it aside so as to get smaller.

They wasn't right on us, maybe twenty-five feet away, and we could see them good, crossing in the moonlight. Must have been twenty of them. More than enough to ride down on us and lose a few, but still take us and do what they like to do to them that cross their lands. Story was they ran the Apache pretty much out of Texas, and let me tell you, if there's someone that can run an Apache, you best take heed of them.

So there we was lying down behind them horses, our teeth clamped on a horse ear, which is not tasty at all, though horses themselves are pretty good to eat if you cook them right. The horse I had on the ground was a fellow I called Satan. He wasn't the original horse I called Satan, as I had to eat him, (which is what made me an expert on the eating of horse) but this one was pretty good, black as the one I had before, and about of the same spirit, though less mischievous. He would even come when I whistled. If he was in the mood.

I'm tempted to tell you a story or two about the original Satan, but I suppose what you want to hear about is the Comanche and what happened to us. Since I'm here telling you about it, and I'm not going to talk about Satan the First, I guess there's no use telling the old joke about the frontiersman who sat down with some tenderfoots and told them about the time he got out on the trail and was surrounded by twenty Indians at each of the four directions, mean and nasty and angry and well-armed. But I'm going to tell it anyway.

They was coming down on him in a rush, and all he had was a pistol with six shots in it. He'd tell the story like that, warming it up like he was tossing a log on the fire, saying what them Indians was wearing, talking about the scalps flapping from where they hung on their horses, or on spears or such, and then he'd say how he fired all six shots, and knew he wasn't going to have time to reload. He'd pause in his story then, stop and light his pipe, or scratch his balls, or some such, and wait for the inevitable question.

"What happened?" a tenderfoot would ask.

To which the frontiersman, leaning forward in earnest, stretching out the moment, would say, "Why I got kilt, of course."

Only this night wasn't no joke. I was seeing if I could smell them Indians, but I couldn't. All I could smell was wet horse ear. I kept my teeth clamped on it without biting so hard the horse got angry and started tossing its head and trying to stand up, just firm like to suggest it might be a good idea if it laid still. Some people taught dogs to do that, jump up and grab a horse by the nose or the ear, and bring him down. That was quite a jump, but we wasn't dogs and this wasn't a joke. Them was real live Comanche braves.

Black Hat Jack

We lay there quiet and watched them ride by, wrapped in buffalo robes, scalps dangling from their bridles. Those robes were a little heavy for the June weather during the day, but at night it could get a shade nippy. I had on my heavy coat for that matter, and so did Jack, though mine was woolen and his was buckskin lined with wool. Jack also had on a hat made of buffalo hide that had fold down ear flaps. It was black as the devil's shadow and he always wore it, snow or shine, and that's how he got his name. He had been a mountain man and was now a hunter and sometime scout for the army, but though he looked the part, with beaded moccasins and such, he was always good about his grooming. He got rid of lice and fleas promptly in both hair and beard, and would bathe and soap up, wearing his red flannel long handles as he did. He liked to keep those clean too.

After the Comanche had gone on, we still laid there and didn't move. It was like we had been planted in that ground and was just waiting for a rain so we, as seeds, could burst up out of the ground, mounted and ready to ride.

After a time, Black Hat Jack let go of his horse's ear, and that horse stood right up, and Jack swung into the saddle. I did the same. We started trotting slowly in the direction we had been going, which wasn't the direction them Comanches was heading.

"That was close," I said.

"Comanches riding in a group like that are out to raid, and this is a good night for it. I got no idea where they're going, but they got plans, or hopes, or maybe they're just traveling like us. Sometimes a Comanche can seem to be doing one thing and he's doing another. In other words, I know some shit about Comanche, but I don't know all the shit there is to know about them. No one does. Not even the Comanche themselves."

I, of course, knew all this, as I wasn't exactly attending my first goat roping. I had been all about the business of Indians before, but it was good to have Jack with me. He was a man you'd want at your back you got in a fight. He even treated me good, and him a white man. Or at least whiter than me. My figure was he was some Indian, and probably some Irish or Swede, and a whole lot of horse's ass. He was a hulk, had somewhat dark skin and those hard, sharp features of an Indian. I don't even know what his last name was. I'd never asked. I always called him Jack, and some called him Black Hat Jack, and time has washed his name from history a bit, as I tell this, but there was a time when he was as well known as Liver Eat'n Johnson, Kit Carson, Jim Bridger, and Buffalo Bill. Well, maybe not as much as Buffalo Bill.

Wasn't nobody as well known as he was, except maybe Wild Bill Hickok. I had known Wild Bill some and could appreciate that he wasn't all legend and no sand. Actually, same could be said of all them I mentioned, though Buffalo Bill was the least shy among us about lying and maybe the one with the largest hole in his bag of sand, cause he used lying for more than just entertainment. He made a living out of bragging, and it made me a little jealous.

Lying was something you was supposed to do up to a point. It was the sign of a real frontiersman, someone who had been around. And I have learned myself how to do it, and I have gotten my lessons from the best, like Black Hat Jack. He could lie like a preacher, and look as sincere as a politician wanting your vote, a banker wanting your dollar, or a whore that has just told you how fine you was, even if you was the twelfth in line that day.

But at the core of it Jack was honest. Stood up for his friends, and he was a straight shot when it come to a rifle, though not as good as me with pistols, and a straight shooter with words when he wasn't yarning, and maybe as good as me there. I do stretch the truth a little, though I want to assure you I ain't doing that now. This is all the truth as it happened without any stretching of facts, though some of the facts are a little hard to remember, and therefore have to be filled in some. I don't consider a fill a stretch.

Another thing about Jack, wasn't no one knew how old he was. He carried himself like he might be forty at the top, but his wrinkled face, his thin, gray hair, marked him up at about sixty or more. That said, I never heard him complain about hard or cold ground or bad weather or shitty food, though there was one exception as he made quite a point to me that he wouldn't eat mash potatoes unless he was held down and they was shoved down his throat. I don't know what he had against mash potatoes, but the feelings didn't extend to the tater in its truer form, as he would eat those raw, or baked for that matter, certainly fried up in buffalo grease, or lard or butter, but the mash potato had somewhere along the line hurt his feelings, and he hadn't never gotten over it.

We was riding along after our close call, and then we seen something lying out on the ground. It was like a mound of light-colored dirt with sticks in it, but that wasn't what it was. When we got up on it we seen it was a man. He was naked and stretched out, tied down. It was clear the Comanche had been at him. They had probably started on him during the daylight and had worked on him most of the day. Stakes were driven in the ground at his hands and feet, and his arms and legs had been stretched out and tied off to them with rawhide. They had fastened a rawhide band around his balls, and when it shrunk the balls swelled up and burst open. Black Jack said they had used wet rawhide and let the sun dry it. I had once been wrapped up in a fresh killed cow skin, wetted down and left to dry, and not by no Indians. I had barely escaped that one, but I hadn't gotten out of that hide before the sunlight tightened it and I began to feel it squashing me like a mouse between two bricks. I was lucky that day. Some folks I knew come up on me and cut me out of it.

This fellow, he hadn't been so lucky. He had been worked over elsewhere too, had his eyes poked out and something stuck up his nose, and his mouth was wide open and full of dried blood, which my guess was from having his tongue cut out. His beard had been skinned in spots, and trips of skin had been peeled from the top of his chest all the way down to his groin. His stomach had been cut open and his guts was pulled out and placed on a fire that was burned out now and was nothing but blackened sticks. Those guts was still attached to him; they had cooked them while he was still alive, and on top of it all he had been scalped. Like I said, you didn't want to get caught out there in the wild with the Comanche, and that's the reason so many frontiersmen saved the last bullet for themselves, or for someone they cared about.

It's hard to imagine such things sitting in your house all comfortable, and the frontier having been cleared out a few years back, but that's how it was back then, and that's how you would do if you were smart; you'd use your last bullet for yourself.

"It's a buffalo hunter, I bet you," Jack said. "Comanche don't like them especially, killing off all their food for the hides. They wouldn't like them much better if they took the meat, but seeing that meat rotting out there, just the hides and maybe the tongues taken away, it sets a Comanche's teeth on edge. I ain't fond of it neither."

"Ain't we hired out to hunt buffalo?" I said.

"We are, but I'm not proud of it. Billy Dixon, who's the one told me about these herds out near Adobe Walls, said he hated doing it, but it was either leave them be and be proud of yourself, or make a dollar, and the dollar won. That cleared things up with him, but I got to tell you, more of them I've killed, more I think about it, it's getting a lot more murky to me. I ain't got nothing against them Indians, none of them, though I will admit to being less fond of the Comanche than others, but they're just doing what they need to do to survive."

"Ain't that what we're doing?"

"Reckon so, but I don't feel noble about it. Dollars I make doing this, well, son, they don't shine. I think I am one of a whole pack of worthless son-of-a-bitches, and though I like you and find you better than most, you have to be included. All us humans are fouled on both ends. One we shit out of, and the other we talk shit out of. If god was fair about things, he would have already smashed the shit out of all of us. I know I'm full of it, and I suspect you are. Thing is, just when I think I'm done with it from either end, I fill up with it all over again."

That's how Jack was. He was going to die a philosopher, not a Christian.

Black Hat Jack

We didn't have a shovel, but we used our knives to dig a grave, taking turns in case we got too deep in our work, so to speak, and not see something creeping up on us, like an Indian. The ground was hard, but we got a grave dug that could hold that dead man down under. Parts of him we found in the grass, skin and the like, we put that in there with him.

When he was packed away, wearing a coat of dirt, we got back on our horses and rode on. I had never been to Adobe Walls, which was our destination, in the north top of Texas. We was to meet up with Billy Dixon and the others Jack knew. Jack had been there before, and knew the way. Once he'd been to a place he claimed he could always go back. I was a pretty good tracker, and wasn't bad with direction, but I was beat out by a lot of others, and especially Jack. I figured you could have blindfolded him, ridden him on a horse over the Rockies, pushed him off his horse and broke his leg, and somehow he'd known the direction to crawl to get back to you and cut your throat, and he would never have to take off the blindfold.

2

We come to Adobe Walls after another day, late in the afternoon, and it wasn't much. It was some adobe walls, as its name suggested, and they was falling down, and there was one dirt street, if you could call it that, a blacksmith shop and a store, and a hole of a room with broad doors that Jack said was a saloon. All of this was surrounded by wagons, stacks of hides, plank-walled outhouses, and out a piece beyond this ruined encampment was deep buffalo wallows where those critters had rolled about tossing dust onto their hides to fight the fleas, which on a buffalo, as well as their hunters, could be considerable. Some attempt had been paid to put up some high posts for fortification, making a kind of wall of them. But the builder had gotten lazy and had quit the job, so there was plenty of open spaces. It really wasn't much protection against man nor beast.

There was a rise beyond the place, about a mile away, and there was a couple of creeks, one thick with trees of all sorts on either side of it, if you can call a West Texas tree a tree. Back where I'm from, East Texas, we call them bushes. Once Kit Carson had fought some Comanches at this place, and on the prairie near about, and got his ass handed to him, though it was called a victory by the whites and he got all kinds of commendation for it. That's the way whites worked. You slaughtered an Indian, it was a victory. They slaughtered you, it was a massacre. In this case it was mostly Kit and his men running and the Comanche chasing.

There was horses tied, and there was some grass bundled for them, for a fee, and there was grain for a bigger fee. This was all handled by the blacksmith who looked too small to shoe a horse, but he made up for that by being skinny and having a small head.

We settled in our horses and unsaddled them, got them paid up, and Jack carrying his Sharps and me my Winchester, our pistols on us, we headed into the saloon, which was next to a store we passed. Store's doors was wide open, and its shelves was visible and there was stuff on them, but all I remember seeing was cans of peaches. When we come inside the saloon it was near dark, or seemed that way at first after us being out in the strong sunlight, and the stink of all them buffalo hunters and skinners met us as we come in and gave us a greeting we wouldn't never forget. Every stinking underarm, crotch, every lice-infested head with greasy hair that had gathered up buffalo blood, every un-wiped butt, burp, fart, and assorted smells that could stick the pages of a book together, was there to say howdy. I tell you, I almost swooned, and it being dark to the eyes was making it worse, because it was like some kind of rotten giant was standing over us and we couldn't see him.

Then the cracks of light that shone through the gaps in the walls and through the windows, which had greasy oil cloth pulled down mostly over them, was clearer and seemed to grow because our eyes had gotten used to things, and we could see who was in there.

There was a bunch of men standing or sitting about in rough-built chairs, and they was festooned with pistols and knives. Rows of Sharps rifles in all calibers you could imagine was leaned up against the wall. There was a bar full of splinters from men sticking their knives into it, and it was made of planks and crates and looked as if it might tumble over with a sneeze. The place was held up with poles, and the pole in the middle looked strained and the roof, which was coated with sticks and dirt, appeared ready to tumble down on things. The center pole especially made me nervous as it was bowed a bit.

We was about six feet in when one of the men said, "Hey, now. No niggers in here."

Black Hat Jack

It was a Southern voice, and I seen him moving away from the bar then, pushing his wide-brimmed hat up a tad. He had left a Sharps rifling leaning on the ramshackle bar, but I could see he had a pistol in his belt. I had pistols too. A Colt on my left hip, and a LeMat revolver on my right. Those LeMats are pretty well forgotten now, but mine was given to me by a Mr. Loving, who was after my Pa a kind of mentor. It fires nine rounds, and if you thumb a little baffle on the trigger guard, another trigger can be worked, and that fires the under barrel load, which is a 4/10 round. It's for close up work. I was also carrying my Winchester, which has a loop cock and a baffle on it, so I can fire it just by cocking it and closing the lever. It's hard to hit anything that way, but it'll sure cause folks to jump, and if they're close enough you just might put a round through them. I say that because that's how it is with most men. Me, I can hit things with it. If it sounds like I'm bragging, forgive me. But it's true. I can shoot a shot up a gnat's ass and knock out its teeth, make them line up like piano keys in front of the little bastard's corpse.

That's a bit of an exaggeration, I admit. Gnats don't have teeth.

The man was swaggering toward me. I said, "Hello to you too, you goddamn peckerwood, shit-eating bastard."

Well now, that caused the air to thin. The other men was silent for a moment, and then a young one laughed out loud, a fellow that was probably no more than a teenager, maybe twenty if you gave him an edge, but walked and talked like a grown man. The young one said, "He knows you, Jimmy," and then the others laughed.

When the laughter died down Jack bowed up and went into a kind of monologue that caused him to sway, way a spreading adder snake will stand on its tail and swing its body above the grass, flaring its head to look scary. "You all know me, the one and only goddamn Black Hat Jack, called such on account of my hat is black and my name is Jack. Nat, standing right here black as the Ace of Spades, is my partner, and due to his shooting prowess in Deadwood, is also known as Deadwood Dick. Paint on the skin don't matter.

You lift a hand to him, I will kill you and skin you and pack you with buffalo shit, and kick you till you are alive and can stand. Then I will kill you again, and if I've got the need, I will fuck your corpse. Is that understood, you bunch of ignorant, buffalo hunting, dog-fucking, shit-sucking, dick-kissing, ass-licking excuses for grown men that ain't even dropped your balls or got hair above your peckers?"

These words hung in the air along with the stink for a while, and then the young man stepped forward, said, "Well, I think that pretty well names us, and there is plenty of buffalo shit out there, and I for one don't want to be skinned, and the thought of Jack's pecker in my ass is enough to frighten me off most anything. Hello, Nat. Step up to the bar and I'll buy your black ass one."

With that everyone laughed, including the Southerner, and he said, "Damn right. You're a friend of Jack's, you're a friend of mine, and your black skin is just as white to me as any white man's."

"Thanks," I said. "That is damn white of you."

"That's my take," he said.

There was more laughing, and me and Jack stepped up to the bar, and a jug came out and the young man who had lightened the mood, who I could now see was dressed as dapper as if he was going to a ball somewhere, his mustache waxed and his hair greased and parted down the middle, said, "Let's knock them back."

His clothes looked clean and he smelled pretty enough to live in France, or some place where the light was bright, the water was pure, and the children and women didn't ever fart.

He stuck out his hand to me, said, "Bat Masterson."

I shook his hand.

"Glad to meet you," I said. "I'm glad you had you a sense of humor."

"It has served me well. Sometimes, when nothing is going my way, I tell myself jokes. It lightens the mood. Let's have a jug, barkeep."

The cup set in front of me looked like it had been used to dip that buffalo shit Jack was talking about, but when the whisky was poured, I lifted it to my lips. Now, you got to understand I never was a man to drink liquor or beer. I always preferred sarsaparilla, which often got me some laughs and some kidding, but considering the circumstances of where I was and who I was with, and the way things had started, I thought it best to suck me a cup and seem sociable. I did that from time to time, though I can't say I ever built me a taste for whisky, and this horror from the jug was worse than anything I had ever put in my mouth. Only thing I could come close to thinking it reminded me of was once, when I didn't have no place to sleep, I slipped under a porch in Abilene and was awakened by a yellow cur pissing on my face, and right into my open mouth. This wasn't quite that tasty, but it was similar.

"What the hell is this?" Jack said, having downed a cup himself. Remember, I told you Jack wasn't a complainer, so this should give you some idea of the rankness of this libation.

"Well," Bat said. "They call it whisky, but it's only a touch of that. It is boiled with snake heads and a squirt of horse piss and some twists of already chewed tobacco by men without teeth."

"Oh, don't tell me that," I said. "You're kidding."

"Nope, he's not," another man said.

I turned to that fellow. He was a tall man with dark hair, a little beard and mustache. Like Bat, he was dressed pretty snappy as far as his type of clothes was concerned, but it was a snappy that had gone dusty and dirty, and he had the smell of skinned buffalo about him.

"Say he ain't?" I said to him.

"He isn't lying," the man said. "I only take a snort of this when I have to, and right now, I have to. Set me up, bartender, and don't hold the horses. To the lip and don't get a match near it."

A cup was poured for the man, and he pushed up between Masterson and myself, said, "By the way, I'm Billy Dixon."

"I know of you through Jack," I said.

Billy turned and looked at Jack. "Why, me and Jack have shared many a buffalo wallow and the fine roof of trees and sky, and we once shared a whore who was so fat you had to take survival supplies and a detailed map with you just to get around her ass."

Billy turned to Jack. "To Fat Ass Willamena, as good a screw as a pretty girl. And I wish she was here right now."

They drank to that, lifting their cups first in a toast, then downing the contents with one mighty gulp. Me, I didn't drink with them, just pretended to, touching the rim of the cup to my lips and putting it down.

3

WE WAS STANDING there in that strained light, and in comes a woman and a man, and Jack, who had taken to the far end of the bar next to Bat, leans beyond him to me, says, "That there is Mrs. Olds and her husband. She ain't available. They run the store."

He said this as if I was planning on asking her for a dance and a possible visit to a hay pile later. She wasn't much to look at, thick and big-boned, and though I wouldn't call her ugly, she was as plain as homemade soap with a wad of hair in it. My take was she could have used a bar of it on herself, with or without the hair, and not just because it was a rough living out where we was. When she come up to the bar with her husband, she said, "Give me the straight stuff, and wipe out the goddamn cup first, and not with your fingers."

Her cup would be the cleanest thing about her. She was six feet from me, and had a smell that was whupping the hell out of that that was already nesting in the room, the one collected from all them men. It was the kind of smell that doesn't come from a sweaty afternoon, but from years of not washing unless she was caught in a rain, and I was certain if she was, she'd run from it to shelter as fast as she could. If she had been available to me, I wouldn't have wanted to venture what kind of stink was under them dark, dirty skirts she wore. She was about the nastiest looking and smelling thing I had ever seen, and considering some company I'd kept, that was some kind of thing to say.

Mrs. Olds downed her cup of poison, yelled out, "Oh good goddamn, that is the shit, there. God-a-mighty, piss up a rope."

Her husband, a stout man with a hound dog face and maybe three strands of hair on his head, had quietly ordered his cup, and now he sipped at it, looked at her as if hoping she might ask for another cup and that a fresh draught of it might strangle her. She did have another, but she didn't strangle. That was when she looked down the bar and her eyes having adjusted good, settled them on me and said, "Is that a nigger?"

"Yes, m'am, I suppose I am." It wasn't any use trying to fight being called that. It wasn't worth the stirring.

"Well, how the hell are you?" she said.

"Fine," I said. "How are you?"

"I got a twitch between my legs, and my old man here has a razor strop for a dick. Loose and floppy, but not as long. A good sized cigar laid next to it would make it look like the nub of a near used-up pencil."

"That is more knowledge than we all need," Bat said. "Charlie, I think your wife might be deep in her cups."

"I ain't had but them two," she said.

"Here," Charlie said. "But you drank a jug-full at the store."

She rocked her head back like that sort of talk was revolting, said, "Well, goddamn you, trying to tell me how to drink and how much of it, and keeping up with it like you're measuring out milk for biscuits. Mind your own dick-jerking business."

She pulled a knife from somewhere then, a slit in her dress, I think. It wasn't long, but in the weak light from outside it shimmered a little and made me believe it was sharp. To Charlie, she said, "I'll cut you from ball-sack to eyeballs, you needle-peckered excuse for a grown man."

Charlie had his right arm on the bar, and he kind of heaved his shoulder and his fist came up and hit her solid on the jaw, knocking her backwards against Jack, who caught her. The knife fell on the floor.

Charlie slipped in then and got his arms around her and hoisted her up like a sack of potatoes over his shoulder. "The lady's sleepy," the weight of her bowing his legs.

Normally, striking a woman wouldn't have settled right with me, but for the first and only time in my life it seemed like a good choice had been made, and my guess was that was to her the same as a goodnight kiss.

Charlie opened the door, carried her out, and slammed it shut.

Billy said, "She cut him up a little not long ago. When she sobered up, she stitched him with a needle and gut-string, kissed him and told him what a lover he was. Next day when he was able to stand, she got drunk again, got into it with him over something or another, ripping out his stitches. She told him after that if she ever acted up, just to slug her. I don't think she meant it, but he took her at her word, I see."

"I think someone asks something of you nicely," Jack said, "you should be ripe for doing it."

"I have to agree with that," Bat said.

Several other men had leant an ear to the conversation, and they agreed that a good punch in the mouth if asked for should be delivered, be it man or woman, horse or dog. Jack backed off on the dog part. He could see the others, but a dog he wouldn't buy into. Dogs were all right with Jack.

I don't guess I have to mention that this was a particularly rough crowd.

4

WHAT WAS LEFT of the day was getting a sack thrown over it, and what light there had been through the windows and the windy cracks in the boards wasn't there anymore. Lanterns was lit.

"I figured I'd let it lay until we was kind of drunk, as that's how I take things better," Jack said. "But me and Nat here, we seen some Comanche, and then we seen what they had been at. A fellow who was cut up and burned and scalped. Had a black beard. Wasn't much to tell about his face, as he was knifed-up good. Color of eyes was two dark holes, and so was the nose. Can any of you put some hair to that, some nose and eyes? He was missing his johnson too."

"Was he tall?" said Jimmy, the man who asked if I was a nigger when we first come in.

"I don't know he was so tall," Jack said. "Do you, Nat?"

"Not as tall as me," I said. "Maybe tall as you. He had a big belly, but that may have been because they cut him open and his guts was pushed out."

"That will swell you," Billy said. "Being dead swells you, but guts right out there in the open in the sunlight, even if the air's cold, it'll swell a fellow. Everything gets bloated in size. A small man can look like a carnival wrestler. I've seen it."

"Where was the body?" Jimmy asked.

"Up near Chicken Creek," Jack said.

"I'm going to guess it's Hutchinson," said Jimmy. "That's the direction he took, and he ain't come back. He and his partner went for a hunt on their own, even though we didn't think there was no use in it. We all felt the herd hadn't come far enough this way yet.

Let them come to you, is what I say. You get so you can tell how they're going to do."

"Only way you can tell," Billy said, "is if someone tells you they're coming or the buffalo show up and stand on your feet. The rest of us can tell, but you can't tell your ass from a hole in the ground."

"The hole is below me, the ass is behind me," said Jimmy.

"Goddamn, he's gotten smart," the barkeep said.

"His partner," Jimmy said. "I figure they got him too, or otherwise he'd be snugged up here with the rest of us, out of the cold. He wasn't one for more hardship than he had to endure. Hutchinson, he might could take it, but that partner of his... What was his name?"

Nobody knew.

"Whatever it was," Jimmy said, "I didn't never call him that twice, as I didn't care for him. I think he liked his hand in his pocket more than he liked a woman, way he talked. All that said, I guess ain't nobody deserves that, being cut up by them savages like they was a link of sausage for breakfast."

"Them savages ain't no worse than us," Jack said. "They ain't ones to keep their word any better than us cause they know ours isn't any good, but they got a streak of honor about them, mean as they are. You might could ask Nat here about savages. His color and his kind have seen plenty of that, and they were white-skins. As far as them redskins go, this is where their people lived before we knew there was a dirt beyond the ocean. Someone come to take land we owned, we'd buck too."

"Ain't like they're doing anything with it," Jimmy said.

"Who says they got to?" Jack said. "And what have you ever done for this country other than slaughter buffalo and shit in the bushes?"

"You do the same," Jimmy said.

"I do," Jack said, "and that's why I say ain't none of us worth a flying fuck in a snow storm. Fill up my goddamn cup again. Let's lift one to poor old Hutchinson and that other dead fellow we don't know the name of. May Hutchinson stay buried, and may that nameless son-of-a-bitch be somewhere alive, and if dead, may the wolves eat his bones and may their shit grow green-green grass." That was the toast, and I actually sipped a bit more, but just a bit. As I put my cup down, Jack turned to it, and knowing my ways, took mine and drained the remains.

There was more toasts and more cups poured, me having turned mine over so as to show I was done, and as the night went on the voices got louder. There was jokes and lies told, and some things that might have been the truth. A man in a bowler hat said how he could throw his bowler hat and make it fit on anyone's head. The barkeep volunteered as victim, as he was hatless, and Bowler Hat, whose real name was Zeke, I discovered, cocked that bowler with careful aim, one eye squinted, and away it sailed. We watched it travel across those darkish quarters, and hit the barkeep in the face, banging his eye. Well, then the fight was on. Bets was placed quick as possible, but it wasn't quick enough. Zeke took a beating so fast, he hit the ground before his knocked-out teeth. Afterward the bar-keep punched his fists through Zeke's hat, so that rain and sunshine would be the same to the top of Zeke's head.

We all decided this was just too mean, and we all chipped in and Jimmy went next door to the store, and come back with a new hat, not a bowler, but a wide-brimmed one the color of wet dirt, and tossed it on Zeke's chest. He then told us he was happy to report that Mrs. Olds was sleeping peacefully in the middle of the floor, her head on a flour-sack, one eye swollen shut. Mr. Olds was watching her carefully, knowing she would finally come awake. He was living in fear of the natural born fact that he had to sleep sometime, or so said Jimmy, though as I have reported, all of us was something of exaggerators.

5

AFTER A FEW pukings and passing-outs, things began to wind down considerable, and there was only a few more shenanigans, among them a cuss-fight, which was seeing who could string the most cuss words together and have it make some kind of sense. Jack won. Well, there was a peach-eating contest. Some fat blowhard said he wished he had some peaches, and that he could eat his weight in them, to which Bat replied, "I judge you about two hundred and ten, and they got canned peaches next door."

"Well," said the blowhard. "Maybe not my weight."

"Let me see you eat twenty-five cans of peaches, and I will give you twenty-five dollars," Bat said.

"That's a lot of money," said the blowhard.

"You fail, you give me twenty-five dollars, or that spare Hawken rifle you got."

"What the hell you want that for," some fellow said to Bat. "Now that they got a Sharps, them Hawkens ain't the gun you need."

"Call me a fucking historian," Bat said.

So it got called that there would be a peach-eating contest, and somebody went next door to the store and bought the peaches with money we all chipped in, and they was opened a can at a time with a pocket knife. Damn if Blowhard, as I had come know him with some affection, take to them without pause, lifting the cans and pouring them peaches and the syrup they was in down his gullet like a wet fish sliding between mossy rocks. About the time he got to the fifteenth can and was looking spry, Bat started to pale. I was wondering if he had twenty-five dollars. On went Blowhard, volunteers opening the cans for him, him lifting them to his lips, gulping them like water, and then when he hit can twenty, he began to shake a little and took to a stool, sat there with the sweats.

This heartened Bat, but there was still some worry, as there was only five cans more.

"I got to pause," said Blowhard. Then he burped real loud, cut a fart that made the nastiest among us ill, and went back at it. He swallowed all twenty-five cans of peaches, took twenty-three dollars and a pocketknife from Bat for the rest, had a whisky, lay on the ground and cried.

More time passed, and by then we was all sagging, especially them that had been about serious nipping. It was decided that we'd hunt in the early morning, so some of the men went to set their skinning wagons and clean their rifles, and make necessary preparations. Me and Jack was shooters on this trip, not skinners, so all we had to do was wait until first light, which was going to come mighty early.

Jack and me decided we'd stretch out on the floor of the saloon, like some of the others. We got our bedrolls and laid them flat. We took off our coats. The night air was no longer cool. It was already growing hot from the oncoming day, though darkness was still about us. We was slipping our pistols and knives off our persons when Blowhard began to roll around on the floor moaning. "Oh, my pancreas. I've busted my pancreas."

Jack hooted. "You goddamn idiot. You wouldn't know where your pancreas was if I cut you open and laid your hand on it. Go to the outhouse, jackass."

Blowhard got up with a lot of effort and went to the outhouse, saying, "I still believe it's my pancreas."

Me and Jack laid our weapons at the sides of our bedrolls, then dropped down on top of them to sleep. I got dunked into a well of slumber mighty fast and deep, and that's why when that loud snapping sound come, I thought I was a ghost already.

Jumping up, grabbing my Winchester, looking around, I saw Jack and a room full of men doing the same. That precarious timber I had mentioned, why it had snapped and the roof was sagging.

"It's got about enough strength to hold a few more minutes if a fly don't light on it," Jack said.

That led to some of the men going outside with the idea to tear down one of the poles that was supposed to be part of the Adobe Walls fortifications, and substitute it for a new support pole. The rest of us took to the roof to pull off some of the sod to lighten the roof, which led to some bad gaps in places. If it rained, a lot of us and a lot of the bar would get wet.

When I was done helping, I went outside. It was still dark, but there was streaks of pink in it like blood poisoning. I looked at that for awhile, then noticed my horse wasn't in the place where I had corralled it. As the blacksmith was up and about, I went over and said, "Where's my horse?"

"It and the others are picketed down by the creek," he said.

"By the creek? Why, that's a good stretch away. Why don't you just offer them to the Indians, and tell them to come back tomorrow for the saddles."

"Now listen here young fellow, you better watch your mouth," he said.

Jack had come up now. He said, "Where's my horse?"

"Picketed at the creek," the blacksmith said.

"The creek?" Jack said. "Why the pig shit would you put him down by the creek? There's Indians about. It's where they live, god-damn it, out there in the nothing, the prairies and the trees. Is your head packed with mud?"

"A horse has got to drink," said the blacksmith.

"Bring the water to them," Jack said. "That's what buckets are for."

"It's a lot of trips," said the blacksmith.

"It is at that," I said. "That's what we're paying for. And besides, you could shorten the trips if you carried the buckets only as far as the well, which is right over there."

"It was just easier to take care of them all in one swoop at the creek," he said.

"But it's still a bad idea," I said.

"What he said," Jack said.

"Oh now, don't give me trouble," said the blacksmith. "It's alright. I'll go down there and get them right now if you want them."

"We ain't ready to ride nowhere," Jack said. "But bring them here close, and watch them. Or give us back our money."

"I got a mind to do it," he said.

"Tell you what," I said. "Take out for the grain and such for the horses, and give the rest of the money back. We'll go down to the creek and get our own horses."

"You do that," he said.

"The money," Jack said.

"Now, tell you what," said the blacksmith. "I'll go get them, and I'll keep the money. I'll keep them up here for you, way you like. I'll be so sweet to them they won't want to leave."

Jack looked at me.

I said, "Your call."

"Oh, what the hell," Jack said. "I have by nature a goddamn sweet disposition. Go down there and get them and keep the money."

So away went the blacksmith.

When he was gone, Jack said, "Goddamn stupid ass."

We walked to where the walls was broken down the most, and as the light had cracked the sky good and was falling over things like sunlight was heavy, we looked and seen the blacksmith hustling toward the creek. There was a run of trees along it, and our horses and others was picketed out, like they was an offering to the Comanche.

"It's like he's lived in a tree all his life," Jack said. "He hasn't learned a damn thing. It's a wonder he ain't dead. I think he's the kind of man that will run for politics when he gets the chance."

We watched as our horses was taken off the picket line. The blacksmith had ropes looped over their heads and noses, and he was leading them toward us. That's when he threw up his arms and let go of the horses and made a coughing sound, staggered forward, then began to run. He headed toward us like he had been born on a hill, one leg seeming shorter than the other. But closer he got, we could see something sticking out of the back of his calf, causing him to limp. It was an arrow. Now our horses was loose, the others was there for the Comanche to take, and the dumb blacksmith had an arrow in his leg, which at that moment was the lesser of it to me.

"We got to get them horses," Jack said.

I had left my Winchester inside for the moment, but I had my handguns, and so did Jack, so we broke for the creek like we was running to a party, and in a way, we would be if them Indians got us. They had to be situated down in that creek.

The blacksmith ran right past us, saying, "This way, you fools."

I realized then he might actually be smarter than we were. We kept running though, and when we reached the picket line some arrows whizzed by us like hornets. I pulled my pistols, one in either hand, and started firing toward the creek. I heard a grunt from there, and then we was at the string of horses. Some of the other men from the fortifications, such as they was, had come to do the same, rescue their horses. Bullets barked and arrows whistled. Pretty soon all those horses was free, and we might actually have hit some Indians. I know that grunt I heard sounded serious enough. Here's the thing though. We didn't actually see none of them.

The horses was loose, and we started running them toward the walls, and there was other men there now, trying to run them into the corrals. The only horse that wasn't there was Satan. He had taken to the prairie or was already captured by a Comanche. Jack's horse walked from where he was and went into the corral as if he had just remembered he forgot something there.

We looked up and seen the ridge that was beyond the creek and the trees was filled with mounted Indians. Not ten or twenty, but more of them than you could count with a pencil and paper.

There have been all manner of estimates since the fight at Adobe Walls, and I don't think any of them have nailed the truth to the wall. Some said we was eighteen men and one woman, some we was eighteen counting the woman, and others have said we was twenty-eight. And though I must admit I didn't take a head count and write down everyone's names, I would say to you that we was over thirty, maybe thirty-five.

Problem was there was a lot more Indians. At a guess, I'd say there was at least five hundred of them. I've heard said there was a thousand, which is too much. I've heard two hundred, which is too few. Let's just say there was enough there to give concern. And let me tell you, they was a sight, them redskins. All festooned in war bonnets, or plumes of feathers stuck to the side of their heads. Them that was bare-headed had hair greased out with buffalo fat, and it shined in the sun. They was all half-naked, or full-naked, but for strands of leather around their necks, wrists, waists, and ankles, from which hung ornaments of brass and silver and bright-white bone. Many of them had round shields of wood and folded buffalo hide. Their horses was painted up in all kinds of colors, yellow and reds, and blues, and enough scalps hung from their bridles to supply hair enough for every white man in the state of Texas to have a wig made, and one that would soundly fit them. I just took it in at a glimpse, mind you, as it didn't seem standing still was a good idea, but it was a sight. Majestic and wickedly beautiful, but at the same time enough to make you wet yourself and look for a hole to crawl in.

From the side come running a couple of men waving their arms, one of them yelling, "The wagons, there's dead men in them. They done been snuck on and kilt."

They meant some of the buffalo hunters that had gone to sleep away from the saloon. This all seems mighty odd in the telling, us out there in Comanche country, the blacksmith picketing the horses at a creek, and then them men going out to sleep in their wagons, away from the main gathering of us, and all of us armed. But that's how it was. All of them, and I have to include myself, had become too confident; the confidence afforded to us not by common sense, but by lust for the dollar.

Another man ran up from behind us and was almost shot by all of us. "They got the peach-eater. He's out in the shitter, they turned it over on him and killed him with his ass hanging out, the sons-of-dog-bitches."

"Get inside the saloon," Jack yelled. This was like asking a fish to swim or a bird to fly. Men was already swarming for the door, and at the same time them Comanche was whooping and howling and riding down off that hill. As we got to the door, we seen there was Indians on foot that had snuck upon the camp. Truth was, that support pole cracking had got us stirring just in time to discover all them savages. They was starting to surround us.

I was still handling my pistols, and I wheeled and shot one of those Indians that was on foot dead, just as he reached a low point in the wall. I was about to shoot another come from the same direction, a little man with long, dark hair in braids, wearing all white buckskins, or at least they had started out white, when he jerked both hands above his head, started waving them like he was trying to catch hummingbirds.

"Don't shoot me," he said. "Save me a place inside. Don't shoot my ass. I'm a white man."

It was reckoned, by me at least, that it might be some kind of trick, but that voice was pure Texas, and as he come on closer, bullets darting by him and slamming into the low walls near us, arrows flocking around his head like birds, it was clear he wasn't no Indian. I might also mention that though he run with some vigor, he was a sloppy runner, his elbows flying all over and his arms now flapping at his sides like he was trying to fan a fire out on his ass.

When he got to the wall, however, he proved quite nimble. He come over it with a leap, landed on his feet, and passed me on his way inside the saloon.

Well, here come them Indians then, and I seen then that they wasn't all Comanche. There was Cheyenne out there too, but I didn't stop to make sure I was correct on the matter by checking out their hairdos and such. We rushed inside and closed the door, and hadn't no more than thrown the latch over it, than they was beating on it with fists, bows, lances and rifles. They was hooting and a hollering so loud it was setting my teeth on edge.

Now they was at the windows, breaking them, firing in. They hit somebody, cause I heard him yell out, and when I turned he was on the ground at my feet, having passed his shadow to the other side. That's how close I come to getting elected.

I had a clear path view to the window, because many of the men had dropped to the ground or cuddled up behind something like it was their best friend. I cut down with that loop-cock Winchester, riddling the frame of the window something furious, knocking out what glass was left, as well as sending lead bees through it. One of them plowed a furrow through an Indian's scalp, dropping him like a bad habit. The others that had been swarming there at the window, even planning on crawling through, was now gone, having decided on another game.

Men was up with their weapons now. The few windows in the place was all on one side of the building, and they was in a flash protected by men with rifles. Thing was, not everyone there was a crack shot or a hunter. There was some that was just skinners, others that was teamsters, and so on. All of them could pull a trigger, but that didn't mean everyone there could hit what they was shooting at.

Jack was at one of the windows, and like the others was firing as fast as he could send a round out there into the air, throw out the casing, and load a fresh one. The Indians was firing back, and bullets was tearing into the walls, and in some places cutting through them like they wasn't no more than bed sheets. I fetched up behind a barrel and got low, knowing a good round might go through a weak spot in the wall, the barrel, my head and whoever might be behind me, and maybe through the other wall and knock off an unsuspecting prairie dog lingering over his breakfast. Those Indians was well armed. They had bows and arrows, some spears, but they had modern shooters too, and when I thought about the number of them up on that hill, the number of us inside the store, I figured we had about as much chance as a block of ice on hot stove.

Black Hat Jack

They was still banging on the doors, and some had crawled on the roof. That was a bad thing for us, as the roof had gaps in it from where we'd peeled off the sod, and the place that had been fixed up there wasn't anything that was going to thrill a professional home builder. We fired up through the ceiling a number of times, heard grunts and yips, and was rewarded by seeing one roll off the roof past the window and hit the ground hard enough a cloud of dust puffed up. Them others lit out of there like their breech cloths was on fire.

After furious shooting at us from outside, none of us was hit solid, though there was minor wounding. Our shooters was claiming to have cleaned the clock of four or five Indians. The men near the windows stayed there, and while they did, the rest of us stacked feed and flour sacks up against the walls, three and four thick. We piled them up to the window bases, so that men could stand at them for protection and see out and pick off targets that presented themselves. I tell you, it was touch and go all the while. But finally we wasn't being set upon like we was before, and the shots fired only came now and then, being most likely snapped off by those who was bored or felt they hadn't gotten their chance.

It was then that we turned our attention to the white Indian. He was squatting behind some flour sacks pushed up against the wall. Questions was being called out to him.

Jack said, "I know you. Ain't you I Got A Hand In My Ass?"

"Hair," the man said. "It's I Got A Hand In My Hair. It's an Indian name."

"No shit," Jimmy said. "We thought maybe your old Mama from New York City called you that."

"My white name is Happy Collins," he said. "I come from a long line of Happy Collins, and I'm not from New York. I'm from Nacogdoches."

"You don't look all that goddamn happy to me," said the barkeep.

"At the moment, I am feeling somewhat dour," he said.

Bat said, "We can see that."

"What in hell are you doing out here without no weapons, running like a school girl from a bunch of Comanche?" Jack said.

"It's not just Comanche," he said. "Cheyenne as well."

"I knew it," I said.

Everyone gave me a look. It had just kind of slipped out. But hell, I did know it.

"There are Kiowa too," he said. "Led by Lone Wolf. And the Cheyenne are led by Big Bow, Little Robert and White Shield. But it's mostly Comanche, and they got none other than Quanah Parker as their leader, and Quenatosavit."

"Translates White Eagle," Jack said.

"Now that there is good to know, and if we just knew all their wives' names, and kids', maybe their favorite horses'," Jimmy said, "we could sleep tight tonight, though our throats might be cut."

"No, it's good to know who's who," Jack said. "I know of all of them names, and it tells us what we're up against."

"We have all been out of the city, Jack," Billy Dixon said. "We know those names as well as you do."

"There's a chief named Little Robert?" Bat said. "I didn't know that."

"That's because you're a kid, still wet behind the ears," Billy Dixon said.

"Well, I'm all up for any man here wants to try and dry them," Bat said.

Bat just got laughs.

"I mean it," he said.

He got more laughs.

That's how them hunters was. They was the sort to laugh when another man would be crying.

"I have lived with the Cheyenne off and on over the years," Happy said. "Until today I got along fine with them. I have a Cheyenne wife, Horse Woman, and she is fine. Or I did have one. I have been taken out of the family, it seems. A divorce."

"And why is that?" I said.

44

Black Hat Jack

"I have been someone who works both sides of the street for quite some time. I like certain aspects of being white, but the Indians are really good about not making you work, at least in a common way. The women do all the work, and the men sit around and watch them work, hurry them about it, tell stories, go hunting and fighting."

"Sounds like a goddamn paradise," Jimmy said.

"It has its benefits, but Quanah, he's done got the ass itch for the whites, and wants to run them out, and he's got the Cheyenne in on it, some Kiowa, and even though Quanah is half-white himself, he has decided we all have to go. He actually talked White Shield, my father-in-law, into giving me the option of having my nuts cut open and stuffed with hot pebbles, or I could try and run back to the white people and take my chances here. I liked my father-in-law, and am surprised he turned on me like that. Now I may have to go back east and go to work for my father's law firm again. I hated that."

"You might as well had your nuts cut and packed," Jack said. "This here isn't going to end well neither."

"I see that now. You know there's a lot of warriors out there, and they are in a bad mood, and they think they got magic on their side. Or did. There is some dissension now. I heard some bad language exchanged from some non-believers, right before they asked me to leave."

Right then we heard some pounding on the wall from where the outfitter store was, and the adobe began to break, and then the head of a pick-axe come through. Rifles turned in that direction, waiting. The hole got bigger, a face appeared there, but it wasn't an Indian face. It was Mr. Olds, he of the right cross to his wife's head.

"Don't nobody shoot now," he said, "it's me. Doors in here won't hold as good as yours, and there's four of us here, counting my wife. We want to come through."

"Then we got a goddamn hole in the wall to contend with," Jack said.

"It's not like we can run outside and you can let us in. We'd be scalped and skinned before we could get halfway there."

"Oh, hell," Jack said. "Come on through, but leave the hole small as possible. We got to plug it with something."

So the pick-axe worked again, and the hole started growing, and after about fifteen minutes it was wide enough for two men to come through, and then Olds pushed his wife through the hole like he was shoving a log into a furnace. "She's still out."

"You hit her hard enough," Bat said.

"Naw, she's mostly drunk, but it was a good punch, don't you think?"

"Try that with me," Jack said, "and see how it turns out."

Between his previous comments and then, Jack had turned chivalrous.

Mr. Olds slipped through. "Naw, I only like to fight people I know I can whip, if I take them by surprise. Me and her have tussled before, and I mostly win. Hell, she cut me pretty bad, you want to know."

"No one's asking," Billy Dixon said.

When they was all through that hole, me and a few of the others went in there and grabbed some supplies, a barrel of water, some jerky and some bags of beans, and when we got that inside the saloon, we put sacks of grain that was in the saloon at the hole and pushed an anvil that was in the corner, being there for no reason I could figure, up against them. It wasn't much, but it was something. They came through that hole, they'd have to come one at a time, unless they took time to break down the wall. If they started on that, we'd pull aside them sacks and start on them.

"I Got A Hand In My Ass here was just telling us about some Indian magic, wasn't you?" Jack said turning back to Happy Collins.

"It's I Got A Hand In My Hair, but Happy will do," he said.

"Go on with your story, Ass," Jack said.

Happy sighed. "Quanah has them all wound up tight as a cheap watch. He's told them how this medicine man, this White Eagle—"

"That's your father-in-law?" one of the men asked.

"No. My father-in-law is White Shield. White Eagle is a medicine man."

"Just tell it," Jack said.

"White Eagle said he has enough magic to take care of the whole of the Indian nations, except the Tonkawa. Nobody has much for them. Comanche, pretty much everyone else, thinks they're toadies for the whites and are said to be cannibals. White Eagle told the others that he had a vision. That he went up in the heavens and seen the Great Spirit, and the Great Spirit told him he was going to lead the Indians against the whites and drive them out. He even got the Comanche doing the Sundance, way the Cheyenne do. You know the Comanche, they are the orneriest bunch of warriors this side of Genghis Khan, but they went for it like a perch on a cricket. That Sundance, that is painful business. I have watched it a few times, but have never had any urge to do it. It is best seen from afar."

I ought to pause here and lay this out to some of you so you'll know what he was talking about.

What the Cheyenne called the Sundance was that they had bones or sticks stuck through their breasts, and then rawhide strands was tied to them, and then long strands to a pole that was stuck up in the ground. Some of them would take a buffalo skull and tie it to bones ran through the meat in their backs. The skulls made them heavy, made them fall back and pull against the bones through their breasts, those rawhide strands. They danced and chanted and pulled back until the bones or sticks snapped out of their chests, or some of the other Indians would tug on them, helping break them loose. During this time they was supposed to have a vision. I know I'd have one or two, and most of it would be trying to figure out how I had got talked into such a thing in the first place.

"I'll say," Bat said.

"He told them if they attack with full vigor, they will win and will not be bothered by your bullets."

"So far he's not a shining light," Jack said.

"I agree," Happy said. "I think that's why they've backed off for the moment, trying to figure what to do, what went wrong."

Billy, who was at a window looking out, talking over his shoulder, said, "Which is which here, Hand In The Ass?"

Happy didn't even bother to correct, just sighed, got up at a stoop and made his way to the window.

"Who is who?" Billy asked.

I had eased over too, my curiosity being stronger than my common sense. It was quite a view, all them Comanche bunched up on a hill near a mile away. Happy studied the crowd up there, said, "One ain't got no drawers on of any kind, just swinging it in the wind, painted yellow, that's White Eagle."

"He doesn't seem to have much faith in his own medicine," I said. "He's got some distance there."

"They have all sort of made for the rear," Billy said, "and I know that ain't from lack of courage."

"No," Jack said, as he came over for a peek. "It is not, but they don't like surprises. They see signs in deer shit and flying birds and most anything. If they think the sign is good and it ain't, it pees in their soup. They have to take time to wrap their head around it. Right now, they're up there figuring how they're going to kill us. If they was mad before, they are more mad now."

"That's right," Happy said. "That's how they are. But if they decide things was not just right, or White Eagle can tell them something that soothes the fact that they lost a few warriors, in spite of his assurances, they will come on, and it will be busy."

"Who is that next to White Eagle?" I said that as a big Indian on a white horse had ridden up, and was looking out on us.

"That there is Quanah his ownself," Happy said. "There aren't any chiefs that run all things for the Comanche, or the Cheyenne neither, but him and White Eagle is close to it as of these days. They don't like the way things are going and are trying to group up and have leaders. I note my father-in-law has hung to the back, even farther back than White Eagle. That was something that was said of him, from time to time. That he liked a good fight when he and his warriors outnumbered their enemies, but that he had a tendency to linger otherwise. He's lingering. I don't see any of the other leaders... Oh, wait a minute, there's Robert. He is kind of hunkered down over his horse. He does that when he's pissed about things. I figure he's mad at White Eagle, and I figure White Eagle is pretty much aware he's in the shit house now."

6

QUANAH PARKER WAS part Comanche and part white. The son of Cynthia Ann Parker, who was stolen when she was a child, and became a squaw of a Comanche named Nocona, which made him a Scotch-Irish Comanche, though they wasn't as rare as you might think. The Comanche was among the most common for killing everybody and their dog, cattle, and keeping only horses and children if they wasn't babies, and therefore trouble. Them they would kill as quick as too many cats, banging their brains out or sticking them on cactus and such. They wasn't a sentimental sort. But the children that was older they'd sometimes keep as slaves, or add into the tribe, as their numbers was declining due to disease from frontier folks and rifle shot, as well as folks like us killing their traveling grocery stores.

Cynthia was rescued some many years later, having bore Quanah, and another son, if memory serves me, and a little daughter named Prairie Flower. She wasn't all that happy about being rescued, though. She had been taken so young, she didn't know shit about the whites, outside of remembering she was Cynthia Ann Parker. That didn't stop white folks from making her stay with them, though. They was certain wasn't nothing better in the world than being a white person, living the way they wanted you to live. I understood a bit of her concern, having been among whites as a young slave. On the frontier, I was better treated, and by some folks a lot better. Buffalo hunters and mountain men was down right democratic compared to others, even Yankees. Therefore I can see her being more than a smidgen nervous amongst the whites.

She run off a few times, but they wouldn't let her go, caught her and brought her back. Her baby died, and then she died too. Starved herself to death. After she was taken, Quanah never saw her again. She died four years before this time I'm telling you about, and I apologize. I can't seem to stick to anything straight away, and get distracted as easily as a cow by a blue bottle fly.

So there we was, surrounded by hundreds of Indians, and we was now less than thirty, some having died in the wagons outside. A couple of the men that had been wounded wasn't doing so well either, and there was a couple that was talking about putting on the sneak if we could hold until dark. There was also a man or two thinking about breaking out in broad daylight for the horses and making a run for it. This was something that got our best wishes, but not our support, especially that whole daylight runaway plan. Besides, the horses had at this point either been taken by the Indians, scattered, or shot in the barrage of gunfire that had gone on earlier. They wouldn't be waiting politely for us in the corral.

It wasn't that I didn't consider escape plans, but outside of tunneling straight down to China, nothing seemed better than those rickety walls, the hunters and those buffalo rifles, me and my pistols and that sweet Winchester.

Well, there I was contemplating, thinking that the bullet I ought to save for myself ought to be that 4/10 load. I figured I put the barrel in my mouth and let it rip, there wouldn't be any wounding and surviving, left to be worked over by the Comanche, Cheyenne, and Kiowa. I would be missing a head. One thing I decided I would do, if time allowed, was shave my head. A good load from the 4/10 might make my part a bit too wide for scalping, but I didn't want to leave my hair to hang on their scalps. I was a Negro with what we called good hair. I wore it long because it made me look like a real frontiersman, which I was, and the girls liked it. Also, it covered my ears, which was a little like two ends of a hallway with the doors thrown open.

I pulled my knife and was going to get some water from one of the water barrels, and then I realized we needed all the water there was to drink, not wasted on me shaving my head. I put the knife away. I hadn't no sooner done that then a barrel was dragged around with a dipper in it, and we all took turns. The man dragging it was the barkeep, and he said, "This here is it, boys. Unless one of you would like to go out to the well."

That got a short laugh.

"They done cut up a horse or some such and dropped down it," Jack said, "you can bet on that. Maybe they all peed in it. That's how they work. How much whisky is there?"

"Plenty," the barkeep said.

"That's what we need," Billy said, "a bunch of us drunk and trying to make a clear shot."

"I been thirsty enough I would have drank piss and thought it a treat," Jack said.

"I'm shooting myself first," Bat said.

"You say that now," Jack said.

"Ask me about it later," Bat said. "See if the view changes."

I eased up by Jack, said, "So, you think this is where we toss in our hats?"

"Could be. Never say never until never is done. Or almost done. You save a load for yourself, Nat."

"Planned on it."

"You know, that fellow ate all the peaches, it was me told him to go to the shitter."

"Everyone has to shit," I said.

"That's true, but I told him right then. Maybe it was his pancreas."

"He'd have gone to the outhouse soon enough," I said. "It's just how it all shook out."

"Reckon so," Jack said.

Then Olds got our attention. He called out, "They come, bet you they come through the roof. That's the weak part."

No one disagreed with that.

Olds put his hands on his hips and looked up at the ceiling. "There's still a hole where that support pole cracked. I think I can ladder up there for a peek, see when they're coming. My head will be between the support poles, and the sod is pushed up there, so I might get a look-see before they note me up there."

"All right," Bat said. "But you ought to let me do it. I'm a bit more nimble than you."

"You ain't nothing but a green kid," Olds said.

I looked around for Mrs. Olds, see how she felt about such concerning her husband, but she was still on the floor asleep. The Indians could be scalping her and cutting off her toes, and she wouldn't have known no difference. She was drunk as anyone I'd ever seen and snoring like wind blowing through the mountains.

Olds got a Henry rifle from the stock against the wall, and Billy pulled a ladder from behind the bar, and propped it up.

"I'll just go up there for a gander," Olds said.

"I ought to do it," Bat said. "I'm small. That ladder looks rotten to me."

"I've climbed that ladder many a time and it's held," Olds said.

"That may be why you ought not to climb it anymore," Bat said. "Your fat ass is bound to be wearing it down."

"Oh, go diddle yourself," Olds said.

The ladder was propped and a man held either side of it, me being one of them, and up went Olds, that ladder squeaking like it was in pain. But up he went, hoping to see better what was behind us, as there was no window on that side.

He reached the top, gently poked his head through the hole in the sod, between the two support poles. After a moment he said, "My, my. I can tell you one thing."

"What's that," a man called up.

"There are a lot of fucking Indians out there."

"Thanks for that bit of news," Jack called out from the window.

"I can also say, for whatever reason, they ain't behind us. I figure they got some braves tucked out there in the grass somewhere, but I don't see them. Why ain't they surrounding us?"

"Why should they?" Jack said. "When they charge down off that rise and out from the trees, they'll flow over us like water. We can run for it, but without horses, we wouldn't have a chance. They're doing fine. They can wait us out if they like."

"They won't do that," Happy said. "They are in for the kill, and are hot for it. I think they are holding back a little due to some disappointment. They was all supposed to be untouchable. Meaning bullets wouldn't hit them. They are now uncertain, and the medicine man will have to make excuses for the ones that got killed. I saw him this morning looking for a sign, which meant he knew he had got himself on the edge of a cliff with them predictions. I was figuring that right then, before I was asked to run like hell. He gave the braves instructions on how they were to conduct themselves, and if he can prove someone killed a skunk, which is bad medicine when on the war path, then he can claim they are the ones threw off the magic. Medicine man has not only got to come up with predictions, he's got to plan excuses for when things go wrong. It's part of the job."

Olds called down. "Still a lot of Indians… Wait now. Here's something. Two riders coming this way, way off, and they ain't Indians."

"Well," said Jimmy, "they're skint."

Right then the ladder squealed and a rung cracked, and down come Olds, and he hit the ground in such a way his gun went up under his chin, and obviously being set on a hair trigger, the jar set it off, sending a round through chin and out the top of his head. He didn't move an inch after that. Wasn't no kicking or moaning, he was dead as a bag of hammers.

Jack turned from the window at the sound of the shot, seen Olds on the ground, men gathering around him. Jimmy said, "Well, he's out of it."

Bat scurried up the ladder without weapons, avoiding the missing rung, and when he was up there, Billy said, "Here go, Bat," and handed him the Henry Olds had dropped.

I glanced over to Mrs. Olds, but she wasn't aware her husband was dead. She wasn't aware of anything. For all she cared she was dead.

If it seems we sort of took this all in stride, we didn't. It wasn't that we wasn't caring, but we had learned to put that sort of thing in our vest pocket, or most of us had. We could save our upset feelings for when we could afford them.

Bat yelled down, "Those two are coming hell bent for leather, but I don't think they're going to beat the Indians. There's a wad of them coming around to the side of them, on their left."

We heard a couple of shots then.

"There's ten, maybe twelve Indians on them. Oh, shit. One of their horses stumbled... Ah, hell, the other tumbled over it. I think one took a shot, and the other is up, got a broke leg way it's standing. Those two's scalps are good as taken."

"I'm going out after them," I said. "Open them doors."

"Son," Jack said. "You can't."

"I can and I am."

"Niggers can run," Jimmy said. "Only one of us got a chance of doing it. I only knew two niggers couldn't run. One of them had a bad leg and the other had a wrenched back. No offense, Nat."

"A little taken," I said.

"They're to the right of the doors, and way out there, not so far you wouldn't be able to make it easy enough if you were on a picnic and there were no Indians," Bat said. "I'd stick, Nat."

"Open the doors and keep your eyes and ears on," I said.

They pulled the planking and the doors came open. With rifle in hand, away I did run.

7

I AM A fast runner, but I made a note that if me and Jimmy didn't get killed, I was going to punch him in the mouth.

Went for all I was worth, I can assure you of that, and it was fairly flat there, so I had a mighty smooth run, considering the circumstances. I knew that Bat wouldn't fire at those Indians near that pair until necessary, because when he did, they might note I was coming. Right then they was concentrated on sending arrows and shots at them two out there on the ground. Soon as they noticed me, he would commence if he was thinking clear, and maybe not even then. I might be out of reasonable range. But when I started back, and with them coming after me, because I assumed they would, he could cut down on them then. I had no doubt he would.

I could see the limping horse and the one already down, and I seen one of the men stand from behind the dead horse, grab the injured horse's bridle, put a pistol to its head and bring it down in such a way that a V was created with the two dead animals. That was smart thinking.

The Indians, and they looked like a small band of Kiowas, was riding up fast now, and when they seen me, an easier target than someone behind a horse, they started firing. I fired back on the run, cock-firing that Winchester until it was empty, hitting two Indians, maybe killing one, and dropping four horses, throwing their riders in the grass. About that same time Bat started shooting that Henry.

The Kiowas dropped off their horses and left them, got behind their dead ones and started shooting arrows and gunfire. By that time I was near the V that fellow had made with the dead mounts, the person who had killed the horse turned to look at me. I had already been noticed, of course, all that gunfire had drawn attention to me.

"I'm coming in," I said.

I took a leap, landed between the two horses. A series of arrows plunked into the dead animals and their hides sputtered with bullets. When I was down between the horses, I seen the survivor was a woman. She had her hair pushed up under her hat, but there was no denying she was a woman, young, in her twenties like me. A white woman with a bit of dark hair showing under her hat.

I turned to look at her partner. He was stretched out on his back with his hands at his sides, like maybe he had laid down for a short nap.

"My brother," she said. "They've killed him."

I had already taken to pulling shells out of my gun belt, slipping them into my Winchester. I said, "Listen here, I'm sorry, but we can't hang our thoughts on that right now. We're going to have to run like rabbits in a second. We stay here, all them other Indians are going to be on us. They can't get them that's in the saloon, they'll settle for us for now. So we're going to run, and as we come up out of here, we got to be shooting their way, even if we can't take time to aim. We got to make them nervous and busy ducking, and we got to move, run for all we're worth."

"All right," she said.

"What's your name?" I said.

"Millie."

"Millie, when I say go, do not hesitate, just go."

"I have shot buffalo and been in some scrapes, so you don't wait on me. I got a fully loaded Winchester, and I will not go down easy."

"Good then," I said.

I took a deep breath, said, "Go."

Away we went. It was one hell of a run. I kept thinking in the back of my mind I was going to step in a hole and go down, or catch a bullet or some arrows in the back, but when we come up out of there we come up firing. As we ran, I turned and started running backwards, and firing my Winchester, and I was good at it. I used to do it on the farm for fun, run backwards like that, and I could even out-run some of the other kids running like that, so maybe Jimmy was onto something about colored being able to run, but still, I was going to punch him in the mouth. I fired at those redskins like I truly hated them, which I didn't. There wasn't any use in that. They was who they was, same as me. I had been whipped as a child slave for nothing more than spilling milk. I had been told if I got a cold and gave it to a white person it was worse than if a white person gave it to you. That I was second to everything in life, and that's why I had come west. I let all that anger cover me like a shield. It wasn't a real shield and it wouldn't have stopped a gnat from flying through, but it was everything that had ever made my blood boil, and before I realized it I had emptied that Winchester and was cocking on empty.

I wheeled then, found that Millie was really hauling freight, was more than halfway to the doors. I run to catch up with her, shifted the empty Winchester to my left hand, drew the LeMat, and come even with her.

Millie's hat blew off and her black hair popped out in a long trail, like ink blown in the wind, and now there came a sound from the warriors up on the hill and behind us. They wanted Millie because they knew there wasn't no greater humiliation to a man than to rape his women to death. It was better than cutting off their balls, far as they was concerned. So they come then in a sea of Indians, Quanah leading, riding down from the rise ahead of us, others whooping it up behind us, some rushing on foot. Out from the creek come more Indian stragglers.

The swarm came, arrows flew, the bullets tore holes in the air. It looked like we was as good as nabbed, and I was preparing to shoot Millie, then myself, when the doors to the store opened. There came from that open doorway, and from the roof where Bat was, a withering round of Sharps rifle fire. There was screams and yells, thunks and thuds, and flurries of sod being thrown up as men and critters struck and rolled on the ground.

I was in fear of being shot down by our own bunch.

To the left of me, having circled the walls, came a handful of riders, and one of them fired a shot that tore through the top of my left shoulder, burned like a branding iron. I cross-fired with my right hand, shot his horse through the neck, and down that horse went, almost sliding into me. I can't tell you much after that, but I emptied that 9 shooter, and clicked the baffle for the 4/10 load. We were almost through the doors of the store now. Men filled it from side to side. Me and Millie was running low. Our people was firing over our heads, just to keep a stream of lead in the air, then they parted and Millie made it through.

A crazy Indian come off from my right and was about to grab me. I fired that 4/10 load in his face. Then I was inside and the doors was being slammed, the wooden bar thrown back into place. Outside came a ferocious pounding of arrows and gun shots and fists. Bullets tore through the door and made holes that light peeked through and the room was riddled with these sticks of light.

Inside, Millie had gone to the window, was standing by Jack, firing her pistol. I knelt down on the ground and reloaded my weapons, went to another window where a man had just fallen, stuck the Winchester out and started firing, not so fast this time, and more accurately. Bullets was plunking into the walls, tearing through in places, pieces of adobe flying around, and then—

It was over.

8

FOR THE TIME being anyway.

Them Indians had regrouped out there on that ridge, feeling good about being just out of rifle shot. One naked brave stood up on horseback, turned his back toward us, and showed us his ass. No one took a shot at him. Too far.

Then Quanah rode up, and so did White Eagle, all naked and yellow-coated with clay. They sat on their horses side by side, checking out the battlefield. What they saw was a pile of dead Indians. We had lost a few ourselves, along with Olds and that fellow out there lying dead between the V of those horses, but them Indians had taken a beating.

Bat called down from his perch, "They are chopping up that dead man at the horses."

He meant Millie's brother.

"Oh, the goddamn savages," she said.

All the men had now noted that she was not only a woman, but that she was one who spoke right up and didn't faint.

Jack said, "She shot two of them Indians with good pistol shots. I think she might have killed one of them, and the other will be lying mighty still later tonight, as he took one in the balls I think."

It was a compliment that you gave a man, not a woman. Least not normally.

"She did all right out there too," I said. "I think she dropped a couple."

Millie heaved a little, like she was going to cry, but then she cinched it up.

"She can run too," Bat called down, "sort of lopes like an antelope," and then he come down the ladder. His hat was full of bullet holes and his face had been streaked with cuts from where shots had come close. He didn't seem in the least fazed about having been nearly shot-up, but when he was on the ground he took a good look at Millie, and that fazed him. She was a pretty thing, and about as on the far end of womanhood from Mrs. Olds, who was still peacefully sleeping, than a buffalo is from a deer. She wore buckskins that fit her loose, but you could tell there was something nice and soft under them, and her hair was long and tumbled down her back and there was something about the way it swung that roused the blood. She looked taller than she was, as she was wearing boots, and those boots cocked her ass up nicely. It doesn't sound very gentlemanly to talk in this manner, but none of us was gentlemanly right then. We all figured our days were numbered, so we enjoyed our last moments by really giving her the once over.

Then she knocked the wind out of us.

"Listen, you piss-ants," she said, "I have ridden the trail and fought Indians before, and hunted buffalo, and I can ride like an Indian, shoot like Wild Bill Hickok, and drink like a fish, but I do not sell myself, and I'm not for free unless I choose it, so any of you fellows get the wrong idea, you'll be wearing your nose on the other side of your face, if you don't end up with a bullet in the head. Are we understood?"

We all agreed that things were well understood.

Jack, still at the window said, "Look at this."

Those of us who could get to the windows in time and was willing to take a chance on there not being some Indians hid close, flocked over there, shoving and pushing for a look. There was a fistful of Indians dragging White Eagle off his horse. They had sticks, and when he was on the ground they went about beating the puredee dog shit out of him.

Binoculars was found, a couple pairs, and a bunch of us got a look, but even from that distance there was a clear view without them. You could easily make out what was going on, and what you couldn't make out, you could figure on.

One of those who had managed a window view was Happy, a.k.a. I Have A Hand In My Hair, and he said, "They've decided White Eagle's magic failing the way it did wasn't just because someone killed a skunk or shit on a scared rock, or some such. They have decided it failed because White Eagle is full of that which comes loose from a goose, and they are teaching him a lesson."

"It's a good one too," Jack said.

It was indeed a good lesson. Sticks was coming down on his ass so hard and fast, it looked like Chinamen hammering down spikes on the railroad. This went on until they was tired, and then they rested on their sticks. White Eagle wallowed around on the ground for awhile. Then he got to his feet, went to his horse, and tried to pull himself up on it, but that was when Quanah turned with the rifle he was holding, and shot the horse in the head, causing it to topple and nearly fall over on White Eagle, who proved spry enough after that beating to dodge the falling critter, which fell with its legs kicking and shit spewing out of its ass. I really don't know about the last part. It was a good distance, but that's usually how it was.

The Indians with the sticks was rested now, and so they came again, and damn if I didn't start to feel sorry for White Eagle. It was a serious thumping.

While all this was going on, another Indian come riding up to sit on his horse by Quanah, and then another, and while they was beginning to clutch up on the hill, some more Indians took to chopping up White Eagle's horse, and now they was all pulling out their johnsons and pissing on White Eagle while he lay on the ground.

"They sure don't like him," Millie said.

"Seems that way," Jack said.

Billy was watching all of this quietly. He said, "I got a fifty, but I want to borrow one of those 50-90's, someone's got one to loan me. I'm going to take a shot."

"Too far away," Jimmy said.

"Yeah, but I'm of a mind to do it anyway," Billy said.

Bets went around about how many yards or feet the bullet would fall short, some money, pocket knives and a cigar went into a hat.

Billy took the fifty in one hand, wet his finger, poked it out the window for a second, pulled it back, "Said wind's not kicking, so what the hell."

He laid the rifle on the window frame, coughed once, wiggled his ass and shifted his feet, said, "Now, don't nobody say nothing."

"You couldn't hit anything up there if we was a hundred feet closer," said Jimmy. "Give me that hat. I got more money to put in against this shot."

"He said shut up," Millie said. "He don't make the shot, I'll pull the wagon with any and every one of you, long as I'm allowed rest time."

Everyone shut up and was hopeful of Billy having the bad eye, all except me. I had bet on his side of the matter, but only in my head. Billy did the thing with his feet again, got his ground, leaned into the Sharps, and with both eyes open, took his aim.

He pulled the trigger. The Indian to the right of Quanah fell off his horse, and then the sound of the shot echoed against the ridge. Well now, there was a bit of excitement up there. Them Indians thought for sure they was out of range, them being about a mile away, and frankly, so did all of us, and that included Billy.

"Well fuck a hairy goat ass," Billy said.

"That's a relief," Millie said, "I was already trying to figure if there was axel grease in the house. You missed that shot, at some stage here in the day or night, figured I might need it."

"Holy shit," Jack said. "That is the most amazing goddamn shot I've ever seen. Except for one I made once where I shot the Sunday hat off God's head."

Everyone laughed. It was like we had all bottled up something and could uncork it now.

Up there on the hill the Indians was gathering their dead man, and riding away, all except Quanah who sat on his horse and looked down at us. I know he was too far away to tell for sure, but you can bet his eyes was blazing.

Course, White Eagle was still on the ground. And while Quanah sat there, we saw White Eagle rise and wobble away, heading in the direction the others had gone. I figured he had a few more beatings to catch up with.

After a moment Quanah lifted his rifle and fired a shot in the air, let out with a whoop, wheeled his horse and was gone.

"You should have took a shot at him," Jimmy said, now an enthusiastic supporter of Billy and that rifle.

"Naw, it was a scratch shot, and a good one, and if I missed next time, it would be said I was lucky. Which I was. I think what helped me there was they was all bunched up together, and maybe a wind kicked up at the back of my shot, pushing. But still, it was a good shot, wasn't it?"

"It was," Jack said, and clapped Billy on the shoulder.

We all stood there for awhile, and then Happy said, "They have had enough."

"Maybe," Jimmy said.

"No," Happy said. "They are through. The magic failing, that long shot, and that was Black Buffalo Hump you killed. He's one of the more respected Comanche. You took the wind out of their sails. With their magic coming apart like that, they think that shot is a sign from the Great Spirit that White Eagle was a false prophet as well as an asshole."

"A sore false prophet," Jack said. "I bet them sticks left marks."

"Hey, Jimmy," I said.

"What?"

When he turned toward me I hit him as hard as I could, knocking him down into wherever Mrs. Olds was keeping her soul.

9

THAT WAS IT for what has come to be called the Second Battle of Adobe Walls, but it wasn't over for me and Black Hat Jack, or for that matter Millie.

After the battle, what bodies the Indians didn't collect, some of the men hacked up or pissed on or did pretty much the same thing to the bodies the Comanche and their partners had done to the whites. Neither me nor Jack took part in that, though Millie did so to avenge her brother, though when she was finished doing what she did with a hatchet, her brother was still dead, and the Indian she had chopped on hadn't been taught any sort of lesson that I could understand. Anyway, they did that, and the bodies of our men killed was buried, including them in the wagon, along with Millie's brother. They took the Indians out away from Adobe Walls for the crows and vultures and ants to have them.

Mrs. Olds they loaded up in the back of a buffalo wagon with the body of her husband. She didn't never make a move, still being under the influence. She may still be passed out at this very moment, even though some years have passed; that woman was drunk.

During all these goings on, I looked up and saw out on the same ridge where the Indians had been, my horse Satan. He had turned back up and was looking down on us with the same contempt that Quanah had. He could be like that. I told you how he would come to my whistle when he was in the mood. Well, thing was he wasn't in the mood right then, cause I wore myself out trying to whistle him up. He just stood there looking, like he had no idea what I was doing, or who I was.

I found my saddle and started out after him, and Jack decided he'd come along and help. He'd found his horse easy enough, saddled it. He loaded up my spare saddle bags full of ammunition, flapped them across his horse, over his own bullet-filled bags, and rode along with me as I walked, that heavy saddle on my back.

I guess because I was the one who rescued her, Millie decided she'd go along with us, ending up on the back of Jack's horse.

Carrying a saddle like that is hot and heavy work, and about the time I got to the creek, I put the saddle under a tree. And then, just carrying the bridle, decided I'd go on after Satan and ride him back to the saddle bareback.

I gave my Winchester to Jack to strap on his horse, and I just wore my handguns. The Indians did appear to be gone, but you couldn't be sure, and my damn horse seemed to be heading out toward the way they went. I decided if he went too far, I was just going to have to let him go and see if he might send me a letter as to his location later in the year.

After a bit, we seen Satan, and he was moving away from us, prancing like he was a wild pony, and in some ways he was.

Finally I decided I'd have to go after him Indian style, which meant I would take hold of Jack's stirrup, and he would get his horse up to a mild run, and I would run along beside the horse, letting its body carry me forward, just being alert enough to get my feet up and make with leaping motions. You could run quite a ways like this if you had the stamina, and I did.

We come to another rise, higher than the one we had gone over. We stopped there to let me get my wind. From that vantage point we could see far in the distance the Indians riding away slowly, going home without some of their dead, their tails between their legs, having been whipped by believing in White Eagle's horseshit. I didn't have a mind to be sad about their circumstances, just then. I still had my hair and was grateful of it. It was that Adobe Walls battle, their loss there, that some said was when the Comanche decided they was finished. That the buffalo wasn't coming back, no matter if they did the Cheyenne Sundance, believed in medicine men, or force of numbers. Their way of life was pretty much over, as far as Texas went. On up north there was still to come the Battle of Little Big Horn, and that would do in the Sioux and the rest of the Cheyenne, but that was still two years off. What we now call the Wild West was winding down like a worn-out clock.

Those Indians decided us on turning back, letting Satan go his own way. It was while we was going back down that ridge, me clinging to Jack's stirrup, jumping along like a jack rabbit beside his horse, that we come by some buffalo wallows. We paused at the wallow to let me blow and get my breath back. It was at the same time about twenty Indians, mostly Kiowa, come out of what seemed like a straight run of prairie, but was instead a low spot that the grass covered unless you was right on it. They just come riding up as if out of coming up from the center of the earth. We was all surprised. They looked at us, and we looked at them. You could almost see them thinking: Why here are some of those that run us off, and we are twenty and they are three, and one of them is a woman. We are in good shape here.

Thing that worked against them, though, wasn't but two of them was armed with rifles, the rest had bows and arrows. I should point out that those are weapons serious enough. A good bow shooter can set a dozen arrows in flight faster than a man can cock a regular set-up Winchester. I, of course, had a different sort of Winchester, and could fire rounds as fast as I could jack, which gave me a slight edge.

I think them Kiowa decided that the day was going to end on a happier note than they had anticipated. They took to yelling, and as we knew what was coming next, Jack rode his horse down into the buffalo wallow, dismounted, jerked Millie off its back, shot his horse in the head faster than them Indians could figure to ride down on us.

It was the right thing to do. Wasn't no use trying to outrun them Kiowa, not with Millie clinging to the back, and me running alongside. They'd have been on us quick and things would have been over for the three of us before we could have gone a hundred yards.

The horse tumbled back and kicked once, but Jack had pulled it in such a way that its legs was pointing into the wallow, and the depression of its body there gave us something to hide behind, as long as they came from one side. Another thing we had going was the wallow was deep, and there was a deeper depression on the far side, and therefore the rim of the wallow served as a kind of fortification. It wasn't the best you could ask for, but it was more than you could hope to get, all things considered. Of course, we was also hoping all our shooting would bring some of the men still at Adobe Walls on the run, but it also occurred to me that shooting might be just the thing not to bring them. We hadn't told anyone of our plans to chase my horse, and there wasn't any reason they might not think it was the Indians firing off shots in anger. I was more concerned that some of the other Indians, having broken off from the others, like these, would hear the firing and come to the aid of their companions, making short work of us.

I won't bore you with all the shooting we done, as you've already been told how it was at Adobe Walls, and this was more of the same, but with less Indians, though our situation was no less dire. We was three and they was twenty, and we was in a hole in the ground with a dead horse for cover. Before nightfall, that horse was littered with arrows and holes from bullets that had missed their mark. We had killed one of them and two of their horses, to put them afoot, but far as we knew, no stray bullets had put anybody down under. They pulled the rest of their mounts back down the hill out of shooting range, as killing their horses and putting them on foot was a good strategy anytime.

Them Kiowa lying out there in the grass would pop up from time to time and take pot shots at us, but they didn't keep their heads up long. They knew we could shoot.

Why they hadn't tried to crawl around behind us, I can't say. Maybe they wasn't fully committed after being defeated the way they was. They might even have seen some sport in it.

It was a bright night and we could see good, and we was keeping our eyes peeled in a serious manner. I have heard that Indians do not like to fight at night, and that's true of some of them, and to be honest, it's not my first pick neither. You're just as liable to shoot one of your own as one of theirs, getting all worked up by the battle. But again, it wasn't a thought we was holding to, as plenty of Indians have put the sneak on folks at night, and did them in before they knew there was something to be worried about.

Way we was arranged was we was all behind the horse. Jack had pulled the saddle bags with the ammo free, and with it I could load both rifle and pistols. Millie had only a pistol, but she looked determined there in the starlight, and I will admit that her bravery gave me a feeling that might have seemed odd for the moment. There are white men who will cringe to hear this, but I had a mighty strong taste for her right then. I'm not saying even had she been of the same mind at that moment, or that it would have been a smart move for us to drop our drawers and take advantage of romance right then. That would have most certainly led to us having as many arrows in us as that dead horse. But she was mighty fetching there in the starlight, her black hair dangling, her lying on her back, looking away from the horse, watching for any of them Kiowa, coming around behind us.

After awhile, Jack said, "Nat," and he said it in such a way, I knew he was trying to draw me near to him. I inched up, and soon as I did, Millie said, "You might as well tell the both of us outright. It's not like I haven't grown accustomed to bad news, and am fully aware we are in a tight spot, so don't hold the horses."

"If only we had one," Jack said. "I think I did the right thing then with this old nag. She could hardly outrun me. But there's one that might serve to do better, provided there was a distraction. On that rise beyond."

Jack pointed. I turned and seen it was Satan. The bastard was about a quarter mile away, just standing there looking, and in that moment I told myself I caught up with him and was able to ride him out, I was going to shoot him and eat him and have a pair of boots made out of him just on general principle.

"We don't want to draw attention that he's there to them Indians," said Jack. "They may already have seen him, but then again, they have a strong eyeball on us, waiting for us to make a mistake. Another bit of news is I didn't fill my canteen at the creek before we went after Satan. I thought it would be less of a journey. I hoped for water in this wallow, but damn if it don't seem to be dry."

"So we got a possible horse," I said, "but no water. I don't see how a horse would do us good, other than shooting him to hide behind."

"Hell, Nat. Satan, that one is a runner and you know it. There ain't nothing on four feet can catch him."

"Probably true enough," I said.

"Now, there's actually a worse bit of news," Jack said.

"What could be worse?" Millie said.

"Well, they want you, little lady, you know that much," he said.

"I do," Millie said. "There is nothing better to satisfy their taste than the rape and tortured murder of a white woman."

"It is similar to what we have done to their own, so they are even more spiteful about it," Jack said. "And Nat here will tell you about how white folks have treated black slave women, but this ain't the spot for politics, since I ain't running for any kind of office. But considering I may not get to speak on it at another date, I thought I'd toss a loop on it. The other problem I'd like to mention, and this is a personal problem. I caught a bullet a short time back. One of those times they threw a few rounds in this direction. It come over the top of this dead cayuse and caught me in the gut."

"Damn, Jack," I said.

"Bad?" Millie asked.

"I'd say so, yes," Jack said, "which is why I call it bad news. And I didn't even know it right at first. I mean, the pain set in pretty quick, but not right at first. I didn't know for sure what it was. Felt like I'd been stung. I been shot before, but not like this; them was all nothing more than a case of sun burn. Now that the sting has passed, the wolf is here, chewing at my guts. I thought I'd save the information until it became important. As I can feel me draining out, I thought it was time to mention it."

I put my hand on the ground next to Jack. It was dark and the ground was damp and sticky.

"Kept my jacket closed up, even hot as it was, holding in things. Now I'm feeling a might more comfortable, there being a snap in the air, and me being pretty near out of blood."

"We got to get you out of here right away," I said. "I'm not sure how yet, but we got to. You and Millie, you got to take Satan and ride out and let me give them the business for awhile."

"No, Nat, that is right manful of you, but I couldn't ride nowhere. This coat is keeping my guts inside. Not all of what we been smelling is dead horse. My innards are raising quite an aroma."

"Tell me what you want," I said, "and I will try and move heaven and earth, and piss hell's fires out for you."

"I know that, Nat. And I'm going to tell you what you both got to do, and I can't really measure much of an argument from you. You got to listen to me."

"We're listening," Millie said.

Jack looked out over the horse and checked on the Indians. We couldn't see them. For all we knew they were finally sneaking up behind us, or some of them was.

"I don't want to die in a wallow behind a dead horse, leaking out the last of me. I want to die fighting, and I'm going to do that. I don't think I can stand till morning. But there's one small chance, and it depends on the disposition of that goddamn horse of yours, Nat. He looks to me like he may have had his fun and would like to be caught up and taken to some grain, so we'll play it that way. It don't work like that, then it's going to be the same for me either way, and I advise the two of you if there's no fight really left, to do what you got to do; that whole last bullet business."

"That's exactly what I'll do," Millie said.

"Good," Jack said. "I got my rifle here, a pistol and a knife. And what I'm going to do is rise up out of here, if I got the strength to do it, and I'm going to them. Going right at them like a derailed train. I am going to fire the shot in my Sharps and toss it, then go in on them with pistol and knife. I won't live long enough to be tortured, but I just might take a few of them down and give you time to catch that contrary horse. You can bet though I'll keep them busy till Old Man Death comes to collect me up in his croker sack."

"That's crazy, Jack," I said.

"Yeah, it is, but what other plan you got?" he said.

"They'll get tired and go on."

"Might, but they are pretty moved to kill somebody after how things worked out. They'd like to take our scalps back to all them others, and say, boys, you done slid out of there when the doings was still good, and we got the scalps to show it. It would put them in good with their fellows if they killed us and maybe brought Millie in for further activities, such as they are. Maybe they'll just want to rape and kill her here."

"Neither is appealing," Millie said.

"You take that Winchester, saddle bags of ammo, and while I'm up and about my business, whistle up that horse. He don't come, you just keep running. It's a long ways, but you just might get away if luck is on your side and they go blind in both eyes and their legs break and their horses won't mind them."

"Hardly sounds hopeful," I said.

"It isn't. Satan is your best chance, and then you still got to get on him and get out of here riding double. It's all we got, Nat. It's what we're going to do. You two get ready to run."

"Jack," I said. "You know I don't want to leave you."

"I do, and if it was just you, I'd still ask you to do this, cause I'll be dead in an hour or two, if I make it that long, and you'll still be in the same spot. But it's not just you. It's her too. Now here I go."

"Take my Winchester," I said.

"No, you'll need that. I'll be in too close a quarters to use it. We rode some good roads and some bad ones together, you dusky demon, but we rode them like men, didn't we?"

"Reckon so," I said.

"All right, then. You may have to help me up and hope you don't take a bullet. I've gathered myself as much as I can. Soon as I'm over the lip and making noise, you two go for Satan. Go fast as you can. My heart is with you. Help me up now, Nat. I'm going to surprise the shit out of them, but first I got to cinch up this jacket with my belt so my guts don't fall out. That shot has made one hell of a hole."

10

"I AM GOING to let the pain have me," Jack said. "I been holding in a yell something terrible, and I am about to let it out, so when you hear it, don't piss yourselves. I am going now."

I grabbed his arm and helped him up. My hand brushed against his hand as he let go of me. It was cold as ice. He stepped up on that horse in a lively manner, as if he was a young'n and full of piss and vinegar. He was one game rooster. Out of the wallow he went, and then he was running, that jacket belted up tight around him at the bottom. He let out with a blood-curdling scream, fired into that grass with the Sharps, threw it aside, and drew his pistol.

Me and Millie was already moving then. I wasn't looking at Jack anymore. We came out of the wallow on the side, me with them saddle bags full of ammunition thrown over my shoulder, the dead horse's bridle there too, carrying my Winchester. We ran toward Satan, who stood in his spot, tossing his head. He had gone to nickering too, and I hadn't gone but a few steps when I tried to whistle, but my mouth was too dry. I didn't stop though, just kept running, Millie beside me. Any moment I expected Satan to bolt, and there we'd be, out of what protection the wallow offered and on foot.

Behind us Jack's pistol was popping something furious. I heard gunfire from the Kiowa too. I glanced back once, and them Kiowa was all over Jack, like coyotes trying to take down an old buffalo bull. They was swinging hatchets and clubs and knifes, but Jack, bad off as he was, was making a hell of a stand of it. He had lost that black buffalo hat, no longer had his pistol, but was gripping his skinning knife instead. It flashed in the starlight as it went up and down and slashed right and left.

When I turned back to what was at hand, here come Satan, trotting toward us like he had just been waiting on us. He come right up to me and nickered. I gave Millie my Winchester to hold, patted his nose, then put that bridle on him. I swung up on his back, stuck out my hand, and pulled Millie up behind me.

We was facing the Kiowa then, and I felt mounted I could do Jack some good, come swooping down on them, but it was too late. I saw him fall beneath a rain of blows. But I'll say this for Jack, their numbers was thinner now. Jack had killed three of them that I could see. The live ones was shoving at one another now, competing for who was going to take Jack's scalp.

Turning Satan with a touch of the reins, I put my heels to him and he began to fly.

Millie said, "They're coming."

I turned to look. Four of those Kiowa was coming after us, having lost interest in Jack now, and maybe lost the tussle over his scalp. They was excited and whooping and really urging their horses.

I hooked my right heel into Satan, swung out to my left so that I was hanging way out from him, him at a full gallop. I had the reins in my teeth. I hung out there in the wind and cocked my Winchester. I didn't have the baffle down, so I cocked and took my time. I aimed and squeezed off easy, and though the world was jumping, my timing was right on. I shot one of them off his horse, and then the others began to slow, and then they was dots way back behind us. I swung back in position, and away we did ride.

Pegasus his ownself couldn't have caught us.

11

We stopped at the creek by Adobe Walls, got my saddle, couple of canteens from the store, filled them from the creek. We got jerky out of there too, blankets, some odds and ends, and continued on, still double on Satan.

As we rode along I wasn't thinking about getting scalped as much as before, and I became aware of Millie's arms around my waist. She leaned her body and head into my back. I could feel her warmth and her breath on the back of my neck. Even with all we had been through, and her in those dirty clothes, she smelled sweeter than a spring flower.

That night we camped and she cried and I just lay on my bedroll across the way and let her do so without saying anything. Finally she got cried out and said, "I wanted to be a tom boy until yesterday. I was good at it. I ran off to go hunting with my brother. I shot buffalo and skinned them, and I went dirty and nasty for weeks at a time. I fought off men who wanted to get in my britches, or fought off those thought I ought not wear men's clothing. I did all that and I was fine with it until Zeke got killed. That took the starch out of my drawers, right there, that's what I've got to tell you."

"That's understandable," I said.

"Do you think I did wrong as a woman to go out west with my brother and do things like I've done?"

"I hadn't given it any thought," I said. "I think it's fine whatever you do, long as you don't steal something or kill somebody doesn't have it coming, be mean to animals, unless you have to kill and hide behind them or eat them. I think you do okay. You got sand. I can say that for you. You got more guts than a lot of men I known. Back there in that wallow, you was strong, girl, strong. You don't buckle down and hope for the best. You fight your way out."

"You have saved me twice, Nat. Both times I was being attacked by Indians and was with a dead horse. Once two of them."

"Jack saved you the second time, saved me too."

"I didn't mean to sound like I'd forgotten him."

"I know you haven't. How could you? How could anyone?"

"He was brave," she said.

"I'd have died behind that horse," I said. "I'd have just bled out before I'd have done what he done. That took guts."

"I think you'd have done it had it been you shot, Nat. I think you would have."

"That makes one of us."

She got quiet for awhile, said, "Do you think it's wrong for whites and Indians to be together, you know, to marry?"

"I got nothing against it," I said. "Jack had an Indian wife. I never met her, but he held her dear to him. Digging Wolf she was called. They wasn't never married in an American way, but in an Indian way they was. She died of some kind of white man disease. He missed her everyday, talked about her all the time. I reckon he liked her just fine, and she was Indian. Course, I'm not sure if Jack might have been part Indian, or even colored. I don't know."

"Do you think it's okay colored and Indians mix up like that?"

"You mean be together?"

"Yeah."

"I can't see no difference in that than in a white and an Indian or a mixed up blood like Jack. He once told me that somewhere along the line all our blood has mingled."

"How about colored and whites, what you think about that?"

"It don't bother me none, but it sure bothers some, you can count on that."

"What about me and you?" she said.

"I'm going to ask you to explain that one."

"What if I was to take off my pants and come over there and get under your blankets with you?"

"I think I'd have a hard time keeping my own pants on."

"That's what I was hoping for," she said.

She got up then, standing there in the starlight, already barefoot, her boots beside her blankets. She went to unbuttoning her pants. I started to tell her I hadn't meant what I said, and she ought to stop. I knew that was the right thing to say, cause no matter how much the color line didn't bother me, it would damn sure bother whites. But I didn't say anything. I couldn't. My heart was in my mouth.

Well, she slipped off her pants, and her shirt hung down over her womanhood, and then she unbuttoned that and threw it open. I could see her breasts and I could see the darkness between her legs, and then she came to me. I threw back my blanket and she laid down. As I had predicted, my pants came off.

The next few days was a delight, and I remember them as clearly as if they happened this morning. Sometimes I think I can smell her. She had that sweet smell I talked about, and she smelled even better when she was hot and at it. That kind of wild animal smell dipped in mint and lilac water.

We traveled slow, moving everyday farther away from Indian country. That's not to say we dropped our guard, but it is to say we frequently dropped our pants. I worried about getting her with child, and was careful as I could be not to, cause if ever I would have been creating a sad little bastard, it would have been that poor, little fellow. Half white and half black and not too popular with either crowd.

Considering all that happened to us, we was reasonably festive. Or more likely, we was that way on account of what had happened to us. I knew that was what most of Millie's interest was about. We had come close to death, and now we was celebrating life, and doing it with all our abilities.

When we come to a town, there was some men who come up to us right quick, looking angry, wanting to know what a nigger was doing with a white gal snuggled up behind him. Nothing sets a white

Texan off his feed quicker than the thought that a colored might be dipping his rope in a white woman's well, which as I said before was one of my great worries. Things could have got testy, but when they started asking, rumbling about what we was doing, Millie slid down off Satan, praised the lord, said how glad she was to see them, said how I had been kind enough to help her, had given her a ride back from the Battle of Adobe Walls and fought Indians for her.

At first they didn't believe her, but she went to telling about her brother, and how things had gone for us, about Billy Dixon's shot. By this time all that news had already been heard, and they took her story to be true, which it was for the most part.

Millie told them too about the fight at the buffalo wallow, and how Jack had died. When she come to that part she tossed in some sniffles, which I like to think was sincere. If not, they was damn well convincing, cause men took off their hats, and women, who had gathered around us, wept. A young boy wanted to know if we got to see Jack scalped. I wanted to scalp that little shit, but held my tongue and held my piece.

She didn't mention what we had been doing under our blankets the last few days. I was just a colored man who had been at the fight and helped her out. I was immediately branded a good nigger, got some pats on the back, and was offered a dinner, as long as I didn't come in the house to eat it. It was a long shot from being out there on the prairie with men who lived by gun and knife. Coming back into civilization I found it had less civilized behavior. Them old boys out there in the wilds could be rude and smelly, forget to wash their hands now and again, but they at least stood back a bit and was willing to take a man's measure. Here, though they took off their hats and didn't spit in public and cleaned under their nails at least once a week, I was already measured, cut and folded. I was a colored man, and though I had done good, I was still a colored. Had I reached out and touched Millie, even on the arm, in a familiar way, I'd have had done to me pretty much what those Comanche had done to that hunter me and Jack found.

Black Hat Jack

Millie got taken to a couple's house to clean up. I had to take my horse to the livery, and then I was blessed to sit on the front porch where the family that had taken her in lived. I sat there watching the sun set with a yellow cat for a companion.

A woman brought me out a supper of cold cornbread and some warm beans. A moment later she came out with a saucer and a bottle of milk, and poured the cat some of it in the saucer. Now both animals were fed.

From the porch I could look through the windows. The lamps gave the rooms inside a nice glow. Millie sat at the dinner table with the family. She now wore a fine white dress, her black hair washed and combed, mounded up on her head and pinned. Her neck was long and slim, her shoulders narrow and straight. The light lay on her smooth face as if it was a thin coat of gold paint. She was very lovely.

When she moved her hands, shifted in her chair as she talked, she did so in a delicate way, like a woman that had never stepped one foot out of a parlor. Like a woman who had never shot a buffalo or skinned one, had never fought Indians, or nearly died in a wallow out on the prairie.

I could hear them talking. I heard the man and woman asking her about her family, and Millie telling them her brother had been all she had, and now he was dead and she was all alone. She talked about how she had to survive on the trail because that's what her brother wanted. He was the one had her dress like a man so she wouldn't be noticed as a woman right off. He had her do it as a form of protection. She said it was a hard thing, but her brother was all she had, and she had to do his bidding. She didn't mention what she had told me on the trail, about how she had gone off to be different. She damn sure didn't mention what me and her did under them blankets. She spoke kindly of me, the way you might a stray dog.

I knew what she was doing. All that time in pants with a six-gun had worn thin to her. She was trying to find her way back into feminine graces and polite society. Some place where it didn't rain on your head and the wind didn't blow cold and you didn't need to go hunting for your supper and maybe fight a bear or an Indian over it.

I looked at her for a long time, and then she happened to look toward the window. I think she could see me sitting out there in the dark. She looked briefly, then looked away, like she had seen something disturbing, and in a way she had. Now that she was among white people, and I was no longer a warm comfort on a cold, dark night, she felt she had to look at things different. I didn't blame her. There was nothing to come of it, me and her, even if it had meant anything to her, and maybe it had at the time. She had been brave about the color line out there on the plains under the stars with no one to see us but the wildlife, but she couldn't be like that now, not here in a well-lit house, wearing a nice, clean dress. Not where a couple might take her in and make her days more pleasant.

I didn't know exactly how to feel, but in a strange way, I think I wished I was back in that wallow, fighting it out with them Kiowa. I realized I felt more at home there than here.

I finished up eating and left the plate on the porch, gave the cat a pat, and walked over to what served as the livery, which is where I had left Satan. It was one small building and looked to have been put up in a windstorm, way it sagged. It could house three horses and a couple of men if they didn't swing their arms any. There was some covered sheds out to the side, and that's where Satan had ended up. I had wanted to shoot him and eat him before, but now I was glad to have him back.

The livery operator asked that I tell him about the fight out there on the prairie, as he had missed the story first hand. I did the best I could to not be impatient. I told it, and I was sure to build up the white boys more than myself. He let me have my horse for free, including the grain Satan had eaten, and even gave me a bit for the road. He told me that the couple Millie was with had lost their daughter to the influenza. I told him they might well have found another daughter this very night.

I mounted up and rode away, and I never saw Millie again, though along the trail for many days after, I would think of her and our blankets out there on the trail, and those thoughts made me feel good.

12

SOME YEARS LATER when I was working as a Marshal for Hanging Judge Isaac Parker, I was walking along a boardwalk in Fort Smith, Arkansas, proudly wearing my marshal badge, and who do I see but Happy Collins. He looked up and seen me at the same time. He smiled, and I smiled, and we threw our hands out and shook.

"Why Nat, you black son-of-a-shit-eating dog, how you been?"

"Better than you, I Have A Hand In My Ass, you horse-humping excuse for a white Indian."

We laughed and he invited me into the saloon for a drink, forgetting I wasn't exactly welcome inside. As a marshal, even a black one, I had some perks, but I didn't take advantage of them much, and besides, I didn't drink. I was still a sarsaparilla man.

"Someone has let you tote a badge?" he asked.

"Judge Parker don't care about color," I said.

"I mean why would they let you tote a badge. That's like asking me to be a banker."

It was all lame stuff, but we enjoyed it. Finally he went in the saloon, got a bottle of whisky and a bottle of sarsaparilla for me, and came out. We walked off to where there was a big oak on the edge of town, sat down there and talked while we sipped from our bottles.

"So what you been doing all this time?" I asked.

"These last three years were what you might call eventful," Happy said. "After Adobe Walls, I managed to brave up enough to go back to the Cheyenne. I mean, I waited until I heard they was near whipped in spirit, you know, and that White Shield, my father-in-law, had forgiven me. He had banished me because

White Eagle said he should. Now on account of White Eagle being nothing but a lying asshole, he welcomed me back. You know, the Comanche and the Cheyenne gave White Eagle a new name after Adobe Walls. I ain't exactly sure how it shakes out, even though I speak both languages pretty good, but it's something like Wolf Pussy, or Coyote Ass, or Wolf Shit, Wolf Turd, maybe. Whatever it is, it's not meant as a term of endearment. He gets kicked a lot and women throw horse shit at him. I seen them do it. Thing was, though, even having been welcomed back into the fold, I didn't stay long. My wife, White Shield's daughter, damn if she wasn't humping the hell out of a brave in the short time I was gone. I think she had done him so good he had gone cross-eyed. I sure didn't remember his eyes being like that when I left out of there on the run. Anyway, I got back into camp, I come to suspect it had been going on all along and I had been a fool. I rolled up my blankets and went back to white folks, and have been miserable ever since. I liked being an Indian. You know a thing I miss, though I don't say it too much? It's boiled dog. I guess anyone can kill and skin and boil a dog, but my woman could do it better than anyone I ever knew. I've whacked a few pups on my own, skinned them and boiled them, but it just isn't the same. Shit, Nat. I ain't nothing but a lazy scoundrel and secret dog boiler in white society. Out there among the Cheyenne I was respected for not stooping to woman's work. Hey, whatever happened to Jack?"

I told him.

"Oh damn, Nat. I didn't know."

"He was a brave one," I said.

"He was at that," Happy said. "I knew him and knew of him for a long time. Lot of people hated him, but there wasn't many didn't respect him. Or if they didn't, they didn't let on to his face."

He drank more of the bottle, and we talked for awhile longer, until I realized all we had between us was that day at Adobe Walls. I made excuses, one of which was that it was best I not be seen with a drunk, and then I stood up and so did he.

Black Hat Jack

While he was laughing at my joke about him being a drunk, I stuck out my hand, and we shook. He had tears in his eyes as we parted. I don't know if it was the whisky, or memory of that day, or if Happy was just the crying type.

13

IT WAS ANOTHER two years before I pulled off my badge and rode out to Adobe Walls. I still had Satan, and he was still one hell of a runner, but he couldn't run as long or as far as before. He had gotten old. But, in a short burst, there still wasn't a horse alive that could beat him.

Took the old trail out there, come to where I thought was about where me and Jack had found that dead man, scalped and cut up. There wasn't any more wild Indians about, least not in packs. The Comanche had all gone tame, or so it was said. I didn't see a single buffalo. It was if that hunter and the Comanche and the buffalo had never been.

When I came to Adobe Walls, I tied Satan off to a broken pole sticking out of one of the walls, and went inside where we'd had the fight. A lot of people had camped there. There was all manner of things thrown around, piles of shit here and there, where lazy ass-holes hadn't bothered to go outside. The roof was long gone. There was only the sky.

I stood at the window where Billy Dixon had made his shot. Over the years there was them that doubted it, and them that said he made it from the loft, but there wasn't any loft. And he didn't make that shot from the roof. I know. I was there and seen him shoot.

There was them among the Indians and the whites who said, yeah, he made that shot, but the Indian didn't die. He got hit in the elbow, or just got the breath knocked out of him by that long shot, and he lived. I doubt it. I seen him fall, and I have seen too many dead things drop; that shot killed him, I am certain.

Looking out the window at that rise near a mile away, I was overcome with emotion. Had Billy not taken that shot, them Comanche might have worried us down like a dog nipping at a wounded animal, worried us plumb to death. Thank goodness he took the shot. That shot had let them know White Shield's magic was no good.

But I hadn't really come out to see Adobe Walls. Oh, that was part of it, but there was more to it. I had ridden this way remembering those nights Millie and I had together. They hadn't meant that much to either of us in the long run, but we had been young and bold and I wondered now if she was a school marm. Not that I planned to look her up.

But even those memories of her wasn't why I had really come.

No.

It was Jack.

Shadows were growing long by the time I reached the wallow where the three of us had fought the Kiowa. Actually, the wallow had filled in a lot, mostly with grass. The grass was long and green there, and where Jack had fallen, not too far from it, there was a greater growth of grass, and there was blue bonnets and yellow flowers. The ground was rich there. Climbing off Satan's back I looked over that spot, turned my head and looked to where we had seen that trail of Indians traveling along, defeated not only that day, but forever. The prairie went on and on except where it was blocked by great rises of red and rust-colored rock. The sky, though beginning to darken, was so blue it near made me weep. Clouds tufted like cotton balls against it and there was a flock of birds racing across it. A light wind blew. I took in a deep breath. I felt as if I was taking in one of the last free breaths there would ever be.

I let go of Satan's bridle, because unlike in the past, he was now willing to stand and wait for me, having finally decided I was someone worth knowing and would supply him with grain. I strolled over to where Jack had fallen, got down on my hands and knees and plundered through the grass. I turned up bits of rawhide and finally a skull, or what was left of it. The top of it had been bashed in and where there should have been a left eye socket there was only a big hole that spread from socket to nose gap. There was smaller splits in the bone at the back of the skull—knife or hatchet strikes.

I prowled about some more, found more bones. Not many. Weather, animals and time had hauled the others away. I gathered up what I could, pushed down a swathe of grass with my foot and laid the bones on top of it. There was a small shovel in my gear. I got that and dug a hole that would hold all the bones. I put them in it and pushed the dirt back into the hole.

When that was done I stood up and tossed my head back and howled like a wolf. Why? I have no idea, but it sure felt good. I went back to Satan and pulled a short board I had brought out from a bag strapped across the side of his saddle. I had prepared it before coming. Carved into it, the carving filled with white paint, I had put:

BLACK HAT JACK.

HE DIED LIKE A MAN. RIGHT AFTER
THE SECOND BATTLE OF ADOBE WALLS.

I didn't have any dates on it, but I thought that better somehow. Besides, I had no idea when he was born, no hint of his age. Jack would have liked it simple. I sat there until the shadows widened and the clouds was no longer visible, and there was only the stars and the moon.

I rode by moonlight back to Adobe Walls and camped there, in the store part with Satan in there with me. I took off his saddle and blanket and curried him and gave him grain. I hobbled him, though I felt he would be willing to stay with me now, even through the night.

There was some firewood and kindling someone had hauled in, and I used that to make a nice fire as the wind was turning chill. I had a cold dinner of jerky and water. I had chosen the store for the night because the idea of lying down in the saloon where I had been holed up against them Comanche didn't appeal to me. It was silly, but that's how I felt. Above me was only sky, and that made me feel less cramped. The walls about me cut the wind. I was glad of that and glad for my fire, as there was much wind that night. It came howling across the prairie and down from the high rocks and moaned all night.

When I awoke the sun was not yet up. The fire had died down, so I took a stick and stirred it up and put on more wood so I could boil coffee and bake biscuits in my little pan. They didn't bake too good because I was in a hurry. I ate and drank, put out my fire and saddled Satan.

I took my time. The wind was still now. The sky was starting to lighten.

I thought about riding back to where Jack had fallen, one last time. But I didn't. I knew it didn't matter. It mattered not at all. Me and Satan went north east.

Author's note

THE SECOND BATTLE of Adobe Walls really happened, though I have used the fiction writer's privilege of telling it my way. Bat Masterson was really there, as were a few of the other characters. And Billy Dixon did take that shot, and its effect on the Comanche is as I described. Many of the events mentioned happened, though as with most Western history, there are considerable conflicts as to who did what and when and who was there and who was not, and so on. You finally have to decide on what seems the most real and lie about the rest of it, which is the bread of butter of a story writer. I have done that freely.

Blacks in the West have been mostly ignored until late. They took part in many great historical events, and did much of the

Black Hat Jack

Indian fighting as part of the Ninth and Tenth cavalry. Racism kept their accomplishments under wraps until recently. I know nothing of a black man being at Adobe Walls, but they were at many Western events, and there sure could have been someone like Nat there. History for African-Americans is growing richer. For Nat's background I read slave and ex-slave narratives, and a considerable number of historical tomes, as well as the remembrances of those who had lived through those times and wrote about it.

As described in the story, African-Americans got a better shake out West, as the tradition there was more of a wait and see before deciding a person's worth. This was not always the case, of course, but it was preferred by many African-Americans to the slave states, and by many, to the northern states, which were not always comfortable for the dark of skin either. Many famous mountain men and deputy marshals for Judge Isaac Parker were black. One of the most famous deputy marshals was Bass Reeves. The list of accomplishments by people of color is long and varied. There isn't room for all of it here, but I hope you will be encouraged to find out more. It's there if you look for it.

Finally, though real historical characters are mentioned in this story, this is my version of events, and even the real characters are not meant to be represented in an exact and accurate manner. They have become mythology, and I have played with that mythology, attempting like all story tellers, and tall-tale advocates, to give them their own sweet myths.

A last note. Western language was colorful and varied. I have tried to capture it here, though I haven't made any attempt for it to be on the money, but Nat's use of was instead of were was common for many. Even now, listening to pure East Texas accents, I find them variable. Not just the sound of the voice but the use of the words.

My father was born in 1909, and memory of him, and stories he told me that were told to him, are very much alive here. Not any exact story, but the tradition of story telling, which when he was in the right mood to do, could be riveting. I also got the feeling when listening to him that I was hearing an authentic voice not much removed from the era he was talking about, stories passed down to him by kith and kin. I am keeping the tradition alive.

I should also add that though there have been two other stories about this character, and there will be a forthcoming novel, the time lines don't entirely jibe. I wasn't sure what was what when I first started writing about Nat. I have also changed his speech patterns a bit for this novella and for that forthcoming novel.

As for history, I love it and care about it and have researched all manner of things, but as I said, I have not hesitated to shift certain things slightly when I felt it was in service of the story. Also, for those who are highly knowledgeable about guns, I want to thank you in the past for sending me a lot of contradicting, expert information. I should add that I appreciate your support, but if you feel that I have made an error here concerning any weapon or any piece of history, well, keep it to yourself.

Joe R. Lansdale
January 1, 2014

On Lost Worlds

by Poppy Z. Brite

Who among us has not dreamed of discovering a lost world? Who has never wished to come upon the secret tunnel, the magic door in the wall, the rabbithole that leads not just to another location in our known world, but to a world unlike anything human beings have ever seen before? This longing is almost instinctive, and surely as old as our capacity for curiosity.

The genre of "lost world" fiction arose in the late nineteenth century, a creative response to the real-life lost worlds that were being uncovered by explorers of the era: the city of Troy, the Valley of the Kings, the step pyramids of Mesoamerica. These discoveries fired the collective imagination in an enjoyably shivery way—jungle treks! Mummy's curses! Human sacrifice, beating hearts pulled right out of chests!—and fed an appetite for hi-test fiction that explored the possibilities of such realms. One of the genre's most important authors was H. Rider Haggard, a Victorian fabulist whose echoes are still felt in modern genre fiction (in *Misery*, Stephen King compares psychotic kidnapper Annie Wilkes to "the graven images worshipped by superstitious African tribes in the novels of H. Rider Haggard," and the novel Wilkes forces captive author Paul Sheldon to write is heavily influenced by Haggard). After failing an army entrance exam, Haggard traveled to Africa to take up a job with the lieutenant-governor of the British colony of Natal. He spent the next several years in what is now South Africa, working at various paid and unpaid government positions, and found a rich vein of stories there.

Often credited as the first lost world novel is Haggard's *King Solomon's Mines*, published in 1885. Set in an unmapped and unexplored region of Africa, it concerns the search for an aristocrat's lost brother and the discovery of a fertile land of treasures. It also introduces Allan Quatermain, a character Haggard would revisit in several more novels. Quatermain is a British explorer, big game hunter, and general old Africa hand who leads other characters into adventure and trouble; he also appears in Alan Moore's graphic series *The League of Extraordinary Gentlemen*, and is one of the inspirations for Indiana Jones. Though he is cast very much in the white-savior mode, Quatermain at least recognizes Africans as human beings capable of being noble and brave, a progressive attitude in comparison to many of Haggard's contemporary adventure writers.

In "Fishing For Dinosaurs," Joe Lansdale reintroduces us to a modern version of Quatermain, and also to a character named for another Rider creation, Ayesha of *She* (the novel that made the phrase "She who must be obeyed" a part of the language) and its sequel *She and Allan*. Haggard's Ayesha is a white queen who rules over an African tribe, while Lansdale's is "a long, lean black woman who look[s] like an African goddess" and trains people for incredible feats of adventure: in this case, capturing a plesiosaur. Lansdale's hapless narrator gets roped into this scheme, and…well, that way lie spoilers. Suffice it to say that "Fishing for Dinosaurs" also echoes Ray Bradbury's sad, lovely story "The Fog Horn," in which a creature that sounds very much like a plesiosaur revenges itself upon a lighthouse that mimics its cry but cannot return its ardor. "It's learned you can't love anything too much in this world," Bradbury's lighthouse keeper muses. "It's gone into the deepest Deeps to wait another million years. Ah, the poor thing! Waiting out there, and waiting out there, while man comes and goes on this pitiful little planet."

As a writer, Joe Lansdale has explored more worlds than most people can even imagine. One of the great things about a wide-ranging writer is that he takes you along for so many different rides. He has taken his readers to interdimensional drive-ins, zombie-infested deserts, weird Old West towns, the Dixie Mafia underworld, and as many more fantastical locales as there are spaces on a bookshelf. "Fishing for Dinosaurs" suggests that old-school adventuring is obsolete and the best thing to do when encountering a lost world may be not to rip away chunks of it for later analysis back in the known world, but to disappear into it. As Quatermain tells Lansdale's narrator, his employers seek to discover only to destroy with no clear idea of why: "When they decide they have learned all they can from him, or can no longer use him for anything, he will cease to be of importance to them... Like me, who has killed everything in this world that flies or crawls or walks or swims. Like me, who has helped capture one beast after another, bring it into their realm, where they can torture it with their experiments in search of the secret of longevity. I am their awful puppet. Or have been."

Heavy tunes in the era of global warming, mass extinctions, and bulldozing the Amazonian rainforest to raise beef. It doesn't seem too far-fetched to think some future author may end up writing about our lost world. If so, let's hope their storytelling voice is as distinctive as Joe Lansdale's.

Fishing for Dinosaurs

WHEN I CLIMBED out from under the bridge that morning, it was raining hard and a cold wind was blowing and I guess that's what turned me, that and the fact my coat was as thin as cheese cloth and I was so hungry I felt like my backbone was trying to gnaw its way to my navel. Being wet, cold, and hungry, as well as homeless, can affect a man's judgment in all manner of ways. It damn sure affected mine.

I thought about waiting for the rain to stop, but then decided the rain was what I needed. It was a Sunday morning, and if I was going to break into a house or building to find warmth, and mercy help me, something to steal and sell at a pawn shop, it was as good a time and as good a cover as any.

The rain beat me like chains, it was coming down that hard, and by the time I walked along the highway, which was empty of cars, I had a throbbing headache from the constant pounding of the rain. Finally, I came to a row of buildings just outside of town, and I decided they were my best bet. I felt drawn to them, in fact.

Most of the buildings were part of a series of warehouses, and that made it all the better. At the worst it would be warmer and drier inside, and maybe there would be that little something I was talking about. Something to steal.

It was like the place was made for me to break in. Underneath one of the windows someone had laid a barrel on its side, and I managed to get up on that without it rolling out from under me, and by using my elbow, I broke the window out. I spent some time picking the glass free because it was a good position, out back of the

Community Library of DeWitt & Jamesville

warehouse, away from the road, and with the rain and lack of traffic, I could take my time.

When I crawled inside, I moved away from the window and through a row of barrels that contained who knows what. Through cracks in the stacks, I saw bits of this and that, but the truth was I wasn't interested. I felt bedraggled and just needed a warm place to rest, and as I said, I was looking for something easy to steal. But it occurred to me that I could hole up in the warehouse until morning, maybe even beyond. It didn't seem like a place people were coming to often. *If I could find a way to get food, this might be my home away from home for a while.* I tried to think about my own home, but my mind didn't co-operate; I had a hard time visualizing it.

Winding my way through the rows of barrels, knocking aside a cobweb or two, I came to a door and gently pushed it open. It was nicer in there, and I could see it was a factory floor. It looked old and unused for quite some time, a deduction I made from the fact that it, like what must have been the store room, was gently covered in dust. There were all manner of machines, and I walked between those and found an office, which I peeked into. There was a desk in there and a chair, and on the desk I could see a little plaque with a rotating world symbol with certain spots on the continents dotted in red. I had no idea what that meant, or if it really meant anything. There was an old-fashioned rotary phone on the desk. I hadn't seen one of those since I was a kid. My grandparents owned one forever ago. I thought of them for a moment, but couldn't seem to hold their faces in my thoughts, and I let it go. There was also a coat rack, and on the rack was a nice wool coat and a pork pie hat on one of the spokes.

I walked away from there and found the break room. There was a candy machine and soft drink machine in there, but I had no money, so outside of turning one over and beating it until it gave up the goods, it didn't look likely that they'd do me any good. I didn't think I was strong enough to break it open. Not the way I felt right then anyway.

Back in the office, I sat in the chair and opened the desk drawer. I found a tin of paper clips, a box of old-fashioned kitchen matches, a few sheets of paper, the nub of a pencil, a plastic container of business cards, and about four dollars in quarters. I took the coins and went back to the machines and bought myself a bag of animal crackers and a soft drink with someone else's money, then went back to the desk to enjoy it. While I ate, I fiddled with the box of cards. They all had the same emblem that was on the plaque on the desk. A globe spread out and broken open to show all the views. I studied that world, determined it wasn't the earth as I knew it. It was similar, but there was a slight rearrangement of continents and the continents were marginally out of form. It didn't fit my geography lessons, but there was something about it that seemed right and sane to me, as if I had seen such a map somewhere, once upon a time.

Texas, the state I was in, was on the map, but the panhandle bent and went higher and twisted up through Colorado. At one time what became part of Colorado had been Texas. I remember my dad used to say "Why Texas gave that part up, I can't say. There's good skiing up there."

There were a number of other things, including a large continent in the center of the Atlantic. I didn't know what that meant.

I studied the card for a while and read the words at the top. LIMBUS, Inc. Below it was a phone number. I fanned the cards out, saw they were all the same, but noted something odd. The phone number on each of them was different. That made little sense. I turned one of the cards over. It read:

> LIMBUS, Inc.
> Are you laid off, downsized, undersized?
> Call us. We employ.
> 1-800-555-0606.
> *How lucky do you feel?*

I studied the number. I looked at the phone on the desk. I thought, don't be a dumb ass. They won't give you a job. They've probably been out of business for years, and besides that, they don't even know how to make a proper map of the world. It was my hunger and desperation that was thinking about calling, not my common sense. It may have been one of those scam jobs where you worked for them and turned out in the end you owed them money. Forget it, I told myself.

I ate my animal crackers and drank my drink, and when I finished, I was still hungry. I scrambled around in the drawer and found some more quarters, a few dimes, got myself another drink from the machine and this time went for a bag of peanuts. When I finished eating, I got the coat and tossed it on the floor and lay down on it, using the hat to cover my face. Lying there with a full stomach, I went straight to sleep. I slept warm, and for some time.

It was dark when I awoke. I fumbled about and got the drawer open and found the matches. I struck one and looked about for a light switch, and found one. I flipped it, and a light so dim that to see well by it you would have to set it on fire glowed on the ceiling.

I shook out the match. I picked up the phone. It had a dial tone.

All right. This place was not out of business, just not used frequently. Or maybe it was just this section. It was a large complex. Very large and this was just one end of it. Maybe there was more going on here than I thought.

I picked up the coat and put it on and sat back down in the chair and looked at the business cards that I had fanned out on the desk. I picked up one and studied it for a long time. I thought, well, what the hell?

I dialed the number on the card.

A man answered on the first ring.

At first I was a little startled and said nothing. Then the voice said, "If you're looking for a job, it is highly possible you've called the right place. My name is Cranston. How did you get our card?"

I told him.

with flecks of what looked like bronze fragments in them. Strangest eyes I had ever seen. The other man wasn't quite so tall, but like his counterpart, he was broad shouldered and muscular, a more lithe muscularity than his partner. His hair was jet black and his eyes were as gray as gun metal. His tanned, handsome face was marked with numerous small white scars.

They came in and stood looking at me, not saying a word. I got up and went with them, walked down the long hall between them, feeling like an antelope between two lions. We turned a way I hadn't been, and I saw clear, glass vats visible between the barrels, and odd, fleshy things floating in the vats, but I didn't get too good a look because the men on either side of me took up my view.

We came to a big door. The dark man slid it aside, and we went out of it. Outside, a long, black car was waiting. There was a man behind the wheel, short and squat, wearing a black chauffeur's cap. He looked like one of those middle-list drawings from a chart of the evolution of man—appeared as if he ought to be squatting in a cave chipping out flint arrow heads.

He rolled down the window, looked at me, and said, "I'm Bill Oldman. I will be your driver."

"All right," I said. "Don't they talk?"

"When they take the urge," he said.

One of the men, the dark-haired one, got in the front passenger seat. He said something to the driver in an odd language that contained clicks, exhalation of breath, and few words that sounded like a monkey hooting. The driver nodded.

The bronze man sat in the back with me. He said in a voice as melodious as bird-song, "You will need to take a sedative."

"Now wait a minute," I said. But I was too tired and too weak, and the man was incredibly strong. He stuck a hypodermic needle in my neck, and as the plunger went down, I was certain I was going to die, that I had been taken for body parts or was being put to death by the vengeful owner of the warehouse, or at least by one of his henchmen. I don't even think I had time to raise my hands. I know

I couldn't speak. My eyes began to close. The last thing I remember was the squat man driving us away into hot sunshine. The rain had passed but there were still clouds over my head.

The world crawled with fuzzy light. The light went from top to bottom in waves, and then from bottom to top. There was movement in the room, and there was sound. Footsteps. I felt like a wounded porpoise floating to the top of the sea. I had the sensation of tiny particles moving throughout my body, looking for a place to lie down.

A blond nurse wearing blue and white smiled at me. She was pretty. I tried to smile back, but moving the corners of my mouth away from my teeth was just too large a job. She moved out of my view and then a man came into my sight. He had arrived without the sound of footsteps. He was either a very light stepper or my mind was only picking up a bit of this and a bit of that. He bent over me. He wasn't as pretty as the nurse. He was what you would call roughly handsome with an emphasis on the rough. He wore a suit so dark it was the color of the end of time. He was lean and bony, had a long, long, crooked nose and hard, gray eyes. His black hair was slicked back from his high forehead. Something about his face didn't lend itself to smiling. In fact, there was a cruelness to it.

"I'm the man you spoke to," he said.

I tried to call him a son-of-a-bitch, but I hadn't the strength for it.

"My name is Cranston," he said. "You can call me Mr. Cranston."

I managed to make my top lip quiver, but that was it.

"You called about a job. We have a job. It's an unusual job, but then again, all our jobs are unusual. We like to choose people who don't really have a lot of options. Desperate people. Sometimes the people we choose, or the ones who choose us, don't live through the job. No one will know what happened to you. Someone might care, but no one will know. It will be as if you have fallen off the face of the earth. If you succeed, it could still be the same. You may never go back to the life you lived, not in any manner, shape, or form. It isn't always that way, but frequently it is."

I didn't have a life to go back to, so that part didn't concern me, though the part about not surviving almost allowed me to speak. But not quite. Phlegm rose up in my throat, but no words. I was too weak to spit it out, so I had to swallow it. It was like trying to swallow a grapefruit.

"If you don't want the job, well, I have to say this. We have a man, the big bronze man who helped bring you here. He's a doctor, and he can wipe your mind clean and set you down wherever we like. We can give you new memories. It might even be a good life. But you won't be you, and you won't remember any of this. I realize right now it's a bit difficult to speak, so I'm going to leave you and let you think. There's an IV in your arm, and there's a drip feeding through it. It will put you asleep again. When you awake the next time, we will feed you, and it will begin. Or, we can make the other arrangements I mentioned."

My eye lids felt like falling boulders.

He moved away.

I tried to keep my eyes open.

I couldn't.

A mouth moved close to mine. I could smell sweet perfume. The nurse. "I suggest you take whatever they offer," she said. "By the way. My name is Jane."

Someone turned out the light. It might even have been the one in the room.

When I awoke the second time, I felt less weak. I couldn't get out of bed though. I had a leather band across my waist and my ankles were bound. I was propped up in bed and my hands were free and there was a tray in front of me. At first I thought I might make a show of things and toss it across the room, but the smell coming from it was divine. It was a big juicy steak with grilled vegetables and wonderful, aromatic seasoning. The pretty nurse, Jane, was sitting in a chair across the way. Sitting there in her white and blue dress and her white nurse cap, her long legs crossed. She was reading a magazine. She looked at me and smiled. I couldn't help myself. I had the urge to smile back, and this time, I was strong enough to do it. It was a thin smile, but it was friendly. It was hard to look at her and not be friendly.

I ate my steak.

No sooner had I finished up my meal than Cranston came in.

The nurse came and took the tray away. Cranston pushed a chair on rollers next to the bed and sat down.

"Feeling better?"

"Enough to cuss you now," I said. "All you had to do was ask me to come."

"We didn't really want you to see the route. Did you know you slept in the car for two full days? Well, part of it was in an arranged house, but you slept the entire time. It took that long, with a stopover, to get here."

"How long have I been here?"

"This makes four days. We wanted you to get a deep rest. You needed it, and you will need it for what's in store, provided you choose to accept our employment."

"And if I don't, then I get my brain sand papered?"

"That's true. I can't say it's something I disapprove of, not when it's someone like you. I found out a lot about you."

"How do you even know who I am?"

"We have our ways here. I know you are adding nothing to society, and I think if you do not add, you should be taken away."

"You do, do you?"

"I do," Cranston said.

"Where is here? Is this a Limbus headquarters?"

Fishing for Dinosaurs

"Limbus finds us employees. We have what might be called a complex and sometimes complicated relationship with them. We are independent of them, and dependent on them. But this is OUR headquarters. One of them."

"What do you do here?"

"Lots of things. Let me tell you something, Richard Jordan—"

"How do you know my real name?"

"That part was easy," he said. "Don't let it worry you. You have a chance at a better life. Here's what I know. You started out good, smart with possibilities, that kind of kid, but your father committed suicide. Or tried to, failed, and then was killed accidentally. Comical, actually."

"Not to me."

"Tried to hang himself from a light fixture. The fixture broke. He fell, banged his chin on the desk, broke his jaw, received a concussion, died in the hospital a week later having never regained consciousness. You went to the university. Two years if memory serves me, and it most likely does. You went through one job after another. Failed relationships—"

"How can you know all this?'

"Not your concern. But there's no use in me continuing. Pretty much, your life is a wreck, and you were just on the verge of that shipwreck washing up on a rocky shore. All that's left was for the seagulls to peck out your eyes and devour your body."

"Enough with the metaphorical bullshit," I said.

"We can offer you a job. We can give you a new back story. A new life. We can also wipe your brain, give you new memories, and send you out in the cold, cold world to survive. To be honest, over time, the ones we send back tend to lose the back story. The depth of it anyway. They cease to believe it, but they know nothing else. Psychosis often results. And frequently they go back to their old ways. Now and again we have someone who succeeds as a new individual, but it's not really all that successful in the long run."

"So you're trying to convince me to take the job."

"Just stating the facts. You get to choose."

"I get to choose between two choices you've given me. One sounds bad, and the other one might be. I don't even know what the job is."

"True. But I can promise you this. It is unique. There is nothing like it. You will be part of a small crew. It is adventurous. We will prepare you for it, as much as someone can be prepared, and we pay extraordinarily well."

"How well?"

"One job and you're fixed for life."

"Are you with the government?"

"No. Unlike the government, we are efficient. We are not with or associated with any known government. You might say we are mostly unknown and a government unto itself."

"That doesn't sound like a good thing."

"Crime bears bitter fruit, Richard, but unlike the government, at least it bears fruit."

"So it's a criminal enterprise?"

"Only in the sense that it's off the books, not answerable to any government, so yes, it's a criminal activity with all manner of jobs, some of them sketchy by the standards of many citizens. That is neither here nor there. Here's how it will be. You agree to work for us, we get you in shape for it first. Some solid meals, exercise, a bit of preparation. You were once a top javelin thrower."

"You do your homework. I was being groomed for the Olympics. Things went wrong."

"That no longer matters. Do you accept the job?"

"May I ask why it's important to know I was once training for the Olympics with the javelin?"

"I didn't say it was."

"But it might be?" I said.

"It might be, but probably isn't. Still, the muscles for the javelin may indeed need to be aroused and rejuvenated to help with what we may consider you to do."

Fishing for Dinosaurs

"You have something in mind already?"

"Yes, but it all depends. Mr. Jordan, are you in or out?"

I thought for a moment. What did I have to go back to? A bridge over my head. Cold winters, hot summers, stealing to survive. That was the world I knew, and I didn't find any of that enticing. Here I was warm and fed and being offered payment for a job. If I didn't like the job, I figured I could find a way out later. They might not think I could, but I felt like it was a better shot than having my brain wiped—if they could actually do that—and being sent back out into the world.

"You're thinking you can say yes and maybe escape later, aren't you?" Cranston said.

"It crossed my mind."

"You can't. If you're in, you're in. Let me put this simply. There are nine, sometimes twelve members of our board, and frankly, they run a lot of the world's affairs. Any one of them is smarter than you, and together, they are considerably smarter."

"Perhaps they could do a better job running the world," I said. "Case you haven't noticed, it sucks like a vacuum cleaner out there."

"They fail from time to time. They are unique and wise, but they are also human. There are other factors, of course. Fate, humans, climate. Our group control more of that than what might be expected, but they can't control it all."

"The climate?"

"Yes," he said. "They work on a theory of balance. Sometimes bad things aren't all that bad, good things sometimes aren't all that good. They have to be balanced."

"You lost me at bad things aren't always that bad."

"You needn't know any more. Are you in?"

I thought it over again. I still believed I had a chance to get out if it came to it. And then again, I might just like the work. Whatever it was.

"I'm in," I said.

✾

I guess I was there about a month. I didn't keep up with the time. Couldn't even tell you what day of the week it was. I saw the bronze-skinned man and the dark-haired man from time to time. I saw them in the gym, wrestling, nude, like in the old Greek contests. Neither seemed to be trying to win out over the other. It was almost as if they were afraid of discovering who was the best. Instead they practiced moves and throws and did so with an eerie kind of grace. I even saw them walking alone through the halls, gently touching hands, entwining fingers. It was obvious they were lovers.

I saw the nurse from time to time, but she never smiled at me again. She didn't smile at that pair either, but she watched the dark-haired man in a way that made me think of a chained dog smelling meat from a butcher shop.

My assignment of the moment was to eat right and exercise. My teacher was a long, lean black woman who looked like an African goddess. She put me through my tasks as if she were a drill sergeant. She sprang about with cat-like grace, taught me a few martial arts moves for muscle tone, had me kicking a heavy bag, and running along the track outside. Where the outside was, I couldn't tell you, and to be literal, it really wasn't outside. Just seemed to be. There was a huge dome over the track, and though it was transparent in spots, it was mostly covered in camouflage. A birds-eye view from above, and it would look like forest, or jungle. The flooring of the track was the color of swamp water, so even views through the gaps would make it appear wet and uninviting. I wondered if it were possible to see us from above on the track, running. I found the idea of that amusing, an aerial view of us running on what appeared to be the surface of water.

Again, I had no idea where I had been transported to, and still had no idea for what reason. But I decided in for a penny, in for a pound, and maybe a ton. I felt it was best to dedicate myself to the preparation of the task ahead of me, whatever it might be. I never lost the idea that I still could escape if I found my job odious. It was hard to imagine it being a positive assignment, what with all the secrecy. I felt like a character in a comic book.

I began to throw the javelin again in time. The goddess brought it to me and I was rusty at first, but I found my stride after a while. It didn't feel all that familiar though, in spite of remembering how good I had been at it in the past. It built my arms up, throwing it again.

I was also fed a very foul-tasting milkshake every day. I drank it without hesitation after the first week. I realized it was doing something to my body. I felt stronger, quicker. More than felt—I *was* stronger and quicker. Partly that was due to the training, the diet, but that milkshake had something in it besides the usual ingredients. I could feel it seep into my bones and innards. I didn't measure myself, but I was reasonably certain that not only was I leaner and more muscular, but that I had grown an inch or more in height, which I would have thought impossible.

They increased the size of the javelin over time, but I continued to be able to throw it with ease. In time the drinks were stopped, and when I inquired of the goddess as to why, she informed me it was no longer needed. Its effects by this time were permanent.

It had other aspects that were beneficial as well. I was not tired at the end of a day, and on a fine, dark night, after a workout, the goddess became quite human, and the two of us shared my bed. It was as if we were competing in a sexual Olympics. By morning, she was out on the track. I showered and ate lightly and met her there. It was as if nothing had happened between us. She looked at me with all the warmth of a cobra.

One day the African goddess came to me and said, "Today, we take a day off from training."

Actually, I didn't want a day off. I had begun to truly love the workouts. They made me feel good and powerful.

"You have a meeting with Mr. Cranston," she said.

I went to meet Cranston with the goddess leading.

It was a large office with a desk about the size of a landing field. There was a computer on the desk, a chair behind it, and a row of chairs in front of it, eight to be exact. It occurred to me that with eight in front and one behind the desk that could be the nine who ruled the world. It was a crazy thought, but there it was. Cranston had said as much, and though I hadn't yet decided if he was crazy or not, no doubt the resources available to him seemed unlimited.

The rest of the room was lined with shelves of books. The books climbed three stories, and there were stairs that led upwards to the other levels, and there were long rows with railed pathways where you could walk along and look at the books.

The black goddess left me there and went away. I stood waiting. A short, older man was on the far side of the room sweeping with a large push broom. He swept and then used a whisk broom to push the small, almost invisible dust pile into a hand-held whisk pan, and then dumped it into a trash can on wheels. He put the broom in the can so that the broom itself stuck up in the air. He pushed it past me, said, "Good luck to you," and was gone.

After a while I walked about, looking at the books on the floor where I had been left. There were what you might call classic literary titles. The entire collection of Twain, Kipling, Dickens, and so on. I pulled a few out for examination, and saw they were first editions. I was even more impressed to find that many of them had been signed by their authors.

I strolled along and found a section of books with titles I didn't recognize. Like *The Book of Doches*, something called the *Necronomicon*, *Those Who Rule the Earth*, and *Outsiders and Insiders*. Volumes that were sometimes attributed to certain authors, others without author recognition.

I had just pulled one of these books from the shelf, *The Hounds of Tindalos*, when Cranston, standing at my shoulder, said, "That one I wouldn't look at. It will make you nauseous, not just due to content, but due to how words and images and numbers are placed on the page, the shape of the letters are quite baffling."

Fishing for Dinosaurs

That didn't make a lick of sense to me, but I returned the book to its position on the shelf. I was shocked to discover Cranston had been able to sneak up on me so easily, so silent.

I turned and watched him glide toward the desk and seat himself in the chair behind it. He motioned to me and I picked a chair directly in front of him and sat down.

"I hope everything has been comfortable," he said, "and to your satisfaction."

"It has, though I do feel a little kidnapped, baffled, and abused."

"Do you now?"

"Just said so, didn't I?"

He almost smiled. The corners of his mouth rose as if they were hats being tipped, then settled back down.

"Do you believe that beneath our world there is a hollow that contains another world?"

"What?"

"Do you believe in global warming?"

"Yes," I said. "And as for the earth being hollow, no."

"Okay, you believe in global warming, but you don't believe the world is hollow."

"I know it isn't," I said. "I didn't sleep through all of science class. I even found out about things like gravity and evolution, and believe them. I also believe the core of the world is molten."

He nodded. "All right then. What if I told you that inside our world is another?"

"I'd say you are nuttier than I first suspected."

"Fair enough," he said. "Let me lay it out to you in a different way. The center of the earth is not hollow."

"Now you're making me dizzy. Didn't you just say—?"

"I said beneath our world—to be more specific, inside the earth—there is another world. But not at the core. There is a hollow band beneath our earth and it can be best entered through a gap at the South Pole, though there is, in fact, a North Pole entrance."

"The place where Santa lives," I said.

He ignored me. "I might also say that the hollow is not strictly hollow. There is a world within the hollow."

"Well, sounds like to me you may have had a bit too much coffee, so I'll just go back to the track and you can call me when you're ready for me to start work."

"What I'm ready for you to do involves both global warming and the world within our world."

I could see that he was absolutely serious.

"All right," I said. "Tell me."

Cranston leaned back in his chair, placed his hands together, and steepled his fingers beneath his chin. He said, "At both poles there are entries into the earth. They are subtle openings. It's like sliding down gently into a bowl. You don't realize the depth of the bowl because its sides slope gradually. The bowl has large openings in the walls of what appears to be a cavern of ice. Through those gaps are more direct entrances, many of them large enough for an aircraft to enter, or even for a boat to sail through. We'll come to that consideration shortly."

"Sailing to the center of the earth?"

"No, it's not the center of the earth, but those entries are how the stories were started. People who went there and came back claimed to have gone to the center of the earth, but they were within a rim world that circles the world completely around."

"It would be a dark world," I said.

"It is not completely explored, but has its own sun, or a substitute for it. The high roof of their world blazes with volcanic fire. This is something the writer Edgar Rice Burroughs knew, though he called it a sun. No one knows how he came by those stories, who told him about the inner light, but he knew. A large number of the things he wrote about were accurate, the bulk of it fabrication."

"If this is true, what has it to do with me? And I don't know who Edgar Rice Burroughs is."

"Doesn't matter. Let me backtrack. The job we had for you was uncertain. It might have been menial. Someone, for example, has to clean this library."

"You were considering me for a custodial job? You went through all of this to possibly have me sweep up? You have someone for that. I saw him."

"It was truly a consideration, having you replace the old man. He's been of service to us in so many ways, but right now, we feel he best serves us here, doing a menial, but important job. You could take his place."

"Again, I have a hard time believing you brought me here the way you did because you wanted me to sweep up and swab toilets."

"True, but the custodial job here comes with added chores you would never encounter elsewhere. It doesn't matter, however. That's not the job. You have been researched thoroughly. Your mother leaving you and your father, taking off for parts unknown. Your father's death. But I've told you I know about all that."

"That has nothing to do with anything," I said. "He was an unhappy man."

"Obviously," Cranston said. "But genetics has a lot to do with inclination, and so do events in your life. The two make you a great candidate for us. As to why, it's a long story and a study of psychiatry and genetics would be necessary to understand it."

"I'm not a total idiot," I said. "How do you know all about me?"

"For us, information comes easy. So does certain kinds of manipulation."

Cranston paused for dramatic effect. I said nothing. I waited him out.

"You are of a good type, blood and bone and flesh and genetic makeup. We ran tests while you were, shall we say, asleep."

"As in drugged?"

"More accurate, yes. I think the best way to short-story this is to say certain flaws in your DNA have been corrected, and strengths have been enhanced through the drinks and the diet we have been feeding you. We like a long employment, so all of these alterations will allow you to live a long, long time. You won't be immortal, and you will still be subject to accident or attack, and some rare diseases, but otherwise quite hale and hearty for years to come. As long as we attend to you. As for your employment, your job, sir, is to fish for and catch a plesiosaur, or at least a beast similar to it. An unknown cousin, to be accurate. Well, unknown to the rest of the world, but not to us."

"A dinosaur?"

"A very large one," he said. "Technically it's a sauropterygian. Unlike the plesiosaur it greatly resembles, it has serviceable legs for taking to the shore, though not well. To simplify what we have in mind for you, I'll just repeat what I said before. You'll be fishing for a dinosaur."

The wind was cold enough to make a polar bear scream and sharp enough to shave with; the water was high and vigorous, and the icebergs cracked and moaned as they melted all around me. The contrasting warmth of the water rose up and heated the great tuna boat we were in, warming my feet and legs; the howling wind in contrast gave me a cold head and body, in spite of my layered clothes, my fur-lined hood and heavy coat.

For all his abilities and knowledge, I could have told Cranston that while fishing for a dinosaur (and this conclusion I drew without any experience in the matter whatsoever), it is best to have a very large boat, and better yet, best not to do it, and if it has to be done, it should be done from shore with a very long line, not caught on the water and dragged to shore, which was their plan. They wanted it alive.

Also, I preferred a different sort of bait. Sticking the remains of dead bodies on a hook the size of a Town Car was not my idea of a good time, even if the corpses belonged to what might have been the last surviving Neanderthals.

But I got ahead of myself.

Fishing for Dinosaurs

So it turns out I was fishing for a dinosaur because it had come up from a world beneath our world. Not a Center of The Earth world, but a world that lay below the crust, a Rim World, Cranston called it. Still, it was deep down and may not be everywhere beneath the earth, but it is certainly beneath the poles, including the South Pole where I was at the moment.

Down deep in this world was a roof of burning fire that served as a sun, and there were clouds and an atmosphere, and all manner of people who lived there in a primitive state, and oh yes, there were dinosaurs and mammoths and mastodons and ape-people and even pirates. I had not seen these things, but Cranston had told me. I thought he was out of his mind, but if you see one dinosaur, it's easy to believe that there were others, and that all the wild and wooly things Cranston told me were true. That the ice caps were melting from Global Climate Change was obvious, but the worry for Cranston and his Secret Rulers was that the world beneath our world would be revealed. Why that was their worry, I couldn't say. But, you see, the water-going dinosaur likes to eat people. It was envisioned that it might swim through the newly acquired waterways because of the ice melting and find its way to warmer waters and make its way to our civilization. Then, much like an old Japanese monster movie, start tearing down cities and eating fleeing citizens, stomping pedestrians, and receiving an air strike.

When that was said and done, the next step would be for our current civilization to find and invade the world below, destroying it in all its primitive glory, just because we can. This is Cranston's and the Secret Rulers of the World's concern. I guess that's a good thing, but with Cranston, it's hard to tell. As for the remainder of the Secret Rulers, I assumed the two men who had brought me to the compound were part of that group, and after that, I'm not sure. Maybe they don't all live there, or stay there, and the others are spaced here and there about the world.

Not only had the climate changed, but when the ice melted, it affected deep pockets of water below the surface. With it came hundreds of dead bodies, drowned victims. Among them animals and dinosaurs and what I call Neanderthals because I can't think of anything else close enough to how they look—large brows, short legs, stocky bodies—all of them drowned and bloated and convenient fishing bait. They are cousins to the man who drove the car that brought me to the compound. Oh yeah, he's one. He came up from the earth through a passage of some kind many years back, or so I've heard. He ended up with the Secret Rulers, went to work for them. They called him Bill Oldman. I think there was a weak joke in there somewhere. He and I got along, were friends actually. That said, when it came to the Secret Rulers, he didn't answer many questions. And contrary to what I thought about Neanderthals, he has the power of speech and is an A-1 thinker. You should play him in a game of chess.

The thing though was the water. A dormant volcano became less dormant. It heated up, and with the air temperature increase from global warming, this part of the world started to melt like a block of ice on a hot stove. The water that filled the dormant volcanoes rose to the surface of our world, brought with it the drowned from down below. And if that wasn't enough, the rising water contained one angry dinosaur. It survived by eating all manner of swimming creatures, not to mention at least one climate investigation team.

So there I was, with Bill Oldman and Cranston and sometimes, the two giants, and a crew of men and women who wore blue and white parkas and carried guns, all of them studying me with jaundiced eyes.

Oh yeah, the goddess is with me too. She's my fishing companion. Ayesha by name, that tall African-looking woman with legs that seem to begin somewhere near that mythical world below, a head with a halo of black hair like a threatening storm cloud framing her face, drawing attention to her strong features and eyes so dark and deep they seem like tunnels leading you straight to hell. But oh that mouth, and how it tastes, and those legs, how they wrap, and that face shiny with beauty. Finally, we had become lovers. Not just sex partners. During our long and fruitless fishing trips for the dinosaur, we had become not only sticky close, but soul-close.

I had never known a woman like her. Enigmatic, strong, purposeful, and someone with a bit of dinosaur fishing experience—and with something in her background I didn't know about, but something that lay coiled there like a snake about to strike. I could sense it. She was unique and wonderful, but inside her head not all was right with the world.

⚜

I climbed up the railing that led to the chairs in the conning tower. The tower was open to the sky, though the chairs we sat in for fishing could, with a touch of a button, cover our heads with a shield against sun and rain, sleet and snow.

Ayesha sat in one of the chairs with the great rod settled into a steel boot on squeaking swivels. The rod was a hundred feet high and made of steel and fiberglass and things I had no idea of. It rose up tall in the sky like a fat finger pointing to the clouds, then it bent at the tip, way up there, and a cable about the size of my thigh spun out of that and went off in the water with its great cork (aka bobber or float) the size of a kayak, and beneath that was more cable, dipping down deep in the water with that mighty, sharp hook with its meaty portion of a drowned Neanderthal.

"They're already dead," Cranston had said. "I see no sense in wasting the opportunities their corpses provide."

Bill Oldman had quivered slightly at that comment. But he said nothing.

That was then, this was now, and it was me and Ayesha on the tower in our fighting chairs with our rods, Bill Oldman down below, manning a cannon-sized harpoon launcher if things went wrong and we couldn't bring the beast in alive. Killing it was supposed to be the absolute worst-case scenario.

I fastened my shoulder straps and waist band, then glanced at Ayesha in her heavy clothes and close-fitting hood, her hands on the gears that worked the rod and the great spinning reel that was six feet above us on our rods. It was the size of a large industrial drum with coils of cable squeezed around it like a hungry anaconda digesting a meal.

Our chairs were about a foot apart. She with her line in the water, and me sitting with enough cable reeled out so that it and its huge hook were resting on the floor of the ship below. A stout, tall woman wearing a blue and white jumpsuit, an electronic cigarette hanging from her mouth, was struggling to stick a corpse on my hook. Thing I had noticed about the blue and white uniformed folks was they were not as strong as me, or Bill, Ayesha, Cranston, and the others. Oh, they were all solid and in shape, but they had not been given the tonic that had been given to me. I didn't know why. I didn't know a lot of things about my employment. What I did know was the world was far stranger than I had imagined. Dinosaurs and Neanderthals were in it, and down below it, living in a land with air and water and fiery skies.

As for our quarry, we had seen the beast a few times, even got hits on our lines, but the meat had been taken and the hooks had been straightened. New, bigger, better-made hooks had been brought in, but we got the same results. What I remembered most was seeing the beast rise up out of the water, massive as a whale, long as a train, flexible as a rubber hose, pulsing with color, blue and red and aqua green, grays and browns mottled about its head, an elongated mouth so full of teeth that when the sun hit them, they threw off a glow that nearly blinded me. I thought then that we needed stronger hooks and a better place to be, but here we were, fishing for a dinosaur, re-equipped, courtesy of the Secret Rulers. More importantly, they had brought in with the new hooks and stronger cables, peanut butter and wheat bread at my request—that was for me to eat, not for the dinosaur, though the idea of the big beast going smacky-mouth over a huge peanut butter sandwich had its appeal.

Fishing for Dinosaurs

In the chairs the wind was cold and the heat from the water did little to warm my feet. The heat rose through the metal but became cooler with height; those icy winds negated it in the end, up there in the chairs where we perched like birds. I pulled my scarf over my mouth and reached out and touched Ayesha's hand. She rolled her knuckles in my palm, then removed her hand.

She looked at me and said, "I have to concentrate."

"On what?"

"Fishing."

"Yeah. Well, when it hits, then you can fish, until then we can hold hands."

At that moment there was a call from below. My baiter had the corpse on the hook. Romance was over. I hit a lever and the cable began to roll up and curl beneath the tip of the rod, dangling the hook and the bait. I hit more levers. The rod flexed back and flung out, tossing the cable and the bait (the arms were still on the torso and they flapped in the wind as if trying to fly) into the water with a significant splash. I took hold of the toggle and worked it. My chair spun then, and the cable and its bait swung around our ship, and within instants, my chair's back was against the back of Ayesha's chair.

"I think tonight," I heard Ayesha say, "you get to be on top."

"That would be nice," I said, "but just so you know, positioning doesn't matter much to me. Just as long as you are connected, so to speak."

"Everything in life is about position. Everything."

We waited and waited, touched the mechanisms and swung our chairs to different positions, but never got so much as a nibble. The daylight was constant; we were in that part of the world where night could go on for months, and then it was daylight's turn, which was how it was now.

I could hardly believe it, but even fishing for a dinosaur, with my intent to save the world beneath us from discovery and exploitation, I was bored. The clock moved, the daylight didn't. My inner workings didn't respond properly. I looked at my watch, the fine one they had given me. We had been at our chore for four hours. Lunch time. I went below. I had peanut butter on bread, went up and Ayesha went down, came back with a kiss for me and caviar on her breath.

Time crawled on as if its legs were broken. Finally, twelve hours from the time I began my fishing shift, it was over. We hit the switches and rolled our lines, and the rotten corpses that remained were deposited in the freezers on the boat, ready for tomorrow's baiting.

The boat toiled its way through the boiling waves toward shore. It docked and we disembarked into a great fortress made of ice. It was beginning to melt around the edges, but was mostly firm still. Oddly, it was heated, and the heat held and the ice held. It was the changing of the climate and the boiling from below that was gradually eroding it. In our massive igloo rooms were large, inviting beds. Ayesha invited me into hers.

"You will think of me tonight as She Who Must Be Obeyed," she said, and showed me a grin that made me tingle from ears to toes. Later that night, I can assure you, I would have called her anything she wanted, and I would have called myself by any name.

In the morning we went out again on the ship. The light was still the same and the waters were still the same, and the job was just as it was before, except for one thing. An hour into our shift, Ayesha got a bite.

Plesiosaurs bite big.

Okay, not technically a plesiosaur, but the thing in the water bit big.

The beast was strong, even when it nibbled. A nibble and slight pull could make the boat quake and feel as if it were about to be yanked below the waters like a cheap, plastic float. Today we learned there were two of the monsters. They swam as a pair, and we just hadn't realized it before.

Fishing for Dinosaurs

We had our chairs back to back and were talking about this and that, sort of flirting, building up for another night in the sack that would involve wet gymnastics and happy determination. Then my reel screamed like an injured panther. Screamed so loud my ears felt as if they would bleed. The cable darted across the water, way out wide, and then it dipped.

I yelled out, "I got it."

This wasn't entirely true. It had me.

As my cable sliced across the water, Ayesha's reel whined and her line hummed, and she had a hit as well.

Since her line was on the opposite side of the boat, her chair having been swiveled back to back to me, it was clear that we both had a bite. And our bites were heading in opposite directions.

"Oh, hell," Ayesha said.

"Took the words right out of my mouth."

Now her line turned and went beneath the boat.

That wasn't good.

Oldman was at the wheel, and he saw the situation immediately. He turned the boat wide, letting the line glide out, and by this time, Ayesha had turned in her chair so we were side by side.

My catch rose up out of the water, showing us all its magnificent beauty and horror simultaneously. Drops big as my head flared off of its shiny teeth. It let out with a howl, if you can call it that. Frankly, the sound was indescribable. It reached down in my gut, deep in my soul, and ripped at me. I could see one great, dark eye, big as a subway tunnel, and then it dipped down and the water exploded and the boat washed heavy.

"By the gods, it is so beautiful," Ayesha said.

Now the cables were swinging so close to one another there was no doubt that within instants they would cross. And they did. They came together with a whine of metal cable and a screech of our reels being strained so hard the oil on the reel and on the cables smoked with friction. Then the boat, I kid you not, spun like a top. I felt the hilt of the rod vibrate in my hands like a washing machine coming apart. I let go of that and went at the gears, trying to disengage, but no dice. It was hooked up tight as a banker's vault.

That's when one of the cables snapped. Ayesha's cable. The cable popped, whipped and flew back. It came with an explosion of glistening drops and what I think must have been blood from the mouth of the beast, and along with that came the hook, minus its bait, and minus its dinosaur.

It came back at Ayesha like a missile. Struck with an explosion of red and grey, black skin pieces and fragments of bone. Ayesha's decapitated body sagged in the chair. The side of my face, shoulder, and chair were soaked with her blood and brains.

My cable locked tight, pig-squealed, and then it too snapped. I yelled as if I had been struck. But I was unharmed. My cable swung loose in the water, minus bait and hook, and the reel's kick-switch went to work on its own and recoiled my cable.

I unfastened my belt and moved to Ayesha's chair. Her hands were still on the levers. Her right leg, which I knew when unclothed would show a fine little scar in the dent of her knee, was pushed out as she were trying to stomp a brake pedal. I watched as her leg went limp and her body sagged.

I sagged myself, right to my knees.

When the ship was brought in that night, Bill Oldman came to where I lay on the upper deck in a pool of Ayesha's blood at the foot of her chair. He tried to lift me to my feet, but it was as if I didn't have any feet. I couldn't get my mind to do what my body needed to do. Finally, Bill picked me up like a rag doll and carried me down the stairs effortlessly off the ship and onto the shore. I think he may have carried me as far as my room. I don't remember anything after that. Not until I came out of a deep pool of shock, floated to the surface, and screamed; that's when the fine-looking nurse I had seen before, when I had first been taken in by Limbus, appeared with a sedative, which I fought against. But Bill and two other men, thin men with gray faces as slack as paper sacks, helped hold me down as she gave me the shot.

The nurse said, "Let yourself go," and I went, racing along a string of smoke, or was it blood? Sweat? Or was it a string of thought? I couldn't tell you because I don't know, but that was how it seemed, as if I were crawling like a spider along a string of matter that was sometimes soft and sometimes hard, sometimes the color of smoke, sometimes the color of blood, and in my mind's nose were scents that couldn't be, the cinnamon smell of Ayesha's skin, the stench of blood and brain matter, of feces and urine that soiled her body when she died, of the wet air and the strange odor of those huge beasts as they leapt out of the water and their stench was mopped up and absorbed by the air.

My sweat and fear were part of the stink. Along that line I crawled, and then I swung under the line, clung for dear life, scuttling with six legs and then no legs and there was no line anymore. There was just a wisp of smoke and the smoke had all those aromas and stinks in it, and then I was falling into a deep black pit that popped with electricity and contained the warm water of the ocean, but when I awoke, the pit was my bed. I lay there strapped down and weak in a pond of my sweat. It was the position I had first found myself when I had been brought to the Secret Rulers by connection to Limbus. It seemed a popular method of sedation and control. A theme was at work.

Cranston came in and sat in a chair by my bed. As he sat, he carefully adjusted his trousers so they maintained their crease, then looked at me and said, "Sometimes it happens. An agent dies in the field."

"I'm going to kill that dinosaur and its mate, or cousin, or butt-hole buddy. Whatever it is," I said, "I'm going to kill it."

"Catch, not kill, that is our desire."

"But it's not mine. I'm going to kill it."

"As I explained—"

"Sometimes an agent in the field is killed. I know. But that doesn't change that sometimes a dinosaur in a vast expanse of water is sometimes killed, and his pal as well, and that's what I'm trying to explain to you, the sanctimonious ass-wipe."

"We can't allow that."

"You certainly aren't one for feelings, are you, Cranston?"

"Not particularly, no. But I will tell you this. Ayesha has been with us for some time, except for occasional trips back to Africa. She has been a good employee. She may have just naturally weaned herself out of her position."

I wasn't entirely sure what he meant by that, but I didn't care. Nature may have been involved in her death, but there was nothing natural about how it happened. All I wanted right then was for those dinosaurs to die, and if I could make them suffer, all the better. I suppose I could look at it as our fault. We were fishing for them. They were dumb beasts. They had no particular intent but to survive. Cranston was right, why kill them? But I wanted to anyway.

And then it hit me. Why did they want to capture them? What was the point? They were trying to keep the lost world below the crust from being discovered, what purpose did they have in capturing a dinosaur, or dinosaurs?

I asked him what I was thinking.

Cranston nodded at the question, as if it were the first time he had ever considered such a thing, which, of course, it was not. "Very well," he said, "but it's not that mysterious. I've told you our main purpose, which is to protect the world down under, but there's also the scientific research we'd like to conduct. There is much to be learned from captured aquatic dinosaurs, and nothing to be learned from vengeance against a dumb creature."

"They are not that dumb, trust me."

"They are merely trying to survive. We have large places where they can live, where they can be contained."

"Why don't they just go home?" I said.

Fishing for Dinosaurs

"Because they are trapped in a volcano of boiling water. They are comfortable this high up. We find the water uncomfortably warm, but they do not. Down deep, however, it's another matter. We've dropped devices into the depths to measure the heat, and for them to go to those depths, it would be like dropping a lobster into a pan of boiling water."

"After today," I said, "I love that idea."

"Ayesha understood the risk. We have global warming to contend with, which has made larger holes in the ice, larger gaps to the world below, and that in turn has been filled with volcanic activity and dinosaurs. Now, I'm leaving. You will continue to be held. That will give us time to decide if you are in fact going to be useful, or if your employment for this job was a mistake."

"I'll kill those big bastards."

"That's what we don't want," Cranston said. "That is not your job. That is not what you were hired on to do."

"It's all I want to do," I said.

"I know, and that gives me pause for consideration. I think your wiring may not be just right."

"That's one way to put it," I said.

🌿

In the middle of the night, I heard a noise and came awake, but the thick straps around my shoulders, middle and legs, the leather clamps on my wrist and ankles didn't allow me to rise and investigate. I had gone down so deep into sleep again—perhaps a secondary rush of the drug—that I awoke as refreshed as I had felt in years; I felt brand new. No less sad, but brand new. It was like electric-hot spiders were crawling about in my brain, giving me juice.

It was dark in the room. Then there was a light. A single light. The light moved across the floor and came to rest by my bed. The carrier of the light sat in the chair by the bed and turned out the light. But as he lifted it to push a sliding button on the instrument,

I saw standing behind the chair Bill Oldman. I got a glimpse of the man in the chair as well. Short, middle-aged, ruggedly attractive in a ravaged sort of way. He looked as if he had seen all there was to see and hadn't liked much of it, and what he had liked he was suspect of. It was the man I had seen cleaning the library.

"I know you," I said.

"My name is Quatermain," he said. "Alan Quatermain."

"What do you want?"

"I am thinking I might want you. Bill and I, that is."

"Bill, you're with him?"

"Yep," Bill said.

"He is a man of true source," Quatermain said, "as am I, though for a while I was tainted with a uniqueness of a sort that has worn me thin in spirit, something that was in me, eating away at my character like carnivorous worms."

"I'm not up for riddles," I said.

"Nor do I mean to bring you a riddle without a solution, though the solution may be hard to understand, as your brain is little more than a bundle of frayed impulses and a mess of contradictions. Let me begin this way. You, according to Bill, want to kill the dinosaurs."

I gave an honest answer. "I've thought it over, or rather I did so in my sleep. I don't want that anymore. My mind wasn't working right. They're just beasts, as Cranston said."

"You could just be saying that," Quatermain said.

"I know. But I mean it. Killing them makes no sense."

"It makes all the sense. That's why you must kill them," Quatermain said.

I didn't know how to answer that. Quatermain sighed and stretched his legs and then tucked them under the chair and leaned forward. He turned the flashlight on and flashed it on my face. The light was a pool of yellow against my eyes. I turned my head.

He said, "You didn't turn your head right away. Something in your skull made you think about it. Something short of common reaction. Something that has to do with quicker adjustment to light. You didn't like it, but you could take it."

I didn't know why this mattered, but I said, "I've been drugged. I've been under a bit of stress, as Bill might have explained to you... Bill, what are you doing with this guy? What is this about?"

Bill didn't answer.

"Let me say this first," Quatermain said. "They want the dinosaurs to examine. Bill, would you come around in front of the chair, please?"

Bill came.

"Show him," Quatermain said.

Bill took off his shirt, pulled his pants over his shoes and stood before me naked, except for his socks and shoes which he had not removed. Quatermain flashed the light over him. He was covered in huge scars, some of them puckered from stitches, others mounded up like some kind of huge animals had burrowed beneath the skin. Some of the scars were light-colored, nearly healed, others were angry and red. Even his penis was scarred.

I said, "Why are you showing me this? Put on your clothes, Bill."

"This is what happened in captivity," Quatermain said. "He would be there still, except on a whim, the professor, the doctor, the fellow with the bronze skin, decided he needed someone as an aide. And finally, Bill, fortunately, at least at the time, began to work for The Fucked Up Rulers of the World. Goddamn shit-eating bastards."

Bill was putting his clothes back on.

"I'm growing old and weak," Bill said. "Not by common human standards, but by their standards, and I am denied the fuel."

"The fuel?" I asked. "What in hell are you talking about?"

"You drank it," Quatermain said. "Ayesha fed it to you. It was to be absorbed by your body. I used to have the drink too. They say it is permanent, but it isn't. It lasts for several years, and then it begins to fade, and so do you, faster than you would have from old age if you don't get it. But once they give that drink to you, and you learn how good it feels, and they finally let you know you really do have to keep drinking it, and they are the providers, well, then you owe them. You will want that drink. The things you'll do for that kind of strength, that near immortality."

"He said it was in my DNA—"

"You don't have your own DNA, friend."

"Of course I do… Come on, man. What is this?"

"I am your salvation if you choose it."

"Oh hell," I said. "And now you're going to tell me I'm going to be sucked up to heaven in some kind of rapturous blast. You may have converted Bill here, but I'm not interested. I went to church when I was young. I had enough of it then."

Quatermain leaned back against the chair and stuck out his legs again. He turned off the flashlight. "Church," he said. "Tell me about it."

"What?"

"Where did you go to church?" he asked. "Where was it? Tell me about it."

"Mud Creek Methodist, Mud Creek, Texas. Minister was Reverend Crutcher."

"Tell me about Crutcher."

"Tall, dark-haired."

"No. Tell me about him, the man."

"I didn't know him that well."

"Tell me about your father. What happened to him?"

I hesitated, but finally went on with it. It was the same story Cranston had known.

"That is such an odd and unique story it would be hard to believe it isn't true."

"Of course it's true."

"And your mother running off, leaving you, that's good too. That way you couldn't have known her past a certain age. You've got a back history, but nothing else you have to remember about them. They are gone."

"I don't understand you at all."

Fishing for Dinosaurs

"You are made of flesh and bone, but it's not yours."

"Bill, please take this man with you and leave."

Bill had returned to his position behind the chair. I could see his shadowy shape more clearly now, quite clearly actually. My eyes had adjusted well. I saw him gently shake his head.

"You have microcosmic creatures running through your veins, pumping in your blood, the blood from transfusions. Bill here was one of the transfusions. Right, Bill?"

"Right," Bill said.

"You are not truly human," Quatermain said. "You are not born of man and woman. You are cells and borrowed blood and bone and skin. Your brain tissues, so wormed with microscopic wires, were essentially grown in a jar and fed little wires so small they are smaller than capillaries."

"Wires? A jar?"

"Well, a beaker and such. Large vats and electrodes and crawling flesh that attached itself to bone with the aid of microcosmic assistance. Nano stuff."

"Yeah," Bill said. "It's little. I mean small. You can't see it with the eye. It's like if a gnat were compared to them it would be, relatively speaking, to them, the size of an elephant."

"You're crazy. Both of you."

"I am crazy," Quatermain said, "but not as much as you might think. What you have in your head is information, stuffed there like cotton in a teddy bear. You have experiences you never experienced. Knowledge you never learned. A childhood that never happened. No parents. No dogs or dates to the prom, no connection between the two meant there.

"None of what happened to you happened. Ayesha, hell, boy, she was a fine looking woman, smart, but she was playing you like a cat plays with a mouse. They all are. You aren't but a few months old. You haven't even had your first birthday. You think you've had ass before, but I got to tell you, Ayesha, she was your first. You didn't screw that cheerleader from Mud Creek I read about in your computer file. An advantage I have of having been more important to the Rulers in the past and knowing what kind of codes they used in their computers, and being the fucking janitor and go-to-guy for all manner of shit. But that's beside the point. Thing is, none of the girls they gave you memories about ever happened. Now, close your eyes, think on things. See what you really know. Compare your long past to your recent past. The recent stuff, that's the real deal. You can feel that like a thorn in the side, the rest, it's not even as substantial as a cloud, now, is it? You got loose from where you were born, broke free, picked up some old clothes that were meant for the trash, put them on, made a loop like a homing pigeon, and then didn't quite understand why you escaped. You had a moment of clarity, my man-made boy. You are a type of Pinocchio, but made from a chemistry set, not wood."

"You're reaching now, Alan," Bill said.

"Yeah, that was a metaphor too far, like trying to cross a bridge with bad support posts. Listen here, boy. You had a moment when you knew you were being bamboozled and buffaloed and filled with their shit, and then it was gone. In that moment you proved, man-made or not, you have free will. Then the coding kicked in. You circled back, came home. Your real home. That was no storage building, was it, Bill?"

"Nope," Bill said. "Least not all of it was storage."

"And that little trip you took from the warehouse to the infirmary, the library. Same building, son. They knocked your ass out and drove you around the block and turned that car into the glitzier side of their operation. The ones with the elevators that went down under, the compartments where they did their Doctor Frankenstein business on you in the first place.

"That building was your true-ass home, and your natural desire was to return to it, though your false memories were starting to kick in at the same time to confuse you. Those memories were made of little nano-bots, racing about, running up your cortex and flowing through your blood, tossing mini-miniature wires and doo-dads all about. And when they were finished, you knew what you were meant to know, nothing more. You're a human-made machine without the machine oil and the squeaky wheels. By the way, that DNA they made you with? Part of it's mine. You are my son in a sense, or at least part of you is. There's some of Bill in there too, the big guys, the hot blonde, Jane. You are the son of many fathers and mothers, a mass of meshed DNA. If you have a big pecker, that part is me. Ha!"

"He gets silly when it gets late," Bill said.

"Ah, hell," I said, because right in that moment, I knew they were telling me the truth. And not just about the pecker.

I had memories, experiences, a childhood fall when I was ten that left me in the hospital for a week, lots of cuts and scratches. The fall broke my leg and left me in a cast and crutches for three months. But there are no scars. I attended school, college, but never really did much with my life, went homeless. All because my father killed himself accidentally while trying to kill himself on purpose. My mother ran off and left me.

Except none of it was true. I was the product of large machinery and small machines not visible to the eye. I was made of bone, flesh, and blood transfusions, none of it mine. I have knowledge, except I didn't actually learn anything for myself. I had never thrown a javelin in my life until Ayesha put one in my hand. I had been geared for the knowledge to see how it translated from brain to muscle and bone, but until then, I had never touched a javelin. I realized that now.

Bill Oldman is a Neanderthal from the Rim World. He had been brought to the upper crust against his will because he and his kind reach the age of about forty in appearance and stay there. They do not continue to age. They live for over a thousand years and then die suddenly, their clock runs down, their light goes out. That was where Cranston and his people who rule the earth got their juice, blood and bone transfusions from Bill and others like him, others from way down under. And then, when they didn't have enough of it, they began to artificially create it. The only problem was, made from Bill or his kind, or synthetically made, they have to be injected over and over. And the originals, those like Bill, begin to fade after a hundred years above ground. So it may be their DNA is activated by the strange fires of the Rim World, flaming warmth and light from miles up, fastened to the roof of their world.

Same with the dinosaurs. They had the natural juice, same as the primitives down below. They needed to be caught to be experimented on. Sliced and poked and cut and pulled and clipped and burned and twisted some. It was a way the Secret Rulers might discover a better formula to make them live longer, maybe with only one injection.

But those experiments, as Bill's body revealed, were ugly stuff for men and creatures. Terrible slicing and dicing, harsh chemistry and surgical operations so a bunch of men and women, Ayesha included, wouldn't get any older and wouldn't need injections to stay young. Ah, the vanity of it. The conceit. And me. I had been handmade as an experiment. That's all I was, something else for them to study tissue and wiring and new ways to live forever. They had already decided I was a failure. It was the damn free will.

"Bill," Quatermain said, interrupting my thoughts, "is fading, and he knows it, and they know it, of course. When they decide they have learned all they can from him, or can no longer use him for anything, he will cease to be of importance to them. Just like me, who no longer will accept an injection or drink their smoothies, and therefore has been demoted from a position of prominence to a position over a mop. Like me, who has killed everything in this world that flies or crawls or walks or swims. Like me, who has helped capture one beast after another, bring it into their realm, where they can torture it with their experiments in search of the secret of longevity. I am their awful puppet. Or have been. The water beasts should die rather than be subjected to such, don't you think?

"I am here to take you with me, if you wish to go. They have tired of you quickly. You have changed and matured rapidly. You see them for the shit stacks they are. Like me, they were once heroes. People to look up to, but then they got the immortality shots, and with that, they got power. Then the shots backfired, didn't do what they thought they would, and that realization gave them fear. The fear of losing youth and power. It soured them, made them bitter as unripe persimmons. Have you had one of those, it'll make your lips suck in behind your teeth. Wait a minute, of course you haven't had them, and I bet that isn't something they put in your brain. That's too unlikely. Too rare."

"Nobody gives a shit, Alan," Bill said.

"Sure, of course. Forget the goddamn persimmons. Richard, as they call you, don't you want to live your own life? Find your own rareness? Use your pecker more? Damn it. I got to go pee."

Quatermain peed in the corner of the room and made quite a moaning production of it.

"Kidney stones," Bill said.

They unstrapped me and gave me cold-weather clothes and put on their heavy stuff they had left by the door. They had a suit for me. They told me their plan as we went outside into the cold air and the constant sunlit sky the color of wet pearl. It was a simple plan. Kill the dinosaurs to avoid them being experimented on for days, months, years.

Outside the air nipped at us like pinchers.

The blond nurse, Jane, lay dead by the doorway, her neck twisted around.

"Bill fixed her," Alan said.

"Snapped that bitch's neck like a chicken," Bill said.

"She was always nice to me," I said.

"Supposed to be," Alan said. "At some point they may have wanted you to reveal your true feelings. They were using her to gradually gain your trust. She would have cut your nuts off with rusty scissors if they asked her to."

I looked down at her, her mouth open, her tongue hanging out of it like a sock from an open drawer. There was a blood drip dangling off her tongue, frozen there like a dollop of strawberry jam.

One thing for sure, Quatermain and Bill weren't messing around, and now I was in the mix too. The thought crossed my mind that I had been bamboozled by bullshit and a fast shuffle, but it wasn't something that would stick. Deep down in my brain cells, I knew the truth, and it wasn't what Cranston had been feeding me. I was brand new with old knowledge of many things. I could tie a bowline. I could toss horse shoes and a javelin, recite poetry and quote books. I knew special secrets of cunnilingus. It was odd to know I was so young and yet the size of a full-grown man, a young man with tremendous muscles and endurance. I was—

I busted my ass on the ice and it hurt, so that put some perspective on it. I was human enough. They helped me up and we hustled past more bodies in blue and white uniforms, scattered about like turds in a dog park, their weapons lying on the ice. And there were other bodies there, minus the blue and white. Men and women in white parkas, splotched with blood. I realized immediately that they had been on my new team, Quatermain and Bill's team.

As we passed, Quatermain said, "If we had time, we'd bury them, but we don't. We have to kill those poor beasts before the word is out and we're dead as stones."

"Wouldn't it be better to make a run for it?" I said.

"Of course," said Quatermain, "but every creature I ever killed for sport and mounted, every possible redemption I might have is in those big ass swimming fish-lizards. I want to make amends."

"And if I don't want to help you make amends?"

"There's the ice," Quatermain said.

I looked about me. Yep. Ice. Melting. Out in the middle of nowhere. It wasn't like I truly had a lot of choices.

"You help me do this, and we kill the beasts, then we'll sail away. Or motor away and do our best to hide, because hide we must. They'll be coming. They don't even let small things go. With the drink comes not only muscle and speed, there's also intense focus. They'll lock onto us and won't unlock until they kill us."

"This is only starting to sound marginally better than the position I was in."

"That's exactly how it is," Bill said. "It's about doing the right thing because it's right and no other reason."

We had reached the edge of the ice now. Our dinosaur fishing boat bobbed in the water before us at the end of the dock.

"In or out?" Quatermain said.

"In," I said.

We hurried across the dock. I could feel it wiggle beneath our feet. The ice it was imbedded in was melting. We climbed on the fishing boat. It was crewed with other rebels. They were of various sizes, races and sexes. All four of them. Those four and us made seven. It was a small revolution.

One of the revolutionaries, a woman, was our captain. She was small and dark-skinned, but most of her face was hidden by her fur-lined parka hood. Nothing was said. Once we were on board, she disappeared into the wheel house. A moment later, the boat was kicking about in the churning water. The three of us climbed to the upper deck. Steam rose up from the once cold sea.

"Stay to the middle," Quatermain called down to one of the men on deck, who rushed to convey the obvious to the captain. But that was all right with me. I surely wanted her to keep us in that middle, away from those crumbling towers of ice.

As we chugged out to the more central part of our icy "lake," the bergs continued to groan like old men on the john, sliding and scraping like shoes on tile. It was a horrible sound, and it was frightening too. Melted fragments larger than our boat dropped loose, sloshed and slid under water, bobbed up near us, or clanged against the side of our puny craft as if they were battering rams. But the boat held.

Into the fighting chairs went me and Quatermain, back to back. Ayesha's blood, brain, and bone matter had been wiped clean, and the rods were ready with new cable that smelled of fresh oil. Hooks dangled, and from the hooks, there were no longer the bodies of Neanderthal, but instead they were baited with great chunks of what looked like beef to me. At least we had enough class not to use the bodies of the fallen, theirs or ours.

"We pull those dinos up, and then we shoot them," Quatermain said. "Right through their tiny brains."

He made it sound simple. He had two very large rifles up there, bagged. He opened the bags, gave me one, which I put in a kind of well at the side of my chair, as did he.

He said, "You've been taught to shoot, but you don't know it yet because you've never done it. But it's in your brain. I laid out all that information myself, they coded it, and in it went. Also, you have my DNA, so you may have the basic attributes that helped me have my skill. And let me tell you something, boy. I'm the best shot who ever lived with any gun or tossing tool. The javelin, hell, you got that from me too. Let me add something I've already told you. Let me speak with perfect conviction once again. Hook them up and shoot them down. It's for their own good. In time the ice will melt, just as you were told, and out they go. Most likely, before that, they would have been caught by you and Ayesha, carried away and tortured for the sake of experimentation. Longevity drugs being the goal, maybe some toothpaste, or hair grower, or something that makes the dick hard would come out of it. But the bottom line is they will suffer, most likely without a drop of pain killer, because the experimenters want the full experience. It's horrible, and we humans, just as always, will be the cause. Screw up the water. Fuck up the air. Cut down the trees and shit on the world. We'll call it science. We'll call it sport. We'll…"

Bill yelled up from below where he was hustling out of the wheel house. "Alan, shut up and pay attention. He gets it."

"Yeah. Right. Sorry."

Bill came up to the chairs then. He was wearing thick goggles to protect his eyes from the glare of the ice, the shimmer of the water. He said, "I'll be your spotter."

Fishing for Dinosaurs

"You have binoculars?" I said.

"Don't need them," Bill said.

"He doesn't," Quatermain said. "He can see a shit spot on a frog's ass from across these waters where we now float to the ice palace from which we came, can't you, Bill?"

"Probably. But it would have to be a large shit spot."

"Naturally," I said.

"Spot away," Quatermain said to Bill. He clambered up a long tower that rose out of the upper deck near us and nestled himself in a little crow's nest at the top. The thin tower shifted and rolled with the wind and the waves. There was a small harpoon gun with cables attached to a reel up there.

The tower hadn't been there before. It had been welded into place since yesterday. The boat chugged forward.

🌱

No sooner was Bill in his tower and us in our chairs, strapped and ready, our hooks in preparation for mechanical toss, when Bill said, "There be them two unfortunate sea-goers, Ar, Ar, shiver me goddamn timbers."

"He saw a pirate movie once," Quatermain said.

True to Bill's sight, along they came through the water swiftly, partly out and partly in, the sun lighting up the ridges of their backs and making the water running down their exposed flesh shine like silver.

"I think they are mad from yesterday," Bill yelled down. "They hold grudges."

"He's not kidding," Quatermain said. "Today, they are looking for us."

The beasts lifted their snakey heads and kept on coming. I touched my controls and my chair came alongside Quatermain's. Our mechanical devices tossed our lines with our baited hooks, and no sooner had they splashed the water than our angry dinosaurs hit them, thinking them maybe less as food, and more as an extension of us. Couldn't blame them.

Under our boat they went, dragging our lines. One line went left, one right. Our chairs rotated about on squeaking bearings and kept turning, us to the back of one another, pivoting the circumference of our platform. Then they dove deep. The reels spun, the cables sang and split the water with a sound like someone tearing rotten sheets.

The boat went dragging across the water.

"They are way down under," Alan said, "and they are dragging us toward the ice."

"Reverse the engines," someone below yelled, and the engines were reversed. There was a straining sound like an apple being forced through a straw, followed by a grinding. The boat locked down and ceased to move quickly. The dinosaurs tugged. The boat's engines billowed with black smoke.

"Cut the engines," I heard another yell from below, and the engines were cut. Now the boat was going across the water like a wagon being hauled by two great horses.

"Harpoon them," I heard Quatermain yell out.

Chunk, came a sound from above. I looked up to see a cable unreeling from the harpoon gun, then glanced at the water as it hit one of the great shadows beneath the water, striking the beast square in the back. The harpoon went in smooth. A dark wetness trailed up and spread over the water. Another harpoon was fired, but now the hit beast was diving down, and the harpoon missed its mark. The other dinosaur followed its companion.

Down they went. The boat bobbed and tipped. For a long, agonizing moment, it seemed as if we would be pulled under. Finally, the boat rested firm, but you could hear all manner of squeaking and scraping as the cables tugged at us. A chunk came out of one side of the boat as a cable effortlessly cut through it like a hot knife through butter.

"They have gone down and intend to pull us with them," Quatermain said, "but the boat will hold."

Fishing for Dinosaurs

"Are you sure?"

"Of course not," he said, "but would you have me say otherwise?"

The cable with the harpoon attached snapped loose with a *ka-ping*, ripped out of the water, whirled around our heads in a fan motion, and wrapped around the tower like damp spaghetti.

"You dead up there?" Quatermain called out to Bill.

"Yeah," Bill said.

"Good," Alan said. "Don't get no deader."

Then to our surprise, the fishing lines stretched out again and the boat began to move, and the beasts were pulling us in a new direction, but with the same intent. We were once again heading directly toward a great iceberg that rose from the water like the Empire State Building.

We were moving fast. We could ride it out and see what happened or release our cables.

"We got time yet," Quatermain said.

I tried to believe he sounded sincere.

Trails of blood from the injured beast were causing the water before us to look like spills of ink. The iceberg loomed closer and closer, and we had no idea how much of it was underwater and in which ways it projected. We might feel what parts of it were below long before we reached the visible part above water.

If this wasn't enough of a consideration, there came a noise like someone beating a thick pillow with a belt. I looked up.

A black helicopter.

One at first, then two.

Bullets slammed into the boat and pinged all around us.

"Shit," Quatermain said. "Someone got word to Cranston and the Rulers. There's rat shit in the soup now."

Bullets pinged on the tower above as the copters flew past. Quatermain yelled out, "Bill, you dead again?"

"Yep," Bill said.

"Good," Quatermain said. "Hang on." Quatermain looked at me and said, "That's a joke. He isn't dead."

"Yeah," I said. "I got that."

So the monsters were pulling us fast as an arrow toward the icebergs, the boat was starting to come apart, black helicopters (five now) had appeared, and only luck had kept us from catching a bullet in the teeth.

Another pass from one of the copters. Bullets buzzed by my head like wasps. By this time we had thrown up our head shields, designed to keep the rain out, not bullets. The shots struck the head shields, and one came through and buried itself at my feet like a lawn dart. Before the shield had slipped into place, I looked up at the chopper. Saw Cranston. He was dressed in a sharp black suit, as if off to the opera and not an employee-killing spree. He had one leg hooked inside the copter and was hanging out of an open side with a .45 in each fist, spitting metal bees at us. I only glimpsed the pilot.

The copter dipped and rose and moved on.

Quatermain pulled a rifle from the well beside him, an old elephant gun. Another of the copters came near. He lifted the gun and fired. The glass eye of the copter exploded and there was a burst of red. The copter buzzed just over us, almost hitting the crow's nest, then hit the water and broke into pieces. I looked toward the water, saw the big, bronze man swimming with the speed a porpoise might have envied.

Quatermain fired again. His shot caught the bronze man in the back of the neck. I saw meat and water fly, and then the bronze man was gone beneath the waves under a wide swath of blood.

That's when my hooked creature worked the hook out of its mouth and leaped high in the air. For something that large, it seemed like an impossible jump. Its jaws widened, then snapped around one of the low-flying copters, dragged it down. I saw the big, dark-haired man inside of it; it was just a glimpse, but it was him, and the inside of the copter was splattered with blood. The beast landed hard, swirling beneath the water with the machine in its teeth.

The wave caused a backwash. It hit the boat like a giant's fist.

The hook cut loose of the dinosaur's mouth. It whipped high on the cable, its tip catching sunlight.

I hit the levers, recoiled the cable so fast it was nearly subliminal, and saved us from that disaster.

Looking up, I saw Cranston's copter coming at us, the others behind it in formation. He was still hanging out of it, firing. I noticed now that on the front of his copter were the painted letter and number G-8. The pilot at the controls could be seen clearly through the great windshield. He looked as cool as the icebergs. They were so close I felt as if I were in the machine with them. Cranston swung out through the opening again, fired those .45's. A shot plucked at my shoulder and banged off the metal chair behind me, leaped up, kissed my ear lobe, and whistled away. Neither wound was major.

I swung the rod, disengaged the cable, swirled the hook, and splattered it against the front of the copter's windshield. The hook knocked through the windshield, hooked on something, and the copter spun. I wheeled my chair and flung the hooked machine way out over the water. But it wasn't enough. Something went haywire with the reel. The copter was jerked back toward us.

"Shit in a pan," Quatermain said.

For a moment, it looked as if the loose line would drop it short. But not quite. It caught the edge of the deck and there was a fiery explosion. The boat came apart like wet cardboard. We were dragged down by the warm waves. As I went under, I saw the shadow of one of the copters beating its blades above us.

Right before going under, I had instinctively gulped in a breath of air. The water was warm, but not boiling, as too much ice had melted into it. It wasn't pleasant though, and I was down deep.

I stayed down for as long as I could, and then I had to come up. When I did, there was Quatermain clinging to a large plank from our boat.

"Hi, kid."

I grabbed hold of the plank, feeling no more confident of it than if I had clutched a straw. There was an explosion in the distance that made the water rise high, and there was fire in the sky. The remaining helicopters, too low and too near the explosion, snapped and crackled in the flames like insects caught in bug zappers. Their great blades went sailing across the sky. Icebergs shot upward and came apart, and their fragments floated above us like clouds against a blazing sunset, then began to fall down. The water heated up considerably.

"Balls," Quatermain said.

The volcano way down below had exploded, just to make sure we were awake.

A whirling blade from one of the helicopters whistled over our heads. Smoldering body parts splashed in the water. Ice chunks plunged down all around us.

The water began to move, fast, and then drop. It sizzled and smoked.

"Cheers, kid, nice knowing you."

The water plunged even more, and we went down with it. Then we were sailing along toward a great iceberg, and the water became lower before it. We came to a massive gap in the ice. The water was flowing into it, and we went along with it.

I glanced back along the icy tunnel, could see the sky, the water. Fire was blowing out of the water, spewing high. Rolls of lava tumbled into the waves, turned them to steam. So steamy I could no longer see.

Down we washed, so far down that I accepted I was doomed. Lava flowed in behind us, sizzling the water, creeping up on us like a cat on a crippled mouse. Then there was a strange rush of water as if we had been caught in a vacuum of some sort. We shot along as if taped to the head of a bullet. We went so fast I lost grip on the plank, lost awareness of Quatermain. I didn't know if I was up or down, dead or alive, still under that bridge, in the warehouse, on a gurney, or if anything I knew was true, or if it was all just a bubble somewhere in my brain.

Water gushed through my nose and mouth and flooded inside of me. The world went dark. I knew my short, real life had ended.

Okay. Sorry for the cliff-hanger. But that's how it was. I was doomed.

Except I wasn't.

I sat up. I don't know how long I had been out, but there was light and it was hot and sticky. Above me, the sky rippled with fire. There were clouds, odd looking, bluish, sparked with pink. Through gaps in the clouds I could see a sky of fire.

There was a vast inland lake before me. I was on its shore, bedded down in deep mud. To my right I could see Quatermain. Down a piece from him I could see Bill. He was standing. The rushing water had torn all our clothes off. We were naked as the day we were born, or in my case, made in a vat.

I leaned to my side and coughed up water and tried to get to my feet. That was no harder than dragging a bus up a high hill with a rope, so I lay back down in the mud for a while. In time, Bill was looking down at me.

"Home," he said.

I sat up, not wishing to lie there with his penis swinging above me.

He grabbed me under the arms and backed up, pulling me out of the mud. Quatermain was already out. He was sitting with his back against a tree.

"This is my world," Bill said. "The volcano collapsed in on itself, opened a path, and we all came down it. Slanted easy and came down under, sliding down the sloping bowl that leads here. Had it been a straight drop, we would have drowned. Might have been drowned anyway. But we weren't. We're lucky to be alive."

"You can say that again," I said.

"We are lucky to be alive," Bill said.

"Not up for the humor," I said.

"By the way, there didn't use to be a lake here," Bill said. "Come walk with me. Come see."

I was able to get my feet under me this time. Quatermain got up too. We went along after Bill. We came to a bend in the shoreline. To our left were great and primordial trees, and to our right, that vast lake, or perhaps a better name for it would be inland sea.

Scattered about it, close to shore, were fragments from the copters and our boat. There were bodies as well. I saw the great dark-haired man wrapped up in a propeller. His head dangled down and that was the only thing about him truly recognizable. His features were perfect, serene even, as if he always expected it to end this way. The rest of him looked like dirty taffy wrapped around those blades.

"Irony," Quatermain said. "They wanted to live forever. Now they're dead and we're alive."

"You haven't noticed," Bill said.

"Noticed what?" Quatermain said.

"Me," Bill said.

"So you've done something with your hair?" Quatermain said.

"Damn, you're dumb," Bill said, then extended his arms and turned around and around a few times.

"Your scars," I said. "They're gone."

"The air," Bill said. "This place. My home. It's healed me. Well, there are some little white scars, but the serious stuff, it's healed up."

"So the question is solved. It's the DNA mixed with the air that keeps people here young," Quatermain said. "Look there."

It was the two plesiosaurs. They were swimming amongst the wreckage, around remaining fragments of melting icebergs, pausing to eat an available snack of mutilated and burnt corpses. The one that had been harpooned looked healthy enough, as if it had received a nasty pin prick.

"We don't need to fish them now," I said.

"Or kill them," Quatermain said. "Of course, now we have a new problem. This world."

"My world," Bill said.

"No one owns a place like this," Quatermain said.

"We can live a life of our choosing," I said. "I'm only a few months old, and I'm ready to have some real experiences."

"I bet that will be possible," Quatermain said. "But as for the Secret Rulers, they aren't all gone. We may see them again."

"Then we will," I said. "But for now, we have this and we are free of obligation, our indentured servitude is over."

"I can show you how to survive, how to live here," Bill said. "I remember all that shit. Making fires, weapons, finding things to eat. It's right here in my head and in my heart. I have sort of lost the taste for grubs, though."

"That sounds all right," Quatermain said, "but what I wouldn't give for a pair of Bermuda shorts, some flip-flops, right now. This is no way to go about."

We stood there looking out at the wreckage in the water at bodies both of our revolutionaries, and those from the choppers. That was done and couldn't be undone. We looked out at the beautiful and foreboding forest, touched by shadows, dappled by sunlight. It was full of fleeting figures, the sounds of birds and growling animals.

After a while Bill located a trail and we took fallen limbs to serve as clubs and went along together into the dark of the trees.

I Should've Known Better

BY RICHARD CHIZMAR

I'LL LET YOU in on a little secret.

You'd be hard pressed to find a bigger fan than me of Joe Lansdale's fiction, but for some reason I've always steered clear of his more gonzo works. Books like *Cold In July, The Thicket, The Nightrunners, The Bottoms, A Fine Dark Line,* and a whole slew of others occupy a sacred place on my office bookshelf. And don't even get me started on the Hap and Leonard novels—classics all. Lean and mean and stuffed full of oddball humor and wisdom, I've long admired and championed Lansdale's unique brand of suspenseful and soulful storytelling. I've also learned a whole lot from Joe's writing. Maybe even swiped a thing or two when I thought no one was looking.

But the more "out there" works—books with wacky titles such as *In Waders from Mars, Zeppelins West,* and *The Ape Man's Brother* (hell, I'm pretty sure Joe even published an entire book or novella about a damn duck once upon a time; I could be wrong, so don't quote me on that)—well, I've always just sort of given those projects a yawn and a pass.

I'm going to let you in on another little secret: I'm a dumbass.

Come to think of it, according to daily reminders from my wife and kids, that might not be much of a secret at all.

Anyway, what the heck was I thinking? After all those years, all those wonderful stories and books and comics and films, you would think I would have learned to trust Joe enough to give anything he'd written a try. He'd certainly earned that much along the way.

So, yeah, the dumbass in this case is clearly yours truly.

Worst of all, I don't even have a good excuse. I mean it's not like I'm some kind of literary snob or stodgy traditionalist. Far from it. I love weird fiction. Hell, I've made my life's work out of being weird and my favorite magazine of all time, the late, great Dave Silva's *The Horror Show*, used to launch each and every new issue by proudly proclaiming: "Better weird than plastic." And didn't I spend a good chunk of my twenties quoting outrageous dialogue from Joe's supremely "out there" *Drive-In* novels—"One day suddenly you're out of high school, happy as a grub in shit, waking up with a hard-on and spending your days sitting around in your pee-stained underwear with your feet propped up on the air conditioner vent with cool air blowing on your nuts, and the next goddamn thing you know, you're crucified." As a matter of fact, yes, I did.

But for whatever reasons, like many dumbasses that came before me, I somehow formed a prejudice later in life. I developed a blind spot—and was all the poorer for it.

Take *The Ape Man's Brother* for instance. Was I a fan of the original slim hardcover when it was first published back in January 2014? Nope. Never even bothered to read it. SubPress publisher Bill Schafer was kind enough to send me a copy hot off the press. I remember digging the Ken Laager cover art and then sliding it onto my bookshelf. And there it stayed until a couple of weeks ago.

I should've known better.

The Ape Man's Brother is wild and wonderful and different than anything I've ever read before—but it also clearly comes from the wonder-filled heart and typewriter of Joe Lansdale.

I won't give away much of the plot. That wouldn't be fair to all you lucky readers about to experience this fine tale for the very first time. Instead, I'll simply say this: it's all there, what I've come to expect (and cherish) in a Lansdale work of fiction—a fantastical plot, razor sharp prose, moments of heart-stopping suspense, laugh-out-loud humor ("The Big Guy, the most powerful being I have ever seen, was on the ground holding his melons like he was testing them to see how ripe they were. Me, I'm just standing there grinning. My race is like that. We grin. It may look friendly, and sometimes it is, but it's a grin that can mean a lot of different things. From, how about you and me go over in the bushes, to I'm about to bite your face off, or how about we share that dead snake. Even we have trouble sorting out meanings from time to time, and mistakes are sometimes made."), and smartly drawn characters you immediately grow to care about. There's also generous dashes of love and hate and jealousy and greed, not to mention friendship and loyalty and betrayal. Toss in a sprinkling of wild beasts rampaging across a mist-shrouded lost civilization, troops of fleas, womanizing apes, dinosaurs, and one unforgettable scene where an unnamed screen legend sodomizes a dead lion—and there you have it, a book that only Joe Lansdale could write.

Wait, did I forget to mention the instantly unforgettable dialogue? ("Your age doesn't matter," said The Big Guy, which was spoken like someone who had never fucked an old lady. I am not suggesting that I have... Oh hell, a few times, at fundraisers back in the States.) Now how delightful is that?

A brief personal aside before I let you get on to the enjoyment of reading:

Despite knowing Joe Lansdale for going on thirty years now, I've never met the man in person. Joe hits plenty of book and movie conventions, but as many folks will attest, I don't get out much. So, ours has been a long time, long distance relationship. Back in the late 1980s, Joe was one of the very first supporters of my magazine and small press. I remember dozens of phone calls during those early days. Countless stories listened to and lessons learned. I tend to learn things the hard way—by making large and small mistakes and working hard not to repeat them too often. Because of that trait, I came to listen closely to and trust Joe's advice. He's not a smoke blower; he's a truth teller—even when that truth might hurt a little bit to hear. I've always been grateful for those early words of encouragement and wisdom. I've never forgotten them. All these years later, Joe is very much the same man I knew then: weird and wise and talented, and working hard to tell his truth—in both his fiction and his life.

The Ape Man's Brother

1

I AM NOT a chimpanzee. I am not an ape. The guy who played me in the movie was an ape.

It's true. I did love that woman, that beautiful, blond woman, and it was not a platonic love. It was much more than that. And in line with that, here's something I want to correct.

Because I'm not a chimpanzee, and am more accurately somewhere closer to an Australopithecus with a larger brain—which, of course makes me neither ape nor modern man, nor actually Australopithecus, but a humanoid off-shoot—what happened between the lady and myself was not technically bestiality, no matter what the tabloids say. But there was a crime. It was the breaking of the bond of brotherhood, and I regret it from the bottom of my heart.

Now the true events can be told, because other than myself, everyone involved with the sordid affair is now dead or missing, except that goddamn chimpanzee. He's got the constitution of a redwood tree. Then again it's not his fault. He was an actor. He was never actually involved, but the way he's treated, living in a retirement home for animals of the cinema, photos and articles popping up about him on his birthday every year, his fuzzy face covered in birthday cake, you'd think he'd at least have been President for a term.

Me, I was the real thing, and my raggedy ass has been left to its own devices. So, I thank you for coming to me to get the real story, and I will tell it true without dropping a stitch on the real lowdown.

2

It begins with The Big Guy.

The Big Guy, truth to tell, had few friends. There were some humans he liked, and many he tolerated. A few he killed. His true friends were that lovely woman, and me, who they came to call by a fictional name because of all those stupid movies. I'll not even repeat that name here. The whole thing makes me angry. The way I'm presented in the films, doing all those little tricks and throwing my feces—they didn't show that in the movie, and it never directly appeared in the books, but it's commonly known chimpanzees haven't any pause about filling their hands with their own mess and throwing it. Well, yes. I did it too. But that was when I was uncivilized. I have learned how to act, so that no longer applies to me.

I guess there's a little jealousy there, that damn ape stealing my thunder. But let me get back to what I was saying, and let me start with how I came to know The Big Guy. Forgive me if I trail off from time to time. I'm healthy, and all my external equipment still works, but my mind, though good, has many alleys, some of them blind, so I apologize in advance. Now, having come to a dead end in this alley, I'm turning about and coming back, looking for the light.

Let me start by saying I was there when the plane went down. Some accounts say it was a great sailing ship and that it crashed on a faraway shore, or that it was taken over by pirates, or that the child and his family were set adrift in a small boat.

All of these versions are false. These storytellers, these experts, also place events farther back in time as to when they really happened. This is partly so The Big Guy, as I call him, can be seen as ancient as Methuselah, but with muscles; a hero of folklore, not reality.

But, it wasn't a boat, and it wasn't a ship, and there were no pirates. It was a plane crash. We had never seen a plane, me and my tribe, and we had no idea that it had flown in from Greenland.

It looked like a great dragonfly falling out of the sky, buzzing and coughing and churning smoke, soon to explode. I know now, these many years later, that it was a small plane and it carried a husband and wife and baby. The parents were archeologists, scouting what they believed to be abandoned ancient ruins in the jungle of a lost, walled-in world.

They were right and they were wrong. The ruins were not abandoned. They were our home and had been the home of our ancestors for many years. Some of our culture had been lost, and the jungle had crept around the stones and swallowed them up and mossed them green. Our great scroll books had turned to dust. Our history was by then nothing but rocks, some scratches in the dirt, some huts, fuzzy memories passed on carelessly from the old to the young. Bottom line, we were pretty ignorant and there was a flea problem.

There were lots of reasons for our decline. No doubt we had fallen back into ignorance due to disease and human sacrifice. That sort of activity cuts down on the population. Offered sex organs were popular. Cut those buddies out and lay them on a sacrificial stone, set them on fire, and everyone thought the rain was coming.

But there was no rain for a long time, and there weren't enough private parts to go around for sacrifice, and by the time it was decided the gods weren't listening, or that perhaps they didn't have quite the taste for privates as were first assumed, half the population's genitals had gone up in smoke, and therefore half the population.

Our folk started disappearing into the jungle to stay attached to their equipment, and finally the sacrifice thing died out, and then the priest died out, and pretty soon we were eating bugs off trees and digging for grubs and trolling for anything edible that didn't eat us first.

Anyway, a lot of wing-dang-doodles were saved and we lost our faith in gods, which, though we were a primitive lot, put us way ahead of most everyone else in the world.

3

OUT THERE IN the depths of the jungle there was only greenery, and as seen from above I'm sure our primitive city was nothing more than a few flashes of white stone gripped in the clutches of moss and vines. Flying up there in their little plane they must have seen it and decided to come closer. But they came too close, and the top of a tree caught the bottom of the plane and ripped it.

I was young then, and I saw it happen from a perch in a tree. Saw the belly of the silver bird rip, saw it twist and spin and finally fall, spewing goods out of it like guts, throwing oil and gas like blood. It hit the top of one of our pyramids, bunched together like a wad of paper, and blew up, sending shrapnel skyward and amongst the trees in a hard, sharp rain. A piece of it killed one of my cousins, but I never liked him anyway.

The pyramid, the tallest one, the one the plane struck, was not Egyptian high or Egyptian grand, but it was well up there, and as I said, cloaked in moss and vines. From where I stood, even watching through the trees, I felt the heat from the blast of the plane lick at me like a baboon's breath, saw some of the vines curl and blacken, smoke and crumble. There came from the wreckage a horrible howl. All of us raced to the source, and as we came closer, I could smell meat cooking.

Then I heard a whine that turned into a gasping cry. There, lying on the moss-covered steps near the top of the pyramid, as if he had been placed there, was something I had never seen before. A near hairless thing, naked; its little bit of dark hair was smoking on its head. I ran over and beat out the flames gently with the palm of my hand, and lifted the thing high. It stopped crying immediately. As if in salute, it lifted its little pecker and pissed straight into my face.

✿

Much has been written about The Big Guy, and I want to say right here and now, the one who wrote the most about him, claimed he was my man's main biographer, had no business telling the story in the first place. He wasn't there. But that didn't stop him. It didn't stop him from telling it wrong and making up facts and situations so he could sell a novel, and later profit from the motion pictures made from the series of stories he wrote about my good friend, The Big Guy. Well, we profited too, I have to admit. But I resent any profits he made. It was our story, not his, and he didn't deserve a single penny.

First off, the name in the books and movies is way wrong. I can say the name but you can't. I can say it because it was given to him in my language. It sounds a little like a cough and a fart to say it right, but it is hard to repeat in human language. So, that's how he came to be known by the name in the books and movies and so on. In the books a monkey takes my place, and in the movies it's that chimpanzee. They gave the chimp a name close to my name but it's not my name.

Everyone now just calls me Bill.

✿

So, here I am, holding this young human child in my arms, him pissing in my face, and all the others laughing. I admit, I was about to toss him from the top of the pyramid, when my mother, who had recently lost her child to some sort of jungle disease, comes up and takes The Little Guy from me and holds him to her breast. A moment later, she and The Little Guy disappear into the trees. I didn't know exactly what was going on. I thought maybe she was going to eat him in privacy, because it had crossed my mind to do just that. There wouldn't have been a lot of preparation and very little hair to spit out. Just swing him by the feet, whack him on a rock, and a hot dinner was served.

But Mother carried him away from me, went swinging through the foliage. We can move amongst the jungle tree tops better than any human or ape our size. We are swifter than the chimpanzee because we are lighter, but stronger. I should also add that we have larger brains than the branch of humanity that survived. That would be you.

All I got to say is, "Good for you, you survivor you." But we were very good too. It was just fate that made you the main human branch and led to our dying out in the jungles of our lost world, amongst the trees and stones of our forefathers. If we just hadn't gotten religion for a while, no telling what we might have accomplished.

4

THE LITTLE GUY, who became The Big Guy, was a real whiner, and if Mother had not been sad from losing my little brother to a hungry panther, he might well have been, as I stated, a nice hot lunch. But he clung to her tit with the enthusiasm of a leech, and her milk filled him and he grew.

Even when he was quite old for it, he still sucked that tit. I wanted to suck the tit, but nope. Only The Little Guy, who was hairless, and in my view a little on the ugly side, got the tit. Full grown, he'd come to the great nest in the trees, give our mom the fruit he had gathered, or the animals that he had killed, and before the feast, he would suckle. No one ate until The Big Guy was through drawing milk through the tit, and he liked to stretch this out, hugging Mother, closing his eyes and sucking slowly, occasionally popping one eye open to see how the rest of us were taking it. The rest of us being my two sisters and myself. The best thing to do was to not look perturbed, but to just go about some business of a sort, and forget it. He was more likely to quit that way and let us all get down to eating.

I will admit, however, there was something about him that made him special. We could all see it. We could all sense it. I would learn later that he had been the subject of an experiment. Dr. Rice, who you will learn more about, told me this. He never told The Big Guy. I'm not sure why. Maybe he planned to when the time was right. I don't know. But the time didn't get right and he didn't tell him. But I will come back to that later. What I know is this: His parents allowed The Big Guy, before birth, to be injected, right through his mother's stomach, with an experimental drug that was designed to give him elevated intelligence and great physical prowess and grant him an extraordinary life span. In the books his so-called biographer says this was achieved by the workings of a witch doctor, or at least I think he said that. As I was telling you, things are starting to slide off my brain like greased butts on a grassy slope. Important part is the injection worked. More on that later.

At the time, all we knew was that he grew up to be tall and muscled and gold of skin and hung like a zebra. He could travel through the trees with the best of us, though he had to take to cinching up his snake with vines, least he catch it on a snag or drag it through thorns, something he once did, and something that took a couple days of careful work on my part to pull the thorns free. I don't know how I ended up with the job, but there you have it.

To say the least, this endeared him to me, and I to him. Why the latter, I'm a little confused. But, once again, there you have it.

He learned our language and customs quite comfortably. In time they were his language and customs, and he became my brother. He is still my brother, and will forever be. We lived a wild life, a good life, and there were many great adventures. We found lost cities containing civilizations thought long dead. We stole all manner of jewels and raped women with and without tails. Sometimes we did the men. This was just the way things were, so don't get highfalutin'. We chased creatures that your kind would call dinosaurs. We wrestled with saber-toothed tigers and wild boars as big as horses.

When they were in heat we fucked our sisters. Mom was off limits, being dry, but the sisters, they got to that time of the month we were all over that stuff. We couldn't help it. That was the custom. That was biology. We were no different than most jungle apes. I should add, technically, none of these sisters were The Big Guy's blood kin, and he couldn't impregnate them, and fortunately, I never did.

By human standards we were stinkers. By our lost world standards, we were just growing boys. But even in our world, we had a reputation.

Watch out for those Monkey Boys (euphemism, I might add), they'll steal your stuff, whip your ass, and then fuck you. Hell, it's how we were brought up. As to who was referring to us as Monkey Boys (again, I'm using a euphemism), it was our neighbors, who were of our own blood, but who had branched off and taken up customs that we disagreed with, mostly having to do with hair-dos and the like. We killed off the bulk of them during our religious days, and the rest of them we killed off to have something to do when times were boring.

So, there we were, living in the jungle with our asses hanging out, our numbers decreasing faster than a baked pig at a luau, and then a little something happened that turned things around and gave us culture.

Well, it gave me culture.

What happened was HER, THE WOMAN.

5

ONE DAY ME and Big Guy were out there in the depths of the jungle, beating an antelope to death with sticks, and we heard a noise that wasn't our antelope expiring, but was something else altogether different.

It was a melodious sound that reminded me of a bird. I often sat and listened to their sweet songs for an hour before I took a rock to one of them, ripped off the feathers and ate it, but this was different.

We left our dead antelope for the moment and took to the trees. Down there on the trail we saw a string of individuals, that except for the fact that their bodies were covered in what I was to learn were clothes and pith helmets, looked a lot more like The Big Guy than me.

One of them was a delicate looking thing (actually she wasn't that delicate) with a long, blond mass of hair bound back by a blue ribbon. At that point in time I had never seen blond hair. Big Guy's hair was black as night. But they had the same eyes—blue like water. She had a bag on a strap slung over her shoulder, and when she stopped singing, she started talking to the man in front of her, that fellow with enough dark whiskers he could, at least in the face, pass for one of my kind. The rest of him, not so much. He was plump in the belly, which we are not. The way he walked was funny, and reminded me of how Big Guy would walk from time to time when he wasn't climbing trees or moving about on all fours. Later I would learn this was the blond female's father.

The Delicate Thing struck me at that moment in time as ugly as Big Guy. Reason for this, I'm sure, is obvious. My view of what was beautiful was based on my upbringing, my culture, and my own appearance. My idea then of attractive was fur-covered, no sores, both eyes worked, they had a vagina, and the fleas were minimal, though sometimes you could eat fleas while you mated, which I suppose for us could be classified as a cheap dinner date.

In time my views on attractiveness changed. That's another can of worms, and I'll come to it.

But even then I liked the way she moved that butt. And I realized that though she wasn't making that bird-like sound now, it had been her voice I had heard, and to me in memory, it had sounded like music, which, except for clubbing a log with a stick and hooting wasn't something I was familiar with at that moment. I use it as a reference as I think it can be more immediately understood. I was also thinking when she quit singing maybe we could club her to death and eat her same as the birds, peeling that stuff that covered her off the way we would yank out a bird's feathers.

Me and Big Guy watched them from the trees, swung above them silently as they moved along the jungle trail. It must have been especially interesting to Big Guy, because he had never seen any of his own kind before, not remembering his parents at all. I remembered them slightly, but only as crispy shells of cooked meat. I never did tell Big Guy that a few of the tribe, one who will not be named, later partook of that flesh in a waste not want not attitude.

We followed them along, and it grew close to night. The moon was about half full, and shining through the trees. We could see clearly into their camp as they put up tents, built a fire, and so on. They had some long things with them that at the time I thought were clubs, but would later learn were rifles.

We watched as they ate from their supplies and went to bed. When we could hear them breathing deep in sleep, we climbed down and made our way cautiously on all fours towards where their packs were. We silently went at unfastening them, looking through them. Another trait of our kind is we're dadburn thieves.

What we found were cans of food, though we didn't know that, and we tossed those aside in favor of dried meat and fruits;

the kind of drying used for keeping something way past the time it ought to be kept.

They had also, stupidly, left a number of their pots and pans they had prepared their meals in unwashed. It was just the sort of thing that could call up a beast or one of us Jungle Folk. I found a kind of goo in one of the pans with chunks of vegetables I didn't recognize. I scooped it out on my finger and tasted it. I was suddenly aware—except for that one really swell meal after the plane crash—that what we had been eating was nothing more than grass and worms and ticks and stolen bird eggs and raw meat and such. This whole cooking thing was all right. You see, we Jungle Folk, smart as we were—and this is embarrassing to say—had fire, but we rarely cooked with it, unless something caught on fire by accident. Making a fire and preparing a meal was a lot of trouble, and when we weren't scrounging for food, we were a lazy bunch. And I might as well mention that we hadn't found out about the wheel either, or the missionary position.

So, me and The Big Guy are licking pans, and all of a sudden, The Woman is standing there. Next thing I know she's jabbering in a language that at that point in time I didn't understand. But I knew enough from her tone to know what she had to say wasn't pleasant and had something to do with us.

Next thing I know The Big Guy is walking up to her. He had a look on his face like he had just been born and was seeing the world for the first time. He reached out to touch her, and she gave him a kick in the old melons that would have made an elephant go to its knees. Damn sure made The Big Guy drop. Strangely, he had a smile on his face when he looked up at her.

Frankly, she had me feeling a might warm and contented myself. I wasn't sure why a non-hairy, clothed female should make me feel that way, but she did. And to reiterate, I never felt quite the same for the hairy women folk of my tribe after that. One look at the woman had spoiled me.

I had seen gold and I no longer wanted silver.

6

I HAVE TO go backwards a little, because as I said before, I tend to wander. But I should say that where we lived in that deep jungle was a kind of bowl. It dipped deep down on the sides and went wide, and as far as we knew, there was no way out. It was miles and miles across, in all directions. If we climbed up any one of the sides, moving through the trees, eventually, the trees played out. When that happened there were some rocks to climb, and caves, if you were willing to go up that high. There were nasty things that roosted in those caves and they had lots of teeth and could fly, so we were extra careful. Finally, above that, there were straight slick walls, all around, and way up for miles. And when I say slick, I mean slick. The stone that made up the walls was like glass, and often damp. It wouldn't even hold moss that you could grab onto. There was no way to climb. For us, that deep bowl of jungle, and all it contained, was it. A plane flying over might not even know what it was looking at, with all that jungle hiding what was down below, and the fact that a mist rolled high and over most of it much of the time like a roof of sun-leaking cotton.

At one time, Dr. Rice (and you will soon know who he is) in his zeppelin, exploring, saw our world. He had made an aerial expedition all the way from New York City, based on old records written by an Italian sailing captain and navigator who claimed to have found a large island, possibly a continent, rising out of the ocean. It was thought for centuries to be a myth, or an incorrect sighting of some known land, but Dr. Rice had taken it seriously and flown over our world by zeppelin, feeling sure that through the mist he had seen a flash of green, lush land. He told his colleagues, The Big Guy's parents, and they thought they could follow Dr. Rice's navigational information, fly out of Greenland, but the navigational charts were off, or they misread them. It was a longer trip than they expected. Even though they wouldn't have had enough fuel to return, they made it to our world, had seen the ruins of our civilization, and were most likely looking for some place to land when the accident happened that turned them from archeologist to well-done with no sides.

I learned all this later, of course. Dr. Rice's guilty feelings about his report leading to The Big Guy's parents trying to come to our world and losing their lives, led to his coming back on a possible rescue expedition, something it took him years to finance. He had hopes they and their baby son might have survived, some nineteen years later by the way they calculated time.

But, there we were, me and The Big Guy, The Woman having caught us in their pans. She was mad, surprised, and there was sweat on her forehead, her hair coming loose from being tied back, falling on her cheeks and neck, one leg bent forward, the back leg ready for another kick.

The Big Guy, the most powerful being I have ever seen, was on the ground holding his melons like he was testing them to see how ripe they were. Me, I'm just standing there grinning. My race is like that. We grin. It may look friendly, and sometimes it is, but it's a grin that can mean a lot of different things. From, how about you and me go over in the bushes, to I'm about to bite your face off, or how about we share that dead snake. Even we have trouble sorting out meanings from time to time, and mistakes are sometimes made.

So, there we stood.

That's when one of the men, a tall, flame-headed one, came running up, pointing one of those clubs at me. I'm thinking he can't do much business with it, the way he's holding it, part of it tucked against his shoulder and all. And then The Woman hits the end of it and the club goes up and barks, and fire comes out of the tip of it, and something rattles off in the bushes, like a rock has been thrown, and then an unsuspecting monkey falls dead out of a tree without so much as a squeak.

I shit all over the place. It's not an unnatural reaction to fear, I might add. It's just I didn't know it was unseemly or might even be thought of as cowardly by those of your race, so I just let it fly. There's a comfort in it, and I want to add promptly that though I had this problem for quite some time, and the chimpanzee that played me in the movies certainly had some similarities, I was quickly civilized on the matter. I know. I've brought this up before, but I'm bothered by it, and I want people to know I've moved on from my primitive state, and though I'm a little embarrassed by the subject, I feel it is only fair that I trudge ahead and be honest and stress my developmental growth.

Next thing I knew, The Big Guy was up, and stirring. He could always recover from something bad quicker than anyone I have ever known. He grabbed that banging club and jerked it out of that man's hands and hit him on the head with it, knocked him down. Then he held it by what I now know to be the stock of the rifle, and grabbed the barrel, and he bent that barrel like it was a green vine. Bent it and tossed it into the greenery. Damn if he didn't bang another monkey. It fell out of the undergrowth and into the moonlight and thrashed around on the ground, then sort of crawled off to cower inside a flowered bush and quivered for awhile before it went still. It was not a good day for monkeys.

All the others of The Woman's group came running up then. They all had the same kind of clubs. They were pointing them at us. During all this action, I had rushed up beside The Big Guy. I thought it was going to be a fight to the death, and I was more than willing, maybe even a little anxious to try it out, see how we'd fare against all those men. I had no idea about the guns, then. I had heard one, and I had seen it spit fire, but I didn't know they threw bullets. I thought that first monkey had just fainted at the sound of the shot. I thought it would be us against them, arms against arms, legs against legs, fists against fists, skulls against skulls, and their clubs against us. But, of course, that isn't how it would have been. That many armed men, no matter how strong and quick The Big Guy was, no matter how savage the both of us were, we'd have lasted just about long enough for our balls to swing once between our legs before we hit the ground, torn apart by bullets. What saved us was The Woman raised her hand and yelled at the others. Everything stopped. She stood staring at The Big Guy, and he stood staring at her.

The Big Guy had never seen anything like her, all curved up in the right places, wet, red lips and shiny blue eyes. And she was looking at a very big man with dark hair and a body that was all long, lean muscle, dirt and scars and deep suntan; from the way her face relaxed, I had a pretty good idea she liked what she was looking at as much as he liked what he was looking at.

It was while they were looking at one another, The Woman with her arm raised, holding back action from those behind her, that there was a screech loud enough to make my backbone shift. A great shadow flowed across the moon and a flying, feathered lizard as big as one of your airplanes, swooped down and grabbed The Woman by hooking its claws into her shoulder.

Those damn things were all over our part of the world. A nuisance is what they were. So, it was pretty much over for The Woman, I thought, and then the next thing I know The Big Guy is running. I mean, he is moving. He took to one of the tall trees, and went up it swiftly. Those flying creatures have an odd habit of grabbing something, then circling back, maybe to see if they've left part of it on the ground. This habit was something The Big Guy, of course, was fully acquainted with, and he took advantage of it.

It was circling back, true to form, and The Big Guy having judged its circle had quickly climbed that tree, and as the thing winged by, The Big Guy leaped and effortlessly landed on its back. He wrapped one arm around its neck, went to beating its hard head with his free fist. You could hear him whapping it all the way from where we stood.

As the thing flew over us, blood and brains sprinkled down on us from The Big Guy's blows, and the next thing you know, it's crashing into a tree and letting go of The Woman. The Big Guy, moving faster than a snake can strike, leaped off that flying, twisting, falling wreck, grabbed The Woman's arm as he went, and swung them both into the leafy boughs of the tree.

There they were, standing on a limb in a tall tree, her shoulder slightly wet with blood, bleeding through the cloth of her torn shirt, and there he was, standing without clothes, staring into her eyes; his pecker standing up like a snake rising to strike. She moved the short distance between them, took hold of his long, tangled hair, pulled him to her, pressed her mouth against his, and even from where we stood, that kiss sounded like someone pulling their foot out of a deep mud puddle.

"That son-of-a-bitch," said the flame-headed guy, who I would later learn was called Red.

The Big Guy picked her up with one arm, leaped off the limb, grabbed another limb with his free hand, swung them up into the cover of a thick-leafed tree, and they were gone. Let me add as an aside, swinging from limb to limb with one hand while holding a very fine and sturdy female is not a feat that anyone else I know of, other than The Big Guy, could accomplish.

I took off.

The men were so shocked to see what had happened, that they didn't know if they should yell or turn in a circle or draw pictures in the dirt. By the time they looked for me, I was across the clearing and into the trees.

7

I caught up with The Big Guy and The Woman about nightfall. The Woman had removed her coverings; she was as naked as The Big Guy. There were streaks of blood where the great winged beast had grabbed her, and that attack would leave a scar on her shoulder, three slash marks. The two of them were in the cup of a big limb that had been struck by lightning and hollowed out by it. There were soft leaves laid out in the cup, and they were resting on top of them. What they were doing wouldn't pass for anything other than what it was; I'll use a more common English phrase. They were fucking like there was no tomorrow.

They were so at it I didn't even announce that I had shown up, though The Big Guy could smell me. As he did his business, her screaming and him grunting, he waved a hand at me that let me know to keep my distance. I did. But I watched. Carefully. I had never seen such goings on. Usually, in the jungle, we jump it and do it and get on with looking for something to eat.

This was different. He moved her in different positions, and she let him, and it was well midday when they quit cooing and fell asleep in the cup of the limb. I sat around for awhile, then went out and found some fruit to eat. I brought some of it back with me.

They ate the fruit I brought, and then they went back at it. I think somewhere in all this The Woman realized from the way The Big Guy and myself interacted, that I wasn't a pet. I didn't know that's what she was thinking at the time, but I can look back on events now with acquired knowledge. I think it's a little different knowing the family dog is watching you go at it, but once you realize that what you thought was a pet is a best friend having secondary thrills, that changes things.

When that realization settled down on her, she got downright prudish. I was surprised The Big Guy didn't just make her do what he wanted, because as I said, we were primitive, but he didn't. He seemed hurt by her reaction. He pouted. He made hooting noises, clicking noises, and screaming noises for complaint. For her complaint, she slapped him so hard it knocked him off the limb.

He grabbed another. Climbed rapidly back up. His face had a red mark in the shape of her fingers on it. I thought this was it. Now we were going to kill her and eat her. But no, that didn't happen.

When he was back up there with her, he hung his head and whimpered. She looked at him for a long moment, her face softened, and she took him into her arms and held him, looking at me over his shoulder with a glare that was nearly strong enough to kill the fleas in my fur.

Me, I went hunting.

8

Now, I COULD go into a blow by blow recreation of what happened next, but frankly, that part is not all that interesting. Simply put, The Woman, having covered herself in her coverings again, took The Big Guy back to the camp with her, or to be more precise, nearby, and I went along with them. She had somehow developed a way of making The Big Guy understand what she wanted, mostly with hand motions, and I believe this was possible because they were so naturally attracted to one another.

Anyway, she went into camp and did some talking while we watched from hiding, tucked back in the bush. There was some yelling from the flame-headed man, who had tried to shoot The Big Guy, and there was a lot of conversation from the others, but she finally came to collect us and led us into camp. The Big Guy went without hesitation, being so caught up in The Woman's spell. I on the other hand was nervous. The flame-headed man, Red, was eyeing us and then looking toward his rifle which was stacked against a tree nearby. He wanted that thing as bad as a worm wants a corpse.

We walked for a ways with them for no other reason than we were invited and wanted to, and in time, just before the sun melted down into the jungle and the ground, we came to a long, dark thing that looked like some kind of giant vegetable. It bobbed in the air on ropes. It was not high off the ground, and underneath it was a kind of box-shape with what to me then looked like eyes that went all the way around, but were in fact glass housed in the frames of a cabin. I know now that it was a zeppelin. There was a wooden ramp that led up from the ground to the opening of the cabin. We were easily convinced to go up that ramp and inside, and then the ramp came up and became our door, and we were closed in.

There wasn't any panic. We had not been forced, and in fact, it was something we wanted to do. For uncivilized wild men, we proved to be putty in the hands of The Woman. A smile and a laugh and everyone was inside and the ropes that were looped through metal pegs on the ground, were let loose with a crank and a groan of machinery. The ropes threaded through the pegs and the pegs were left, and we were aloft. We rose quickly and smoothly, into the mist that covered our world, and then we lifted up through that roof of mist into clearer air. Up there I saw a great winged lizard flying. I never knew they came this high, because I never knew how high was high. It flapped its wings and the crew of the zeppelin oohed and ahhed, and on we went, high and then wide, over the tops of the slick walls that contained our world. We stood by the glass and watched as that world moved away from us and the world below turned blue. It was water, but we had never seen so much water. It went on forever, and we sailed across it, rising higher and higher, moving quickly away from our home.

We were in a way captured specimens, but we didn't know it. The old bearded man was ecstatic. I don't know what he truly thought about his daughter's escapades with The Big Guy, not what he was thinking down inside of him, but he seemed fine with it. I didn't think about that then, of course, because as I said, our ideas about what is proper and improper varied considerably from those of the civilized, of which I am now one, but later I would think on it and decide whether the old man was very progressive about such matters, or the idea that his daughter had lured in such unique specimens as The Big Guy and myself, surpassed any sort of fatherly propriety he may have possessed. At this late date, and it's still only a guess, I am going with the former view instead of the latter.

So there we were, as stunned as if we had been run over by a water buffalo, looking out the window glass of the cabin as the zeppelin rose up and our world became a dark line in the distance capped with fog, resting there in the great blue water in such a way it seemed the sky had been turned upside down and the dark line of our home was a wound in the fallen sky, blanketed by a cloud.

Inside the cabin there was plenty of space. There was a man in a funny hat standing at the wheel beside the captain, a position I learned of later. The captain's name was Zeppner and he worked for Dr. Rice. There were many other crew members, and there were a number of jobs they did. During the time we were aloft, and that was a goodly time, we would find out that the cabin branched out through a door and there was a place where the cook prepared meals and there was a mess, and there were rooms off of it. One of these rooms we shared with The Woman's father, so perhaps his propriety was wider and deeper than I would think, but it may have been merely a polite custom to separate a man without clothes from his daughter, as well as myself. I think it took a few days for them to decide if I was man or animal. I think the final decision was somewhere in-between.

Dr. Rice was not only our roommate, but a man who began teaching us his language and certain customs long before we reached the shores of Japanese-America, and later European-America. We also made friends with the navigator, Bowen Tyler, of which adventure books have also been written, most of them exaggerated lies, and by the same liar who told the stories about The Big Guy and me, though I will admit he got a few things right, if only perhaps by accident.

Anyway, we were given pants, and I took to mine right away, but had to learn about unfastening them and pulling them down when the urge to let loose with inner workings arrived on the wings of nature. I ruined several pairs of pants before I got that right. The Big Guy wore the pants all right, but he didn't like shirts at all and wouldn't wear them for the longest time, and he never did really take to shoes. I liked them, but there were none in the zeppelin that would fit me.

The days passed. On we went. Over mountains and jungles and more water and land dotted in the water, and finally back to more water again; a blueness that appeared to stretch out until it linked up with the sky.

As I was saying, during the trip I began to learn words of English, which was the main language spoken by Americans, even the Japanese side. I learned that at one time there had been a war, and one side of this huge country we were going to had been taken over by the Japanese, but in time they united. Still, the West Coast was called Japanese-America, the East, European-America. On the zeppelin there were also a few Japanese. During the trip I began to see the differences in them and the others. Before, when I had seen them as a group, except for the hair on the faces of some, I hadn't realized they were different; to me they were all the same, people like The Big Guy, but smaller. I learned to say "please" and "thank you" and "pass the peas," and for a long time I thought all food was called peas. I also learned words like "fuck" and "shit," "damn, hell, goddamn" and the like, but it took me some time to learn how to use them properly in polite conversation.

So we flew and we flew and The Big Guy and The Woman were often together, much to the disappointment of flame-head, or Red as he was known. You could see the anger coming out of him. He looked easily as savage as the wildest things me and The Big Guy had ever encountered. But from previous experience, Red knew going up against The Big Guy would lead to him losing a few parts, so with steam almost blowing out of his ears, he held his temper and watched them stand beside each other, look at each other and smile and say nothing, and sometimes they held hands, and I am sure there were times in secret places that they did more than that.

When we were near our destination, New York, they gave me and Big Guy some fresh pants and shirts, but neither of us wore shoes, The Big Guy because he wouldn't, and me because as I said, none fit. We didn't really need them. The bottoms of our feet were hard as wood and we could step on thorns and glass and not have them penetrate. They also gave The Big Guy a tie for some reason, and he used it to bind back his long hair, which The Woman had trimmed considerably, after combing out burrs and thorns and minor wildlife. She even gave me a good brushing, and I liked it so much, that I did it myself several times a day. I liked the way it made my hair shine.

We had never seen buildings before, and in the wheelhouse, looking out of the glass, those buildings looked like odd mountains at first. When the craft docked at what they called the Empire State Building, I was almost beside myself. So was The Big Guy.

"Son-of-a-bitch," I said.

"Very good," said Dr. Rice. "That is a proper usage of the word, if not the literal meaning."

"Thank you," I said. I tell you, right then I felt like one sophisticated motherfucker, that motherfucker word being something I learned later.

9

ME AND THE Big Guy were all the rage. We were paraded about like circus animals and asked to do all manner of things. Big Guy bent metal bars and snapped ropes with his chest and climbed up the sides of buildings like a big bug. I couldn't bend the bars, but I could break a lot of ropes and climbing was my middle name. It's actually Uchugucdagarmindoonie, but that's not important. Besides, looking at it now, spelled out, I have to say that is only a close approximation, so we just won't worry about it.

Anyway, we were taken here and there, poked and probed by doctors, and on one occasion a greased finger was jammed up my butt, which resulted in an unexpected thrill. We were needled and measured, asked to run and be timed, asked to climb and be timed. They watched us eat, watched us talk English in our peculiar way. They listened to the old language, the language we knew, and they made notes. They were amazed at how hard the bottoms of our feet were. They were equally amazed at the overall condition of The Big Guy's muscles and teeth. Mine they were equally impressed with, especially my more pronounced canines.

Next thing that happened was we had lessons in manners.

We learned to sit in chairs, sleep in beds, take baths, eat with utensils instead of our fingers, and to take our time about meals. We had to grasp the idea that no one or anything was going to spring on us from under the table or out of a closet and wrestle us all over the room for our food. This was one of the more difficult changes for the two of us, due to us having come from a world where when food was found you wolfed it down to make sure you got to keep it, or to make sure it didn't bite you back; and you eyed everyone and everything around you suspiciously, lest they be reaching for your chow. They soon learned how ingrained this was when one of our table companions reached casually for the salt shaker, only to end up with Big Guy grabbing him by the head and flinging him across the room. He thought the man was going for his baked trout.

To make sure the man understood The Big Guy's dominance, The Big Guy not only finished his own trout as quick as a wild pig snuffling up a grub worm, he ate the man's trout as well, jumped to the middle of the table and started stuffing the dessert (a cake) into his mouth as fast as he could reach with both hands.

Instinct and experience taking over, me knowing how much that big bastard ate, and having gone to bed hungry because of him in the past, I too leapt onto the table and started snatching, which led to a mild grapple between the two of us which resulted in my being bit on the shoulder and having a handful of cake stuffed in my ear and a random carrot shoved in my nose.

What could you expect? We were savages. But we did learn some civilized activities. We learned to drink, and I learned to smoke (Big Guy never took to it), and I learned to chase women. Big Guy had his woman, and he stuck with her. They had even taken to living in the same hotel room. But me, well, I was a goddamn celebrity, and I had groupies. They all wanted to hump Mr. Hairy. I rush in here to say this was a title given to me by the newspapers for a time (fortunately it didn't stick) and one I never embraced. But the women embraced me, and I came to find them attractive, not just usable. I began to like to wear suit coats and ties, well-creased pants, and shoes, though I always had to cut them open at the front so my toes had room. In short time I took to wearing open toed house shoes. It became all the rage with the kids. The sale of house shoes went up, and pretty soon I was modeling them in magazines, wearing a tux with those fuzzy shoes on my feet. They pretty much became my trademark. I was loved by the young and the sophisticated, disliked by parents and the clergy.

The Ape Man's Brother

I went to fine restaurants and learned to order wine. I will tell you truthfully, I took to the life. It beat climbing trees to flee wild animals. It beat looking for fruit and eating bugs and worms, or chasing down some swift animal with a stick or a rock. I liked the nice rooms in the great hotel where we were kept. I liked the bed with its clean, cool sheets better than I liked a leafy nest on the ground or the crook of a tree. I liked room service. I liked the women who slept with me; or rather I liked what we did. No particular woman ever stayed with me more than a day and a night. I wouldn't let them, even though there were many who wanted to. There were just too many opportunities, too many offers, and I took advantage of it.

I was drinking until late, smoking cigars and sometimes a pipe. I was learning to tell jokes and talk in a sophisticated manner. I knew how to get my arm around women's shoulders without being awkward, and I had gained quite a reputation in the tabloids as a ladies' man.

And I was becoming famous and admired. Maybe not as much as The Big Guy, but it was a new experience for me. Back home I was, to sum it up in crass and modern terms, just another monkey, because even though he was different from the rest of us—perhaps because he was—he was always held in higher esteem than me. At home, I was just like everyone else there, but in New York, I was special.

In time this fame led to The Big Guy and myself becoming movie stars.

At least for awhile.

10

You went to the movies, you saw all manner of things in the news-reels about us. Saw us climbing trees and doing this or that, Big Guy bending those iron bars and so on, and it was only natural that Japanese-America and Hollywood came calling.

This was sometime after we had been in New York, and we had learned the language reasonably quick and reasonably well; well enough to do simple interviews.

We flew out there in a smaller zeppelin than the one that had brought us to New York. We landed in a field near the ocean. There were reporters and cameras everywhere. We did interview after interview.

"What do you think about our world?" a reporter asked The Big Guy.

"Busy," he said.

"What do you think about our women?"

"I think about The Woman all the time." He called her that, same as me, but they thought he just didn't know how to say women, and so it was reported that he thought about women all the time. This led to women throwing themselves at him in even greater abundance than before. He ignored them even when a fine doll would toss a pair of underpants in his face, or a room key. It wasn't a moral code that kept him from humping them; it was a sincere love for The Woman, who was back in New York teaching anthropology at a university. Me, I was damn near screwing anything except a hole in the ground. But The Big Guy was truly lonely. While we were out there in moving picture land, sometimes he would go out on the hotel veranda and look up at the moon and howl. Sometimes

he whacked off. This was a behavior he had been taught to modify
in public; out there he just put his hand in his pocket, but he knew
I didn't care. That was just SOP for us back home. While he was at
it I read a magazine and drank a cup of coffee. This was the kind of
activity that our handlers were always afraid of. Fearing we might
go primitive during an interview, and frankly, it was a legitimate
concern. It was hard to figure things out.

"Where is your home?" reporters asked.

The Big Guy shook his head. They thought he was being coy,
but it was an honest answer. We had no way of knowing where our
home was, not after that long flight. And in fact, old Dr. Rice wasn't
telling either. The crew had been sworn to secrecy due to scientific
research and Rice wanting to keep the place unknown due to fear
that it would soon be swamped by explorers and curiosity seekers.
There was also this: No one except him and the navigator truly
understood its locale, and to be honest, most people thought it was
a big publicity hoax, that The Big Guy was some Hollywood muscle
man, and that I was a fellow with a disease that caused me to grow
hair all over my body. We never did shake that whole hoax business.
It still follows us around.

Anyway, there were all these interviews, and then we were given
lines to learn and deliver. We made two pictures.

We got a few calls from the desk about the howling, but that
didn't stop him, and being the celebrity he was, no one wanted
to really corner him on it. Besides, he had a look in his eye when
approached about such behavior that made you feel as if he were just
looking for a reason to reach down your throat, grab your asshole,
and pull it up through the big middle of you.

As for the pictures we made while we were out there, they were
terrible. We were the real deal, but we couldn't act our way out of a
paper bag with a pair of scissors. We didn't really understand what
acting actually was. They had these scenes where "natives" would
attack, and me and The Big Guy would just actually beat the hell out
of them. We had to really work to play at it; play of that sort wasn't

in our nature. You showed up with a weapon, even if it turned out to be made of balsa wood, and waved it around, it triggered our defense mechanisms. We broke up a lot of stuntmen.

Also, on the second picture there was an unpleasant incident with a lion. There were lions on the lost world where we lived, but they were lions without manes, and they were much bigger. Our greatest fear in the form of jungle cats on our world wasn't actually the lion. It's what are called by those who study bones, saber-toothed tigers, thought to be extinct. Maybe everywhere else, but not where we are from. And the dinosaurs in those two pictures we made—stop motion and men in suits—were just plain silly, and didn't look anything like the real deal. But damn it, there I go again. Distracted. I was talking about the movie we were in and how a supposedly tame lion on the set went wonky and jumped on the girl who was playing The Woman (we portrayed ourselves, The Woman did not), and The Big Guy strangled it as easily as a kitten. He was a hero up to that point, because there had been considerable panic on set, but when the cat was dead, The Big Guy jerked off the loin cloth they had given him to wear (we, of course, never wore any), yanked it up by the tail, and diddled it in its dead ass right there, then threw it on the ground, put his foot on its neck, lifted his head and howled. This was his way of showing dominance, acceptable behavior where we came from when there had been a life and death struggle. It wasn't necessary for an antelope, and some of the creatures were a bit too large for this act of dominance, but, still, it was considered just part of our way of life when it came to big dangerous predators. It was a way of showing who was boss. This, in civilization, however, was looked down upon even more than whacking off in public.

Observers on the set took this out of context and thought it to be deviant. The set was abandoned for the day and no one would talk to The Big Guy for awhile, and certainly wouldn't turn their backs on him. Me, I was proud of him. That said, the rest of the shoot was a nervous event.

Anyway, Hollywood is Hollywood, and there was money in the picture and money in us, and the public was waiting, even though the first picture had gotten the worst reviews of any film ever made. What counted was it had been a big financial hit. The director, who was devastated, and not anxious to do another film with us, or anyone else, retired from the movies and went into advertising, but when asked about his work in later, nostalgic interviews, said he had worked at shooting pornographic slides.

That was the end of our movie career as actors, even though that lion screwing incident didn't end up in the last picture we made. It had been filmed, but that part of the movie was removed, though there was gossip about it from some of those on the set who had seen it. That gossip grew into a larger crowd that claimed to have witnessed the incident. If all of those who claimed to have seen it had, then the movie set that day would have been packed with a thousand people for a scene that only contained The Big Guy, the actress, me, and the lion, a skeleton crew, and a mess of false tree and brush props.

We went back to New York.

The rumors didn't kill our popularity. Not at first, (we'll come back to that) because there wasn't any actual revealed evidence it ever happened; it seemed so bizarre to Americans on either coast, and in the middle of the country, it was mostly thought of as an anecdotal story.

As for future pictures, they hired an actor to play The Big Guy, and got that damn chimpanzee to play me. When the actor pretended to kill a lion, or some beast in the movies, he put his foot on it and howled. No diddling allowed. The chest beating and the howling were correct, but the other thing missing just sort of dulled the situation. But, from an acting standpoint, our replacements were better and the movies still made money and made us even more famous. They made eight movies back to back about us with that actor pair, all of them major hits. There were lunch boxes and thermoses and T-shirts and bread and milk products with our pictures on it. I still have a lunch box with a thermos, and for the right price, I'm willing to let it go.

By the time the first four pictures came out, the two with us, and the first two with the other guy and that chimp, we were rich as fresh-whipped butter. Something I learned about my adopted land was that if you had money, and if you were making other people money, you could diddle a lion at high noon in Times Square and most everyone would get over it, even the kids, as long as you didn't have the actual film to prove it, of course.

11

Now the odd thing was, in a short time, the actors who played us became better known than us, and many people forgot that we were the real ape-men of the jungle—me being a little closer anthropologically in that department. We were old news, and that damn chimpanzee, even after he quit playing the part, as I said earlier, got special attention each year on his birthday. Cake and candles. We didn't get that. But, we did get royalty checks, so there was a trade-off. In that way I prefer what we got to what that damn ape got, though I still bristle at his popularity, and that now, so many years later, me and The Big Guy are mostly forgotten and the memory of the actor and that chimpanzee have taken our place.

The whole thing began to get to Big Guy. The whole thing being the world we were living in. He just couldn't understand it. He discovered alcohol, and he could drink a lot of it. That stuff was to him like nectar to a bee. He became bourbon's bitch. He was so drunk most of the time The Woman began knocking on my door late at night to ask if she could sleep on my couch while he raved and cursed in our ape-man tongue. Sometimes when he drank up all the hotel room booze, he climbed out the window, down the side of the building and into the street, and away he would go, dressed in clothes but not wearing any shoes.

He drank his way from one end of town to the other. One night he climbed over the walls of the zoo, bent bars, and let all manner of wild animals out. It was kept out of the papers, but a couple of tigers ate a bum and two orphans who were sleeping under a bridge. They weren't tax payers, so it was easy to sweep under the rug. Way Big Guy saw it animals were supposed to be free. They could kill or be killed in a wild world situation, but cages, that bugged him, bugged him big time. In a way, I think he came to see the hotel, and even the whole of New York, as nothing more than a kind of cage that held him back from where he wanted to be, from the life he wanted to live.

Me, I was digging it. I got so I kept my body hair trimmed close, dressed nice, wore a monocle and a top hat and very nice suits. I took to going to jazz clubs, learned to play the bongos, smoked big cigars. I liked having an evening martini, wearing my bathrobe and slippers. I even did a little record album with a couple of those cool jazz cats; one of them on bass, one on sax, and me beating the skins. I got so I could lay down quite a few French phrases and a smidgeon of Italian. And there was another thing. Me and The Woman, all those nights she slept on my couch... Well, we got close. We talked about The Big Guy. We worried about him. We cried over him. We hugged each other in sympathy. In short time I was laying the pipe to her like I was running a gas line from here to Cuba. We didn't mean for it to happen. It just did. The Woman told me that before I took her to bed, she and The Big Guy hadn't had sex in three months. He had found a substitute for sex: whisky, beer, wine and vodka, as well as his favorite, bourbon, and sometimes a little rubbing alcohol taken from the medicine cabinet over the sink. He had even been known to drink hair oil. He had the itch bad.

He had also became a bigger spectacle and public disgrace. Shedding his clothes. Running naked through the streets. Climbing the Empire State Building, all the way to the top where the zeppelin dock was. Swimming in public fountains, pulling one of the stone lions down from its pedestal at the New York Public Library. Just got hold of it and yanked that big sucker off its pedestal and broke it to pieces. He even swam out to the Statue of Liberty. Can you imagine that. I can't swim at all, but he swam all the way out there, climbed it because he can, had a hot dog from a vendor, and swam back; all of this done without a stitch on, just like in the old days.

Here's something I'm really ashamed of. I began to be embarrassed of The Big Guy. My best friend. My brother. We had done a lot of things together in the old days that were no worse than the things he was doing now, in the new days. Bless me, but I was starting to shake my head and cluck my tongue. To be honest, I really enjoyed banging his old lady. That doesn't mean I quit feeling for him. Late at night, holding The Woman in my arms, after I had drunk my martini and had my fun with her, I would think. Shit, that's tough on the old boy, me with his girl and him not knowing, and me not telling, and her not telling. But that didn't change me. I stayed the same. That sweet, warm, woman and the cool, clean sheets, and the toilet where you could sit and read without fear of being attacked by some manner of beast, were much too satisfying to want to give up.

Now, I told you about that red-headed man who had loved The Woman and thought he was going to end up with her, but after The Big Guy came along, he might as well have been the balls on a brass monkey. She had no interest in him, and now, of course, her interest was in me. Or at least it was to some degree. I won't kid you. Sometimes I would awake and find her missing from my arms. She would be sitting in a chair by the great open window that led out on the veranda that overlooked the light-winking city, naked, her blond hair dangling, the moonlight nestled in those scars on her shoulders, her breasts spear-tipped from the cool air, and I could tell she was thinking about The Big Guy. Somewhere, maybe he was thinking about her. It was hard to say. He seldom came back to the hotel anymore, which is why he didn't miss her from his bed. He slept atop buildings, or in the park, or on a bench, usually clutching a bottle of booze in a brown paper bag. I had brought him home many a time in that condition, until I finally gave it up. Nothing changed him. I even talked to him about The Woman. I didn't mention that me and her were doing the nasty—though I would never have thought of it that way in the wild—but it didn't change him. I like to think had he come to his senses that me and The Woman could have shook hands and just been friends and they could have gone back together, the way it was supposed to be. But he didn't change. The alcohol had numbed his senses—a lot. But he knew something wasn't right between me and him and him and her, even though he didn't know it was what it was; he trusted us both too much for that. I could tell the way his beautiful eyes rested on me that he knew our friendship was washing up on the rocks, yet I'm certain he didn't actually suspect me of such treachery as taking from him the thing he loved the most in the world, The Woman; well, that and his freedom, his desire to go back to the way things were. I think he might have been willing to share her, and maybe The Woman would even have gone for that—she was progressive, but it just didn't occur to him that she needed him in her arms and in her bed. Like I said, that ole John BarleyCorn had him by the nuts.

I have wandered again. I was telling you about the red-headed man.

You see, Red, as most people called him, never gave up on The Woman. One look at her and you would know why. She was a stunner, as I have said, but there was something else about her. It was—and this is going to sound like a cheap romance story—her soul; it reached out to you and embraced you. Corny as that sounds, I don't know any other way to describe it. She was something. For Red, though, I think it was that he thought he had her locked down, and when the lock broke, he couldn't accept it. Maybe if he had been the one to break it off he would have been fine. He was that kind of guy. Everything on his terms. Only thing was, The Big Guy wasn't interested in terms. Red knew that any interference there would just lead to him having his head pulled off like a grape plucked from the vine, so he bided his time. When things fell apart for The Big Guy and The Woman, he was waiting, and I am certain (without actual evidence, I admit) he was the one who finally leaked the lion diddling event to the public. We were told at first it was destroyed. Another time we were told it existed, but that it was lost, and finally that it was stolen. And then it showed up. I think Red bought it from someone, maybe the director who had gone into advertising. I can't say. But he got his hands on it.

That wasn't what happened first, though. That wasn't the first brick pulled from the pile. There were several. I guess I should have snapped to it, but I admit that I had been for the most part civilized and my instincts were not as sharply honed as they once were. Two or three times I thought I was being followed, and had noticed someone in the streets that I had seen twice earlier that day. New York is a big city, but people cross paths with one another now and again, so I didn't think much of it. It wasn't until The Woman and I had come back from a party, a little liquor-buzzed and hot to trot for the old bedroom, when I smelled something. We had just come in through the door, and even though I was a bit drunk, and as I have said, civilized, something kicked in. I got a whiff of someone having been in our hotel room. Not a maid. I knew all their scents, and had had relations with several before me and The Woman took up together, and once or twice when she was out of town. This was the scent of a man with too much cologne. I peeled The Woman off of me, told her to wait, and sniffed about. My sniffing eventually led to a little camera fastened into a light fixture over our bed. Way it was rigged, when you turned on the light it came on and started snapping pictures, and when you turned it off, it still snapped for awhile. That way it had you in full light, and then, because our window always had the big curtains thrown back, and there were lights from the city resting on our bed, we could be easily photographed doing whatever we were doing, and frequently we were doing a lot.

At first, I was elated, thinking I had found the camera before any photos could be taken. Then it occurred to me that the only reason I knew someone had been in the room was the cologne. A strange thought passed through me. What if, with my senses dulled, I had missed somebody having entered our room before, when they weren't wearing cologne? The camera could have taken many photos, and it only had to have its film replaced from time to time, something that could easily be done when we were out of the room. What if there were already photos of us?

I pulled the camera out and showed it to The Woman, who gasped. You see, there was some part of us that played like this was all a momentary fling. That when it came right down to it, all was right with her and The Big Guy, or soon would be, but that camera made us realize otherwise. We knew he didn't know and that things weren't right between them, and if he saw photographs of us together, it might be too much for him. He might turn savage, or even do something to himself. He just wasn't right anymore.

"Perhaps it's blackmail," The Woman said.

I nodded, thinking perhaps that was it. I suppose The Big Guy could have had someone do it, to check up on us, but that didn't seem likely. Unlike me, he never learned guile. I learned it when we lived in our lost world, and I had perfected it in civilization. Maybe whoever had set this photographic trap would want money instead of showing it to The Big Guy, but I tell you, right then I had a hunch who it was and what it was about. It came to me like a tick crawling into my armpit that Red was behind all this, that he had hired someone to follow us, and to plant that camera, and what he wanted wasn't money. He wanted revenge.

12

YEAH, I HADN'T thought of Red in ages, but right then I knew down deep in my bones, it was him, and what hit me the hardest was that there was something for him to find, something he could let The Big Guy see so that it harmed his pride and took away the only reason he had allowed himself to be hoodwinked into coming to this world.

The Big Guy trusted us, especially me. We had been brothers since he was a baby. Right at that moment I felt the way I should have felt all along. Like a traitor.

I smashed the camera on the floor.

But you know what? I still went to bed with The Woman.

The next day that lion bumping film was released and seen in private by a number of newspaper men who reported on it. It wasn't seemly for it to be shown to the public, and wasn't, at least at that period in time. But it was written about, and a few stills were published in the rags, and though they weren't explicit, it was clear what was going on. Shots of the dead lion facing us, its tongue lagging out of its mouth, The Big Guy clutching its tail, lifting it into position for... Well, it was obvious. There had been rumors before, but now there was the film. I told you how it is with money, how it offered lots of insulation. But The Big Guy took a hit with the public. Not that he cared, but that's what happened. Our two movies were removed from circulation, and even to this day they are seldom shown, and only on late night television.

But the day it hit I found out about it in the morning paper. I tried to hide it from The Woman, but too late. She saw it. It made our souls and stomachs sink, and you would think we would just lock our hotel room door and hide. Or maybe at least have the guts to somehow talk to The Big Guy, own up to what we had done, and try to commiserate with him over the news, though that part about the lion probably didn't bother him the way it would others. For him, that was an accepted ritual. And once, it had been for me as well.

As I said, you'd think we'd do that, commiserate with The Big Guy, but we didn't. We took the cowardly way out and tried to make things better for ourselves. We went out for a drive. It's not that we weren't concerned, but we were determined to not let some asshole with a camera ruin our life, and like I said, we were cowards. We drove outside of New York and into the country. There was a nice place there where we could have a picnic. We parked the Packard and rolled our blanket on the ground, set out our picnic basket stuffed with very fine foods, a thermos of good wine, as well as a thermos of Italian coffee. We had paper plates and cups, and we ate and laughed and kissed, trying to make our worries go away, but the truth is they hung over us like a rain cloud even though the sky was clear and beautiful. After awhile we lay back on the blanket, in each other's arms, digested and looked at the sky. I rose up on one elbow to pry off the thermos lid to the coffee, and that's when I saw him.

The Big Guy. He was a pretty good distance away, on a hill covered by trees. In the tallest tree, mostly hidden by leaves, he sat in the fork of a limb and watched us.

I knew then that Red had not only had the camera put in my hotel room, but that most likely shots from that camera had been put in an envelope and somehow slipped to The Big Guy, just as we feared.

The Big Guy knew I saw him. He dropped from the tree, light as a bird, disappeared behind the hill. I expected he would come rushing down that hill to destroy us at any moment, and I didn't intend to put up a fight, not even to protect her.

The Woman had seen him as well. She had tears in her eyes.

We waited.

He didn't come rushing down after us.

The Ape Man's Brother

I heard a car start up behind the trees and race away.

I could tell by the sound of the engine that it was his Buick, the one he hardly drove and really shouldn't drive at all. The Big Guy could do many things, but he never really learned to drive too well. He was always being pulled out of ditches and having to pay other drivers for banging up their cars. But he had been smart enough to ease up behind that hill silently, get out and climb that tree. Now he didn't care. About anything was my guess.

You want to know what hurt me the most right then? That he didn't even have the courtesy to kill us.

13

After that, it was over with me and The Woman.

I decided what I had to do was confront The Big Guy, lay it all out and hope he didn't yank off my leg and beat me to death with it. I desperately wanted to make amends. But he wasn't in his room. I couldn't find him. I walked all over the city, took taxis and trains to his favorite haunts, but nothing. I must have gone through every bar in New York City that next week, but I couldn't find him. The Woman had gone back to their room to wait for him, to hope for the best. But he hardly ever went there. Up until the other day he didn't seem too concerned about where she was, or even where he was. But I could imagine him seeing those photos, my hairy ass on top of her, doing the deed. It made me sick to my stomach.

I didn't really want to see her again, but I went to her and told her that I had searched everywhere, and had pretty much given up.

"Any ideas?" I said.

"The hospitals," she said.

"Beg pardon?" I said.

"He may have been injured. You know how he drove. He may be in the hospital."

Well, that got me to a phone right away. I started checking around, and sure enough, we found him. Downtown, right near the hotel, in a hospital room. Two broken legs, a broken arm, smashed ribs, and a concussion. He'd been there all week, under an assumed name. He hadn't done that, a doctor had, knowing there was so much publicity afoot concerning the film of him and the lion. It was a damn noble thing to do, I thought, though later I found out he sold his story to one of the cheap-ass rags, and for not that much money, I might add.

When I finally saw the police report a couple days later, it was revealed that he had driven down a hill on his way back into the city at top speed. A motorist behind him said, "He just yanked the wheel to the left, off the curve, and over the side of the big hill. The car flew like a plane. Was in the air all the way down until it hit a brick fence around a sheep farm. Tore that fence down, and one of the sheep died of a heart attack. It didn't do the car any good either."

The Good Samaritan drove to a nearby farmhouse, called the law and an ambulance. That's how The Big Guy ended up in the hospital, wrapped up like a mummy, his legs lifted in traction. The nurse told us that three days later he came around, but they couldn't get him to eat or drink. He seemed to want to die. They finally used heavy drugs to put him completely out, help him deal with the pain. I thought, yeah, the pain. The only thing he was pained about was seeing me and The Woman together like that. Broken bones were nothing to him.

After he was knocked out, they kept him that way, ended up hooking him to a feeder tube and an IV. We went and sat by his bed, and when they tried to make us leave because visiting hours were over, we wouldn't. They finally gave up and let us stay. The Woman held the hand of the arm that wasn't broken, and I just sat in my chair with tears in my eyes and looked at him.

The Good Life had ruined all three of us.

One morning, The Big Guy still on the mend, The Woman at the hospital with him, I went to see Dr. Rice, and laid out my plan. I said, "Doctor, The Big Guy, he's not doing so well. Civilization hasn't taken with him like it has with me. He needs to go back."

The old man nodded. He said, "And back he shall go."

Remember, the location of our home on the world in the mist had been kept secret by Dr. Rice, and a couple of other individuals, including the navigator, one Bowen Tyler. Red and a few others had been on that trek, but they were all trusted individuals, except for Red, who had been there due to the fact he was then The Woman's boyfriend, and a known hunter and tracker. He could find his way through the jungle, but no one thought he knew the path to our world across that vast ocean, so any knowledge he had wasn't a great concern. And at that moment, no one knew where he was. Nothing had actually been proven to suggest he had been the one behind the lion-fucking leak, or for that matter, the camera in our room, so there was nothing to do legally, though it was in the back of my mind to give him a visit if I got the chance so that what was inside of him could be found painting the walls of his abode, wherever that was.

Remember too, for the most part we were considered the perpetrators of a hoax to sell tickets in Hollywood, so that gave us a bit of insulation, and was part of the reason crew members had been silent in regards to discussing where we had come from. To talk about us in a positive way was the same as telling their neighbors they had seen the Abominable Snowman in their backyard having a cookout on their barbecue grill with a nude female leprechaun.

We made plans. The Big Guy was going back, and I had a pretty good idea that The Woman was going back with him. While The Big Guy was on the mend, it was pretty obvious that he and The Woman had found their connection again. It was also clear, though I had betrayed my friend, he had forgiven me. He said so. I suppose that he actually had always known. The photographs that he found in his hotel room were just the icing on the cake. In fact, it was a rare thing for him to go back to that room, but he had, and they had been waiting. Yeah, the photos were the icing, but he had known about the cake for a long time, or certainly suspected it was baking in the oven. I think he forgave me because he understood. The Woman was a force unto herself, and he felt he had been as responsible for our situation as much as we had. I didn't agree. Friendship should have stood steadfast, woman or no woman. But, then we come back to that part about it being her, and if you've ever seen her, you would understand. I don't mean photos of her. Oh, she looks fine, no doubt. But if you had actually ever SEEN her in person, you would know. No other woman could hold your fancy after that. She was a goddamn goddess.

In our old world The Big Guy would be away from alcohol and things he didn't truly understand. He would be with The Woman. He could speak the old language and live the old ways. And me, I could come back to New York City where I truly belonged, among the civilized. I didn't find that savage life all that appealing anymore. It was different when it was all that I knew, but I liked my winter heat and summer air-conditioning and no flying beast and saber-toothed cats. I liked what my money from the movie royalties could buy. It was my intent when I came back to get a college degree. I thought I might teach anthropology. Lots of college girls around, nice cushy job, retirement, and all that shit. It beat working, which with the money I had coming in from the films I wouldn't have to do for a long time to come; but truth be told, it wouldn't last forever. Already the checks were slightly smaller. It was a matter of time, and I had to plan for the future, and I didn't have any plans where I would be out in the jungle with my ass hanging out in the wind, glancing over my shoulder for predators.

It took about two more months for them to get the zeppelin refurbished and for Dr. Rice to get the old navigator on the task. Turned out Bowen Tyler had retired from navigating air flights and was living in Greenwich in England (the half that belonged to Germany; he was there on a visa), and he was teaching at a small college in the area. He really didn't want to go back into the air, but, as he was one of the few who knew how to get to our little lost world, we told him it was necessary, and he kindly agreed. We also knew we could trust Tyler, as he had refused to give the location of our world these last few years, though he was constantly asked. He had written about it, but never in any detail. His work was a fictional account, and I will be quick to add it is very fictional and has little to do with the truth. He got the part right about how savage the place was, about the creatures that lived there, but the rest of it, about evolutionary pools and submarines, and so on, that was just pulp magazine junk. Another reason we have been marked down to nothing more than a hoax. But hell, that's alright with me.

Bottom line is it all got planned. The Big Guy healed up good as new. That's how he was. He could mend quickly, and considering how many injuries he had from that car crash, it was amazing. The doctors who worked on him were astonished. One of them, a nice man named Dr. Cupp, told me that there was something different about The Big Guy's insides, that it appeared as if everything was unique about his body. That would have been the injection he received from his parents, but I didn't say that, though I had done a bit of research on the matter, and figured that the drug he had been given not only gave him long life, but made him capable of healing rapidly and perfectly. He could be hurt, and he could die, but because of that drug, he had advantages over you and me.

Now, if you are paying attention, I bet you are thinking about now what I was thinking about then, and it was simply that The Woman didn't have that serum in her blood. What happened when she aged, and he did not? It was an ugly thing to think about. I decided for the time being to be silent.

14

ON AN EARLY morning with the copper sun edging into the city, we launched off from atop the Empire State Building and into the rising light. No cars and no people visible; the city had not truly awakened yet. It was so quiet up there you could have heard a gnat fart. As we rose, a flock of white birds flew before us, and I took that as a good omen.

Let me tell you what I know now.

Omens are for shit.

The zeppelin had been worked on and retooled. It was larger, but swifter. It had less of a crew than when we first rode in it, and it was, according to Dr. Rice, a trustworthy crew. The zeppelin was stuffed with food and water and even a few barrels of beer and a stocked wine closet. There were two biplanes as well, one on either side of the wheelhouse. They were held by clamps that could be worked from the open cockpit of the planes to release them. There were a number of guns on board. There were some trade goods. The Big Guy had tried to discourage this aspect, trading with the natives, as he had seen what civilization could do to us (I, as I said, liked it. He didn't), but Dr. Rice was determined that if he was going to lose The Big Guy and his daughter as well—for he knew the score and wanted her to be happy—he demanded an opportunity to work among my people, explore the island, bring back native items, write about his experiences, but not give away its location.

By the time we were four days out I couldn't shake a feeling of doom. Perhaps it was because I knew I was not staying with The Big Guy, and The Woman was going with him, and I was going back to civilization. Fact was, I had already started to crave it, yet, still I hated to leave them. I loved them both.

On the fifth morning the sky darkened. It began to rain and the zeppelin began to jump. I was airsick until late afternoon when the darkness split and the sunlight sliced in and the rain died out. I went to the huge storage room for some bicarbonate of soda to settle my stomach, and while there I saw that some of the food goods had been broken into. A lid on a crate near the back had been lifted and replaced awkwardly, and a wax paper container of crackers was missing from the box. I also noticed that the tins of sardines had been disturbed, many of them strewn about on the floor. I didn't think much of this at the time, as it seemed to me that it was likely one of the crew members that had broken into the goods; far as I was concerned they were welcome to it. I found the bicarbonate of soda, and on my way out I sniffed the air, recognized human urine. Some years back I would have thought nothing of someone pissing wherever they wanted, whenever they wanted, but now this bothered me. Had it only been a bit of the food, I could have stood that, but pissing on the floor? I had become too sophisticated for that.

Angrily, I straightened the askew wine rack on my way out by pushing it with my shoulder, not giving much thought to it being out of place, and determined I would bring these doings to the attention of Dr. Rice. By the time I left the storage room and went to my cabin to put the bicarbonate of soda in a water glass, my anger had subsided. I even considered that The Big Guy might have done it. Gone down there to get some food and mark his spot. He was still a savage. Years back, I could have sniffed that urine and known who it belonged to, but now my nose was cultured, and all I knew was someone had taken a leak in the storage room. I decided to forget it. I was beginning to be as fussy as an old lady, and I was a little ashamed of myself.

For the next few days the weather was fair. We came to a place in the ocean where a huge mist hung in the air like a veil. A bit of excitement stirred within me then, for this was the world from which I had come, a huge island, or continent—I actually have no idea how large our world really is—clothed in fog produced by the volcanic humidity that warmed our lost world. And even though I liked New York City, I did suffer more than a bit of nostalgia at that moment.

The zeppelin dipped into the mist; everything was a white cloud. Then the zeppelin dropped down even more and the mist thinned. Below there were high, slick, flat gray walls of rock that rose up to incredible heights. As we slipped over the top of that wall there were more clouds. We descended into them slowly. They broke, and what we saw then was mine and The Big Guy's fine green world. Windows were opened on the sides of the wheelhouse, allowing the warmer outside air to stir about. Great leathery lizards flew about, and for a moment there was some consternation that one of them might attack our ship, but we glided down, easy, unmolested. There was a gap in the forest, savanna, and we coasted toward it. As we did, we saw a herd of large, feathered lizards running on their hind legs, their heads leaning forward as if to show the way. We slowed to observe them continue their path until they were out of sight, then we stopped hovering and headed in for a landing.

Instantly, things went wrong.

I have thought about this a lot, and I don't know that I have an exact answer, but I have a strong speculation. At first I thought it was just because he had hidden so long, waited so long, was so goddamn angry, he couldn't wait anymore. Instead of waiting until we landed, he came out of hiding and rampaged into the wheelhouse where everyone on board had gathered. He was carrying a revolver. He looked crazy. His red hair was standing up on his head like a blaze of fire. His face was near red as his hair. His eyes were wide and there was saliva drooling from the corners of his mouth. He looked like a man about to blow a major hose, and in that moment I knew his hatred of The Big Guy had driven him somewhat mad.

You have probably guessed by now that Red had stowed on board, and that he had been the one who had been at the crackers and sardines, pissed all over the place, and when I pushed that wine rack back in place, all I did was help conceal him better, hiding back there behind it, probably on some makeshift bed. I curse myself for not being observant enough to have noticed.

Red came storming into the wheelhouse carrying a revolver, calling The Big Guy a goddamn whoremonger, and calling The Woman a whore and a shit poke, and to top it off, he called me a fucking, chattering monkey. I will admit that I am sensitive to the comparison. The ape comparison is bothersome, but a monkey is a much more annoying association, perhaps because I do chatter a bit. I was a talker in my own language, but the English language opened up all manner of possibilities, and I have most likely taken advantage of all of them multiple times.

That said, even I should know it's bad storytelling to stop a story in the midst of momentum when someone enters into the wheelhouse with a gun, and especially since I'm trying to describe true events and let you know how things went. But there's that chattering problem I just told you about. I may go off on a tangent at any moment; I think all the coffee I drink adds to it.

I would like to say there was a big heroic moment that occurred, an immediate battle for the gun, but to be honest, we were all as stunned as if we had awakened to see the sunrise was blue. Red pointed the gun and fired. The shot hit The Big Guy in the stomach. The Big Guy dropped like a pig in the slaughterhouse. Red fired again, at me, but I was moving and the shot tore through the windshield. The Woman dropped to her knee, grabbed The Big Guy's head, lifted it up. Everyone else hit the floor. It sounded like a wash woman had dropped wet laundry in there.

The Ape Man's Brother

As I said, I was moving. I went crazy. In that moment everything about me that was civilized went out that hole in the windshield, same as the bullet that blew it open. I sprang forward and grabbed Red as he fired. I felt a pain like a hot iron against my side, and then I had Red by the head with both hands, lifting him off his feet. I threw him toward the side windows, one of those that wasn't open. He hit with such force the glass shattered into thousands of sun-winked stars; he went right through the opening his body made, out into the wind, the revolver flying from his hand as if it had gone to roost.

I jumped to the window, looked down.

He had fallen onto the top wing of one of the biplanes below, and was swinging himself to the lower wing on the port side of the craft. I suspected he was planning to open the cockpit, release the clamp with the wrench that was inside for just such a purpose, and try and fly away. I doubted he had any real flight knowledge, but we were still high enough over the lost world he might well have glided to the ground, and to safety. He might even try to fly the plane into the zeppelin if he had any understanding of how the craft worked. I couldn't take any chances.

I went through that gap in the broken window and clung to one of the metal windshield struts. There was a coiled rope ladder to the right of me where there was a door that led out to it and the plane below. I could have climbed back inside and gone out the door and used the ladder, but I hadn't become that civilized. I kicked off my toeless house shoes, stretched my leg way out and kicked the ladder loose. It tumbled down until it was even with the bottom wing of the biplane. By this time Red had managed to reach the cockpit, had lifted it up, and was climbing into the plane.

I leapt and grabbed the ladder, was down it and onto the bottom wing of that plane faster than someone on the ground could have looked up and seen me and said, "Is that a monkey or a man in a wool jacket up there?"

What I didn't expect was for him not to be in the cockpit. He had opened it and taken out the wrench, and was standing on the bottom wing, clinging with one hand to a wing strut, and in the other he had that wrench. He hit me with it. It was a glancing blow, but it knocked me off the wing. I was able to twist my body and catch the edge of the wing. He scooted forward and stomped one of my hands, hard. I swung out, grabbed the plane's propeller, which of course was stationary, scrambled along it, up over the nose of the plane, and back onto the bottom wing. He was gone. The ladder was visible and it was vibrating. He was going back up.

I don't know if he was truly bug-shit crazy, or just afraid he hadn't finished the job on The Big Guy. Or maybe he wanted to do The Woman harm. Maybe he wasn't thinking at all, just working off instinct. I scrambled up after him.

Feeling the pull of my weight below, he pivoted and saw me. He had stuck the wrench in his back pocket, and now, hanging on with one hand, he grabbed hold of it with his free hand. As I came close enough to grab his ankle, he leaned down and tried to hit me with the wrench. I dodged, grabbed at the weapon and ripped it from his hand. It was such a violent motion I lost my grip on the ladder. I spun out and landed on the top wing of the biplane with enough force to knock the breath out of me.

I got my air quickly, hustled to my feet, glanced down and saw the earth was coming up fast. In all of the confusion, something had gone wrong up in the wheelhouse. I leaped off the wing and snatched at the ladder, climbed up to the broken window glass just in time to see that the bullet that had grazed me had caught Dr. Rice. I hadn't noticed this before I went out the window. Dr. Rice was down, not moving. Bowen Tyler was struggling at the wheel, which looked bent. Keep in mind that while it takes me time to describe all this, it all occurred rather quickly. I assumed Dr. Rice, after being shot, had fallen into the wheel with such force that his weight had done something to it. Maybe the bullet that had grazed me and killed him had gone through him and done damage to the control panel. I can't honestly say, but the craft was flying erratically. I could hear the rear propellers cutting out. The great gas bag was starting to dip its nose. The Big Guy was on his feet. He had ripped off his shirt, and his stomach was covered in blood. He was a little wobbly. The Woman clutched his huge arm, as if to help. The Big Guy pulled free of her just as I was trying to climb through the window after Red.

Red went at The Big Guy. He swung the wrench. The Big Guy, wounded as he was, dodged it and grabbed Red's arm. There was a cracking sound, like the weight of heavy ice breaking a rotten limb, then there was a savage yell from The Big Guy; the sort of war cry that would have made that actor who played him in the movies crap himself.

And then I, one foot hanging through the broken window, was splattered in blood, and so was everyone else. It was like a geyser full of red plum juice had erupted. The reason for this wasn't only that The Big Guy had twisted Red's arm off at the elbow and it was spurting, but as they went down together in a tangle of limbs and blood, The Big Guy bit out Red's throat with a wild gnash of his teeth. You could hear flesh ripping like someone tearing old bed sheets. The Big Guy sprang to his feet, leaped up and down on Red a few times, put a foot on Red's destroyed and bloody throat, bent down and grabbed that flame-head, and yanked that sucker off as easy as jerking a cork out of a bottle with a wine screw.

This would have held our attention longer had not Bowen said, "I can't lift it."

He was talking about the zeppelin. It was dropping fast. I had just managed to climb completely through the gap in the window (which should give you some idea how fast The Big Guy took care of Red) when it listed to starboard, then turned completely over. I hit the roof of the wheelhouse, which had become my floor, glimpsed through the windshield at a huge, leathery, flying beast grabbing at the zeppelin with its claws, screeching loudly. I thought, perfect. If it weren't for bad luck we'd have no luck at all.

I don't remember much after that.

15

I NEVER KNEW when we hit. Or at least I don't remember it. Perhaps it was the impact that knocked that part of my memory away.

When I awoke the wheelhouse was wadded up around me as if I was a chocolate in tissue paper. The zeppelin had landed on its top; it had stayed completely turned over. I was close to one of the windshields, which had lost all its glass, and managed my way through it, receiving only minor cuts. I got hold of one of the support ropes that contained the gas bag, worked my way briskly to the ground. The leather-winged monster, or at least part of him, was poking out from under the gas bag, dead. I could hear helium leaking from the zeppelin like a slow fart from a grandma. We had been low enough to the ground, that with the zeppelin turning over, the gas bag itself had cushioned our fall. It was still a hell of a drop.

No sooner was I on the ground than it occurred to me that I had left The Big Guy and The Woman in the wheelhouse, or what was left of it. I was about to climb back, when I heard The Woman call out to me. Just hearing her caused a sudden rush of memories to flood through me; our picnics, our talks, sitting on the hotel balcony with a glass of wine or a cup of coffee, screwing like mongooses.

I turned and saw her kneeling over The Big Guy. They had been thrown free of the crash. Bowen Tyler was nearby, sitting up, looking dazed, a hand to his bleeding head. I hurried over to The Woman and The Big Guy. The Big Guy wasn't moving. I pushed her aside and put my head to his chest, peeled back an eyelid and looked at his eye.

"He's still alive," I said. "I'll see if I can find some first aid."

Most everything that had been in the cabins and the storage rooms was scattered about on the ground. I scurried amongst it all, running on all fours as I did in the old days, and quickly came across the small trunk that contained our medical supplies. I dragged it over to where The Big Guy lay. I tore the locked lid off as easy as you might rip the top off a box of cereal. I still had my strength.

To make a long story short, I bandaged him up. The bullet had hit him in the stomach, and there isn't a much worse wound, normally, but with the bullet having gone through him, and by some miracle not having destroyed anything major, and with him having such incredible recuperative powers… Well, let me make this story even shorter. He was going to live.

Our first order of business was we buried Dr. Rice and all the others who had died on the zeppelin; that was everyone but those I've mentioned. I dragged what was left of Red off a good distance from us and each day I would watch the huge buzzards of our world descend on him and finish off what was left of him. I stopped there nightly where he was rotting and being eaten away to piss on his corpse. I never did find his head.

We ended up staying near the wreckage of the zeppelin for a couple of days. We had found and broken out the firearms for safety. Bowen, like The Woman, had only minor injuries. We stayed there a couple of days, and all manner of beasts showed up, as I knew they would. With our weapons, and having built a large fire, we were able to keep them at bay, as well as provide ourselves with breakfast, lunch and dinner.

Better yet, I knew where we were. It was about a three-day walk from where my people congregated. We made a litter, put The Big Guy on it, and started out. It took about five days. It was slower than three days with me and Bowen having to carry The Big Guy, who was no feather, let me tell you. We also had to stop and change bandages. Those ran out after day two, but there were plenty of large leaves, some of which could soak up blood as fine as cotton. I had also sewn his belly shut with a large thorn and some fibers from a plant I knew made good stout thread. Anyway, we took five days to reach my country, across the savanna and deep into the jungle.

I began to see our people before we arrived at my old homeland. They were up in the trees, hiding carefully at the edge of the narrow trail, watching. I actually recognized one of them, and in my own language, said, "Hey, picking many fleas?"

It's a kind of a greeting we have.

My old friend came out of the brush then, a little nervous. He said my name. I agreed that it was indeed me. He recognized The Big Guy, and though The Big Guy may have fallen into our midst, he was considered one of us. More of my people melted out of the jungle and onto the trail. Bowen looked nervous, but I reassured him.

That's how we came to spend about six months among my people. The Big Guy healed up quickly. Within what I estimate to be about six weeks he was fine. We even went hunting together like in the old days, and though I had lost the taste for our hairy females, what the hell, I humped a few of them; it seemed the least I could do so that no one might think I had gotten too high above my raising.

The Woman, who I thought might find this a pretty uncomfortable world once she was introduced to it with the idea of staying, fooled me. She took to it like a cow to grass. Like The Big Guy, she had abandoned her clothes, and had gone native. I gotta tell you, she looked fine like that, brown-skinned and sweat-glazed, her hair standing out from her head like an electrified halo.

She and The Big Guy even built a home. A tree house. Constructed between two massive trees with spreading limbs and great overhead foliage so thick it could hold off a pretty serious rain. Not that it mattered. The Big Guy put a thatched roof on their house, and those digs were quite large for being built so quickly; four big rooms and a veranda that ran all the way around. The Big Guy even rigged up some kind of device that held rain water and could be tapped into for drinking, and bathing if they chose, though most of their bathing they did in the nearby rivers, streams or ponds.

His time in the civilized world had made more of an impact on him that I expected, and his ability to construct that house out of native materials surprised me. When we had lived here in the past, a crook in a tree was good enough for us, but now, with The Woman, he wanted to give her the best of both worlds. I think another thing that made it easier for her was that she didn't really have any family to go home to. Her father, Dr. Rice was the end of it. Her mother had died when she was a child. Dr. Rice had raised her. I think she liked the idea of being near his grave.

As I have said, I had grown to like civilization, and missed it. Bowen was ready to go home as well. So on a cool night with all of us up in the tree house, drinking wine we had gone back and rescued from the zeppelin crash (surprisingly most of the bottles had survived), I said what I had dreaded to say. Me and Bowen were going home.

The zeppelin was beyond repair, but the biplanes, both of them, were in fine shape. We would have to release them from the zeppelin and turn them over on their wheels, but I thought with the help of a lot of my people, that could be done. A plane couldn't carry us all the way back to America, but Bowen had charted out the possibility of Greenland, the place The Big Guy's folks had flown from. It was a close possibility, and he wasn't sure we could make it, but since there were a couple of intact cans of gas along with the plane's filled reservoir, and me being quite nimble and able to gas it up in flight by means of a can and hose and good strong rope, we thought there was a good chance we could manage it that far. I reminded Bowen that The Big Guy's parents had made it from Greenland to here, and that gave me hope. He reminded me the wind patterns were different, and we would be pushing against the wind in spots. Still, we missed home bad enough we were willing to give it a try.

The Big Guy cried. I mean he cried, just let loose with a howl and started leaking tears. He clutched me to him, and damn near broke me. He begged me to stay, but I was stalwart in my plans, and told him so. The Woman cried and hugged me to her naked body as well. I clung to her as long as I could without getting an erection. I thought, considering past events, that would be bad form. Another thing, I couldn't stay close to her for much longer because the old feelings still existed, and I didn't want anything to fan that little blaze into a fire.

Bowen shook hands with them, went on down. I stayed for one last drink of wine. I should add that I was drinking and The Woman was drinking, but The Big Guy was not. He had sworn off the stuff forever, in any shape or form. He drank a kind of coffee made from jungle nuts. It was pretty awful, and hard to get used to. It tasted to me as if it were goat shit boiled in sewer water, but he had a hankering for it and drank it by the cups.

When we had our drinks, I said, "You know, there's something I feel I must tell you." I told them about the serum, and that The Big Guy had, at least according to Dr. Rice, received it when he was a child, that it gave him everlasting life, and that he might remain as he was forever, provided he wasn't killed or got some kind of disease. I explained this as best I could, and The Big Guy sat there mulling it over. The Woman let out her breath and jerked a hand to her mouth. "He won't age. And I will?"

I nodded.

She buried her face in her hands.

I said, "I think there might be a way where you can both continue to be as you are now."

The Woman peeked through her fingers. "Really?"

"Maybe."

I had brought a little box with me that night, along with the wine, and now I opened it. Inside were items from the medical supplies. Hypodermic needles and big glass syringes.

I put a needle in a syringe. I said, "If I can draw some of The Big Guy's blood, and then put that blood in you, it may serve as a serum for you as well. I can't guarantee it, but we can try. It's one of your father's theories."

"He told you all of this," she said.

"He did. Me and him, we got along well."

"I knew you did," she said, "but this... It's amazing."

"I can't guarantee it will work," I said. "But I thought we should try."

"Oh, my heavens," The Woman said. "We must. The idea of growing old, and losing him... I can't face it."

"Your age doesn't matter," said The Big Guy, which was spoken like someone who had never fucked an old lady. I am not suggesting that I have... Oh, hell. A few times, at fundraisers for charities back in the States.

"You should inject yourself as well," said The Woman to me.

"I can try," I said, but Dr. Rice and I had discussed this, and it was possible that I was a different enough species it might not take. I didn't mention that to them, but as you can tell, sitting here with me, my fur as gray as cigar ash, it didn't work.

I drew The Big Guy's blood into the needle, gave a shot of it to The Woman, in the rump, which was a pleasant experience for me, if not her. When it was done, I put the medical tools away, hugged them both, and climbed down to sleep until the break of light. That was when Bowen and I would start our trip to Greenland, and then home. Or we would crash in the ocean when our fuel ran out. I was, of course, hoping for the former.

16

WE DIDN'T MAKE it to Greenland. We crashed in the ocean, and damned if the plane didn't float for a full day and night, and only began to sink the next day. By then we had spotted a steamer and it had spotted us. We were rescued by the crew, and as the ship was on its way to New York City, we were saved.

So, now, here I am, in my modest apartment, quite aged, having never gone back to my lost world. For the most part, my money is gone, except for a little old age pension, which, of course, is why I have to charge you for the pleasure or my company. And need I mention that I prefer cash, not a check?

Bowen died some fifteen years ago of a heart attack. Dr. Rice is now a figure of ridicule, as am I and The Big Guy. Who we were, what we did, and where we came from, has been poorly remembered, taken out of context, or forgotten. What is remembered has been mixed with lies. People these days believe more than ever that our story is nothing more than a swindle.

The entire world from which we came, all that happened to us, is now thought to have been a big fat lie, that I am a man with a strange, hairy condition, and nothing more. Finally that lion screwing event has become even better known, and with the crassness that has become the Americas, it is now shown at a number of venues, and presented frame by frame in numerous magazines. It has robbed The Big Guy of what reputation he once had, and with the money mostly played out from our films, both our reputations have taken a greater hit. Money keeps the paint fresh. When it plays out, the paint begins to peel.

It's not all bad. Explorers say there is no such place as we claimed those years ago. There are also plenty who have said my insistence on its existence is merely senility, that I have come to believe the story myself. This protects The Big Guy, and I know you don't believe me either. I can see it in your eyes.

That's okay. I have aged. The serum didn't work on me. I think it has to do with a different number of chromosomes or something. Yet, I am not senile. I have described it as it was. My mind still works and I still like to visit the ladies. It's probably a good thing that my species can't reproduce with yours, or the world would be filled with hairy folks with long toes.

I am growing tired. I doubt there is anything else left to say that is worth saying. I sit here and remember the old days, and from time to time wonder if I made the right decision to come back to civilization. It's not a thought that occupies a lot of my time, however. I am for the most part quite happy being civilized; in my old world the weak, tired, and the wounded die young.

Looking back, it's strange the way The Big Guy's path crossed mine. Stranger yet, the ape has become the man, and the man has become the ape. I was fortunate to know him, and to know The Woman.

I wonder what happened to them. Did the injection I gave her work? Are they still alive in the jungles of the lost world, hale and hearty, dwelling in their tree house, having adventures, lying together, loving together until the end of time?

It is certainly nice to think so.

The Yarning

by David J. Schow

Novellas are fascinating beasts, aren't they?

Particularly in the realm of what we might call the "scary story."

A few words about Joe Lansdale and scary stories, and a few general tenets.

I have come to believe that the short story is the first and best form of storytelling—the most primordial and essential; the formalized campfire tale.

I further believe that the short *scary* story is likewise the best *kind* of short fiction, for my taste.

You're ticking off your favorite horror *novels* in your head, right now, and that's fine. There are some terrific, immortal ones. But they are far outnumbered by the roll call of famous and memorable horror short stories written to achieve what Edgar Allan Poe famously called the "effect"—the frisson, the kicker, the mood, the build to the short, sharp shock that reverberates in your brain. The furniture of the horror tale changes, but the quest for the effect is always foremost, the idea or core concept that fevers the brain of the writer.

Remember that a century and a half ago, Mr. Poe did not fret about what "category" or "genre" his next work might fit into. He believed short stories were at their best when they could be read in a single sitting. He believed in the "unifying emotion" that provided a basic superstructure for any story—beyond category, if you will. (That is to say, other effects besides the horrific were possible, even though Poe's works are mostly recalled, today, as horror…whatever *that* is.)

Poe further believed that his much cherished "effect" needed to be obvious from the first line of the story, and registered as such by the reader.

And most pertinently, Poe often wrote of impossible circumstances and deeply bizarre events, but he firmly believed in the truth of human behavior—that is, he was dedicated to the idea that the characters in his tales acted as though ordinary people would react to the same or similar bizarrerie.

(Yes, that's not a typo—*bizarrerie* is actually a genuine word, and don't you just love the way it seems to conflate "bizarre" and "eerie"?)

Jump from Poe, then…to Joe, now.

Joe does not fret about what "category" or genre to kneel before. His writing generally suggests a free-associative waterfall of ideas resulting from an igniting spark. He takes the idea off the leash and lets it run around the yard inside his head, to see what it does.

"Do you think he was yarning us?" Bernard asks in "Prisoner 489."

Yes, Joe is yarning us, from his comfort zone as storyteller, or tribal mythologist. He affects an informality that strives to make his tales as inviting as possible. More than that, his tone excludes very few readers and insists that you need no special qualifications to partake—no insider education or elite knowledge is required for the enjoyment of "mojo storytelling." The tale also feeds one of Joe's favorite themes—guys just sweating out existence or hanging around between feedings; fellows (usually men) who are bored to death… until something happens to them, or they initiate something that obliterates the boredom yet makes it preferable in hindsight. A learning experience they might not survive, and sometimes, a glimpse of a larger world that's not so welcoming as the dull plod of routine.

The basic what-if of the yarn involves a very new application of a very old monster—old in the sense of venerable, classic. What if you tried to electrocute the Golem? Not only has Joe seen that immortal Paul Wegener silent film, but it's a pretty good bet that he's also cherished the 1960 B-movie potboiler *Dinosaurus!* and almost certainly has a good working knowledge of Theodore Sturgeon's *Killdozer* as well. (Ted's 1944 short story was adapted as a pretty memorable TV-movie in 1974.)

Indeed, as *Der Golem: How He Came into the World* (1920) was originally intended as the first in a trilogy (a sequel, *Le Golem*, was eventually realized by Julien Duvivier in 1936), one could say that the field was wide open for *the further adventures of...*especially in a modern-day context.

In an introduction to his own 1985 long-form tale, "Sailing to Byzantium," Robert Silverberg summed up the *have-your-cake-and-eat-it-too* appeal of the novella:

> *(It) is one of the richest and most rewarding of literary forms...
> it allows for more extended development of theme and char-
> acter than does the short story, without making the elaborate
> structural demands of the full-length book. Thus it provides an
> intense, detailed exploration of its subject, providing to some
> degree both the concentrated focus of the short story and the
> broad scope of the novel.*

Simple, right? No snap-backs, no twists; merely relentless pursuit of the single effect, which in this case is the otherworld of ancient myth brought crushingly home to the entrenched drudgery of island prison exile.

In writing, you have to be really deft to pull off something that looks really simple.

See, there's these guys bored out of their skulls, just sitting around on an island, and...

Prisoner 489

BERNARD THOUGHT HIS small island was beautiful, though it served an ugly purpose. A necessary service perhaps, but ugly just the same.

The island across the way was larger and less beautiful. It didn't have the trees of the smaller one, and there were the great and imposing walls of the prison, one side visible from the lesser island's small but sturdy two-story sanctuary made of shell and rock and shipped-in materials. It was wide and high with seven large rooms and plenty of garage space for a bulldozer, front-end loader, and a workshop, all of those positioned at the center of the building in the wide dog run that could be sealed on both ends by large metal doors with strong locks, as if theft was a problem. This building, which they called Island Keep, had rows of windows on all sides, and the windows could be opened wide to let in the cool sea breeze. There were trees around the building, and they were tall and gave shadow to the structure during the days when the sun was high and the air was hot. At night they wrapped the place in moon-shadows, and sometimes Bernard would sit at the open window in his bedroom and take in their mystery. There was a gap in the trees, and between them Bernard could see the big island and the walls of the prison. At night the lights of the prison were savagely bright. The prison could be seen clearly from along the shoreline, which was a white sand beach that curved halfway around the island. You could also see the prison clearly from the dock that stuck out in the water. The dock was built of sound, black-painted wood that creaked and moved in high winds and high seas, but held firm.

On all other sides of the small island, once you made your way through the trees that bordered it and that were slightly bent from frequent night winds, all you could see was the sea. On one side was a straight-down wall of rock that ended in jagged pokes of rock and smooth, round boulders, shiny white and large like the backs of partially submerged hippos. They called that part of the little island The Big Drop. It was rumored an earlier caretaker, fed up with isolation and a lack of black tea, his favorite, had thrown himself off The Big Drop and had exploded like a watermelon on the rocks below. Bernard, when he stood on the edge of The Big Drop and looked over, could understand the urge to leap. It was like a siren call. He had experienced it many years before in a car, when on a near whim he nearly weaved his machine right into the path of an oncoming semi. It wasn't something he had thought about at all, but watching those trucks come toward him he thought of it suddenly, felt his hands tighten on the wheel as if he might do it. Sometimes he wished he had. There were times when he felt that way looking over the edge of The Big Drop.

From his bedroom window in Island Keep, Bernard often looked at the prison as if he might be able to see through its walls, knowing full well if he could he wouldn't want to. Those pale concrete walls of the prison rose high and thick and stole in the heat of the day like a thief, and the walls from any angle shimmered with ripples of sunlight. If you were to touch the walls on a hot day they could burn you as surely as touching a hot iron. At night when the moon was bright, the walls were the color of clean, white marble. They cooled slowly, but by midnight touching them was like touching a corpse freshly washed in cold well water. Bernard had been on that island for only a short time, as an observer, as part of his training, but he remembered it well, and almost pitied the souls inside, held there by nature and guards and the United Nations. It was a bad place and he didn't like it, and only went there now when he was to leave for awhile. He exited out from the prison island, went out into the Real World, as it was called, for a week of R&R. He went back to the Real World mainly to flog the dog in some prostitute, but it never really made him feel any better. The whores liked to talk more than he did. He felt as lost in that world as this one. He had served out his prison time, but he had stayed on the job. Why go back when back was nothing he missed. He didn't always like the isolation here, but ashore on the mainland, he felt pretty much the same way, even though he might be surrounded by people. He had been thinking seriously about giving up his "home" time altogether.

Below Bernard's window was the garden, and Bernard always thought of it as the Garden of Gethsemane, though why he chose to think of it that way was beyond explanation. It was lush with smaller trees and all manner of plants and hardy flowers; red and yellow, orange and white. A patch of vegetables was grown there from time to time. Bernard didn't grow them and he didn't work the garden. Wilson did.

Wilson wasn't much more than a kid, but he had a way with the greenery. He could grow tomatoes and cucumbers with a wet, rich taste that would make you cry with satisfaction. Wilson had come from a farming family, and he knew what he was doing. He spent a lot of time there, building trellises for tomato vines, hoeing hills of squash and cucumbers and even a few mounds of potatoes. Not to mention beans and random stalks of corn that on some nights you could actually hear growing. The corn gave off a sound like a small man cracking his knuckles.

The white stone path Wilson had built glared in the sunlight, shone in the moonlight, wound like a snake toward the sea but didn't quite reach the beach. Wilson said he planned to make that happen when he had the time. He had the time, of course; just not the will. The rocks were heavy. He could load them in the scoop of the front-end loader, bring them back and put them in place with it, mostly. But it was time consuming, and Wilson preferred the plants and vegetables in the garden. Bernard was glad he did. It was a nice garden and seemed right for a beautiful island. Wilson also did other work: driving the digging equipment, fixing this and that. He was handy with many things and dependable, but Toggle was the main guy on all that. Toggle seemed to have been born with a tape measure in one hand, a hammer in the other. He was the kind of guy who could fix a motor and change a tire with harsh language.

The ironic thing was Bernard had taught both of them how to do it all. But now the things he had taught were their jobs, and they were better at it than he ever was. He was the foreman, or some such thing. Wilson and Toggle called him boss, or Bernard, and behind his back Toggle may have called him a son-of-a-bitch for all he knew, as they had never quite jelled. He got along with Wilson well enough, and Toggle enough to get by, but working on the island was not a case of creating a family.

What blood family he might have had was gone before he had memories, and the memories he had were of an orphanage and later a foster home or two, a priest putting a dick up his ass after he became an altar boy. The priest cried later about it and asked him not to tell because god would forgive them both. Only thing was, Bernard was uncertain what he was supposed to be forgiven for. He was the one who had been raped—and any god that would forgive that priest wasn't worth believing in.

What life he had went to shit after that. Which was why he was here. Too many petty crimes, too much jail and prison time, and then some officials, men in suits, looked at him through the bars, said: "We think you might be made for better stuff," and this was supposed to be the better stuff. And when the sun was bright and the sea was blue, or when the night was white with moonlight and the stars were clear in the skies like animal eyes, it was a nice life. It beat prison, a cot, three squares, and an unpleasant rendezvous with Buster, who insisted you lose the underwear and wear your prison jacket like a skirt. It beat looking out through bars and feeling your life ooze away like water through a sieve.

Prisoner 489

To the far right of the garden, not completely visible from where he now stood at the window, was the cemetery. Like everything else, Island Keep, The Big Drop, they had their name for it: The Lot.

It was The Lot that gave them their duties, though there wasn't a great amount to do. They waited on news about corpses to come, and in between those arrivals, they just waited. The island was a prison in a way, but without bars and with the freedom to walk about and swim nude in the sea.

Twisted trees with dark bark and thorns the length and thickness of a fat man's thumb grew scattered about The Lot. There was one large tree at the edge of The Lot, close to the shoreline. It was not a thorny tree and was wide and not very high, but the trunk that held up the vast number of limbs that sprouted out of it was big enough that four men would have to link arms to reach around its circumference.

The graves in The Lot were indicated with simple markers, nothing more than thin white slats with dead black numbers painted on them. The numbers corresponded to names in the record books Bernard kept. There was no information about the occupants—the executed, to be more exact. Not even their date of birth; just the location of their interment, date of their burial, and their number. 73 is buried here. 98 is buried there. And so on. They hardly seemed like records worth keeping.

All in all, there were 488 graves, and they had been laid out over a period of one hundred years. Bernard had been told by Kettle, the boatman who brought supplies over and sometimes the dead, that one hundred of the graves had been dug at the same time to take care of one hundred bad people who had been put down in some kind of uprising on the prison island. There may have been more to the rumor, but that's all Bernard had heard, all Kettle had told him.

In The Lot there was more space for more graves, and at the current rate of execution—about three a year—it would take some time before the allotted space was filled, unless there was another mass uprising and burial. If The Lot did fill up, Bernard was uncertain what happened then. Maybe a new location, but it was his guess that the graves would be dug up with the bulldozer or the front-end loader, and heaped into one large hole to save space. This would be easy to do when the graves no longer contained anything more than bones. The coffins, such as they were, were made of biodegradable products; cheap wood and hard paper. The bodies were put inside of those after they had been tucked into what looked like long, gray duffel bags. The bags were designed to rot quickly. Like the cheap coffins, they too were biodegradable. And when you got right down to it, so were the corpses. If they did that, he wondered what kind of marker would replace the others. It wasn't much to think about it, but it was something, and Bernard found that he thought about all manner of things that under normal circumstances might not interest him.

The prisoners in the graves had not only been deadly, they had been different. He wasn't sure how different, but he knew they were in fact different. Not like your run-of-the-mill rapist or murderer. They were worse than that. He wasn't sure what it was about them that made them worse, but he knew it was true. They had been evil. Not mustache-twisting evil, but true evil, rotten inside, wearing their blackness deep at the core. It made him shiver just to think about it.

While he was there at the prison for orientation, something all caretakers had to do, one of the guards came to like him and spend time with him. He was kind of Bernard's guide, the one who helped orient him, let him know just enough about the prison and what was going on there without letting him know too much. The man's name was Charlie, and Charlie told him that his was the worst job in the world and that a few of the guards had gone mad. Plain snake-licking, ass-clenching mad.

Charlie told him he knew of one guard who had beat his own brains out on a concrete wall, and several had hanged themselves, and a few had gone down to the ocean to drown. For that reason, the time a man or woman worked there as a guard was limited to three years. You could then take a year off and come back for two if you wanted to, and then you were out for good after that. No coming back.

He said he only knew of one guard who returned after leaving, and that he lasted two days before he cut his own throat with broken glass. Charlie said he found himself thinking about bad things from time to time, and he felt it was because so much evil was in that prison that it had a presence, like a shadow that flickered along the corridors and through the cells. He said he dreamed of some of the prisoners, and he dreamed they were trying to suck his own shadow out of him. He said the dream was so real he sometimes checked when walking along the halls, where the light shone bright, to make sure he still had a shadow and that it slid across the wall with him as he walked.

"They are here without writ and without trial, and for these people, that's how it should be," Charlie said. "They are the bad of the bad. Only way they leave here is by illness, old age, or electricity."

Bernard had seen a few of the prisoners—though he was only there for a short time, to await an execution. The deal was, you were going to be a caretaker, and you were taking orientation during an execution, you had to attend. If there was no execution Bernard was uncertain what it would have been replaced with. All he knew was it was his misfortune to have to witness one. They had a big room with a wide glass that you could see through, but the other side was opaque. The person being executed couldn't see you back. He watched as they strapped in a heavy woman with greasy hair and one eye turned white as a snowball, the other moving in her head as if it thought it might find a place to hide.

She struggled with them, but they got her in the chair. They strapped her down, a thick belt around her waist, straps fastened to her wrists and ankles. They put a rubber pad in her mouth, held there by clamps on either side of her head. They placed a black mask over her eyes and brought the metal cap down and pushed it into place, the wire coiling back to the generator. It made her look like some kind of weird spaceman about to launch into space. There were no last words, no priest, and nothing said. She was strapped in, the warden and the guards stepped back out of the way, and a man wearing a hood threw the switch, which looked like a big lever in a Frankenstein movie. The air hummed like a million bees, and the execution room appeared to waver a little, the way sunlight will do on water. The woman jerked and rose up out of the chair as if she might levitate, but the straps and clamps held her. Smoke curled out of her mouth and out from under the mask and licks of fire slipped from beneath the cap and toasted her ears and turned them and her cheeks black. Her fingers lifted off the chair like quivering worms trying to escape. Then she was still. A guard fanned the smoke away and leaned forward and looked at her. A doctor came into the room and put a stethoscope to her chest, nodded. He removed the mask and her dead eye eased out of the socket and hung down on her cheek by the tendons. The eye was no longer white: it was red, and there were tendrils of smoke drifting up from it.

At that point, Bernard and the others (he didn't know any of them) left the room. They were let outside into the fresh air the prisoners inside never tasted, and he stood there with the others, quivering, not knowing them, not speaking to them, and then they were all led away, and within moments he was separated from them and never saw them again and never knew why they were there, only why he was.

Now he had that dark remembrance boxed up in his memory like a Jack-in-the-box. He never knew when it might pop up. From time to time he thought he smelled that woman's cooking flesh, like bacon burning in a pan, though he had never actually smelled anything, and he could see that dead eye dangling, the way the smoke curled up white to the ceiling and spread out and misted away.

When Bernard asked the boatman, Kettle, about Charlie, the guard, actually inquiring just to have something to say, Kettle told Bernard about three months after he had begun his work on the small island, Charlie had disappeared from the big island. They thought he might have drowned himself and been carried out and deposited somewhere deep down and forever by the sea. No one knew for sure, but no one thought he had left the island alive. The prisoners couldn't escape, and neither could the guards unless they were taken away by boat or copter. Charlie's disappearance was long ago, but Bernard thought about it from time to time when he went down to look at the sea. Sometimes he imagined Charlie might wash up. Even after ten years he thought about that. It was ridiculous, but he thought about it anyway. What could be so bad you couldn't wait out your time to leave? Though Bernard had seen a few of the prisoners, and the execution, he knew nothing about those barred in the Keep, and from what he could tell, it would remain that way for the rest of his days. It was Bernard's guess he was better off for it.

What he did know was tonight there would be a new one. A freshly dead one would be boated over by Kettle to go down in the ground, out by the big tree near the dock. The call had come, blunt and simple. The phone ringing like a single thought in an empty skull, an accented voice giving him the time of the execution, the estimated time of arrival.

The phone only permitted calls between the islands. There was no way to call out. No chit-chat to the mainland. For that matter, there was no chit-chat between islands. There were only messages of importance. A need for supplies on the little island, the arrival of a freshly grilled prisoner.

Since executions were not common, Bernard sometimes went months with nothing more than his books and magazines. There was no internet either. No e-mail. On that island you took a pledge to stay quiet, and the pledge was backed up by not providing temptations. He hated to think it, but when one of the prisoners was executed he felt a little festive. Something was happening to break the routine.

Wilson was young and was here because he had been full of hormones and youthful stupidity. Two years from now, when he was able to have his break, his vacation, he just might be able to figure things out. Though he had five years to do on the island before they let him go, he would still be young.

Toggle was a lot like Bernard. He neither wanted to be here nor wanted to go back to the mainland. He was merely letting his internal clock tick away his time on earth without trying to do any more than he had to.

Kettle worked at the prison, and when he came from the big island he only stayed a few hours at a time. He brought supplies and he brought bodies. But it was Bernard's guess he wasn't much different from them. Maybe more of a talker, a bullshitter, but still a man with his soul in a sack. He enjoyed Kettle's visits, all the stories he told, the hints he gave of what went on over at the big island, but he was also glad to see him leave.

Fact was, things on the island pretty much ran themselves, and none of them had much to do. You had to make your own entertainment. Like now, waiting on the execution.

Bernard sat in a chair at the window with a book and started to read. The last book he had read was *Catcher In The Rye*, and he hated it. He had heard all about it and how good it was, but within a few paragraphs he wished the kid would die on the first page. He himself had been like that kid in a lot of ways. The kid's story, his point of view, wasn't very appealing unless you were fifteen and thought that's how cool people acted. Now he had a different book, and it seemed like it might be better. But he sat with it and found he wasn't paying attention. He had gone back to his dilemma. He was thinking about how he might leave, and what he might do outside of the island, and the more he thought about it the more he felt he should stay until they carried him away. He tried from time to time to think about leaving because he thought that's what he should do, but then he didn't want to, and the next day he thought about it again as if it mattered. It was like being a poor old chained dog waiting on the next meal, the only thing there was to look forward to, and after the meal it started all over again, the waiting.

The sky darkened and Bernard looked at his watch. Another fifteen minutes it would be night. He would turn the light on and wait. An hour later the lights would flicker here in this place he called a home, and across the way, of course, in the prison, the source of the interruption in service. He wasn't sure how it was done, but both islands received their electricity from the same source. It was rumored there was a great battery beneath the waves, impervious to lashing seas, hot or cold. He doubted that. Most likely it was simply an underwater cable. And of course, there was a backup generator for both islands.

The lights blinked when whoever was in line for their electric dose got it. A short time after it was finished would come the boat, Kettle at the helm, followed by the burying. Down below, he saw Wilson. He was sitting in a lawn chair amongst his plants. He had a tunnel-view of the prison there. He was in shade from the trees. Toggle would be down by the dock, near the big tree, waiting, smoking his cigarettes or chewing his tobacco.

Wilson turned and looked up, called out. "It's about that time."

"Yeah," Bernard said, as if he had only just now thought on the matter. They had been waiting on it all day. The hole was dug. The boat would come. The body would go in the hole and they would fill it, using the front-end loader to fill it, and then the shovels to smooth it out. Tomorrow would come.

Bernard made himself a cup of coffee, poured from a not-too-clean glass pot into a not-too-clean plastic cup, opened a bag of chocolate cookies, and sat back down, the cup and cookies on an end table at his elbow. He remembered reading of executions through history, how observers often brought snacks while they waited for the main event. In a way, that's what he was doing.

He dunked a cookie in his coffee and ate it. The sky swelled with darkness. He watched the prison carefully. Rows of yellow eyes ran along the top of the prison, those savage yellow lights. Bernard had no idea where the execution room was. Kettle said it was on the far side of the prison, and that's all he knew.

Bernard looked at his watch. He sipped his coffee. The lights at the prison dimmed from yellow to pumpkin-orange, and the lights in his room did the same. They stayed that way for a long time. Night was full now and the dimmed lights from the prison shone on the water, orange instead of yellow. Then the lights brightened in the prison and in his room, and the lights on the water became a bright, wavy yellow. The execution was over.

But then the lights blinked again, and this time the lights everywhere went dead black. It had to be his imagination, but he thought he could smell the ozone cooking.

He waited. Darkness still.

Finally the lights jumped back, bright yellow.

Damn, thought Bernard. He had remembered one time before when they had bumped the switch twice. Something didn't go right and it had to be done again, but this time the lights hadn't just dimmed, they had gone absolutely dark for several seconds.

Bernard was contemplating on that when the lights went out again. It surprised him so much that he stood up and jarred the end table, knocking the cup of coffee to the floor. He felt hot coffee splash against his sock, warming him a little. He stood at the window and waited.

One, one thousand, he counted.

Two, one thousand. Three, one thousand.

He went all the way to eight, one thousand, and then the lights kicked on, bright and warm and yellow, poking out of the prison windows, shining out of their great bulbs along the top of the prison, their reflections lying firmly on the water. It was as if a great ship had sunk and turned on its side and its lights were still burning beneath the waves.

"Holy shit," Wilson said down in the garden.

"Yeah," Bernard said, leaning out of the window. "Holy shit."

"You ever seen such a thing?" Wilson was out of his chair now, was turned to look up at Bernard.

"No. I've seen it blink twice. I mean, they had to hit number 486 more than once for some reason. But three times. No."

"486. The one on the end near the row of trees," Wilson said.

"Yeah, her. They had to hit her twice. First time it didn't kill her, second time they got her fixed right. But I haven't seen anything like this. Three surges."

"Who in hell would need three bumps?"

"Something wrong with the link-up is my guess. Probably only that last one hit the prisoner firm and fixed him up right."

"Jesus," Wilson said. "How firm does it have to hit you?"

"Good question."

"Guess we go to work pretty soon, huh?"

It was a question with an obvious answer, so Bernard didn't answer it. He eased back from the window. And then the lights jumped one more time.

Darkness.

The lights jumped back.

"Now that," Bernard said to Wilson below, "is what you call damn unusual."

Bernard felt cold, as if a draft had blown in off the water. But there wasn't a draft. The trees hadn't even moved. Soon, as if by clockwork, the wind would pick up and the limbs would tremble and the leaves would shake, but for now all the island was still as that goddamn corpse strapped smoking in the electric chair.

Bernard picked up the plastic cup and placed it on the nightstand. He picked up the cookie, ate it anyway, figured the floor was clean enough. Besides, he wanted that cookie.

When he finished it, he went to the cabinet, pulled down a bottle of liquid antacid, drank straight from it. It tasted like chalk. He wasn't sure why he had stomach problems, the job being relatively easy, but he did. Maybe it was his life before all this, or maybe it was something inherited. Maybe it was his memory of that horrid execution. Whatever; two or three times a week he had to give the insides of his belly a good coating.

And then, as expected, the sea breeze rolled in. He heard the leaves rattle like a tubercular cough, then the limbs shook against one another like dice rocked in a cup. The breeze slipped cool through the open window. He looked out through the tunnel between the trees, saw the water tossing whitecaps.

Bernard took a deep breath, moved from the window, pulled on a light coat, picked up his flashlight, and went out and down to the dock, Wilson tagging along not far behind with his own flashlight. That's where Kettle would be arriving in a pretty short time. When he got to the dock, Toggle was there. He had the front-end loader parked near the grave, shovels nearby. Toggle had already put the device for lowering the coffin into place. Wilson came wandering up behind Bernard, came to stop by him with his hands stuck down in his light coat pockets.

"Howdy," Toggle said.

Bernard nodded and Wilson greeted them both. He always had the attitude of a big puppy, happy to see you under whatever circumstance. Toggle kept his own company most of the time. He and Wilson got along well enough, but they didn't keep each other company any more than Bernard did. Toggle had his spot on the bottom floor of the garage, and he sat there watching DVDs on his little TV screen. He watched the same movies over and over. Mostly action. Of course, there was no real TV connection, no channels to watch, no news. Like Bernard with his books, Toggle had to wait until a shipment came in with new DVDs. Bernard had watched a few, but grew bored with the process early on and dedicated himself to reading and masturbation, though the latter was becoming more and more difficult. He had a hard time imagining a woman who wanted to go to bed with him. He had a hard time imagining a woman anymore, for that matter, and that distressed him.

Toggle had a thermos of coffee, and he poured himself some. He didn't offer Bernard any, but that was all right with Bernard. He would have had to share the cup with Toggle, and Toggle always smelled of chewing tobacco and dirty shorts.

Bernard took hold of one of the three shovels provided and leaned on it. Wilson started in talking about the weather, like they hadn't noticed it was getting windy and was soon to be wet. Wilson just liked to hear himself talk. Wilson was a friendly kid, and likeable, but even so, Bernard always hated his chatter. Way he figured it, when the kid finished his term, he'd be gone. That's what he should do. Not like himself. He had been here so long he didn't believe he deserved to be in the outside world where people talked and chatted over dinner, made love and raised families. This lonesome island seemed like the only thing real in the world.

Bernard then realized that the reason he hated Wilson's chatter was that he envied him. Wilson would actually leave this island, he was certain, and he was the only one among them that had a chance at a real life. He wanted the kid to leave, but the fact that he could, and most likely would, was something he envied.

Wilson was still chattering on about the weather, when Toggle turned his head, looked out at the water, and as if Wilson were not talking at all, said, "Here he comes."

They all looked, and there was the boat. It was a simple thing, somewhere between boat and barge, painted black, befitting its use. It was like the boat that carried the dead across the river Styx, and this little island was Hades. Kettle was its Charon. The boat churned steadily against the growing pressure of the wind and waves. As it neared the dock, its motor chugged and huffed and puffed like a dying dragon.

"That motherfucker needs some mechanic work," Toggle said. "Some new spark plugs and a completely overhauled engine. Better yet, get it on shore, jack it up, and drive a real boat under it. That piece of shit, one night it's going to come this way and not make it. They'll find Kettle with a swordfish up his ass, and the body he was bringing over covered in seaweed down at the bottom of Davy Jones' Locker."

As the boat neared the dock its struggling motor slowed, sputtered and coughed, gave out with one loud fart, and slid up alongside the dock with a thump. A moment later, Kettle, who was a large, gray-haired man, came out of the water-splashed wheelhouse, onto the deck. Already Bernard and the others had started down to meet him.

Kettle stepped out on the dock and secured the boat with a length of heavy rope. He looked up and said, "Hey, boys. Getting any pussy?"

"That's some funny shit," Toggle said. "It was funny first time you said it, and every time since, and I bet it's funny six months from now. No. From now on each and every time."

"Yeah, well, I got to tell you, over on the big island, they bring in some split tail for us once a month. Last night was the most recent. They always bring the whores in the night before an execution. Female workers get some dick, and men get pussy. The spouse-faithful and the in-betweens do without."

"Bullshit," Toggle said. "I didn't believe that the first ten times you told me, and I don't believe it now."

"Want to smell my fingers?" Kettle said. "I don't wash them for a week after I get them up some snatch."

"Shit, you been eating tuna fish."

"Let's just get this done," Bernard said. That kind of talk always embarrassed him.

"Bernard, you are a boring sonofabitch," Kettle said. "Anyone ever tell you that?"

"Most everyone, and you, frequently. Let's get it done."

Wilson said, "Hey, you bring some supplies this time? Something worth a shit?"

"I'm making the big run next week," Kettle said. "I did bring some coffee and tea. A box of cookies. That's it for now. Next week, all the goods. Oh, Bernard. I have a book from the warden for you. Charles Dickens. I tried to read him once and he made me sleepy."

"I'm glad to get it," Bernard said. "You sure it's in the box? Last time you got me excited about *The Old Man And The Sea*, and it wasn't in there. Some magazines was all."

"Naked-women magazines," Toggle said. "I thought it was a kind of bonanza. You got to get your priorities straight, Bernard. A book on fishing, or some fresh young things with their legs spread?"

"Let's check," Bernard said, and they all went on board. There were two wooden crates there, a smaller one that supposedly held the coffee and tea and book, the cookies, and another large one. That one held the body. Bernard lifted off the lid of the small crate. Inside was a cardboard box. Bernard took out his pocket knife and cut the cardboard box open where it had been sealed with tape. The book was there, so were the tea, coffee, and cookies.

"Good deal," Wilson said leaning over, looking in the box. "I read that book after you?"

"You can," Bernard said.

"Now you're starting bad habits, boy," Toggle said.

"That's the largest crate I've seen for a body," Bernard said.

"Because it's a large body." Some of the humor had gone out of Kettle. "How about helping me get it on shore. I'll be glad to get rid of it. This ole boy gives me the willies, even dead."

The crate was made of good firm planks and there were metal handles along the sides of it. It took all of them to hoist it onto the dock, where they paused to get their breath.

"Damn," Wilson said. "What's in that, an elephant?"

"Inside the box they got a good metal coffin, and inside that they got the Guest of Honor."

"They've never done that before," Bernard said.

What he meant was the metal coffin. It was always the shit coffins, the biodegradable stuff.

"No, they haven't," Kettle said. "But they've never put to death anyone like this guy either. Big motherfucker. Head like a goddamn volleyball, shoulders just a little wider than Boulder Dam. They hit him hard with three shots tonight."

"Four," Bernard said.

"Yeah," Kettle said. "Four. He was still breathing after the last hit."

"No way," Wilson said.

"Way," Kettle said. "They smothered him for the finish by putting a plastic bag over his head. You ain't supposed to know that, and neither am I, but I was there. I was a witness. I always like to see who gets killed. Somehow it makes my job more real."

"I can pass on that," Bernard said. "No more for me."

"Not me," Kettle said. "It gets easier every time out."

"That's what I'm afraid of," Bernard said.

"I don't want to see it either," Wilson said.

"Look, who gives a shit?" Toggle said. "Let's get fat boy unloaded off the boat and in the ground. I feel like watching a movie."

"Like you haven't seen them before," Wilson said.

"I got a bottle," Toggle said, "and you start sipping early enough, and all the way through, no matter how many times you've seen something it feels just like new."

"I brought a bottle of Scotch with me for the big finish tonight," Kettle said. "We get him in the ground, maybe we can all have a little nip before I start back across. They haven't got me on a tight leash."

"I could taste some Scotch and not feel bad about it," Toggle said.

They carried the crate along the dock toward the open grave. They had to stop and put it down a couple of times and regroup.

"Damn," Toggle said. "There may just be an elephant in there."

"What I'm trying to tell you," Kettle said. "They were afraid his weight would tear through one of those cheap-ass cardboard and best-wish coffins. I think they're right. It would have."

"But why the metal coffin?" Bernard said.

"Let me tell you something else," Kettle said. "That metal coffin, it's wrapped in chains."

"What the fuck for?" Bernard said.

"So what's in it won't get out. That old boy still has the plastic bag over his head. I mean, every prisoner on the big island is unique, it's just this fellow was a little more unique than the rest."

"He have a name?" Bernard asked.

"Not that anyone knows. We just called him number 489," Kettle said.

"How do you execute someone and not know who he is?" Bernard said.

"Peculiar, huh?"

Prisoner 489

By the time they got the box to the gravesite they were covered in sweat, and when they tried to place it on the cloth straps that worked the device to lower the coffin, the crate tipped. It tore the contraption loose and dove into the hole with one end striking the ground so hard the crate burst open and the metal coffin was revealed.

"Goddamn it," Bernard said. It was the first time something had gone wrong when he was preparing a burial. He was overcome with a sense of being unprofessional.

"It's all right, pal," Kettle said. "It's not like anyone is looking. We'll just shovel the hole filled. Who gives a shit if that mother-fucker is standing on his head."

"We'll do it right," Bernard said.

"There really are chains?" Wilson asked.

They looked where he was pointing. Wrapped around the coffin they could see chains, padlocked chains.

"Told you," Kettle said.

"But he's dead," Toggle said. "Even an odd one can get dead."

"I think they wanted to be sure," said Kettle. "Let's get him covered and we'll have that drink. I'll tell you what I know. Why the fuck not. I'd like to get it off my chest."

It took some work, but Wilson and Toggle were able to climb down in the grave and tug at the coffin until it lay flat. They pulled loose the pieces of the crate that weren't under the coffin and passed them up, then climbed out.

Toggle worked the front-end loader and filled the grave with loose earth. Then Bernard, Toggle and Wilson firmed the dirt down with shovels while Kettle leaned against the big tree.

"I have the marker for it," Toggle said, and he got it out of the front-end loader where it lay on the seat. It had the number 489 painted on it. He shoved it in the ground at the head of the grave.

"All right," Toggle said, "another one put away."

Kettle poured Scotch all around, except for Bernard, who didn't drink liquor. He had some of the new coffee Kettle had brought instead.

Kettle said, "The big boy. He didn't eat."

They were seated in chairs in the downstairs community room, as it was called, though the community was the three of them, and now a guest, Kettle. They had the door and windows open and the night breeze was blowing in, turning a bit chill as it blew.

"What do you mean he didn't eat?" Bernard said.

"He didn't eat. Not a bite all the time he was there. Took them three years to throw the volts to him, and I'm not sure why it took that long, as they don't have any laws or appeals over there. Not for the folks they bring in. And in his case, I'm not sure he was a folk."

"That's ridiculous, Kettle," Toggle said. "Everyone eats."

"Everyone human."

"Even adding in the weight of the crate and the coffin, there's some serious meat inside that box," Toggle said. "He was eating *something*."

"He didn't eat for three years," Kettle said, and took a long slug of his Scotch. "Let me tell you, I know. I was assigned to him sometimes. You know, guard duty, look in through the peephole now and then, make sure he hadn't offed himself. I had to ask for them to let me out of the duty a time or two, it got to me so much. They let me off too. Everyone there that dealt with him understood. They had a special room just for him, and it had all manner of symbols on the wall. I don't know what they were about, but it was like some kind of incantation."

"Oh, for heaven's sake," Toggle said. "We don't need some stupid ghost story."

"I want to hear," Wilson said, leaning forward. One drink and he was already starting to act a bit buzzed.

"I doubt it was just decoration," Kettle said. "It was some kind of mumbo-jumbo going on there. It was there to keep him in that room. The walls were ten feet thick and the bars were as big around as my forearms, and there was a clear plastic shield in front of those bars, on the outside. There was an electric eye that was set off if he moved too close to the bars, and they gave off a shock of electricity, for what that was worth. You could go in there and stand in front of the plastic when you were on guard duty, but most of us used the peephole on the big metal door. That door was two feet thick and solid steel."

"So he could take that shock, he went too far?"

Toggle said, "Enough bullshit."

"It didn't hurt him," Kettle said.

"He took four serious jolts tonight, and a bag over his head," Wilson said. "Haven't you been paying attention? He could probably take a little shock like that."

"You tell him, kid," Kettle said. "And he really didn't eat. They tried to feed him daily for the first month, but he either left it or threw it against the wall. And he didn't lose a goddamn pound. Not an ounce. They had him recorded as six foot seven, weighing four hundred pounds. He was broad in the shoulders as a beer truck and had legs and arms like trees. Big hands, catcher's-mitt hands. He had a toilet in there, but he didn't use it. He didn't eat anything or drink anything, so there was no shit or piss. He just *was*. He sat on his bunk, sagged it, but didn't move outside of that, except now and then to come to the bars and look at me when I came in, right through the electric barrier. It hummed around him like horseflies, but didn't bother him at all. You could see the damn electricity, blue-white and sparking. Goddamn, that was some look he had when he was staring. His skin was gray, like damp sand, and his eyes were black and round like dry olives. Never smiled. Now and again he'd open his mouth and just let his jaw hang, but it wasn't any kind of smile. He had big, fat teeth, all of them exactly alike. The size of sugar cubes and the color of dirty snow. And he had a tattoo right in the middle of his fat forehead. Blue and ugly, some kind of squiggles and such. You couldn't call it decorative. Looked like this."

There was a notebook and pad on the table covered in coffee rings. Kettle took it, drew a design on it.

"That looks like some kind of language," Bernard said, turning it around to face him.

"Very descriptive," Toggle said. "But you lost me at *he didn't eat.*"

"He didn't. Believe me. He just didn't eat. I swear on my grave, he didn't eat."

"You didn't see him eat," Toggle said.

Kettle shook his head. "No. He didn't eat."

"Why was he there?" Bernard asked.

"They don't tell us stuff like that, not us guards and boat men. Well, I'm the only one drives the boat. But there were rumors, you know."

"What kind of rumors," Wilson asked.

"He could fly and throw lightning bolts," Toggle said. "Oh yeah, and he didn't eat, but he could fart cannon balls."

"You don't want to believe me, you don't have to," Kettle said.

"I want to hear it," Bernard said. "We all know that whoever is kept over there is not just a thief, a rapist, or a murderer. They have some kind of peculiarity about them."

"That's what I keep hearing," Toggle said. "But all I've seen are coffins and them slipping down into graves I dug, rotting like any other dead thing."

"But that doesn't mean that they aren't peculiar," Kettle said. "Governments put together this business, these two islands, for a special reason. They wanted to make sure they held them in a place where they couldn't get out. And over there, I've seen some odd stuff, I tell you that."

"I think you like to hear yourself talk," Toggle said.

"I do at that," Kettle said, "But that doesn't mean what I'm talking isn't true."

"Tell us about the rumors," Wilson said.

"They said they found him in a wall."

"A wall?" Bernard said.

"Yeah, a wall. In some old synagogue in New York they were tearing down. Opened the wall, and there he was."

"Now the bullshit is deep," Toggle said.

"It'll get deeper," Kettle said. "And it may be bullshit. I'm telling you this part because it's what I overheard. They found him in the wall, and he was just there, stiff as a giant tree. They thought he was a statue."

"Here we go, the set up for the big joke," Toggle said. "Ends with, and he killed them all."

"Almost," Kettle said. And the way he said it, even Toggle settled back in his chair. "You see, they had to get a dozen men just to lift him, and they carried him out and placed in a warehouse, and the next morning the warehouse had a hole just a little bigger than the statue, or body as it turned out. It was gone."

"He knocked a hole in the wall, huh," Toggle said, but a lot of his sarcasm had dried up.

"No. They saw tire tracks outside the warehouse. Someone had cut their way through the aluminum and stolen the body, hauled it away."

"Who and to what purpose?" Bernard asked.

Kettle shook his head. "I don't know. I mean there's more to the rumor, but I don't know the answer to that. But there is this. A few days later a couple of Jewish fellows turned up dead in an apartment in New Jersey, and there was a hole in the wall again, but this time it had been knocked open from the inside."

Even Toggle had grown quiet. Kettle poured them all another round, and even Bernard let him dash a bit in his coffee cup.

Kettle sipped and then sat quietly for a moment. "Those two Jews, they had something to do with the old synagogue, I think. If I remember the story right, one was a rabbi. I don't know all the truth, just the rumors. But they were messed up, those two. One had his head pulled completely off, like it was a cork in a bottle. The other, his arms were pulled off, and one of the men's legs was missing."

"You can't know that really happened," Toggle said. There was nothing disdainful in his tone now, though, just curiosity.

"I said as much. Rumor. But the body, because that's what it was, was missing. Something had gone wrong there, and it had got up and walked away. After knocking part of the wall down. There were all manner of books lying about, they said. Most of them in ancient languages or some such shit. Again, this is just the stuff came down from the guards and the hired help, things they overheard, or got told in secrecy, which, of course means it got told to someone who told it to someone. It could be like the game of telephone, where you tell someone something and by the time you get to the end, it's changed. They told me they finally cornered him, and he had that leg. He beat some homeless people to death with it, and had pulled some others apart with his bare hands. He killed two or three cops. Bullets didn't stop him."

"Now you have gone wild," Toggle said. "That's insane. How can anyone believe that shit?"

Kettle shrugged. "Believe what you want. I don't know how they finally got him down, clamped him up and hauled him in, but they did. I believe all that, about the cops, all that stuff they say he did. Because I've seen him. Been near him. From what I know of him, what I saw, him not eating—and you don't have to believe me on that. I don't give a shit. But he didn't eat. He didn't crap. He didn't piss. And he didn't do much more than sit, and he was a solid weight all that time. There was something about him that was just plain scary. And tonight, you know what they did? They had to use a forklift with claws on it to take him from the cell, and he still hurt a couple of guards before they pinned him with that thing. The wall was fixed so it could be unbolted and pulled out. The lift had a wide shield and it had those tongs, and it got hold of him, and then it took a dozen men to put him in the chair when they got him there. And it wasn't the usual chair. It was like a goddamn throne with thick clamps and wraps of chain. I saw all this through the plastic shield on the door. They always let me watch, and I always do. Like I told you. I want to know what kind of shit I'm putting in the hole. Well, they strapped him in, put a special-made cap on his head that made him look like Tom Terrific—"

"Who?" Wilson said.

"Forget it," Bernard said.

"And then," Kettle said, "everyone jumped back and they threw him the juice. No formalities or last words, because he never spoke, ever. And they hit him with those volts and he smoked and cooked and let out with the first sound anyone had ever heard. It was like a giant wolf howl, but harder and meaner, maybe a scream inside a howl. I don't know how to describe it, but it made my blood curdle, I'll tell you that. They saw he wasn't dead, and had in fact snapped one of the leg bonds, and they hit him again. This time the cap had flames coming out from under it, and they singed his head, and still he howled, and they hit him again and, as you said, again. I had forgotten that fourth shot. That time he went silent. They put a stethoscope to his chest, and he wasn't breathing. But his hands were moving, and one of the wrist bonds was starting to break. They put a plastic bag over his head then, and he went still after a time, but I never saw any indication he was breathing inside that bag. They just assumed he had to be, but the bag didn't suck in or nothing. He just finally wasn't howling and was still, and it was done. They were going to hit him again, but decided it was over and crated him out and boxed him up and put him on the boat, and here we are."

"Damn," Wilson said.

"No doubt he could take some volts," Toggle said. "That part I believe. I saw the lights. But all that other stuff."

"Believe what you want," Kettle said. "Ain't no skin off my dick. Look, I got to head back. Well, maybe one more drink. Anyone for one more?"

Everyone but Bernard was for one more. They drank it down quick and Kettle got up and started out the door. "I got to go," Kettle said. "I'll leave you with the old boy tucked tight in the ground."

"I'll walk down with you," Bernard said.

"Me too," Wilson said.

"Hell, why not," Toggle said. "Not like I got anything else to do."

When they were near the dock, Bernard found himself glancing out at Number 489's grave. The moonlight lay on the white marker and made it shiny. The wind was very cool now, and to walk down to the dock he had slipped on a windbreaker, as had Wilson and Toggle. Kettle was in short sleeves and seemed just fine, as if he were impervious to the weather. They watched him climb on board and listened as he started up the boat and sent it out into the waters, which by that time had grown quite choppy. The boat heaved and lurched toward the big island, its lights going away from them fast. It seemed Kettle was anxious for the security of a prison filled with what were thought to be the world's worst criminals, instead of on the little island with a freshly executed prisoner buried down deep in the ground inside a chained-up metal coffin.

"Looks like it's going to come a serious blow," Toggle said, as they turned and walked back up the dock and onto shore.

"Does at that," Bernard said.

"There hasn't been a real storm on this island since I been here," Wilson said. "Just some wind and rain."

"We've seen a few, haven't we, Bernard?" Toggle said, and Bernard felt a strange sense of unusual camaraderie between them. Maybe it was the Scotch Toggle had consumed that made him friendly. Or perhaps it was the aftermath of Kettle's story.

"That's right, we've had two good ones. No. Three."

"Yeah," Toggle said. "Three. Three really good ones. We had one blew the roof off Island Keep, took them three months to get over here and fix it. Lot of stuff got rained on during the storm, and during the three months too. Messy."

"So we could have a good one?" Wilson said.

"You can always have a good one," Toggle said. "Shit, boy. You never know. But the way this wind is picking up, how cool it feels, I can tell you this, we're in for something. Maybe I ought to bring the loader back to the shed."

"Probably should," Bernard said.

"All right then. I'm going to take a moment to have a smoke or a chew. One or the other. Wind doesn't pick up too much, maybe both. I'll be up."

Bernard and Wilson kept walking toward Island Keep.

Toggle turned back to the cemetery and the loader.

Wilson said, "He's an odd man, isn't he?"

"No odder than I am."

"I can believe that," Wilson said. "No offense."

"None taken. But like us, here you are."

"Yeah, I did something stupid, and here I am. But I can tell you this, my time is up, I'm off here. I always thought an island would be a treat. It isn't. I get bored."

"Well, this little rock isn't exactly Hawaii," Bernard said.

"True, but I think I've had it all up and done with islands of any kind. I didn't know how much I hated water until I got here. You can leave, can't you? You served your time."

"I can. I think about it. I probably won't. I don't know anything else. But I tell you, son, if you want to leave, you have the urge to leave, do so, and don't come back. You come back here, pretty soon you're like a bird with clipped wings. You remember flying, but you can't do it anymore. Leave while you still got the wings for it."

"Don't worry, I plan to," Wilson said.

When they got back to Island Keep, Wilson said, "I think I'll go find a girlie magazine and jack off."

"I didn't need to know that."

"Just messing with you. I drank too much Scotch. I couldn't get it up if I had a swimsuit model tugging on my dick."

"Goodnight," Bernard said.

"Hey," Wilson said, pausing as he started away. "That stuff Kettle told us. I mean about that guy we got out there. About him not eating or shitting and such. Do you believe that?"

"No. He said it was a rumor, and Toggle is right. Kettle likes to hear himself talk; he said so himself."

"So you think he was yarning us?"

"Mostly, yeah. I mean, it did take several jolts of the juice to kill him. If in fact he was in the chair when they threw it all those times. It might have been maintenance the first time or two, and then the last two were the real deal. No doubt though: whoever he was and whatever he did, it was bad. But the rest of it, I think you can let that flow under the bridge, so to speak."

"Yeah. Sure. What I was thinking."

"Good story, though," Bernard said.

"Yeah. It was a good one."

Wilson hitched up his pants and started along the dog run. His room was just off of it. He wobbled slightly, but arrived at his door and went inside.

Bernard, when he was sure Wilson had made it, climbed the squeaking stairs up to his room, and for the first time in years, he locked the door. He thought about the big metal door that was open to the outside. It being open bothered him. He hoped when Toggle pulled the loader in he would close and lock it.

Bernard couldn't sleep. He had felt tired, and then all of a sudden he was awake. The wind was whistling in hard through the open window, flapping the curtains and blowing in rain. Bernard got up to close the window.

Before he did, he stuck his head out into the storm and looked toward the cemetery, the orchard of bones. He could faintly see the tree near the dock and the front-end loader was still parked there. Toggle was supposed to smoke or chew and bring it up, but it was in the same spot. Nothing really that could be hurt by the wind and rain, and it was enclosed with a kind of wheelhouse surrounded with glass, but still, Bernard felt it should be parked and put away. Toggle might have had a flask with him, or one in the loader, and was inside the machine enjoying a nip. Maybe he had come home, abandoning the loader, and was in his room drunk. It had happened before.

Bernard decided to be less of a worrywart. He closed the window and walked to his bookshelf. Something was bothering him, but he wasn't sure what. He ran his fingers over the titles, over the old encyclopedias with their loose covers and yellowed pages. And then it hit him. The description of the executed man, the mark on his forehead; the tattoo, Kettle had called it.

He reached for volume G, and his hand trembled slightly as he removed it. He opened it up to *Golem*.

Yes, that was exactly what Kettle's story had brought to mind. But that was ridiculous. A golem was from Jewish tradition. It was made to be used for protection, or to perform certain tasks, and then it was put back to rest. Stories sometimes referred to one golem, an eternal being made of mud or clay, while other stories said there could be many golems, that it could be made by any number of people with the skill and the magic.

Magic? Jesus, what was he thinking? A chill slipped over Bernard's body. According to the story Kettle had heard, the unnamed thing had been found inside a wall, a synagogue wall, and it had been stolen by a rabbi and a helper. They had been killed, and the thing went missing. Could it have been an actual golem, maybe brought over from the old country, or built in modern times, and then put away until it was needed? Could knowledge of its existence have been passed down from rabbi to rabbi? Could it have been brought to life to perform a task, perhaps to wreak vengeance on someone, as it was often used in the legends?

If so, why had it not performed? Perhaps the knowledge the thieves had of the golem was flawed, and something in the process of bringing it to life went wrong. Bernard studied the encyclopedia more carefully. It was said that the golem could be brought to life by writing a certain word on its forehead. *Emet*. Which the old text said was the ancient word for truth. The word it showed in the dictionary, the way it was printed out, it looked very much like the word

Kettle had drawn crudely on the paper downstairs. The way he had drawn it, the letters looked more like symbols, but now that Bernard could examine the word, he recognized it as essentially the same.

The article also stated that to rid yourself of the golem, you had to remove the word on its forehead.

Bernard gave himself a shake. He was being ridiculous; maybe touched by that little bit of Scotch he had tasted. The story Kettle had told them was ludicrous. Toggle had been right. The old man was yarning them, at least mostly, had to be. Probably he had read about the golem, and the big prisoner fit his idea of it, so what a fine way to combine truth and legend and tell a good story. He probably laughed the whole boat trip home, knowing even Toggle had been taken in by it, if only for a moment.

Bernard kicked off his shoes and climbed into bed with his clothes on. He began to read the article more closely, but he had only gotten started when he heard something odd on the wind. A kind of howl, like a wolf, maybe. But there were no wolves on the island. No real wildlife other than birds, a seal now and then, lizards, things of that nature.

Could it have been the wind? A growl of the tossing sea?

But another thought kept coming back to him.

"Oh, come on," he said to himself. "Don't be a nitwit."

Maybe it was Toggle. Perhaps the drunk bastard had run the loader off into the sea by now. That would be about right. The loader was gone, and Toggle was swimming for it, calling out for help.

But it damn sure didn't sound like Toggle—and for that matter, it didn't sound human.

It was most likely nothing but the wind, and he was worrying for no reason at all, other than being a bit worked up over Kettle's story. For the hell of it he got up and tried the phone that connected to the prison island. He had a sudden urge to want to be connected. They didn't like surprises or simple phone visits, but he could claim he was worried about the storm, ask them for weather information. That just might fly.

Dead. No signal. That damn phone died easy, so that was no surprise. If the wind picked up or there was a strong rain, the line was affected. He had no idea how, but that was the long and the short of it. There wasn't even a hum on the line. The phone was just flat dead as the original Christian. It was probably best. A phone call would have done nothing more than piss them off. What the hell was he thinking, calling for a weather report?

Bernard went back to the window and opened it up and looked out. The front-end loader was still partially visible down by the big tree. Toggle had not driven it off into the water. He closed the window, slipped on his shoes, pulled his rain slicker on, grabbed his flashlight, and headed out, down the squeaking stairs. He decided he'd get Wilson for backup. He might need him if Toggle was hurt.

He paused when he came to the bulldozer in the dog run. He put his hand on the dozer. Something about touching that cool metal connected him with reality. He was thinking some pretty crazy thoughts. The dozer was real. Made of metal and plastic, state-of-the-art, able to spin about and go in any direction without actually turning, though it could do that too. The treads flexed easily and were mounted. It had a wheelhouse encased in thick plastic that served as windshields. It was a tough machine. There probably wasn't another dozer like this one anywhere else in the world. He patted it again. Yeah. It was real. A golem wasn't real, and in that moment he felt stupid for thinking such a thing and almost turned around and climbed back up the stairs. But then he heard that howl again, and even with his hand on that firm metal he felt what prehistoric man had felt when he heard a sound in the dark, something that sounded strange and inexplicable. The hair on his neck stood up. He felt fear.

He shook it off. Toggle was out there. Toggle worked for him. It was his job to take care of him and Wilson. He had to go check, like it or not. The door was still open wide, waiting for the loader, and the rain was coming down hard out there, but he had no choice as far as he saw it. He had to go out there and see if Toggle was all right. He could have fallen and broken a leg.

Bernard edged his way around the bulldozer, stopped at the boy's door and knocked.

Wilson took a long time answering. He opened the door wearing only boxer shorts. He looked like death warmed over.

"Did you hear that howl?"

"Howl?"

"Kind of like a wolf?"

"We don't have any wolves here."

"No. We don't."

Wilson studied Bernard. "What's the deal, man? I was about to hit the sack. I just finished a super shit and it kind of sobered me up. Can you imagine that, shit so hard it shits you sober?"

Wilson's face changed as he studied Bernard. He wasn't in the least interested in his bathroom event. "So, okay. What's up?"

"I'm worried about Toggle, thought I'd go check on him. I was going to ask you to come, but frankly, you don't look up to it. Hell, it's probably just me being goofy, the storm and all."

"I'm a bit stir-fried, all right, but hang on."

Wilson stumbled back inside his room, and Bernard waited outside the door. After a few minutes Wilson appeared, dressed and wearing his rain slicker, carrying a flashlight. He did in fact look sober, just beat down by the liquor.

"I feel like hell," he said.

"I said you could stay."

"Naw, it's all right."

They went out and Bernard decided to close the metal door and lock it. They started along the walkway, past the garden, which was being whipped by the wind.

"Looks like tomorrow I'll have some work to do," Wilson said.

"I can help. I'm the boss, but I can help."

"It's all right," Wilson said. "I like it better here when I have something to do. You're thinking Toggle might be drunk, aren't you?"

"Crossed my mind."

"Well, I was kidding about being shit sober. I'm not stone drunk, but I got a few pebbles. So why wouldn't he be drunk? That was some Scotch, and my guess is he's got some more to suck on."

"My thought. For Toggle to get seriously drunk, he needs a lot of alcohol. He can hold it pretty good. That's why I'm worried. He either got into more of it, or something went wrong. He wouldn't have any reason to stay out here in the storm if he wasn't drunk."

And it had become quite a storm, if not of hurricane proportions. Bernard found he had to shout so he could be heard; the wind grabbed his words and sucked them up and took them away.

As they continued, sweeping their lights before them, they could clearly see the tree by the dock had been knocked over. It had been standing not too long ago, when Bernard last looked out the window. This had just occurred.

The tree's long roots writhed in the wind, shaking dirt from them and blowing it away. The loader sat silently behind the fallen tree, like some kind of dark-orange dinosaur.

"Damn," Wilson said. "I loved that tree."

"You and me both," Bernard said.

"That was some wind," Wilson said.

"It's windy," Bernard said. "But it's not that windy. Not yet. It's coming, but not yet."

"Yeah, well it must have been a freak blow that come through, cause there's the tree, lying on its side. It didn't just fall over. Not that big guy."

Bernard didn't reply to that, because he was actually thinking the same thing. They made their way to the loader. It was a pretty good-sized machine and the wind hadn't moved it. But then again, had the wind really pushed over that big-ass tree? Bernard took the two steps to the cab, slid the door open and looked inside. He danced his light around in there.

Nothing. Just a musty smell. "Hey," Wilson called out.

Bernard climbed out of the loader, closed the cab door and went down to join Wilson.

Wilson was holding Toggle's tobacco pouch in his hand. "It's full, and Toggle doesn't litter. None of us do."

Bernard looked about.

"He has to be here somewhere."

"Yeah, but where?"

Wilson shook his head, turned around, glanced along the length of the fallen tree. He turned his head slightly, poked his light in the direction he was looking. "What's that?"

"What's what?"

"That, in the branches of the tree. In the light."

Bernard still didn't see anything. Wilson started forward and Bernard followed.

"Looks like ropes," Wilson said, and now Bernard saw it. Twists of ropes or vines in the broken boughs of the tree.

Wilson pushed through the broken limbs, the ones still attached to the tree, grabbed one. "That's not rope."

He pulled his hand back and put the flashlight on it. "Oh goddamn Jesus on a ass-fucked pony."

Bernard slid up and put his light on Wilson's hand.

It was covered in blood and the rain was washing it away.

Bernard moved closer to the ropes, flashed light on them, bent forward for a closer look. They had a smell. The wind and rain was carrying some of it away, but the smell was of blood and...shit.

"It's intestines," Bernard said. "What the hell?"

"The goddamn tree must have fallen on him."

"Toggle?"

"No, Elvis Presley. Of course Toggle."

"Shit, shit, shit."

"Jesus Christ," Bernard said, and then he and Wilson went back and forth cursing and swearing.

"What a fucked up piece of luck," Wilson said. "Where's...the rest of him?"

They moved along the tree and shined their lights into its branches and found his head. It was on the ground, between two limbs. And nearby was a leg.

Bernard bent down close and put the light on Toggle's head. The man's eyes were wide and his mouth was thrown open and his tongue was swollen and fat and marked with a wound, as if, in the moments before he threw his mouth open, he had bitten his tongue. The mouth was filled with rain water and blood. Pieces of flesh and a fragment of spinal cord dangled from where the neck had been.

"His leg," Wilson said. "When the tree fell, it must have jerked it out of its socket, jerked it right off of him."

"The head too? What are the odds?"

"Pretty rare, I'd say."

"Yeah," Bernard said. "I don't think it could happen like that."

"But it did."

Bernard moved the light away from the tree. He saw marks on the ground. "What's this?"

Wilson put his light on it. It was a big mark. A big shoe mark. "That is one big footprint," Wilson said. "A boot."

"Yeah. But that isn't Toggle's print. Those feet, they would have to belong to Bigfoot."

"A mutant Bigfoot. Hell, Bernard. Those feet, they got to be eighteen inches. Who or what the fuck has eighteen-inch feet?"

"The golem," Bernard said.

"What?"

"Nothing. Thinking out loud. Come on."

"We got to get the body."

"We will. Come on, and watch yourself."

"Hey, man, you're creeping me out."

Bernard made his way to the grave they had prepared. Some of the dirt was gone; there was a gap in the ground where something had pushed its way through from inside. It was a large gap. They could also see the coffin, and they could see inside it, the part near where the head should be. The coffin was knocked open as if by a battering ram. There were bits of cloth from the bags used for burial, and there were bits of orange jumpsuit, the kind convicts wore. The chains were broken and lying loose in the grave.

"Damn, man," Wilson said. "I got to still be drunk, drunker than I thought."

"Trust me, I'm not drunk and I'm seeing the same thing you are."

"Just so I got it straight, what you're thinking is what I'm thinking, and that's that whoever…whatever…was inside the coffin has knocked its way loose, climbed through hundreds of pounds of dirt, come out of the ground and killed Toggle."

"I think Toggle tried to get away from it. Climbed the tree. And this thing, it pushed the tree over and got Toggle."

"That's insane."

"It is," Bernard said. "But I'm still thinking it."

Wilson flashed the light around, first one direction, then the other.

"That means it's out here somewhere."

"Yeah."

"You said a word earlier, then said 'forget it.'"

"Golem."

"Yeah, what's that? Is that this thing?"

"I don't know; maybe."

"What do we do, man? I mean, we can't swim to the big island, and we got no boat, so what do we do? Something like this, I don't want to deal with it. They couldn't kill it with four jolts of electricity and a plastic bag over its head. It knocked its way loose of a coffin, busted some chains, dug its way out of six feet of dirt or thereabouts, pushed a fucking tree over, pulled Toggle's guts out, and then this… golem, yanked off his leg and head. Motherfucker."

"Keep calm."

"Oh," Wilson said. "Now there's some good advice."

"And maybe we should be quieter."

Wilson swallowed heavily. "Yeah. Ten-four on that."

"Best bet is to head back to Island Keep. It's concrete. It has steel doors. It locks tight."

"Yeah. Yeah, that's good. But shit, how can this be. That story Kettle was telling. I don't get it. I mean, that can't be. Can it?"

"I think it's true," Bernard said.

Bernard felt as if the walk back to the compound took about a month, and now and again he'd see what he thought was a shape in the shadows, but where he flashed the light there was nothing. Still, he thought he heard something big shuffling along with them, just out of sight, deep in shadow. But no matter when he flashed the light, nothing was there. He was starting to spook.

The lights of Island Keep, those that fanned out from the top of the shed, were warm and inviting. They finally reached the metal door, and as they were about to slide it back, Wilson said, "Company."

Wilson's voice had been weak. He pointed. Bernard looked. Something was visible, some kind of hulking shape, there in the shadows amongst the trees that were bunched up near Island Keep. It was visible at the edge of the pooling lights emanating from the roof of the building.

They both put their flashlights on it.

It was a big shape, maybe seven feet tall and five feet wide, built like rocks stacked together, but there was no doubt it was something other than shadows or a natural outcrop of rock or trees. Nothing had been there earlier, and now it was, and it hadn't blown in with the storm. It was a shape among the surrounding trees, a hunk of solid darkness, and then it moved, took one plodding step forward, and stopped.

"Stay calm," Bernard said.

"I don't think I can do that," Wilson said.

It took another step, further out of the shadows and into the pools of light, into the beams of their flashlights. It was huge and bulky and its head sat neckless and firm on wide shoulders and the plastic bag, torn and stained with dirt, was still over its head. Parts of the thing could be seen through tears in the orange jumpsuit. It looked to Bernard as if someone had mixed shit and mud and everything nasty, and made this thing. It looked somewhat like a man, moved somewhat like a man, but it wasn't in Bernard's mind anything that could be confused with a man. Kettle had actually underplayed its unearthly appearance. Even though it was partially standing in the light now, Bernard could not see its eyes. Its brows were heavy and its eyes were hooded, shadows lying across them like the visor of a cap—and there was the dirty plastic bag. Its nose was a mound, and its ears were nearly flat against the sides of its head. Its mouth was wide, as if it had been made by a knife-slash. Its lips were dark and long and thin.

Bernard reached over slowly and clutched the handle on the door, tugged, slid it open about three feet. Wilson, as if he were liquid rushing down a funnel, flowed inside. Bernard hurried behind him, pausing to study the shape from the crack of the door. It had not moved since that last step. It stared at him with shadowed eyes, as if locking his image into his head. Inside, Bernard pulled the steel door shut and threw the lock.

"That's six inches of steel," Bernard said. "It seems suddenly kind of thin."

"Yeah. Don't it?"

Without really thinking about it, they found themselves backing up against the bulldozer blade.

"What's a golem?" Wilson asked. "And maybe I don't want to know."

Bernard gave him a short rundown.

"Okay, which one of us is going to take a wash rag and wipe that shit off its forehead?" Wilson said.

"I don't think that would do it."

"No shit. I don't think a rocket launcher would do it. Did you see the size of that thing?"

"I think it's gone mad. Sometimes they do; that's what the article said. They have been known to go berserk and run away from their masters and cause mischief."

"That would be our guy? Mischief would be correct, if understated. Wait a minute, you read this in an article? Not in the back of a comic book or anything, right?"

"Encyclopedia."

"That only kicks it up a notch. I mean, we're talking about something that can't be killed."

"You saw it," Bernard said.

"Yeah. Or at least I think I did. I'm having doubts now."

"According to the legends, it can be killed. It's the how that varies."

"Yeah, that whole wiping-its-forehead-clean doesn't resonate with me all that well. Electricity. They killed it before with electricity. We got any way to do that?"

"They may have stunned it, but that's all they did. The plastic bag, they couldn't steal the breath of something that didn't breathe. That was nothing. It never was alive, not in the way we think of life. But it's not what you would call dead either."

"Right now stunning it is sounding pretty good," Wilson said. "Shit. I'm still wrapping my head around this."

"There's no wrapping your head around it. The golem, it's made of mud and is given life through a spell."

"Magic?"

"In the way we understand it," Bernard said. "It could be something we just don't understand and call magic."

"That doesn't help me feel any better, knowing it might not be magic as we understand it."

"Son, I got no idea. All I know is, that prison island, it has some of the worst of the worst, and Kettle was always saying how the prisoners in there weren't your normal sort of bad, but were something else. That means there can be all manner of shit over there. If there's a golem, why not a werewolf, a vampire and a unicorn? It's more unique than I thought. I mean, like you, I saw an execution, and it did the work, got that person dead, but this thing—"

There was a pounding at the door. Bernard and Wilson startled.

"Shit pie," Wilson said. The door had dents in it.

"That door might as well be aluminum foil," Wilson said.

"It's bent, but it hasn't broken."

"Yeah, you want to wait and see if he can break through?"

"Not really. But if we go upstairs we'll be trapped like rats."

The pounding grew louder. The metal door was pocked all over.

"We'll slip out the back," Bernard said, and his voice sounded weak, almost girlish.

"What then?"

"Good point... Wait a minute," Bernard said. "We got our own golem. The bulldozer."

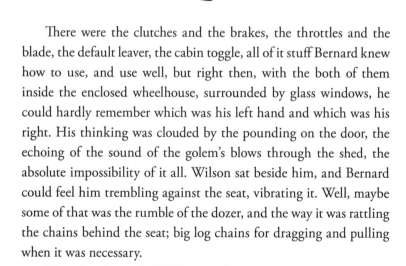

There were the clutches and the brakes, the throttles and the blade, the default leaver, the cabin toggle, all of it stuff Bernard knew how to use, and use well, but right then, with the both of them inside the enclosed wheelhouse, surrounded by glass windows, he could hardly remember which was his left hand and which was his right. His thinking was clouded by the pounding on the door, the echoing of the sound of the golem's blows through the shed, the absolute impossibility of it all. Wilson sat beside him, and Bernard could feel him trembling against the seat, vibrating it. Well, maybe some of that was the rumble of the dozer, and the way it was rattling the chains behind the seat; big log chains for dragging and pulling when it was necessary.

"So, what do we do?" Wilson said.

"Well," Bernard said, "we're not going to sit here."

There were rents in the steel door now, and fingers like great, dark tree roots were poking through the gaps. After a moment, Bernard thought he saw a face against one of the gaps. He hit the lights on the dozer and the shed lit up like a nightclub act. In the light he could see a big black eye looking in at them through the gap. Kettle had been wrong about them looking like olives. They looked like charred stones.

"Let's see which manmade machine is the strongest," Bernard said.

He worked the clutches and the throttle, and the bulldozer lurched a little, smoked slightly, the smell of an abused clutch stinking up the air.

"I got it," Bernard said. "I know how. It's been awhile and I'm scared. But I know how."

"I can drive the loader, not this; least not well. That was Toggle's bailiwick. So you got to do it," Wilson said.

"I taught Toggle and you, but now I don't remember shit."

Then all of a sudden, it came back to him, like riding a bicycle, and he got the rhythm of the clutches, lifted the blade and gave the dozer the gas. The machine lurched forward, gained speed, hit the metal door like a missile, ripping it off its great hinges, pushing the blade forward against the door and the golem behind it.

It was like striking a mountain.

Bernard gave it all he had. The dozer screeched. The blade rocked. The smell of burning clutch filled the air.

The treads flopped, and for a moment Bernard thought he might throw one of the tracks, but then the dozer grabbed the concrete floor, ground down and lunged forward. The door came all the way loose and the dozer blade pushed the door over the golem, knocking it down, driving it into the soft dirt outside of the concrete flooring. The dozer went over the hump that was the golem under the steel, rattled and rolled forward.

Bernard kept the dozer rolling. Wilson turned back for a look.

"The door's moving. Being thrown aside. Oh, my god. It's standing up. Worse. It's coming."

Bernard turned sharply and wheeled right into the Garden of Gethsemane, smashing down trellises and twists of vines, continued crunching over fat tomatoes and mounds of cucumbers, swollen flowers and bristling shrubs.

"Sorry," Bernard said.

"Least of our worries."

"Is it still coming?"

Wilson looked back. "Yes. And for a thing that big, quite briskly, I might add."

"Well, let me see if I can open this baby up a little."

Bernard worked the controls, gave it more fuel, and surprisingly, it did have some get-up in it. The dozer began to pick up speed, and then suddenly Bernard brought it to an abrupt stop.

"What are you doing?" Wilson said.

"Turning."

Swiveling, actually. The dozer wheelhouse turned on its swivel. The front became the rear. The tracks dug in. They were now facing the golem. The lights shone on it. It was coming toward them, and though it was moving pretty fast, it seemed to be loping there in the strong, orange light of the dozer. There was an illusion of everything being slow, like a fat bug struggling in amber. It moved without effort, swinging its giant arms, its legs reaching out with those gigantic feet, splashing in the wet puddles the rain had made. And there was the wind and the rain whistling against the windshield of the dozer, rattling the glass.

"Brace yourself," Bernard said.

"Isn't that what the Irishman tells his wife on their wedding night?" Wilson said. It was an obvious attempt at levity, but it landed cold as an ice cube down the collar.

"I think it is," Bernard said.

He moved the controls. The dozer jumped forward.

Bernard lowered the blade, kept it off the ground, but had it where he could see above it, see the head of the golem growing in size as it came near, as the two juggernauts rushed to meet.

They hit.

The dozer shook and slid back, then gained traction and inched forward. A large hand appeared at the edge of the blade. Then another, and then the golem's head. It had taken quite a lick, and the head was slightly warped from where it had taken the blade's impact. The etching on its forehead was faintly visible in the dozer's cabin light.

The golem started to pull itself over the blade, the plastic bag now a plastic rag clinging to the side of its head. Bernard lifted the blade rapidly and slammed it down, hoping to catch some part of the golem with the edge of it. If he did, he couldn't tell. The golem clung to the blade like a leech to a wound. The remains of the plastic bag shot up into the air and floated down.

The dozer was still rolling forward, and now they were nearing the compound. Bernard gave it all he had, kept slashing the blade up and down, giving it the angles it would allow, trying to throw their rider loose. Nothing worked. It clung.

And then they smashed against the wall of the compound hard, pinning the golem between blade and concrete. The impact threw Wilson backwards over the seat, the heels of his work boots cracking the rear glass. Bernard was knocked loose from the controls, but he quickly reclaimed them. Wilson tumbled back into place in the seat beside him. Blood ran down his face.

"You okay?" Bernard said.

"Think I broke my nose."

The lights from the front of the dozer bounced and shadowed against the wall. Bernard kept the throttle hot, kept pushing forward. The clutch was stinking to high heaven. Bernard figured much more of this and it was going to blow.

And then the dozer moved. But not at Bernard's command.

It was gradually being shoved back from the wall. Bernard was doing all he could to drive it forward, and it was being shoved back.

"What the fuck?" Wilson said.

"It's moving us backwards, and I'm giving it all we got."

"It can't do that," Wilson said.

But it could, and it was. The golem was pushing the dozer away from it, had dug in its heels and put out its arms and was shoving it away from the wall.

Bernard swiveled the cabin, reversing it so he could run the dozer in the opposite direction. He shifted gears, worked the smoking clutch, and lumbered forward. When he swung it around, the blade swung too, scraping the golem along the wall with a smear of gray mud or flesh, or whatever it was that it was made of, and this time Bernard was successful in tearing the monster loose from the blade. Bernard gave the dozer the juice, plunged it forward into the night.

Wilson looked back. The golem had been knocked to the ground. Yet, beyond all that was possible, it was rising to its feet.

"Now that there is some shit," Wilson said. "That's what I'm trying to tell you. It's like the goddamn Frankenstein monster."

"In a way, that's what it is," Bernard said, and geared the dozer toward a not-too-distant gap of shadow, a split in a dense growth of trees near the edge of the island, near The Big Drop.

Bernard drove them to the gap and through it, swerved to the right along the edge of the trees and cut the lights on the dozer.

"I don't like this," Wilson said.

Bernard could feel a fresh chill racing up his spine. This whole night had been a succession of chills, but now he was driving a dozer full out in the dead dark not far from The Big Drop, and behind them, out there somewhere, was a thing that couldn't be, but was.

"Maybe we'll be harder for it to see," Bernard said.

"And maybe we'll go right over The Big Drop," Wilson said. "Jesus, Bernard, I don't know."

"I know this place pretty well," Bernard. "My eyes are adjusting. To the right, the big trees, to the left, The Big Drop. But we got plenty of space between them. As long as we don't miss the curve."

"That's not comforting."

"There's a big curve coming up."

"I know it. You know I know that. I mean, I know there's a curve. Shit, man. I can't see a thing."

"I've been here longer than you. I know it by instinct."

Wilson turned in his seat and looked back. "If it's coming, I can't see it. Maybe we lost it. Maybe it gave up."

"I don't think it gives up," Bernard said. "I think it's a killing machine and it's been set loose, and now it's going to kill until there's nothing left to kill."

"That would be funny. Kettle brings the supplies and that thing is waiting on the dock for him with one of our legs. Well, not that funny."

"No. Not that funny."

"Damn, Toggle climbed a tree and the thing pushed over the tree and got him. Listen here, it looks like it's going to get us, I'm going over that cliff. I'd rather die that way than being pulled apart by some guy made of...what did you say?"

"Mud. Earth. It had been stored inside that wall for a long time. Probably brought over from the Old Country, and someone knew it was there, the rabbi, and he decided to free it, animated it. For what reason, it's doubtful anyone will ever know, but he did, and things didn't go well."

"I'll say. Jesus, can't we turn on the lights, Bernard?"

"Not yet." Bernard turned the dozer sharply for a machine its size, directed it into the shadows. Bernard felt reasonably confident he knew what he was doing, where he was. But only reasonably confident, not certain.

They didn't bang into anything or go off into a gully, fall over the edge into the bottomless ocean. They eased in-between dark rows of shrubs, and then behind a wall of trees, and Bernard cut the engine.

"I think I'm more frightened that we aren't moving," Wilson said.

"Keep your voice down."

Bernard opened the dozer's door on his side and climbed out, shut it gently. Wilson did the same on the passenger's side. Bernard moved through the split in the trees, walking back the way they had came. Wilson caught up with him, obviously not wishing to be left alone.

They came to where the trees broke and stood where the dozer had come. There was a small clutch of low trees along the edge of the taller ones, and they stood behind that, and peered through its branches.

The wind had slowed and the rain had ceased, and even as they stood there, the moon leaked out from behind some clouds that rolled away, oddly oily and silver-looking as they went. The moonlight lay on the edge of the cliff some three hundred yards away, light as a feather, the steam from the rain rising upwards from the edge of the cliff like steam off a cup of hot coffee on a cold morning. And as they stood there, they saw, walking slowly, no longer running, the golem.

It was walking along the edge of The Big Drop, looking down. There was something about the way it moved that reminded Bernard of how he felt those times he had looked down and considered the fall, thought he might throw himself down into oblivion. Could the golem be thinking such a thing? Could it be thinking anything? Certainly it had some sort of mind, even if it was nothing more than that of destructive juggernaut.

As they watched, it clutched at the ragged and ripped jumpsuit, and tore it from its body with a grunting sound. A few moves and it was unclothed. Even there from a distance, in the light, they could see its penis and testicles hanging limp and dark, a rough facsimile of human sexuality. Slowly, it lifted its head to the cloud-touched moon, and that howl, that dreadful howl, that sound that uncoiled from inside the golem, came out. It was both frightening and depressing. It was like the howl of something or someone that had just realized it was missing something important, and that the lack of it was an awareness so dark and deep there was no crawling out of it. It was a sound that made Bernard feel all the evil in the world, all the futility and disappointment of life, of his own life. It was a howl that reached down deep inside of him and touched a hidden nerve so buried, causing it to throb. Bernard felt that his life and all the lives that were being lived, had lived or would be lived were nothing more than desperation personified.

The howl crawled out of the golem's chest, rose to the sky, and seemed to fill it. Bernard had the illusion that the moon quivered. But it was he who quivered. He felt so empty. Felt as if he were filled with empty. How could that be? How could you be filled with emptiness? It was an odd impression of being so fully empty as to be a void, yet the void had weight and awareness. Contradictory feelings, for sure, and strange, and in that moment Bernard felt so damn sorry for the golem. Not so sorry he wished it well, a spot on the beach with an umbrella and a paperback, but so sorry he wished it dead, for that howl seemed to request it, a quick death, a release from that dreadful, spiritless form that had been made for one sole purpose: destruction.

The howl seemed to last forever, and then slowly the golem lowered its head, and even more slowly it turned its head in their direction, and let its gaze settle there. Its head very slowly shifted to one side. Then to the other.

"It's too dark for him to see us, right?" Wilson said.

"It's an *it*, and it sees us, dark or no dark. Run, Wilson."

The golem started to trot. Bernard and Wilson made a dash back to the dozer. Their moment of relief had been brief, and Bernard cursed himself for his curiosity. They should have stayed back at the dozer. But no sooner had he thought that, he knew he was wrong. It wouldn't have mattered. The golem was going to find them. There was no way to avoid it, on this island, in the city, wherever. Once it latched its intent on you, it would stay after you until it was satisfied. Then a new victim, or victims, would fall into its path, and the cycle would continue.

Bernard and Wilson scrambled into the dozer. Bernard said, "You ever play cowboy?"

"What?"

"Ever roped a cow?"

"Of course not. But if you would like to take the time to explain it to me, nothing would please me more, except for that whole giant, bad-ass monster shit."

"Get the chain, make a loop. You're going to rope it."

Bernard had already started the dozer when Wilson reached behind the seat and pulled out the heavy chain. It was about twenty feet of chain, and it took considerable effort to pull it over the back of the seat and have it end up coiled in the floorboard, except for one end, which he held.

"Make a loop with a slipknot. There's a padlock in the glove box. Take it out and clamp it so the chain won't slip, but the knot will."

Wilson fumbled about with the chain. His fingers seemed about as useful for the job as sausages.

"This might be your worst idea," Wilson said.

The dozer was heading back in the direction of the golem, the lights were on and bright and just waiting for the golem to appear in their glow.

"Wrong fucking way."

Bernard ignored him. "When I get right on top of him, I'm going to stop and spin the wheelhouse, and you're going to be at the back of it, and when he starts climbing up to rip our heads off, you're going to throw that chain over his body, and you'll need a big loop for that."

"Why don't I just do some rope tricks with it first?"

"That's your choice," Bernard said, "but I don't recommend it."

"Shit, shit, *shit*," Wilson said.

The dozer bumped along on its tracks, and then there was the golem, running steadily toward them on untiring legs.

Bernard kicked the dozer up a notch. Wilson opened the sliding back window, dragged the chain up to it and put one foot outside on the carriage.

"You might want to fasten the chain to the undercarriage of the seat," Bernard said.

"Oh," Wilson said. He bent down and went at it, trying to link it up underneath the seat.

"You got it? Tell me you got it."

"I don't got it."

That's when the golem and the blade of the dozer collided. Bernard had raised it high, and now as they came together, he dropped the blade to the ground and scooped the golem, knocked it down. It was one good blow for the good guys, thought Bernard. Well, the better guys.

"It's hooked," Wilson said.

"All right; when he stands I'm going to swivel it. Hell, there he is."

The golem had in fact stood up, and as he did, Bernard raised the blade as if for another strike, but hit the toggle switch and the dozer spun its wheelhouse so fast it nearly threw Wilson loose.

Wilson braced his feet, and with the golem climbing up the back of the dozer, Wilson threw the loop of chain. It was heavy, and he knew the minute he let it go that he was fucked, that it wasn't going to work. But he was only partly right.

The chain didn't fit over the golem completely. It went over its head, and over one arm, and cinched up in its armpit as Bernard jumped the dozer forward in a way Wilson didn't think could be done; it sort of bunny-hopped on its treads, and when it did, the golem fell backwards and the chain cinched up. Bernard clutched and geared and throttled, and the dozer began to move away fast, dragging the golem after it.

Bernard wheeled the dozer to the left, made a wide turn, swinging the chain and golem into a small tree, smacking the tree hard enough it sagged from the blow. As they rode away in the dozer, dragging the golem behind it, heading back through the gap toward The Big Drop, the tree cracked even louder and fell, clipping the golem and striking the back of the dozer. A limb from the tree drove through the back glass and shattered it and knocked Wilson onto the floor board.

From that vantage point, Wilson said, "The chain—it's slipping."

"No," said Bernard, "it's the seat."

At that moment Bernard stood up, and the seat was jerked out from under him through the back of the dozer, blowing out what glass was left, bending the frame that held the glass. But the seat lodged against the frame and held.

Bernard was fighting the controls now. The dozer wasn't meant to be driven while standing. They broke out of the shadows of the trees and into the moonlight, bearing down on the cliff.

Wilson had managed to get his feet under him and was hanging onto the dash. He said, "You *are* going to turn, right?"

"No," Bernard said. "We're going to jump."

"Shit, man! I don't want to jump."

"Get ready," Bernard said and unlatched the door on his side, slid it open.

"I don't want to jump," Wilson said.

"One," said Bernard.

"What part of *I don't want to jump* do you not get?"

"Two."

"Shit." Wilson swung his door open.

"Three."

Wilson jumped. He landed pretty wide, but the golem was swinging on the chain, and it swung toward him. He didn't have time to get up. The golem missed him, though its arm reached out for him. The chain didn't miss. It caught Wilson along the shoulder, side and hip, lifted him painfully into the air.

Wilson rolled on his side, glanced at the dozer. Bernard was still in the wheelhouse.

"Jump!" Wilson screamed.

The dozer reached the edge of the cliff and the blade tilted down, and Bernard jumped out of the dozer. Wilson had seen him jump, but from his angle he didn't see him land. The dozer kept going, nodding on the edge of the cliff, and then it went over and the chain jerked along the ground and the golem jerked with it, was rolled over on its stomach. The golem clamped its fingers into the dirt, making grooves in the soil as it went, and then it was at the edge of the cliff, and its fingers caught hold there, and then...*Jesus*, thought Wilson. *Unh-unh.* The golem was hanging there firm, even with the chain around it and the dozer tugging at it. It reached one arm way up, to gain a better hold. Wilson saw Bernard. He had made the jump successfully. He was up and limping toward the golem.

Bernard limped to where the golem struggled. He grabbed hold of a huge rock at the edge of the cliff. He could hardly lift it. He felt his spine strain and his testicles swell as he boosted it to his chest, then dropped it on the golem's head. The golem lost its grip, perhaps because of the blow, but just as likely due to the weight of the dozer pulling it loose of its hold on the cliff's edge. Bernard watched as the weight of the dozer dragged it down toward the ocean. Bernard let out a little laugh of triumph.

"Motherfucker," he said, and then his leg wouldn't hold him. Damn; it was broken. It had finally snapped all the way. Had he not been so high on adrenaline and fear he wouldn't have been able to stand at all, and the pain would have been unbearable. *But, hey*, he thought, *I still have the pain coming, and I have that to look forward to.* He lay on his stomach at the edge of the cliff, watched as the dozer hit the waves below and foamed them white as it disappeared beneath them, yanking the golem on the chain after it.

Wilson came jogging up then. "Did we get him?"

"Yeah," Bernard said. "We got him."

"Good. I never doubted it for a moment."

"That right?"

"Well, a moment here and there, but all's well that ends well."

"Listen, you have to go get the front-end loader. My leg's broken."

"Shit."

"Yeah," Bernard said. "Get it and take me back to Island Keep. You're going to have to set it."

"I don't know how."

"You didn't know how to play cowboy either, but you did."

"Yeah. I did, didn't I. Okay. Wait here."

"You can count on that," Bernard said. Wilson trotted off.

Bernard edged to the cliff again, looked down at the water. He thought about the golem. It was deep there, and dark, and down he would go, and that should be the end of it, chained to that goddamn bulldozer beneath the waves.

He felt the excitement start to drain. Relaxation came first, and then the pain. He lay there for a long time feeling it, gradually feeling worse and worse, and then he looked over the edge of The Big Drop and saw something impossible.

The head of the golem rose out of the stormy waters and its arms clawed at the slick wall, clawed hard, somehow taking purchase on the stone. Bernard actually shook his head, thinking he might be having some kind of delusion brought on by fear and pain.

But nope. He was seeing what he was seeing. The golem was climbing up the side of The Big Drop by grinding its fingertips into the rock wall. It was a slow ascent, and impossible, but yet, it came. The chain was still wrapped around it, shedding water in great moon-lit droplets. And following the chain was the dozer, banging against the cliff wall like a child's toy. Bernard knew the dozer weighed over ten thousand pounds. The golem had swum up from the bottom and tugged the dozer after it. He felt like Wilson now. It couldn't do that. It just couldn't.

Yet the golem was pulling itself and the dozer out of the water with the effort it would have taken him to drag a bicycle uphill.

Bernard tried to stand, but couldn't. His leg was dead, limp as a wet noodle. He thought about crawling away, but there was no future in that. As slowly as the golem was climbing, he wouldn't even make the edge of the woods by the time it reached the summit of the cliff.

It was then he heard the front-end loader crunching over the rocky soil, the roar of its motor. Bernard rolled over and saw the loader's lights.

Wilson parked the loader, left the lights on, got out and walked briskly to Bernard.

Bernard said, "Take a look," and dropped his hand over the edge.

Wilson took a look, and as he did, Bernard looked up and saw Wilson's face go white as the moon.

"Oh, hell," Wilson said. "We got to hustle."

"And go where?"

"The compound."

"It'll come there. It's just a matter of time."

"Hey, I live by the minute, don't you? Come on."

"You have to finish it."

"Me?" Wilson said. "What am I going to do? Give it a lecture? No, man, I got nothing to say to that thing. I got nothing I can do. You're coming with me." Wilson reached down to pull Bernard up.

"No. Listen to me. Its forehead. The mark there. You have to scrape it off."

"So it climbs up, I take a pocket knife to its head, scrape off the symbol and we're done. Is that your plan? So far your plans haven't worked out quite as well as we hoped. And this one, man, it's the worst of the bunch."

"You're pretty good with the loader, right?"

"I'm not Toggle. I'm not you. And who gives a shit? I'm not taking a driving test. Is your head broken too?"

Bernard glanced over the edge of the cliff. The golem was steadily coming, digging its fingers into the rock as if it was made of plaster.

"Listen, son. My leg won't let me work the controls the way it's needed. You drove it here without a problem, and you can use the lift and the bucket pretty well, and you can put it where you want it. I've seen you. You're going to have to tilt the bucket, use the edge to scrape off the word on his head."

"I don't like that idea. That sucks. Seriously."

"I think you just mess up the word a little, and we're good."

"You think?"

"Wilson, it's all we got. That's it. We're just prolonging the inevitable if we go back to Island Keep."

"Prolonging the inevitable was my plan all along."

"When it comes to the lip of the cliff, you have to be ready."

"Oh, man. I just wanted to finish out my term in peace, make a garden." Wilson leaned a little, glanced down. "Oh, good."

Bernard checked below. The seat attached to the chain was starting to pivot and slide through the broken window of the dozer. As they watched, it snapped free, and the dozer plunged back into the ocean with a splash and a swell of waves. It was gone in an instant. The seat swung wide on the chain, then back and forth like a pendulum.

The golem, dragging chain and dozer seat, climbed faster.

🌱

Wilson dragged Bernard toward the loader, pulled him up so Bernard could get his hands on the machine; that way he could help Wilson push him up and into the seat. When Bernard painfully found his position, Wilson climbed up.

"I can cue you if you need it, but you can do it," Bernard said. "You know how. You got this."

"Fuck, fuck, fuck," Wilson said.

"Just take it easy," Bernard said.

"*You* say."

Wilson took the controls, eased the machine forward, hopping a little at his touch. "Nervous," Wilson said.

"No hurry," Bernard said. "Just ease up to the edge."

"Come, on, Bernard, you really think that soft-talking shit helps?"

"I hope so."

"Well, yeah, I mean, it doesn't hurt. Okay."

Wilson moved the machine closer, and then there it was. The golem, its head rising above the rim of the cliff like a dead, blackened sun. Wilson brought the shovel down on top of the golem's head with a ringing sound that drove the monster out of view, except its hands which continued to grasp the cliff's edge. It was muddy there, so Bernard's grip was precarious.

Raising the shovel, Wilson waited until the golem edged over the cliff again.

"You can't just bang it," Bernard said. "You got to scrape its head; otherwise, you knock it down, it'll keep climbing right back up."

That didn't stop Wilson from banging it again when its head poked over the rim, knocking it back down, but not loosening its grip.

"I said it's no use," Bernard said. "It's just a game of whack-a-mole this way."

"I know. But it satisfies."

Wilson backed the loader slightly, lowered the scoop, and then the head came up again. He rushed the machine forward, trying to hit the golem in the forehead, but to their surprise, hanging by one hand, the golem reached out with the other and clutched the edge of the scoop, and when it did, it actually shook the loader, twisting it sideways.

"Goddamn, I may have to leave you Bernard. Sorry. My balls are only so big."

Bernard was wrestling his knife from his pocket. He clicked the blade free.

"You got to be kidding," Wilson said.

Bernard placed the knife in his teeth, eased the side door open, and swung himself out, screaming with pain as he did it. He fell down on top of one of the lifting arms, smacking his nuts in the process. At least it momentarily took his mind off his broken leg. Bernard bellied forward. The loader rocked left, then right, as the golem turned it like a plaything.

"No!" Wilson said. "Don't fucking do it."

Bernard kept sliding forward until he reached the shovel. He lunged over it awkwardly and fell on top of the golem's head, swung around so that one leg clutched over the shoulder of the golem and he hooked a heel in its chest. The other leg, the broken one, dangled along the golem's back, the foot turned in the wrong direction. Bernard was out in the wind. If the golem fell, so did he, all the way to the rocks and the sea.

Wilson tried to back the loader, but the golem held it. At first.

And then it let go of the loader and reached up for Bernard with the free hand, but Bernard took the knife from his mouth and scraped it across the length of the word on the thing's forehead. It was like trying to scrape stone with a toothpick. And then it struck Bernard. He dropped the knife, clutched a handful of mud from the crumbling cliff and jammed it against the golem's forehead, filling the carving on its forehead, causing the word to be filled, obscured. The golem howled that wild, soulless howl, but this time Bernard found it invigorating. Not frightening as before. It seemed to him that this time the howl was one of fear, something the golem might never have experienced before.

Wilson lifted the shovel slightly and rammed it forward so Bernard could easily tumble into it. Bernard grabbed the scoop with both hands, and though his broken leg caught on the back of the golem's head and twisted and cracked so hard when he fell into the shovel he passed out from pain, he made it.

Gearing it backwards, Wilson pulled Bernard farther from the edge of the cliff. He glanced at the golem. Saw a strange and fascinating sight, just as the sun rose up on the far side of the island and became a thin umbrella of pink. The golem's head rocked right off its shoulders.

Then the headless golem pulled itself up so that it could put a knee on the edge of the cliff. It finished the climb, wobbled to its feet.

"Fucking perfect," Wilson said.

The golem's fingers came loose from its hands and fell to the earth like dog turds. Its penis, which looked like a length of black hose, the kind the cops might use to beat you with, dropped off. The testicles dropped off like rotten apples. The arms came loose and fell, the knees sagged and exploded outward, the torso tipped backwards and tumbled over the edge of the cliff.

Wilson just sat there on the loader seat. He called out, "Bernard?"

There was a wait.

"Yeah," Bernard said.

"You okay?"

"That's a relative term."

"Are you all right?"

"Just had a little nap. Fine now. Lots of pain. Leg and balls both hurt."

❧

Wilson helped Bernard out of the shovel, which he had lowered.

"We got to get you back to Island Keep."

"Not just yet. Be my crutch."

Bernard slung an arm over Wilson's shoulder. Wilson helped walk him to the edge of the cliff. There were pieces of the golem's body in the rocks; some of it had darkened the sea near the slick wall, but the water was washing it away and the sunlight was turning from pink to fiery-red, making the water appear volcanic.

"I think we did it," Bernard said.

"Don't say it out loud," Wilson said. "You might jinx it." He helped Bernard back to the loader, worked a little harder to get up this time. The leg really was bad, and Bernard seemed to have turned much heavier.

"I'm really not all right," Bernard said.

"I was sort of hip to that, actually. Sorry. I said I was going to abandon you earlier, and I want you to know I mean it."

"But you didn't. That's all that counts."

When Bernard was in place on the loader, Wilson climbed down. He walked to where the golem's fingers and appendages lay, and kicked them one by one over the edge of the cliff. He saved the penis and testicles for last. He kicked the penis far out and watched it fall with delight. Then he stomped the testicles, and kicked them over the edge.

When he was finished, he went and looked down. He could see a few pieces of the golem in the rocks, but with the cliff wall being smooth, most of it had fallen into the water. He felt like a kid that had just whipped a bully. Or had helped lick one.

"Motherfucker," he said, and shot his finger at the ocean below.

Kettle had left his Scotch, and Wilson had Bernard drink it, all that was left, and when Bernard had a snoot full, he tried to set the leg. He wasn't sure how good a job he had done, but at least the foot was facing the right way and Bernard had only screamed for a short time before passing out. It was late afternoon when Wilson found the phone worked again. He called over and gave them a short rundown, waiting to be called a nut, expecting a boat to come over with Kettle driving and another guy with white jackets with reversed sleeves for the both of them, but that didn't happen. They didn't even act surprised.

When they came up to Island Keep there were four men and a stretcher, plus Kettle was with them.

"So Number 489 wasn't dead?" Kettle asked.

"That's one way of putting it," Wilson said.

"I'm not surprised."

"We sure were."

"I told you he was bad."

"You were conservative in your tone."

"Toggle?"

"You'll find him amongst the downed tree by the dock. A little here. A little there."

"Oh," Kettle said.

"Yeah," Wilson said. "Oh."

"He has a bad break," Wilson said to the men who were lifting Bernard onto the stretcher. "His leg is seriously fucked over."

"Yeah, we figured as much," one of the men said. "I mean, it's our job. You know, we look at it and see it's broke, we figure it's broke. We're smart like that."

"Yeah, and he's my friend. Be careful with him, smart guys."

"We get it, kid."

"Just carry him out," Kettle said. "You guys can talk wise to one another later."

Bernard spent about two months on the prison island with the doctors and a female nurse he liked, and maybe she was worth an extra week of that time.

Wilson took over all work at the small island for a while, doing repairs on the shed door, a little of this, a little of that.

The powers that be decided a new bulldozer cost too much and wasn't used enough. They determined the loader was enough.

When Bernard came back over, boated there by Kettle, Wilson went down to meet him at the dock. Bernard was on crutches. He said, "Kid, I'm not staying. I'm going back to the island, and then me and a nurse named Sharon are flying out of there. I've served my time."

"Congratulations," Wilson said. "I thought you might never leave."

"I had a talk with some of the suits over there. They think you did your part, time served or not."

"What are you saying?"

"I'm saying if you want to, you can pack your things."

"Fuck it. I'm wearing them."

"Then get on the boat," Kettle said, coming out of the cabin. "I got three new meats coming in to take your places."

"How'd you know I'd go back?" Wilson said.

"What would make me think you wouldn't?" Kettle said. "And Bernard. He said you would."

"We have to sign an agreement not to talk, and they say they'll kill us if we do, so are you up for that?" Bernard said.

"Like I'm going to tell people we fought a golem on the edge of a cliff with a bulldozer and a front-end loader, and you scraped a magic word off its head with a pocket knife."

As Kettle helped Bernard and his crutches onto the boat, Wilson turned and looked back. "It is a beautiful island."

"Yeah, and it'll be beautiful without us," Bernard said, looking up at Wilson on the dock.

"Amen," Wilson said, and climbed aboard.

Harryhausen, Houdini, and Hisownself

BY NORMAN PARTRIDGE

WHEN I WAS a kid, I wanted to know how everything worked. I saw *The Seventh Voyage of Sinbad* and had to find out how Ray Harryhausen made that cyclops rear up on its cloven hooves and growl. I read about Houdini's escape from the Chinese Water Torture Cell, and I couldn't rest until I understood how he did the trick. I even spent a few nights during of the summer of '70 at the county fair, trying to figure out how they turned that girl into a rampaging gorilla (Before my very eyes! In a horribly cheap tent! Why weren't they on TV if they could really do that?). And when I was older and had a driver's license in my wallet, my buddies and I used to borrow my big brother's pickup and drive north on Highway 101, where we'd hike in as close to Bluff Creek as we could get just to see if we could spot that bigfoot we'd seen loping along in the Patterson-Gimlin film.[1]

In one way or another, all those experiences opened my eyes. When you're young, that's a good thing. But as I've gotten older, I've decided that there are definitely times I'd rather hold onto magic than poke it with a stick. Because nothing drains magic's tap faster than reality rearing its ugly head, and you can't unlearn a secret. Once you know how a trick is done, it's suddenly a whole lot less interesting.

---

[1] Of course, we never did. But we did hear something strange howling in those woods on a rainy December night, and I'm kind of happy I didn't lay eyes on whatever it was.

I feel that way as a reader, too. I imagine most writers do. After all, learning to write involves a certain amount of reverse engineering. When I was starting out, I used to take apart stories and novels like things laid out for dissection. I learned that particular trick in college. Writing papers like "Shadow and Substance in Edgar Allan Poe's 'Ligeia.'" I got pretty good at it. I cut off hunks of fiction with a highlighter and pinned them to the page with quotation marks. But after four years doing that, I felt like I was cutting the wings off butterflies.

And sure, I learned a lot about fiction along the way. But in the end I decided that there was a simple and undeniable truth about wingless butterflies.

They were all done flying, and that was a damn shame.

So these days I try to hold onto the magic when I can. It's not as easy as it sounds, putting a patch over that critical eye. But sometimes, with some writers, it's definitely worth doing.

You've probably guessed that Joe R. Lansdale is one of those writers for me. Now, I could tell you some things about Joe hisownself, or I could talk about the story you're going to read. Instead, let me peel off that eyepatch and tell you a couple things about how Joe makes the magic work.

Hopefully I can do that trick without cutting up any butterflies. I'll give it a go.

Since I've already name-checked Eddie Poe, let's jump into those cold, calculating waters. Poe posited that "suspension of disbelief" was an essential element in creating fantastic/bizarre fiction. Meaning that the reader's buy-in was a prerequisite for getting those kinds of tales to do the job.

INTRODUCTION: Harryhausen, Houdini, and Hisownself

Seems like a simple enough concept, but getting there can be harder than you might imagine. And for a writer like Joe "getting there can be harder" doesn't quite cover it. Because when it comes to the fantastic and the bizarre, Joe doesn't just climb out on a limb. He lives out there. Not only that, he regularly saws off the damn thing while sitting on the wrong side of the branch. After all, Lansdale has written convincingly about a post-apocalyptic drive-in movie theater ruled by a creature called the Popcorn King, and a mummy named Bubba Ho-Tep, not to mention Ned the Seal and a wrestling ape called Rot Toe.

Which means there can be overflowing bucketfuls of disbelief that need suspending in a Lansdale story. One way Joe does the job is through sheer audacity. He makes the unlikely twists and turns his friends, and he's not afraid to pile them on—he's a writer who always seems ready to take another hard turn in a story and go for it, jumping over genre conventions and jumping back.[2] Fact is, Joe was selling genre mashups before anyone coined the term, back in the days when you were likely to get a note from an editor asking: "Exactly what kind of story is this, anyway?"

"It's a Joe Lansdale story," he'd say.

So there's that sense of audacity, but behind it there's a solid back-beat of story elements that are familiar but not quite. Touchstones readers will recognize, but with a Lansdale twist. There are some in the story you're about to read. Maybe a little Edgar Rice Burroughs and a little P. T. Barnum, too. A slight echo of *McKenna's Gold*. There's even a mad king of sorts in a bowler hat, and a steamboat that has definitely made a trip through a *Heart of Darkness*.

Those are the kind of touchstones that draw you in if you're a fan of the fantastic, but it's Joe that keeps you there. It's not just his solid knowledge of multiple genres and how they work, but also the curious marginalia that bleeds in around the edges of fiction and

---

[2] And since I firmly believe that learning to consistently anticipate a writer's work is the death of the reader/writer relationship, Joe's ability to power through in this regard is a good thing.

life, like those mysteries I mentioned in the first paragraph of this introduction. Which means I wouldn't be a bit surprised to find that there was a Lansdale story about Houdini's Chinese Water Torture Cell, or that girl-to-gorilla carny act, or one with a cyclops stalking through the piney woods in East Texas.

If he hasn't already written those stories, I hope he will.

So what else powers Joe's fiction? His characters, for one thing. I especially admire the way he works with first-person narrators. Often they're the last man paddling water in a sea of crazy.

And when it comes to that metaphor, I'm talking a *deep* sea.

But the thing that never quite occurred to me until I read this story is that it's not exactly the essential nature of those narrators that earns reader buy-in. It's not that they're good guys or bad guys...not exactly. Joe plays a double-whammy game with them, and it involves 1) the honest eye they use to size up the other characters in the story, and 2) the not-so-simple ability to turn that same eye on their own faults and weaknesses.

Unblinking, honest, clear.

Warts and all.

That's a rare trick in life, and everyone knows it. When someone does that in a story, it grabs you.[3] The narrator in this tale is a young man named Rabbit. I'll let you find out what kind of guy he is for yourself. After all, you're the reader and that's your job. Picking up cues along the way, adding things up as the story unfolds...or to put it another way, slapping your money on the bar and buying in.

---

[3] There's a great offhand bit in *The Drive-In* with the narrator staring at a bunch of books on his bookshelf—self-help, religion, numerology, etc.— while he considers where they got him. If you want to be a writer and see how this works, check that out.

I'll leave you with this. Joe would have been a storyteller even if he'd never picked up a pencil. If he was a soldier sitting across a campfire spinning a tale on a starless night a couple thousand years ago. If he was a hitchhiker you picked up on a foggy road in the middle of nowhere when maybe you shouldn't have. If he was a bartender in a saloon in the old West, pouring you a drink and telling a story on one of those ubiquitous dark and stormy nights.

So go ahead. Enjoy the story…and that whisky.

Just watch out for the rattlesnake chaser.

You've been warned.

Sixty-Eight Barrels on Treasure Lake

You want to know how I ended up here?

Well, some of you won't believe it, but that doesn't mean it isn't true.

Gather up close and listen tight. The beers are on me.

🌿

Most nights at the saloon you'd spend a lot of time wiping up messes with a dirty rag that smelled like beer, blood, whisky and sweat, and maybe the stink of fear, because some nasty things could happen in there. I've seen it. Everything from puking to peeing to shitting, to fornication and murder. Sometimes all of it happened in the same night.

This sort of nightly business, except on Sunday, might give you reason to believe I was looking for a way out of my situation when all this happened, and you have all the reason in the world to believe you are right. Thing was, I was still ciphering on that little problem without much progress, when the solution, such as it was, came along.

Preacher was part of it, but not all of it. He'd been a preacher in town for I guess nigh on four or five months before he took to coming in to sit at a table alone and drink. He always wore black pants and a black dress coat, but was changeable in color when it came to hats. Mostly, though, he wore black.

He would always sit at a little table in the corner with his back to the wall and a loaded hog leg on the table. He might preach about how to get to heaven on Sunday, but most any day he was willing to send you to hell.

Let me give you an example. There was a little fellow with a fiddle in the saloon one night, and he was playing, mostly sawing at the strings in a way that sounded like someone mistreating a cat with a pair of pliers.

There was a fat man there too, wearing ragged clothes and a new black hat. He was sitting at a table playing cards, and that screeching moved him. He jumped up so fast it knocked over the chair he'd been sitting in. He started dancing, pounding his boots on the floor, hopping about in a way that made people spread out and pull tables and chairs aside to give him room.

The crowd started hollering and hooting and clapping and so on, and that was like putting dry wood on a hot fire. It really encouraged the fat man. He twirled around and slapped his knee, stood up on the toes of his boots, and hopped.

He was doing a nice little two step at the same time he took a gander at Preacher sitting there sipping his drink, that hog leg in front of him. The fat man decided he needed him as a dance partner.

Preacher didn't want to dance, and one thing led to another, the fat man pulling on Preacher to prance about with him. Preacher told him to stop, but the fat man wasn't having it. Every eye was on him now, and he liked being the center of attention. You could tell that by the way he was grinning.

More Preacher resisted, the more the fat man tugged on the preacher's coat.

The fiddle player was really sawing by then. I think there might have been a tune hidden in that noise somewhere, but I wasn't the one to find it, not even with a posse.

One sleeve tug too many from the fat man caused Preacher to snatch up that hog leg and fire. A bullet went through the fat man's head and came out the back of it along with a mess of blood and brains, and down he went. He hit the floor so hard tables and chairs jumped.

It wasn't all bad. Same bullet went through the fat man's head hit the fiddle and busted it, and that was the end of that nonsense.

As for the fat man's body, no one in the saloon claimed it, and it was put outside overnight, and what didn't get chewed on and eaten by wolves, was picked up the next day in a wagon by a woman and a boy of ten or so. They said they had heard about his demise. They were his wife and son, and they always figured he'd end up this way, on account of his love of drink. They asked how he died, and Daddy, who was the saloon owner, told them. The wife smiled, said, "He did love his dancing."

Preacher wasn't ever asked to dance again, and there was always a little more room than was necessary at his table. The extra two chairs there remained unused, except by me. Preacher liked me because I had learned to read and write and had read a half dozen books or so, couple of them twice. I liked a newspaper when I could find it.

By the way, my name is Tim, but everyone calls me Rabbit, because when I was young my teeth outgrew my mouth for a time and my mother thought it made me look like a rabbit, so I got the nickname. Even after I'd grown into those suckers the nickname stuck. So here I am, a grown man, eighteen at the time, and still called Rabbit. I thought I ought to get that out of the way.

Back to my true story.

Preacher could be quiet, but he always liked me. Some nights he liked to talk. He'd fought in the war, sailed the seas, hunted buffalo, been married three times ("For the pussy," he said) and had somewhere along the way got the Jesus calling, though that sounded kind of tacked on. He ran the local church. The one folks went to when they went, because it was the only one around. The first preacher had died, and that's when Everett, which was his real name, came into town and claimed his spot. It was easy, because there wasn't a lot of competition. Even in the short time I'd known him I didn't find Preacher all that religious seeming.

I'd sit with him at the table, and though Daddy could be angry about any kind of loafing other than his own, he knew by me being there, Preacher would talk and buy lots of whisky and stay steady at it through the night. He had plenty of money for drink, but it wasn't known how he'd come by it. It damn sure wasn't from preaching.

Another thing I think Daddy liked about Preacher, was he felt he made the place more respectable. Which was damn silly, of course. The place was never respectable, though it might have been a bit tamer when Mama was alive. What had kept things in tow before Preacher started coming around was fear of Mama taking a hatchet to someone, which she had done a time or two—bless their souls.

After she was gone the degree of rowdiness went up a couple of notches, then was brought down a notch when Preacher started coming around. Still it was plenty rough, and on some nights the working ladies that showed up there at night not only got pinched on the ass, but so did I. The place was always full of noise and the stink of mostly working men come straight from a hard, sweaty day doing this or that, coming into our saloon to let off steam, get drunk, swear and pass chili wind, which ripened the air all night long.

Another side note, one important to me, and I date it to the time Preacher started coming around, Daddy had gotten so he only beat me on Wednesdays. He figured I'd done something during the week, or would by week's end, so a punishment mid-week with a razor strop was in his mind a corrective measure.

"But Daddy," I would say to him, "what if I don't do anything?"

"Guess you get a whipping anyway, Rabbit," he'd say. "My advice on the matter is you might as well do something you ain't supposed to do, because you're going to get it anyhow. And hell, ain't it better than the old way?"

It was at that. Used to, I got a whipping three times a week. Once on Wednesday, and twice on Sunday. That was Daddy's day off, so his arm was good after noon.

We stayed home Sunday, if you can call a one-room shack nailed onto the saloon a home. It had a roof leaky as a sieve, and the slats that made up the wall had gaps in them big enough to sling a bobcat through. We had another room tacked on as well, and it was for boarders who really might have been better off to sleep under a tree.

After Mama was dead, Daddy took heavy to the bottle, drank all day on Sunday, which was another reason the whippings were cut. It wasn't that he got to feeling sorry for me or spent Sunday contemplating on Jesus. It was that whipping my ass cut into his drinking time. His drinking also cut into our profits, by the way.

Come to think of, he was drinking before she died, and heavy, but he went from drinking like a fish to drinking like a whale when she passed.

He was such a drunk it took him three days to realize Mama hadn't been around. I had noticed, but hadn't brought it up because I didn't miss her none. She was a hard woman and mostly unhappy.

"Where's your Mama," he asked, like maybe I kept her in my back pocket. Well, I didn't know. Didn't even have an idea.

Day or two later, one of the saloon folk came into the saloon on a late afternoon, right about opening time, took off his hat and held it against his heart, and said, "Frank," that was my father's name, "I got to tell you something."

"Tell it," Daddy said.

"I just shit on your wife's face. She's out there in the outhouse pit. I wiped my ass and dropped some corn shucks, looked down, and damn if I didn't see her face. She wasn't swimming, Frank. She's dead."

Me and Daddy went out there and saw that her hatchet was lying just inside the outhouse, and when we looked through the shitter hole, we could see her face poking up through the watery turds and a smell so stiff it moved the air around.

"That's her all right," Daddy said.

It was decided not to get her out, as that would be messy. A new pit was dug, the outhouse was moved, and the old pit was covered with dirt and a cross was put up. It was thought for a time she had been murdered and put in there. An Indian was even hung for it. But later we found a note under the bar on a shelf with a jar of preserves setting on it. It read: I AM KILTING MYSELF BY DROWNDEDING CAUSE I WON'T TO. FRANK, YOU CAN GO STICK A DRY CORN COBB UP YOUR ASS. AND TELL WHAT'S HIS NAME, THE BOY, GOODBYE AND TO TRY AND NOT TAKE ANY WOODEN NICKLES. HA. HA.

It was signed ME.

I guess the Indian didn't do it.

So, there I was, living the life of a millionaire (that's a joke), and thinking on how I could get out of my situation, not knowing the path away from there was already being blazed by fate.

It was late summer and I was sweeping up a busted beer mug when the giant came stumbling in. I swear he was well over six feet tall, and he had to duck his head when he come through the door, bringing in with his size an odor like a dead cat rotting on the back porch. He had a black slouch hat and bearded chin. (Black hats were popular.) There was streaks of gray in his beard and you could see grey in his hair where it hung down from under the hat. His clothes looked like a hog had been wallowing in them, and his boots were coming apart and he'd tied the tops where they were broke-up with twine to hold them. His socked foot poked through the toe of one of the boots, and his toe poked through the sock like a crooked tooth. He had a face like a scratched-on rock. But in spite of all that wear and stink, he had an alligator smile with plenty of teeth, and his eyes were blue like the sky come first break of morning on a clear day. He had a brace of revolvers on his belt, four I reckon, and the weight of those pistols would have been enough to drag an average man down, but he wore them like they were no more than a belt full of wishes.

That night he came in and sat at Preacher's table, which was minus Preacher. He was out back doing business in the outhouse. Delivering a package, we called it.

Sixty-Eight Barrels on Treasure Lake

No one sat at Preacher's table. No one that knew him anyway, and most new people that came in were looking to sit with others so they could play cards, sling the shit and drink.

But there he sat, and I'm thinking things could get sketchy, considering Preacher's temperament. I was pondering on that when the door opened and Preacher came in from his dark night delivery.

The big man saw Preacher, and Preacher saw him, and the big man smiled, and Preacher smiled, and came over to him and laughed a little. The big man stood up and shook hands with Preacher like he was trying to crank his arm off, and they grinned big, and Preacher said, "It took you long enough. And damn do you stink."

"I've had a rough time of it, Everett," said the big man.

"Fate must be changing, because you chose my table where I been sitting and no one else with me. It's like you knew and were guided from above."

"Naw, you left your favorite hat hanging on the back of the chair."

"Oh, yeah."

That greeting between the two was not what I had expected, but it beat a bunch of blue whistlers firing out of pistols.

Well, I swept on past them and went behind the bar and started helping Daddy serve drinks, taking in the money and such, but I had my eye on that pair. They leaned in close to each other and talked, and I could tell from the way Preacher scrunched up his face, the giant's smell was damn near melting.

After a while the giant came over and he and his stink leaned on the bar, said, "You got a room a man could rent?"

"We got a room a goat could rent, if it had the money."

"How much is it?"

I told him.

"Damn, that would put a goat out considerable."

"It's got a tub in it and you can heat water on a wood stove in there, though you got to bring it in from the well, or hire me to bring it in for you and heat it."

"All right, I'll take it, and I need to rent it for as long as I need to rent it. One question of importance. It got a bed in it?"

"It's got a thin mattress on the floor."

"Rats?"

"Not many to speak of."

"Well, then, I reckon I can make a payment on it right now."

After he paid up, I took him outside, around back, and showed him his room. I lit a couple of the wall lanterns, and he studied the place over, bent down and pushed at the mattress on the floor. "It ain't got nothing in it, boy."

"There's some ticking in there," I said, "but it's gotten thin."

"It's gotten absent."

He came and leaned against the door jamb and studied the wood stove, the number ten washtub hanging on the wall, the stack of pots and pans, the wood pile next to the door.

"There aren't any windows."

"You're right," I said.

"I don't think a goat would like it here."

"What about you?"

"It'll have to do, I reckon."

He went back then and spent some time with Preacher, and when the night ended, when everyone had left, including Preacher, the giant came over and asked if I would gather up a bucket and draw him enough well water, and heat it, so he could take a bath.

We close early morning about the crack of day and open late afternoon, and I was wanting to get to sleep so as to have some day left before I went to work again, but the money for drawing and heating was money I kept for myself, and Daddy, who had already gone to bed and left the closing to me, could, as Mama suggested, stick a corn cob up his ass.

I brought a bucket of water into the giant's room, poured it in a big black pot, got the wood going in the stove, and then I got another pot and put it on a stove hole, brought in another bucket. I got those two pots of water going and the room turned warm. I opened the door to let some wind in, and that helped some with the big man's odor which was strong enough to help me carry the water.

While the water was heating, he said to me, "What's your name?"

"Rabbit."

"Your mama named you Rabbit?"

"Not right at first, but I been called that so long, I don't go by nothing else."

"Good a name as any. I knew a fella named Poot once, and that was the name his mama gave him. She had another boy named Scooter. They call me Paul. You know where I can get some new clothes? These are about done for. Boots too."

"Dry goods store. You can go there in the morning."

"You fix breakfast here?"

"You got to fix your own or buy it in town. There's a lady that cooks in a tent on the edge of town."

"I saw it coming in," he said.

"Well, that's where you can get some breakfast, or any other meal, but it'll cost you dear. She charges like a mining boom is still going on, but most of the miners have cleared out, gone on somewhere else to mine, or find another line of work. It was good money around here once. The saloon was doing a hopping business then, what with us watering the whisky down and giving it a dash of turpentine for kick, we were doing all right. We could turn a bottle of whisky into three."

"Seems like a good way to do business."

"Was then."

"Well, you're damn sure skinning me with what you're charging, but it'll have to do." I took the tub off the wall and set it on the floor, and started pouring the buckets of hot water in it. I eventually had the wood crackling good, so the pots heated fast, and it didn't take me terribly long to get that tub filled.

Paul began to peel off to get in the tub. I saw then his body was as scarred up as a chopping block. Some of the scars were angry red streaks, and some were puckered up like a bullet wound would make.

"Don't be wishing on my dick, now," he said.

He lowered himself into the tub, and the steam puffed around him and he gritted his teeth against the heat. I went and got a bar of lye soap and gave it to him.

Before I left, I said, "You can leave the door open for some air, but I wouldn't leave it open at night, we got a bear likes to come up in the dark and walk around. Door's open, he might come inside."

"He'd have a tight fit," Paul said.

Every night I heated and poured his water for him, and put the money he paid me in a fruit jar I placed under my bed. I thought of this as my traveling money.

Paul bought a black suit with a black shirt and some shiny black lace up boots. He shaved himself real close and cut his hair. He had two, pearl handle, converted .36 Navy Colts. He wore one under each arm in shoulder holsters hidden by his coat. He had a gun belt and holster around his waist too, and there was a Peacemaker in that with a yellow ivory grip. The spare pistol he had carried on his belt the first night was tucked away somewhere where I couldn't see it, but I guessed under the back of his coat on his belt. As I remembered, that one had a black pearl handle.

Preacher abandoned his church altogether after a few days, and he and Paul would sit in the saloon and drink, their heads tight together, discussing something in secret, pulling out a goodly sized piece of paper that Paul would unfold every night and spread out on the table. Preacher would do the same, put his piece of paper against Paul's, and they'd study it serious like, point at spots, and keep their words soft.

One day Paul came over to me while I was wiping up the bar with our least dirty rag, said, "Listen here, Rabbit. Me and Everett there, we're watching for a fellow that might be a bit of a problem to us. He's a stringy bastard with a bowler hat and wears a pistol and big ole Bowie knife, and he don't never go anywhere, summer or winter, without a possum hide coat. It's got the fur on it, but it's bald in spots. He's got a look on his face like someone shot at him and missed or shit on him and hit. Got a scar along his left cheek like a lightning bolt. That would be from a Sioux's knife. They got in a ruckus and the Sioux lost.

"Anyway, you see him, let me know if I don't see him first. I'm not here when he comes in, as I'm going to travel off a couple days, me and Everett, I'd like to know he's around. I wouldn't want to come back and be surprised."

"Can't guarantee he wouldn't be in here when you came in."

"That you can't, but if you got it in mind to warn me if the situation allows, it might be to mine and Everett's advantage. Everett asked if you'd remove his table and put it out of the way so no one can sit there, and put it back two days from now and leave it open for him. He told me to give you this twenty-dollar gold piece for your troubles."

I took the twenty dollars, and when Paul left, I removed the table and set it in Paul's room.

I guess it was the very next day, shortly after we opened on a late afternoon, that the fellow Paul had described came into the saloon. He pushed the door open slowly and stepped inside looking this way and that, with an expression on his face that said he seldom liked anything he saw. He may have been a scarecrow of a man, but there was something about him that made a fellow nervous soon as you saw him. The possum coat Paul had described. His bowler hat had a bent white feather in it. That jagged scar on his face.

He kind of glided up to the bar, all beady-eyed and nervous.

"Boy. I'm looking for a couple fellas. One really big fellow named Paul and one named Everett."

Then he ordered a beer and went into describing Paul and Preacher, telling me what great friends one was to him, and how the other was a cousin, though during his run down, he kind of forgot which one was supposed to be which a couple times.

He had a long story about how he was trying to give his cousin an inheritance, and how the man the cousin was with was a close family friend. It was elaborate and as convincing as a whore's promise of true love for a dollar fifty and a clean wash rag.

I let him go on, poured him up a beer he'd asked for, and when he finished telling me his lies, he took the beer and sipped.

"This is warm as spit," he said.

"We don't have much in the way of cooling it," I said.

"About them fellas?"

"Haven't seen neither of them. Then again, folks come and go. I've got so I don't remember much about who's who and what's what in here. I serve beer and clean up."

"You the only one here?"

"There's my daddy, but he's sleeping."

"Could I ask him?"

"Not just now," I said. "He's taken him a jug and gone on to bed early."

"All right, then."

When things got settled there, and the tall man with the bowler found some men to play cards with, I went back to check on Daddy, as he had looked poorly when he and his friend the jug had gone to the back.

He was lying on the floor near his bed and the jug was busted and the floor smelled like blood and whisky. He had his pants down below his ass and his butt stuck up white as the moon. I could see right then that he was dead.

I figured he'd gone out to the outhouse with his jug in tow, did his business, didn't fasten his belt good, stumbled into the room and tripped over his drooping pants. I could see where he'd hit his head on the edge of a chair, because the chair was turned over nearby and there was blood on it. He had ruined my pallet on the floor, as he had bled all over it.

I tugged his pants up to give him some little slice of dignity, then went over and sat on his bed and looked at him and tried to feel sorrowful, but I couldn't get there. What I felt was relief. I now had the good bed and I was the owner of a saloon.

In the next few days I got Daddy buried next to Mom in her shit hole grave. No one came to see him off, and after he was in the hole, I carried on. I felt a little guilty about not feeling sad that he was dead, but I got over it.

Paul said he and Preacher would be gone for a couple of days, but they were gone more than that. Possum Coat hung around right smart, and only left when we closed the doors, and was right there again when they opened.

I kept as best a lookout as I could for Paul and Preacher, so as to catch them early and warn them about Possum Coat, but I thought whatever it was they were worried about when it came to that skinny man might be exaggerated. He didn't look like much to me.

New information can change a viewpoint, however.

One night, Possum Coat was playing cards at a table. He sat with his back to the wall, and he had the bowler pulled down a little in front so that his eyes were shielded. He was chewing on a freshly whittled tooth pick, looking at his cards. He had quite a pile of money, pocket knives and watches, stacked in front of him.

"You gonna study them cards all night, or you gonna play 'em?"

This was from a man only a little smaller than a grizzly bear, and of an appearance where he might be confused for one.

Possum Coat didn't say anything. Didn't bat an eye.

"War of Southern Aggression didn't last this long," the Bear said. "Play the cards or check out of the game. I mean, hell, you been winning all night. Give someone else a chance to cheat."

Well now. There were some rotten people showed up there at the saloon, but even the most rotten didn't cotton to being called a cheat. Next to humping a child, being a cheat was worse than murder.

Possum Coat lifted his head slowly and looked across the table at Bear, and then, all of a sudden, he was up and scampering across that table on his knees like a rabid rat.

I don't know exactly where he had the Bowie knife tucked, but he pulled it and was using it on that big man's face like he might be trying to shave him, and I guess you could say he was, but not whiskers. When the bear fell on the floor, his upper lip was missing, there were holes in his cheeks, and his eyes were gouged out. The last strike with the Bowie is what done it, though. Possum Coat drove it straight down into the top of Bear's head, and it went in as easy as your finger would in a fresh baked pie.

They both hit the floor. Possum Coat rolled and came up on his feet. Bear was done. I could smell where he'd shit himself all the way over to where I stood behind the bar.

"Take him out, he stinks," someone said, and he was taken outside by a couple fellows who knew him, and that was it, except for me having to mop up the blood, and there was plenty of it.

Possum Coat, who had not even lost his hat in all this business, stood up with his blood-dripping knife, said, "Anyone else got a complaint. Or maybe some words of wisdom."

One of the men at the table said, "I think you play a fair hand of cards and deftly wield a large whittler, so all I can say is you play your hand when you take the notion."

"I got the notion," Possum Coat said, and tucked away his knife and put down his cards. The others followed suit, and Bowler Hat won another pile of coins and a silver button or two, and they went on playing a quiet game without criticism. Fact was, at that point, Possum Coat could have said, "Excuse me while I jerk a few cards out of my ass and shake the shit off," and they'd have been fine with that.

I was coming out of the outhouse one late morning, and what did I see coming up the trail, but none other than Paul and Preacher, riding side by side. They both had shotguns laying across their saddles, and they were looking this way and that. When they saw me they rode over.

"And what of that vigil I asked for," Paul said.

"I've seen him," I said. "He killed a man last night."

"Knife or pistol."

"Bowie knife."

"He likes the knife," Preacher said.

"Another thing's changed," I said. "Daddy died. I own the saloon."

"Without stepping too far over the line, and not meaning to sound critical of your kin," Paul said, "but I'm thinking that his death might not be a burden of misfortune and anxiety, but more of an open window to a brighter future."

"It might at that," I said, "if I liked saloon work. But I don't."

"You could always sell it," Preacher said.

I hadn't even considered that.

"This fellow with the Bowie knife, he comes in nightly, I suppose?" Paul said.

"He does, and he was looking for you two."

"Son, we want to make you a little proposition, so as we can make sure not to be killed, and maybe manage some killing."

"I don't know," I said. "That doesn't sound like something in my line of work."

"You are wanting to depart the saloon business, are you not?" Preacher said.

"That's true," I said.

"Then how about we ride off a piece to some place private and talk a spell," Paul said.

***

Paul stuck out a hand and pulled me up on the back of his horse about as easy as picking a biscuit off a plate, and we rode down the trail a piece and into the woods. We stopped, climbed off the horses, and Paul and Preacher led the cayuses over to a spot under a big cedar tree.

"Here's our situation," Preacher said, as he leaned against the tree. "We were once in business with Possum. I think his real name is Garner. Something Garner. Thing is, Possum and me and Everett robbed a bank. We had some accomplices, and what we thought was a damn clever plan. We rented a steamboat and its crew. No passengers on board. Them and the Captain helped us get away with the bank money, which was a gold shipment that was supposed to be stored in that bank for a few days, then later moved to Denver. Don't know all the details there, but we knew gold would be inside the bank due to an inside source we beat the information out of, shot a few times, and left him in a ditch for the worms. We figured him as being too talky. He told us, didn't he?

"Bank president wouldn't open the vault, which was all right, as we'd brought some small crates of dynamite with us. We were nothing, if not prepared. We tied the president to the vault handle, stacked a crate of dynamite at his feet, started rolling out the fuse, and he decided the better part of valor was to open that vault without further argument.

"We stole the gold and cut the president's throat, killed everyone in the bank, except a baby. Beat them to death with iron bars. I almost did the baby too, way it was bawling, and even now I still have a feeling of not finishing the job up right. I hate to think of him growing up without a mother."

"That was our case," Paul said.

"We hauled the gold away by a wagon we had planted out back. Got to the river, wagon lost a wheel right near the steamboat, so us and that steamboat crew, all had to carry those crates of gold on board. Believe me, that shit was heavy coming out of the bank, but it seemed a mite heavier being loaded onto the steamboat, even with all the help we had. Seemed that way as we knew there was a good chance there'd be the law after us once someone came across a bank full of dead folks, and someone said, 'I seen a wagon going out of town with a bunch of strangers in it.'

"But things went smooth. We got the crates loaded, and away we went down the river for some goodly distance, churning that water like we were churning butter. Then the boat captain steered off on a tributary."

"Tributary meaning a little off-shoot," Paul said.

I knew that, but I nodded like it was precious information and wiped sweat off my forehead with my coat sleeve.

"Captain knew of the place," Preacher said. "It was shallow and narrow for a steamboat, so he was taking a chance, but he took it. We sailed along for a day, then through a crack in the mountains, came out on a lake in what I guess you would call a valley."

"I'd call it one," Paul said.

"This valley was the perfect place to hide the goods, you know. Leave the boat there, go ashore, work through the mountains, let the heat get off, come back later with a wagon, and tote the stuff out. We decided first to pull to shore and stay on the lake for a few days. There were plenty of food goods and such on the boat, and there were these barrels on the boat we decided to look into. There were sixty-eight of them, and they were full of salt. Boat Captain had some kind of deal to deliver it, but we made a deal with him to help us rob the bank and split the loot instead. Gold weighs out better than salt.

"One of the Captain's crew told us the Captain had designs to kill us and take the gold, so with the help of this turncoat crew mate, Dub, and our original band, which was me and Paul and Possum, and four others, we killed the Captain and his crew. Messy business."

"We killed Dub while we were at it," Paul said. "He betrayed his own, didn't he?"

Preacher nodded. "It was just practical thinking. Possum told us there were doctors who would buy bodies, no questions asked, and pay good money for them, enough it would be like we had robbed another bank full of fat gold bars. So much money there between gold and bodies in salt, we could move some place far away and exotic, hire some whores to lick the sweat off our balls and have some dogs could do it when they got tired.

"By then there was just us and Possum, and our original gang of four, and with the split of the money looking better, we decided we'd blow up the crack in the mountain, tumble some rocks into the water so another boat couldn't follow. Someone else knew of that little tributary, even by accident, we could be in some serious dog shit, even by accident. Paul ramrodded that operation, and it worked like a charm. We figured we could get out easy and come back and take care of business later, but we didn't have that open entrance by water to worry about."

I tried to keep a pleasant appearing disposition during the delivery of all this information, but I sure wasn't feeling pleasant. I was beginning to realize these brothers could go off their nut at any moment.

"We got ready to ride out, with a bit of the goods, with plans to come back for the others, feeling they were safe on the boat out on the lake," Preacher said. "We rolled up close to shore and let the horses out, took the steamboat back out, as Possum could work it, and then we sailed back in some canoes we had made, got the stock, and were ready to go, but we discovered a lot of the trails were switchbacks, just kind of went up and around and back down. That jammed us up."

"There were other problems as well," Paul said.

"There were indeed, but we won't bother Rabbit here with that business," Preacher said. "Thing was, we eventually found a trail out. Right close actually, but it twisted around a curve in the rocks, hard to see unless you were right up on it. By this time there was me and my brother, Possum and the last of our gang, Elegant."

I didn't ask about the missing members of the gang. I had an idea they too had been dispatched. I tried to look like this kind of information was common business for me.

"We all rode out, and after a few weeks, we decided to split up. This was mine and Paul's idea, as we knew we'd have to let the heat go down for a while, and riding around in a heap wasn't a good idea. We decided to split into two groups, and away we went. Before we split we made a map as to how we had come out of there. We found that to be more difficult than we expected, but we managed something of the sort, then tore it into four pieces, one for each of us. We all knew that our way out of there had been tedious, and our map wasn't exactly spot on, but with it torn in four pieces, wasn't anyone going to go back and find that place alone. Loose plan was we'd travel about a bit, and in a few months' time we'd meet at the first town on the far side of the mountains. We figured there had to be one. Then we'd put our map pieces together, get a wagon, some help, and go back for the goods."

Paul said, "We came upon some pilgrims who didn't own enough to make killing them worthwhile, but they had with them a newspaper that was a couple weeks old, and there was a story in it about a murder over in Boulder, and the one that got dead sounded like Possum's partner, and the other, right down to the possum coat, sounded like Possum. Our take was Possum had killed Elegant and taken his map piece. That meant he had half of the map, and we had the other half.

"Those pilgrims had with them a young lady of red hair and large bosoms, and Everett got sweet on her and decided he wanted to stick around with them and travel up north for a way until he got tired of humping her. I tried to get Everett to pass on that notion, but his dick was pointing the way he wanted to go, and I didn't consider it the right direction and went on to find the town and wait until he got tired of her."

"I'm foolish for women," Preacher said. "After a few weeks, things went sour. I humped her until her father and brother found out I was, and they came after me and I had to kill them. The woman was mad, so I had to shoot her too. I only shot her once, and it was a merciful shot. It wasn't all bad. I took their dog and sold it to a colored fellow down the road for a couple bucks. More seed money."

My skin had started to crawl by this point, but again, I was playing it straight on, like this wasn't surprising news to me. Just everyday business.

"I arrived later than I intended," Paul said. "My horse tumbled down a mountain side and rolled on me and broke my goddamn leg. The horse was killed, which served the clumsy bastard right, and I had to crawl out of there until I got back to the trail. I crawled down it for a quite a while. Days came and nights came, and I was miserable in the nights because it got cold. Had it not been for a family traveling along coming up on me, I would have died. An old Mammy with them set and splinted my leg, and if she hadn't, I'd have died. I don't doubt I was knocking on hell's door, and their arrival was all that kept it from being opened. When I was well, I stole a horse from them, and rode on."

Preacher said, "I come to what turned out to be your town first, and to look like part of the community, I took up preaching as a disguise. My sermons were so bad that my congregation, such as it was, quit leaving money in the offering. I found some rock candy in it near the end of my tenure, but I never could decide if it was a generous giving of what they could afford, or a shitty comment.

"I met this school teacher, and I had to work to get in that, as she had some class. But I got there. Knocked her up and had to drop her, because I have never felt right about bumping hair with a pregnant woman. I felt the same way about all three of my wives."

I suddenly knew why the school teacher had left town, and I knew too she was one of the lucky ones. These two would make Satan seem like Jesus carrying Buddha on his back.

"So, what's with this Possum?" I asked.

"We're thinking we want to be ready in case he decides he needs our pieces of the map. Got to be alert, you see. He makes a move, we make one. On the other hand, maybe we work together. Depending on who gets up on what side of the bed in the morning will determine how he or we will act. We're going to go down there and be prepared with some sweet talk and a loaded shotgun, see where he stands on matters. The other thing is, we've grown fond of you, little Rabbit, and you'll be going with us too."

"I appreciate the invitation, and I'm sure there is a lot I could learn from you two, but I have to work at the saloon, now that Daddy is deceased."

"Our condolences," Preacher said. "But here's the thing, Rabbit, you're still going with us. Way I see it, you ought to throw in with us gleefully, as we plan to make you some money. More money than you would see in a lifetime of work, and all of it in gold."

"Again, I thank you, but I don't think so."

"We think so, though. Right Paul?"

"Dead right."

"You see, Rabbit," Paul said. "You are just the right size for what we need, though we might have to grease you up a bit to make you fit."

I was thinking I best go along with them and wear a smile like a promise of love, because if I didn't, I figured I'd end up resting under a tree with a bullet through my teeth and a buzzard on my chest.

My fascination with the two and thinking of them as possible friends, had for obvious reasons waned. My mean as snakes parents had comparatively begun to approach something next to sainthood.

Still, I had been looking for a way to get out from under the saloon business, and as they rode me back to it, I considered that if they planned to use me for their gain, I might could turn the tables on them, get my share of some loot, sneak off and leave them with only the scent of my passing.

When we got where they had picked me up, I climbed off the back of Paul's horse and stood on the ground looking up at him.

Paul said, "What we need is someone knows the country and can track, can read our map and tell us what the hell we meant by what we put down."

"I know of someone that's said to be like that," I said.

"That's good," Preacher said. "Can he be persuaded?"

"She. And I don't know."

"A woman?" Paul said.

"A girl. I only know her by reputation."

"All right," Preacher said. "That's one of our problems solved, but the other is we still need the rest of the map. Hell, we see it all together, we might be able to follow it."

"But it's good to have a guide, if we have someone knows these mountains," Preacher said, "might even know of that lake. Real problem now, is we don't have those other two pieces of map. Possum does."

"We'll slide on into the saloon later, and try and be easy about it," Preacher said. "But you might want to be prepared to duck."

I walked back to the saloon trying to formulate a plan. The plan should have been run like hell, but youth and greed made me bold.

I was back at my bar wiping up with a dirty rag, when Possum came in and took a table near the front door and laid that big Bowie knife on it. From time to time he'd pick it up and clean his fingernails with it. He also had his possum hide coat peeled back, and I could see hanging in his shoulder holster a Smith and Wesson Model 3, and once when he turned, I saw a shotgun hanging on a cord inside his coat. The barrel and the stock had been cut down, but up close it could salt a room, and that's what I feared.

I was all prepared for a big shootout in the place. I was thinking on a way to not make it too much of a blood bath, and hoping if I ducked down behind the bar that that hickory and oak wood it was made of would protect me enough as to not get killed. That's when, as big and bold as a buffalo bull in striped pajamas and a paper hat, in came Paul.

Paul eye-balled Possum, and Possum eye-balled him, and I eye-balled them, and so did the crowd. The air seemed tight with the feel of a lightning strike which gives the air and mouth a coppery taste.

They locked eyes for a while before Possum said, "I brung them two pieces of map for us."

"Yeah," Paul said, and for a moment the air felt less stormy.

That's when Preacher came through the back way and walked past the bar and came up close to Possum. Possum knew he was there, but his hand didn't move for the knife, his shotgun, or pistol.

Sixty-Eight Barrels on Treasure Lake

"Come sit down," Possum said.

That's what Preacher and Paul did, and the crowd, having felt the electricity go out of the room, went back to poisoning themselves with whisky, chattering, playing cards and blowing farts.

The three gold robbers put their heads close together, and I couldn't hear them well enough to make out what they were saying then. Two pieces of map that looked as if they had been through some hard times were pulled from Possum's pocket and placed on the table. They all took to looking the fragments over, then produced their own pieces, pushed them together and looked those over. They wrinkled their foreheads and twisted their mouths, said something to one another, and then Preacher looked up, said, "Rabbit, come on over here."

Under the bar there's a double barrel shotgun and a double shot derringer. Stealthy as snake sneaking up on a baby chick, I plucked up the derringer and dropped it into my coat pocket, and went over to the table.

There wasn't an extra chair at the table until Possum looked at a man at a table near him, said, "We're going to be needing your chair."

That fellow had been there the night Possum used his Bowie, so he stood up as polite as if he was at the Queen's dinner and toted his chair over to the robbers' table, and gave a smile that showed us his dark, nub teeth. Then he went away without so much as a thank you or go eat shit remark from the three. He was there to serve them. He knew that and so did they.

I sat in the newly arrived chair and let my hand hang inside my coat pocket, clutching the derringer.

"Look that over," Paul said, "see if you can make something out of it. We turn out to be failed cartographers."

I gave the pieces a good examination, but in the end, it was as mysterious as government work.

"I recognize a few things, but when you get here," and I put my finger on one of the map fragments, "I get lost, and I'm not sure what these drawings mean."

"Them's trees," Possum said.

"You'll notice, that the map was drawn by all of us at certain points before it was divided," Paul said. "I think my trees are far more identifiable than Possum's. And what's that, Possum?"

"It's a cave opening," Possum said.

"Looks like an ass crack," Paul said.

"Don't get uppity," Preacher said. "Possum didn't have the benefit of your education and art schooling, him being raised by wolves."

"Both of you can jump off a goddamn cliff," Possum said.

"Let's hold our animosity," Preacher said. "We are on a mission, and it's best we work together. Fact is, we need a bit of help for not only the manual work, but someone to scout and track and locate."

Paul looked at me, said, "You said you knew someone that knew the deep country. A girl."

"Know of, not know. A colored Seminole mix. Name's Bleedhead. First name is unknown to me, but I'm going to wager she's got one."

"She can track?" Possum said.

"That's the word," I said. "She was taught by her Seminole daddy, they say. He was supposed to have been a hell of a tracker, and he taught her. Story goes if you wanted to find a flea named Willie on a dog named Rex, she can do it. I think her family's all dead now."

"But you say you don't know her personally?" Possum said.

"I know she works at a sawmill."

"I see," Possum said, leaning back in his chair. There was an air of disappointment about him, like a man who thought he was about to have a big dump, but discovered he was as stopped up as if he had a cork in his ass.

"We can talk to her and see if she wants to do it," I said. "Figure some money will put her on the trail."

"In that case," Possum said, carefully picking up his pieces of the map, folding them as precisely as the governor's napkins, and placing them in his pocket, "we ought to go see her."

Preacher gathered up his and Paul's pieces of the map and put them away. "Rabbit, you think, for a small sum, you could retire from the saloon business."

Sixty-Eight Barrels On Treasure Lake

"Can I have a day to consider on it?"

Preacher pursed his lips and nodded.

"You can, but we've already decided for you. You're coming with us. We need help to contact this Bleedhead. You have a sharp head about you and look pleasant enough that she might be receptive to you. And, of course, we need you later to grease up and send slithering."

※

I put a fellow in charge of the saloon for a few hours, as he didn't steal as much as some of the others, and wasn't as prone to drink up all the supplies. With him behind the bar, drinking a glass of warm beer I gave him, I walked into town. It was a short walk.

At the General Store, I found the owner, J.T. Simmons, and said, "Mr. Simmons, since Daddy's demise and the need to move on, I'm going to sell my saloon, and thought you might be a prime buyer."

Simmons was as bald as a door knob, except for one gray sprig that poked up like a brave weed on his forehead.

"For sale, huh? Well, I heard your daddy done went and sailed over Jordan, so I say sorry about that."

He said this pushing his hands together and resting his elbows on the service counter. He lowered his eyelids a bit, wrinkled his brows, and gently opened a corner of his mouth before closing it up again as if in fear too many words might escape.

"How much?"

"How much will you give me?"

"Saloon like that, it's in a bad state of repair."

"It's got right smart customers, though."

"I have seen the horses out front, the buggies, men stumbling in and out at all hours. I sometimes sit up in my room and smoke a cigar and drink a little drink in private and watch through window as they come and go, bodies are dragged out."

His window was in a room on top of his General Store.

"Yes, sir," I said. "And someone really wanted to be a saloon owner could do right well with it. I don't want to be, and a boar hog missing one eye, would have been about the same business man Daddy was."

"You got stock?"

"Yes, sir, you just got know to water the whisky down, maybe put something in it to keep it dark looking. You can give it more bite with turpentine. There's enough whisky right now in storage to last you for four months. There's about eight barrels of beer. If you had the mind to set up a sandwich shop in there, have some boiled eggs for the fellows, I figure you could do considerable business. I don't want to, and Daddy always said he didn't like to slice pickles."

"You have to serve pickles?"

"He felt you did, but you take it over, I leave that to you."

He gave me an offer. It was awful.

I said, "Listen here. That's not an offer. There's people get paid more than that to wipe a man's ass. Make me a decent offer. You do, you get the saloon, the supplies, and most of all, you get the steady stream of drunks who come there to spend money. And of course, you get my best wishes."

Simmons wrinkled his brow and the corner of his mouth slipped open again and closed.

"Suppose I could get a card dealer, someone could cheat without getting caught, and start some house run card games. Monte and such."

"Now you're thinking."

He made me an offer. It wasn't wonderful, but it would do. I decided to dress it up a bit by saying, "That sounds right, but I'd like to add me a bag of possibles to take with me, and I want it to be free."

"How many possibles?"

"I'll need a round of rat cheese, a heavy slab of salted bacon well wrapped in oil cloth, some sourdough starter, well contained, some hard tack, salt and pepper, and a pistol."

"What sort of pistol? They cost money."

Sixty-Eight Barrels on Treasure Lake

"The sort that holds at least six rounds. Kind of small. I'll need a holster and a box of ammunition."

"Why don't you have me pull your dick too before you go."

"Can you?"

"Ha. Ha."

I picked out a few more items, and Simmons packed them up good in a travel bag. He then wrote out a contract that made the saloon his on the morrow, and I signed it. He paid me in Yankee dollars, and I put the money in the travel bag.

He said, "What about your Mom and Dad buried out there?"

"One is in deep shit, the other is in deep ground. I won't be visiting their graves because they're dead. I didn't like them anyway."

"That's practical."

I went back to the saloon and relieved my stand in, checked the cash box. He'd only taken a few dollars.

I carried the cash box and the travel bag into my room at the back of the saloon, and put the box in the travel bag with the sale money.

I was feeling scared, but also excited and generous. I had more money now than I had ever imagined, even if I had sold the saloon for a pittance. I called for free rounds of whisky and a glass of beer for everyone. A shout went up, and I served them from one of the less watered barrels of whisky. The beer was bitter as milk weed, but it was beer.

Came time to close, I scuttled everyone out and locked up. I went back behind the counter and looked about, trying to feel sentimental about the place, but I couldn't find a drop of it in me. I felt about it like I did about Mama and Daddy. Good riddance.

I pulled the shotgun from under the bar, along with a box of shells, and carried it and my travel bag back to my room.

I stripped off, went to what used to be Daddy's bed, choked my chicken a couple of times, and tried to sleep.

Next morning, I took Chester the mule out of the shed and feed him a bucket of grain, brushed him good, dropped a blanket over his back, and saddled him up. My Daddy always took better care of that mule than he did me, and I was going to carry on that tradition of care and concern, though I might give myself equal attention, and if things got bad, I heard mule meat wasn't too bad if you cooked it right.

I got my travel bag and blanket roll fastened on the back of the saddle, along with a bag of grain for the mule, along with my shotgun. Hadn't no more than finished when the three Ps come riding up along with two other fellows, a bit older than me. They were in a wagon pulled by two good-looking mules.

I knew them. One of them, the one at the reins of the wagon, was Charlie Clawson, who was a step up from a half-wit, and a step down by choice, but as strong as a bull and could fix things. And then there was Jonas, last name unknown. He was always looking for work that wasn't complicated. He'd do near anything in that range. If you'd asked him to service your milk cow, he'd have done it, provided you could provide an overturned bucket for him to stand on to get to its ass.

When they saw me, they nodded at me, and I nodded back.

Paul said, "Let's go find that tracker, see if we can convince her to go with us. You talk to her, and smile a lot, Rabbit. You got nice teeth."

There was a long stretch of nothing, and then there was something, and that something was well out of town and you could smell it before you got there. It smelled like turpentine and there was a sound like a sky full of angry bees.

When we arrived at the sawmill where Bleedhead worked, we saw mules, men, and women working, white and black and Indian, the mules of varying shades of tan and gray. The air was filled with sawdust, and up close that ripe turpentine smell was as sharp as the blade on Death's scythe.

I climbed off my mule and gave the reins to Paul, who sat on his horse holding them. The others stayed back while I went to a little shack built of broadly spaced boards that I assumed was of some importance. I could see someone in there between the slats. I knocked on the door, which moved considerably when I did. This might be a sawmill, but carpenter skills were in short supply.

A white man in faded overalls wearing a sagging hat that might once have been white, a wad of tobacco about the size of an apple in his cheek, opened the door and spat on the ground between us.

"Excuse me sir," I said. "Are you the owner of the mill."

"I am. Gerald T. Cranshaw, formerly a Colonel in the Confederate army."

"You are a long way from the South."

"Ain't that the truth."

"We are looking for a Miss Bleedhead."

"That bitch."

"May we speak with her."

"She's working."

"Yes, sir. But it's a matter of some importance."

"So is this sawmill."

"I understand. I won't take much time."

Gerald T. Cranshaw, formerly a Colonel in the Confederate army, looked me over like someone figuring the best way to squash a roach, then said, "Make it damn quick. Go back yonder. She's working the boards."

"Thank you, sir."

I left while Gerald T. Cranshaw, formerly a Colonel in the Confederate army, was giving my partners a once-over.

I walked back to them and told them what I was doing, then I walked to where Cranshaw said Bleedhead was working.

When I got around there I saw a colored girl about my age in overalls with hair that looked more Indian than Negro. She had a hook on a pole, and she was using it to push a log along a moving belt that was pulling another log toward a big old buzzing saw blade driven by a steam boiler.

I assumed this was Bleedhead. She filled out the overalls nicely, and I felt something stir inside of me I had never felt move before, and when she looked up and saw me, that thing stirred again, only this time a little more vigorously. She had smooth skin the color of coffee with cream, and she had a way of moving that seemed panther like to me. Her chocolate eyes only studied me for a moment before she continued pushing the log on down the line into the steam-driven saw blade. The look she gave me was like she was pushing my dick into that blade instead of a log.

The saw whined and chewed and dusted the air with sawdust. She was already using the hook to pull another log off a wagon of logs, shifting it onto the belt with the ease and strength of a lumberjack.

I went over close and called to her. "Miss Bleedhead."

She looked at me again. This time the look she gave me caused me to stand up on the balls of my feet for a moment.

"What you want? I'm busy."

"Well, me and some other fellows have got a job offer for you that pays and you might like it."

"I can't talk now. Come back when I'm off at seven."

"Tonight?"

"Yep."

"Very well then. Where should I have this discussion with you?"

"Come back right here."

With that she went back to work, and it was as if I weren't even standing there. I waited a little longer, watching that girl and feeling that stirring some more, then I hiked back to the others.

We waited off amongst the trees, and Paul and Preacher passed a bottle, offering me a snort, and with some reluctance, allowing

Possum a jolt. Charlie and Jacob had their own bottle, and they were sitting up in the wagon nipping on that while we sat on the ground with our mules and horses nearby. When it was time to meet up with Bleedhead, all of us went.

Bleedhead was at the same place, but now there were no logs, and since it was night, she had brought a lantern and had set it on the log runner. She also had a double barrel shotgun. That kind of weapon was certainly popular. It was pointed at us, but the hammers weren't cocked. She had her thumb draped over one of them, though.

"What is it you people want?" she said.

"She's sassy for colored, ain't she?" Charlie said. He had a whisky grin that looked like someone had kicked a few slats out of a picket fence.

"I'm sassy all right, and if you mess with me, chicken neck, I'll blow a hole through you so big your friends can drive a mule team through it pulling a wagon."

"I know I'm not all that smart," Charlie said, "but I don't think the hole would be big enough to drive mules through him, let alone a wagon."

"You're right, Charlie," Possum said, "you ain't that all that smart."

"Let's hear some talking," Bleedhead said. "I'm wanting to get back to my shack and plunk my pudding."

"That's bold," said Preacher, and he laughed.

"What we need is a guide," Paul said. "And for you to lower that shotgun. We're offering gainful employment."

"You like this job?" Preacher said.

"Beats not eating."

"What would you say if we offered you enough to quit for a while?"

"I'd say I need to hear that offer, and then I'd need to see the money."

"Fair enough," Preacher said. He reached in his coat pocket and pulled out his and Paul's pieces of the map. He gave Possum a look.

Possum pulled out his pieces, and they put them down on the conveyer belt and pushed all of them together.

"We got a map," Preacher said. "But we didn't put it down so well, but a lot of it's right. Maybe you could help us find what we thought we knew. We been there just the once."

"That there is Lost Valley," she said, putting her finger on the map.

"How lost could it be if you know its name?" Paul said.

"It's not lost meaning you can't find it, it's lost meaning it's hard to get to and harder to leave, or so Indians say."

"Yeah," Paul said. "We been in it and we've been out of it. No Indians bothered us."

"See anything else when you were there?" Bleedhead said.

"Yeah," Paul said. "It's got a lot of animals, and clean water, and there's fruit and nut trees, though they didn't have any fruit or nuts on them that we noticed."

"What about the animals?"

"We saw deer, and bear and heard a panther scream," Paul said. "They didn't bother us."

"I see," she said.

There was something about Possum, Preacher, and Paul, the way they answered Bleedhead's questions, that made me think I might not have gotten the whole story about their time in the valley.

"I don't know how much truth I'm getting here," Bleedhead said, "but I don't think it's the whole sack full."

"What we want to know," Possum said, "is will you take us there for a good payment, or not?"

"I got a steady job here," she said.

"You want this job back, little girl, would they rehire you?" Possum said.

"Might. But you can cut the little girl shit. I can handle myself."

"Would you look at the maps more carefully," Paul said. "Here's the deal. You go with us you can make a lot of money. You don't want to go with us, and you can look at this map, and figure it better than us, that's worth a bit of money, but not the bigger money if you guide us."

"You sure got a pretty shape," Charlie said.

"You, on the other hand," Bleedhead said, "look like a sack of shit stacked too high."

"That's not nice," Jonah said. "Him talking about how nice you look and all."

"I don't think he means to paint my portrait," Bleedhead said.

"Well," Possum said. "Can you read that map or not?"

Bleedhead examined the pieces in the lantern light. She pulled two pieces apart, and then repositioned them.

"They're torn pretty even, but this one goes here, and this one goes there. Knowing how the map goes together seems like something you'd remember."

"It's been awhile," Possum said, "and we ain't been together. And the other way fits too."

"Not if you know the place you're looking for."

"But you haven't been there?" Possum said.

"Nope. But like I was saying, I know of it."

"So, can you find this place?"

"What's it worth to you?"

Preacher told her.

"That's not enough for it to be worth it to me. They say that valley is haunted. I've heard stories."

"We were there," Paul said. "We didn't see any ghosts."

"No, but I can tell by the way you talk, you found something," she said.

"There were some unexpected events," Paul said. "Let's leave it at that."

It occurred to me that I had some sizable sale money in my pocket, and I might ought to slip away while I was ahead, and do a serious scamper.

I didn't though.

Not after the brothers and Possum raised their offer for Bleedhead's assistance, half now and the other half on completion of employment, and she agreed.

If Bleedhead was going, I wanted to go, even if it wasn't a smart choice. The loins were not meant to make reasonable decisions.

Next morning Bleedhead got some payment in Yankee dollars to start out, the source of it being the three Ps who had chipped in together. She counted it carefully. When she was satisfied, she packed the money on her horse, told Gerald T. Cranshaw, formerly a Colonel in the Confederacy, that she was leaving work and going out on a tracking job.

He didn't like it. He cussed her, and then he cussed us, and then he begged her to stay. She said she might be back in the winter.

He said she wouldn't, as he wouldn't hire her back if she did come back, and then as she walked to mount her horse, he said, "Look, you're a good worker. You feed those logs into that saw better than two men. Come back soon and I'll consider taking you back on."

"I'll keep that in mind," Bleedhead said, and we rode away, leaving Gerald T. Cranshaw, formerly a Colonel in the Confederate army, looking as if he might drop to his knees and cry.

Bleedhead led us along, and near right away Possum said, "Well hell. I can follow the map the way you're going."

Preacher, who rode next to Paul and me, and just behind Bleedhead, turned on the back of his horse to look at Possum. Possum had tied his horse to the back of the wagon Jonah was driving, and was sitting in the bed of it like a prissy lady on her way to a church revival.

"Anyone can follow it a few feet, you blithering idiot. We hired her to get us there."

Possum tucked a wad of tobacco in his cheek, said, "I was just joking."

"Sure, you were," Paul said.

We all hated Possum, and none of us trusted the other, and with good reason, I might add.

The day went and the night came, and we slept out under the stars and moon. The wind was chill but not unbearable when we sat by the fire and listened to the wood crackle and burn, smelled the smoke from it.

Charlie had a little guitar in his travel goods, and he brought it out and played and sang.

When Charlie sang about love lost, I could see Possum's face. It was lit up by the firelight, and there was a tearful gleam in his eyes. When Charlie paused in his singing, Possum said, "Charlie, you may have the brains of a goat, at best, but you can sing like a goddamn angel."

"Thanks, Possum," Charlie said.

"Never took you for the sentimental kind," Paul said.

"Life can change a man, but it don't make him forget," Possum said.

On those nights when we sat around the fire, Bleedhead laid out her bedroll some distance away from us. She lay with her head propped up on her saddle, and I figured that shotgun she had shown us that first night, was under her blankets, near to hand.

I liked knowing she was there. Possum did too, but for different reasons. He licked his lips when he looked in her direction, like a hungry man about to enjoy a greasy pork chop.

The days came and went, and finally, we broke into a thick swathe of forest and started up a trail so narrow we thought the wagon might not be able to fit through. But it did. Just barely.

Upwards we climbed. I began to feel ligh-headed. It was as if two small, but long, nails had been driven into my forehead just above my eyes. I had always lived in the mountains, but I hadn't been up this high ever, and the height was getting to me.

Bleedhead was just in front of us, leading her horse. We were all leading our horses and mules, and they too seemed winded, snickering the way they do when irritated. The mules pulling the wagon were particularly cantankerous, and the wagon rattled like bullets in a tin can.

Bleedhead stopped at a bend in the trail and pointed. The day was beginning to die and its dying shadow was touching on the tips of the mountains, turning them purple and blue, and above that, the last of the sunlight was bleeding strawberry red all over the sky.

"That range there," Bleedhead said. "That's where we're going. And once there, I think I can find the path in."

"Think?" Possum said.

"I said I know about the valley. Never said I been there. I may leave you once you get there. Take my half of the money and go. I'm beginning to think I don't need the rest."

"Not the deal," Paul said. "We're going to need you to stick around."

"In fact," Preacher said, "we insist."

I watched as Bleedhead's face realized what I already knew. We weren't volunteers, we had been drafted.

"And by the way, Bleedhead can't be your whole name. What do you go by besides that?"

"Sally," she said.

Preacher turned on the charm, but it was merely window dressing, and we all knew it.

"We would rather be able to get in and out without losing our way or getting scalped, so we'll put an extra cherry on top of our offer. What do you think?"

"How big a cherry," she asked.

It wasn't that big, but Sally, knowing the score and trying to keep face, to stay as in control as she liked to think she might be, said, "All right, then."

We camped right there on the trail that night. Sally had put a bit of fear into us about the Blackfeet, and though she said they weren't any kind of worry where we were, for the moment, Preacher insisted we take turns at watch, to see if any of them were sneaking up on us.

Sally laughed at that. "You people. A Blackfoot could track a gnat flying through the woods, follow it by smelling its farts. They'd be on your white asses and have you dead and scalped and thrown off the side of the mountain and you wouldn't never know it, unless they paused to torture you awhile. You fellows really don't know your ass from a hole in the ground, do you?"

"How about that? A damn colored girl lecturing us on survival," Possum said.

I thought that Possum might have a point. He and Paul and Preacher had been around the tree more than a bit, and seemed quite capable of survival. I had a feeling Sally might be a bit big for her britches, which she wore quite nicely in truth, but still. She couldn't have been more than in her early twenties. She had seen some stuff for her age, but the three Ps had seen a lot.

Preacher decided on a guard anyway. I drew the short straw, which I figure was bullshit, because Possum held the straws. I think he tricked me somehow.

I found a position above the camp, on a rising at the edge of the trees.

I sat there with my shotgun, my back against a large cedar, and watched the shadows squirm about in the forest and between clefts in the mountains until night was fully settled in. A night bird was calling, and in the distance, another was calling back.

I scanned about from time to time, seeing nothing unusual, though a coon came down out of the woods and sat in the middle of the trail and looked at our sleeping camp. He stood up on his hind paws and sniffed the air, and seeming to not like the smell, turned and went back into the woods as soft and soundless as a shadow in moccasins.

And then a warm hand rested on mine, and I tried to jump up from my position, but the hand had me. It pushed me back against the tree.

"Hold up," a voice said. "It's me."

Me was Sally. She had her shotgun with her. I hadn't even seen her move from her bedroll, though I hadn't had my eye glued on her spot the entire time. At that same moment, below me, in camp, I saw

Possum, still wearing that bowler hat, sneaking toward Sally's bed-roll. As he settled on his knees and pulled her blankets back, there was just her pack of goods and the saddle there.

"I thought he might try that," Sally said.

Possum looked up into the trees. I don't think he could see much up there, the way the night lay over us, and by the time he looked, Sally was up and behind the big cedar.

I lifted a hand at Possum. He made no sign he saw me. He got off his knees and went back to his bedroll like a child that had been sent to bed without his supper and was expecting a whipping in the morning.

"I thought about killing him," Sally said, coming out from behind the tree and sitting beside me. Her voice was soft and her breath was sweet. I could tell she had been chewing mint leaves, something I did myself from time to time.

"You were going to kill Possum?"

"Considered it. You know they're going to kill us, don't you? And those two boys too, and then maybe each other."

"I've thought on that."

"Then why are you here?"

"Why are you?"

"Money."

"Partly the same."

"What's the other part," she said.

"I just wanted to quit what I was doing. I didn't like it."

"Me too."

"What makes you think I wouldn't want to kill them or you," I said.

"I can tell."

"That's no kind of answer."

"All I got, though," she said.

"Your gut?"

"Experience. Had a lot of it early on, as a child. Most everyone I ever loved had either been a slave, or had been hunted down and killed in the swamps back home. You pick up on signals, how people act, how they watch you. I like the way you watch me. I don't like the way Possum does. It was clear to me he was thinking about humping me. His kind would think I'm thinking about it too. He doesn't hold me in high esteem."

"You sound a little different talking to me."

And she did. It wasn't so much the words she used, it was how she used them.

"No matter what tone I take, I fear it comes off cocky."

She was right about that.

"It's a tool of survival. I learned books from my mother. She had secretly been taught to read by the son of her master. This was before I was born, before the War Between the States. He taught her for an exchange in favors."

"Oh."

"Exactly. He taught her reading, writing, and arithmetic, a bit of history and geography. She thought the trade was worth it, since he could have had her without giving anything in return."

"That's not right."

"Why the war was fought, Rabbit. It helped. Didn't cure, but it helped. I was never a slave, but my mama was, and she never completely got over it. She did love my daddy, and he loved her. They got together in the swamps, where they escaped to. He was part Seminole."

"I've heard," I said.

"When my parents died, I got a ride out west, working my way as I went, doing the usual jobs they gave me. Washing and ironing, field work. I ended up at the saw mill, but I was fed up with it. I wanted something new, like you."

"We're taking quite a chance."

"I think we get to where we're going, they get through having us do what it is they want us to do, and they'll do what we think they'll do. They'll kill us. And another thing. I'm figuring what they want us to do may be a lot different than what they're telling us, which isn't much. They don't all have their story together, and they know that, so they don't try to say so much because they might talk crossways of one another."

"Agreed. I know this, Sally. They are wholesale murderers with the conscience of a weasel in a hen house."

Sally nodded, paused. "All right. I'm just going to say it straight out without any dressed-up bull. You mind that I'm not white?"

"I don't mind at all. I don't care one way or another."

"Good. Kiss me."

I did. Her lips were warm and so was her skin where I touched her face and held it in my hands.

When our lips parted, she said, "I'm going back to sleep. See you tomorrow."

"Oh," I said, and might have added to that, but she was already moving away, down the hill toward her bedroll. She looked up at me when she got there. She held up the shotgun to let me know she was pulling it under her covers with her. Then she climbed into her bedroll as relaxed as a pig in a wallow.

Half through the night, Preacher woke up, as if awakened by a rooster crowing, pulled on his boots and came up the hill to replace me.

I won't kid you, the rest of that night I was as nervous as a female goat in a miner's hut. I had begun to realize that acquiring some treasure and slipping off from this bunch might not be as easy as I had first thought.

And now there was Miss Sally Bleedhead I was thinking about. I felt an obligation to her, though, in truth, she seemed quite capable of handling herself just fine.

Early morning, we loaded up and came through a narrow pass, and Possum yelled, "I remember this. I can go straight there from here."

Sixty-Eight Barrels On Treasure Lake

He rode up in the lead. We watched him hoot and holler and race his horse around a precarious curve in the trail, the left side being a dropoff so deep it fell into darkness below due to the thickness and height of the shadowed trees.

We rode on around, saw Possum riding up the trail, gravel tumbling down behind him. He made it to the top of the hill, and then dipped down out of sight.

We followed, and on the downside of the trail Possum was sitting on his horse looking about, his face making all kinds of contortions. "You know, I remember this, but how did we come out of them woods when we left the valley? I can't find the spot."

Possum was so surprised by not being able to find what he was certain of, he had taken off his bowler hat, which until that moment, I had begun to suspect might be a part of his head. I saw then why he wore it all the time. He had been scalped. He had an angry red patch on his head where some Indian had peeled him, thinking maybe he was dead. I had a feeling the Indian hadn't survived the event. He wiped his head with a stained, white rag he pulled from his coat pocket.

"I remember this too," said Preacher, and then Paul agreed he did too, but they were all baffled about where the trail that led through the woods was.

Jonah and Charlie came rattling up behind us in the wagon.

Sally got off her mount and walked to the trees, said, "See this batch of brush here?"

We all agreed we did, and we climbed down from our animals and led them behind us, over to where Sally was pointing.

"Brush is turning brown. It's dead. They've been cut and put there a while back to hide the path."

"I didn't notice that," Charlie said.

"Of course, you didn't," Sally said. "Brush has been broken off and stuck in the ground with the sharp end. First glance, it looks like it's growing. Had it been a little fresher, it might have fooled even me."

"That means someone blocked it on purpose," Paul said.

"Who blocked it?" Jonah said.

Paul and Preacher and Possum all looked as if we'd caught them rotating a finger from their ass to their mouth.

"Whoever," Preacher said.

Sally was standing close to me, looking at the ground. I looked too. There were the faint impressions of bare footprints, but to me, they didn't look right.

"Or whatever," Sally said.

"All right, then," Paul said, "let's move those limbs and take the path."

Sally stepped back and let us at the brush. We went up the trail removing the brush, which at first glance, looked like part of the forest. About thirty feet in, the trail was clear, and we mounted up and rode on. There was barely enough room for the wagon. It wound up through the trees, turned to the right, and wandered down into a valley.

Before we went down, we stopped at the pinnacle of the rise. The trees had thinned there, and we could consider the valley from our great height. The valley was deep and went for miles in either direction. It was surrounded by woods and rocks and rising mountains. A white mist rose from the center of the valley, and as we stood there, it began to dissolve in the sunlight and the wind picked up and pushed what was left of it away. In short time, we saw that the mist had been rising from a big lake in the center of the valley. It was a great sky-blue lake, shiny as a mirror, and I could see a little white something on it, about three hundred feet from shore. I reckoned that to be the steamboat I had heard about.

"Sure is pretty," Charlie said.

As we rode down, we got so we couldn't see into the valley anymore. We were creeping down behind a great rock wall. The trail ended at a tumble of big rocks and the tumble raised up to about a hundred feet high. It was clear it was where the three Ps had dynamited the trail closed.

Sixty-Eight Barrels on Treasure Lake

"We could ride around and look for another way in, but I'm thinking we just use the dynamite we stored here and blow it open again. This was the only damn trail we found that went out."

"Way those rocks are stacked," Sally said, "dynamiting it could go wrong."

"I'm pretty good with dynamite," Paul said. "Worked in mining for a time. But we got this problem. After we came through and blew the place, we only took out the dynamite we needed to blow the rocks. That was considerable, but there's a whole case we forgot on the other side."

Sally laughed out loud. "You fellows are some dynamite experts. You take your dynamite with you, boys. That's what an expert does."

"It was Possum left it," Paul said.

"Don't blame it on me," Possum said.

"It was you, though," Preacher said.

"Wouldn't the dynamite have been covered by the blast?" Sally said.

"It was pretty far back," Possum said. "Way back. Figure it'll be fine if nothing's meddled with it."

"What would?" I said. "A bear doing a little freelance mining?"

"Watch your mouth, boy, or I'll cut you from gut to gill," Possum said.

I had seen Possum work his knife, so I took this as highly instructive and changed the subject.

"So how do we get to it?" I said.

"As fate would have it, there was a little tunnel created in the explosion, and it goes straight down to the ground," Preacher said. "You have to climb up a piece to look down into it, but above it the stones are too slick to climb over. Tunnel is narrow. Too narrow for any of us to go through."

That's when the three Ps looked at me.

"Remember when we told you we might have to grease you up?" Preacher said.

"We might could grease up the girl," Possum said. "I could slather her up good, especially those titties, as you wouldn't want them to hang up."

"Nope," Sally said.

"It's just a thought," Possum said.

"Nope."

"Grease Jonah or Charlie up," I said.

"They're too big," Possum said. "You can see that. We couldn't shoot them through there if we stuck dynamite up their asses."

"Yeah," Jonah said. "Anyone can see that."

Preacher said, "Rabbit. See up where that rock sticks out, makes a kind of ledge?"

I looked where he was pointing. "Ah hell, Preacher. That's a hard climb."

"Naw," Paul said. "Any of us could make that climb. It's the tunnel up there that only you or the girl can go through, and we have already elected you."

I was between a pile of shit and a grizzly bear, and the pile of shit seemed a better choice than the grizzly bear. I took a deep breath, got off my mule, started to go up, but Preacher stopped me by grabbing my shoulder.

"Meant it when we said you might have to grease up. No use going up there and then finding out you'll need to. Jonah, get that pack off my horse, unwrap it and get out the lard can."

"Goddamn it," I said.

They had me strip off right there, giving me no privacy, and when I got down to the long johns, they had me take those off too, so there I was with my hammer swinging in the wind, and them putting grease all over me so seriously it was in the crack of my butt. My pecker and balls were slathered up like a chicken neck ready to drop into the frying pan. It was damn embarrassing.

They didn't put any of the grease on my hands and feet, as those were my climbing tools and they didn't want me slipping.

All the while they did this, Sally watched and smiled and kind of laughed. "You're going to hang your sausage on a rock, Rabbit."

"Nope," Paul said, and brought out a long piece of white cloth and wrapped it between my legs and tied it around my waist.

"Why the hell did you grease that part up if I'm going to wear this?" I said.

"You know, Rabbit," Paul said. "You make a good point. We should have thought of that."

All the men laughed and Sally grinned.

I started climbing, dust sticking to the grease on me, and the rag around my gonads feeling sticky and uncomfortable.

It wasn't really that hard to climb up there. There were plenty of foot and hand holds. I managed to get to that little shelf, and I could then see the tunnel they were talking about.

Rocks had fallen in an odd way and formed a straight shot tunnel, though it had some bumps of rocks in it. There was sunlight slipping down it except where my body made a shadow. I studied it a moment, decided it might not take much to loosen up a boulder that would drop the whole mountain on me and turn me into a pile of shit jelly wearing a greasy rag.

I looked down. Everyone was looking up at me. Only Sally seemed a little concerned.

Possum cupped his hands around his mouth so he could yell up at me.

"Well, go on."

I decided to go in head first and crawl. There was some slant to the tunnel, and I feared I might just slide through it like a turd shooting out of an asshole, but I bent forward and started through.

I felt like I was being swallowed by a snake, and for a moment, I had a bit of panic and considered backing out. But it also occurred to me that I was alive because they needed me. I soldiered on.

It was slow going because some of the floor was jagged and it cut my knees. I bumped my head a few times and had a slight panic as

I came to a narrow section, but the grease did indeed help me slide through, though the tunnel pinched a bit.

By this time, Preacher had climbed up on the shelf and was yelling encouragement to me. His voice came down the tunnel as if brought to me by a freight train.

"You're almost there, Rabbit."

I kept crawling and finally I broke out into the light. From there it was a short drop to the ground, about two feet, but it was still a rough fall coming through head first. I tumbled on the rocky ground, scraping up a bit.

I got to my feet and looked up the tunnel. Preacher was leaning in the mouth of it blocking most of the light up there, but I could make him out all right.

"I'm through," I said.

"I can see that," Preacher said. "Now, work your way down to the lake. You won't need to go all the way there, but to a big ole tree. An oak, I think. But you'll see it. It's the first big tree before a grassy clearing and then the lake. The box of dynamite is there. You find it. I'm going to lower a sack on a rope, and I want you to start putting sticks in it."

"Might it blow my head off?"

"Dynamite needs to be handled carefully, but not like glass. It's the fuse that's going to set it off. Still, I wouldn't be whacking it on anything. We want to get this done before dark."

With this encouragement, I turned and looked out at the valley. It was large and so goddamn blue. I could see the steamboat out there, obviously anchored. I thought that was an odd choice instead of leaving it tied up at the bank, but all of this was odd, and becoming odder by the moment.

I saw the tree he was talking about. It stood out large and alone. The air was sharp as a floor tack and it made me a little woozy, like good whisky sipped too fast on an empty stomach.

I walked down to the big tree. The box of dynamite was there. It wasn't a large box, but it was heavy to carry. I took my time with it, sometimes setting it down on the ground and taking a breather. Being as high up in the mountains as we were was starting to get to me.

Finally, I got it to the tunnel, and there was a tow sack on a rope dangling out of the mouth of it. I looked up the tunnel at Preacher, who was looking down.

"Put some sticks in the bag, and then I'll send it back down for more," he said.

I opened the dynamite box, which took some work, having to use a pointed rock to edge under the lid to open it. The dynamite was dry. Had it been sweating nitroglycerin I would have been worried. I knew that much from being around miners.

My clothes and boots were in the bag. I used the rag that had been tied around my waist to wipe off some of the grease, dressed, then I filled the bag with dynamite, and Preacher pulled it up. Nothing exploded.

We did this time and again. When we got to the last of the sticks, for some uncertain reason, I decided to take a few of them and set them aside.

While they were preparing to blow the opening, I went down with my sticks and put them in a hollow I found in that big ole tree. I didn't know if that was a good idea or not, but like I said, I was driven to do it.

Figured they blew those rocks, a bunch of them might be tumbling my way, so I hastened toward the thick line of woods on the edge of the lake. When I was almost there, I thought I saw something move between trees, and there was an unidentifiable and unpleasant odor that made the hair on the back of my neck stand up like the tines on a wire brush.

I tried to determine what I had seen, but couldn't arrive at any kind of satisfaction. I thought it might have been a young bear, though I had gotten such a fleeting glimpse, it could have been nothing more than a shadow. The odor had lessened by then, as if what had caused it had moved away.

I stood for a long time peering into the woods, until there was an explosion that damn near made me shit myself.

I had forgotten it was coming.

Let me tell you, I was glad I was far away, but I have to give Paul some credit. The path was blown wide open. The gap was about ten feet wide and had blown in such a way that it wasn't littered with large boulders, only smaller ones. That took some experience and some skill. The sides of the path looked shaky to me, still dripping dust and bits of gravel.

We all went about putting the big rocks aside, and then Jonah and Charlie came through with the mules and the wagon, followed by the three Ps leading the rest of the horses and my good ole mule. They stopped the wagon on a flat place overlooking the valley and the lake.

Charlie said, "They didn't use but a few sticks of that dynamite. They did it real good. Paul knows his stuff."

"I can see that."

"Could have done it myself, though," Charlie said. "I worked with miners. I'm not that smart, but I can do stuff like that. Give me something to blow up or fix, and I'm your man."

"Good for you, Charlie," I said.

It turned out that down by the lake there were two canoes fashioned out of trees. They were well hidden in a little weather worn indention where some trees grew close to the shore of the lake. They were pushed up against the roots of those big trees, tied off just out of the water so if it rose they wouldn't wash away.

"We built these to get out to the boat," Preacher said.

"Why not just dock the boat close to shore?" Sally said.

"We have the stolen goods on the boat," Preacher said. "Not likely, but it's possible someone might come out here and find it. It makes it a little harder with the boat out there in the lake."

Sixty-Eight Barrels on Treasure Lake

This sounded dubious.

"Jonah," Preacher said, "you stay with the stock. Curry them and feed them. Chop some wood. Drag in some dead wood along with it. Rest of us will get these boats in the water."

With Jonah going about his business in a grumpy fashion, we loaded some supplies, our personal gear, and Charlie and Possum took one boat, me and Sally took the other with Preacher and Paul in it.

Me and Sally paddled that boat while Preacher and Paul relaxed like big shots. I had my shotgun with me, and I laid it by my side where I thought I could get to it quickly. But the thing that was in my mind was how deadly Preacher was with his pistol, and I could only assume Paul was no slouch either. The shotgun was some comfort, but only a little.

As we came nearer the paddle wheel, I was surprised to see how big it truly was. It had seemed large enough from the distance, but coming up close it was bigger than the saloon I had sold times ten. It was two stories and there was a giant paddle wheel at one end. It shone bright in the sunlight.

There were knobs cut in the front of the canoes and some ropes were coiled up in the bottoms, and these were used to toss up onto the steamboat. There was a rope ladder dangling down from the boat, and it looked a little rotten. Preacher took the ends of the ropes and went up the ladder like a squirrel, and all it did was squeak a little. Once up there, he fastened the two ropes to something, and the rest of us took turns climbing up. Possum and his crew had to step from their boat to ours before they could climb up on the ladder. Both canoes were tied off to the steamboat.

When we got on deck, we could see there were a bunch of barrels on board. The word SALT was painted on the sides of the barrels in thick white lettering. The barrels were lined up, and there were so many on the deck—and keep in mind it was a sizable deck—there was only a narrow path between them to the cabin and wheelhouse.

Preacher went into the cabin, and came out with a pry bar.

"Those four barrels on the end, there," Preacher said, handing me the pry bar. "Pop the top on the one nearest the stern."

I noted those barrels had leaks at their bottoms, and it wasn't salt coming out of them. It was something liquid. I took the pry bar, slipped the edge of it under one of the lids, and pried it loose. A smell came out of it like it meant business. It was the smell of death.

Everyone had come up close by this time. I looked in the barrel and I could see a lot of salt with something black in the center. The sharp smell from the salt tickled my nose, combined with the death stink, I thought I was going to lose my stomach for a moment. I assumed the death smell was from the black round thing in the center. On further examination, I realized it was the top of someone's head.

"There's the same in these other barrels, but these four are starting to turn," Preacher said. "Can see that by the leakage, which is why I let you open it. Body's already ruined."

"There are people in the barrels?" Sally said.

"We got to thinking on a bit of trade I had done in the past," Possum said, scratching his ass in such a way his fingers dug into his pants and pushed them into his ass crack. "These barrels of salt the steamboat was hauling made it an easy choice. Salt is right good at keeping a body fresh for some time.

"This bit of trade I did was digging up bodies for medical schools. They paid mighty good and didn't ask a lot of questions. I made some prime dollars, but I got to figuring it was easier to just go on and kill the bodies fresh. That way you save all that back-breaking labor of digging up graves and hauling them stinkers out of coffins. And you have to wait around for someone to be buried, so it's not constant work. Might have to dig in the rain, and sneaking out to a graveyard added some more pain to it. You kill someone in an alley, sling them over a horse and cover them with a blanket, and you're on your way."

"These, however, were not killed in an alley," Preacher said. "They are the former steamboat crew. We decided the gold was best split fewer ways. We'll want you to push these barrels over the side."

"You mean all them other barrels have dead folks in them?" Charlie said.

"No, but quite a few," Paul said. "Sizable crew. We tried not to mess them up too much when we stuck them in the salt. Medical schools like bodies that are intact."

"I don't know why anyone would do that," Charlie said. "Kill a fellow like that, and sell them."

I was beginning to like Charlie better all the time.

"They're worth money, Charlie," Possum said. "Weren't you listening? Even you ain't so stupid not to understand that."

"How'd you end up here?" Sally asked.

I had heard their version of the story, of course, but they went ahead and told it for Sally, Jonah and Charlie.

When the tale was finished, I noted that it was close to the version they had told me, but not exactly. It was hard to know exactly what was what with those three.

"All right," Preacher said. "Now you know. Toss those leaking barrels over the side, and don't get that leak on your hands. It's hard to get that smell off. Some ways, you never do."

It seemed wrong to foul that smooth water up with barrels of salt and dead bodies, but we didn't have a lot of choice. We did as we were told.

When this was done, the three Ps led us off the deck and down deck into a cabin. In one corner, it was stuffed with gold bars. It wasn't that there were so many of them, but there was certainly enough to make a person rich for the rest of their lives, and have enough left over to bribe the Devil in Hell. I picked up one of the bars. It was heavy. They had to work to load those gold bars onto the steamboat, that's for sure.

Next, we were guided to the engine room. There was a lot of wood stacked there, and even some coal. Paul had us shovel the coal and toss the wood in what I call a big furnace.

They started a fire, and while we rested from the loading of wood and coal, Paul said, "We heat water in the boiler until we have steam, then we switch a valve and feed steam to the engine, and the steam gives the gears power to turn the paddle wheel. We guide the working of the boat with the big hand wheel. That way, we can park right up next to the shore."

"Listen to him," Possum said. "I taught him that kind of business. He doesn't know the difference in a paddle wheel and a paper boat. I worked on steamboats for a couple of years. Captain was training me to be a pilot. But I stole his goods, and he got rid of me. It's a boring job anyway."

Paul grunted. I could tell he wanted to tear Possum's head off and shit down his neck, but he contained himself admirably.

He said, "There's a big room for the animals downstairs, and there's easy access with a ramp. There's hay and grain there already, for transporting stock down the river."

Preacher said, "Very well, since you're the ace on this, to hear you tell it, boat gets heated up, you can work the wheel and get us alongside the shore then, can't you Possum."

"I'll show you how it's done," Possum said.

"I'd like to watch you do it," Charlie said. His simple mind seemed overcome with the excitement of a big steam engine.

"Just don't get in the way," Possum said.

"Yes, sir," Charlie said.

It took a while, but when the steam was built up, Possum, with the help of Charlie, got the paddle wheel churning. The rest of us went up on the deck while this was taking place.

In time the great boat began to move. Possum made a huge circle in the lake, cutting the flow of the water wheel from time to time to direct the turning. It was a tedious affair, but finally he got it wheeled and we made our way toward the shore. As the boat neared, Possum began to turn it so that the side of the boat would come up against the shore line.

The docking was less smooth than intended, and the boat banged up against the bank of the lake hard enough to knock those of us standing on the deck down. One of the barrels tipped over against the railing, and Paul set it straight. That big bear of a man did that as easily as a milk maid turning a milk bucket upright.

I was told to grab one of the docking ropes, Sally took another. Then they lowered the ramp and we went ashore. Paul drove some stobs into the ground in a few spots, and the ropes were tied off to those. The canoes we had come in had been pushed up on the shore.

Paul had us untie the canoes and put them back into their former place in the hollow near the shore. After that we met up with Jacob.

Jonah was glad to see us. He said, "I think there's bears out there in those woods."

"There's all manner of things in those woods," Preacher said.

"One of the horses has done got sick," Jonah said.

The sick horse had gone to ground, its front legs curled under it, its head hung. I looked it over, but except for it being listless and its nose warm, I couldn't have told you if it was sleepy, or about to die.

"Leave it here for now," Preacher said. "Let's get the others on board."

Eventually Possum and Charlie showed, and we led the stock onto the boat and down to the stable at the bottom. There were some port holes there, as Preacher called them, and we opened those to give the animals air.

There was hay and feed and a great water tank with a trough under it. Preacher turned the tap and water filled the trough. We let the animals drink, but dry as they were, we had to be careful they didn't drink too much and too fast, lest they bloat. We were careful with the grain too, so as not to founder them.

We pulled the wagon onto the deck of the boat, not wanting to hitch up the animals for such a short trip. There were rings in the floor of the deck, and Paul got some rope from somewhere and looped it through the rings and we bound the wagon down so it wouldn't shift in case a storm came and the boat rocked.

The day was waning and the sunlight had turned pink and was shining through rocky splits in the mountain. The lake appeared to be bleeding.

"We won't be doing much more today," Preacher said. "Bleedhead, there's a kitchen, a wood stove, and plenty of wood. Go in there and get the stove going. There're some beans in cans, some pots and pans, a reservoir of water. Warm some of that up, and cook some bacon with it. Charlie, get the bacon out of the pack."

"I'm no goddamn cook," Sally said. "I'm a guide."

"A guide that cooks. Now get the fire going, or you'll be a piece of ass that cooks."

"Don't talk to her like that," I said.

"She'll do us good one way or another," Preacher said.

"I'd just as soon she won't cook," Possum said. "I'd love to dip my wick."

Sally glared at Preacher and Possum, but she went inside the great boat to do the job. I think she did it without any real argument because she saw what I saw right then. A kind of darkness came over Preacher, and it was like being able to look through his flesh and see the bones and the night of his soul stitched in between. Now that he had us here in the valley, the real man was starting to show, and that man was a murderer and no telling what all. Sally protested too much, he'd let Possum have her, and he and Paul might take a ride their selves. I tried to stop them, I'd be joining those barrels at the bottom of the lake.

Possum had gone off cackling by this time, and Paul had pulled Jonah and Charlie off to do some chore or another.

"Rabbit," Preacher said. "You're going to have a bit of jerky and no hot food tonight, because you're going to go ashore and watch after that sick horse. I started to shoot it, but I think it's just worn. I want you to see if you can get it to drink, eat a little. We can make it with one less horse or mule, but I'd rather not. That one is a good puller, and I think it just pulled too much. A little rest, drink and food, and it ought to come around. I think you might be more suited for the job than Jonah, and I wouldn't leave Charlie to do much of anything that left him by himself for too long. He might wander off. Horse doesn't recover right away, we'll shoot it. Around midnight, one of us will relieve you. I want you to pay attention to your surroundings and give me a report when I see you next. Might want to watch for bears and such."

I thought he had put an emphasis on the word "such."

"Sally will be left alone," I said.

"You have my word," he said.

I wasn't sure that was worth much, but I didn't say anything. I got my pistol and derringer, and tying a strap to my shotgun, slung it over my shoulder. I took a bucket and some goods for watering and feeding the horse, some jerky and a canteen for myself, trudged down the ramp and onto shore.

The sunlight had about finished bleeding by the time I got to that poor horse. That beast looked like something had let the air out of it.

I rubbed its nose and it made a soft nickering sound, then put its nose to the ground. Using the bucket, I poured water from a canteen into the bottom of it, about three inches, and put it in front of the horse, gently tried to lift its head. It wasn't easy, but finally I got it lifted and the horse smelled the water. It put its head in the bucket and began to drink. I managed to have it eat a bit from a grain sack I opened, and then the horse lost interest. But I thought I saw a bit of a spark in its eyes. That may have been nothing more the last of the dying light.

I built me a fire out of some of the wood Jacob had collected. He hadn't exactly gone all out on the fresh wood chopping, and some of it wasn't any more than sticks, but he had dragged in a heap of dead wood. I mostly used that and got a fire going. I built it up high, because it was starting to chill a bit, and the bright light from a big fire made me feel better.

I sat on a log near the fire and got out the cold jerky I had brought with me. It was wrapped in waxed paper. I placed the paper on the ground and opened the canteen. I placed the shotgun across my lap. I could see the horse from there. Jacob had tied him out to a little tree with a long rope, but he was near the fire.

The horse turned its head and considered the darkness, made a snorting noise. I looked where the horse was looking, but all I saw was blackness. I had this uncomfortable feeling I was being watched, and I remembered what Preacher had said.

"...and such."

I got up a few times and walked around the fire carrying the shotgun, stopping from time to time to put fresh logs on it.

Eventually, I sat my ass on the log and tried to stay alert. The feeling that I was being watched grew so much, I turned around on the log, away from the fire, and faced the dark. Finally, I pushed the log I was sitting on closer to the fire. Close enough the back of my neck felt sunburned. But I was feeling better about having my back to it, facing out into the night. That gave me the left and right sides and the way I was looking to worry about. I wasn't expecting anything to come through that fire from behind, and if it died down even a little, I was quick to load it up with wood.

After a time, I began to hear faint movement beyond the fire. It was at first quite stealthy, and then it wasn't so stealthy. There was that awful stench I had smelled before when I first came into the valley and looked out into the trees.

Then there was the sound of more than one thing moving, limbs cracking, leaves and pine needles crunching. My first thought was bears, because there was a snuffling sound, like they'll make. But this wasn't quite that. It sounded like a fellow with a head cold.

I stood up from my log and cocked the hammers on my shotgun, pulled my coat open so I could get to my pistol quick.

A few times I thought I saw something moving around the fire, getting closer over time, but never fully coming out of the shadows. Then there were quite a few somethings.

The horse was obviously feeling better now. It was standing and starting to turn its head from side to side. And then it jerked back and I thought I saw dark hands grab it. Next moment there was a sound from that horse, like I had never heard a horse make. Almost a scream. My skin shimmied like a snake trying to crawl off.

Sixty-Eight Barrels on Treasure Lake

I pulled a burning stick from the fire and waved it a few times causing the flames on it to grow, then I tossed it high and in the direction of where I had last seen the horse standing. For an instant, the light from the burning stick flared wide and I could see them. They weren't bears, and there were a lot of them. Hairy and man-like, but not quite. Their blood-flecked teeth flashed in the light, their eyes were like flaming emeralds. The horse was down on its side and hands were ripping at it, tearing open its throat and stomach as effortless as ripping cheese cloth.

This was all seen in a moment, and then the flaming stick hit the ground and the torch flickered and went out in a spray of sparks.

My heart thumped so loud I could hear it. I immediately started to build the fire higher, trying not to get too far from the shotgun I propped against the log. I finally had the fire blazing hot and high, throwing its light wide. I caught a glimpse of them moving away, and then I couldn't see them anymore. But I could smell them. They were just beyond the firelight.

Now I knew what Preacher, Possum and Paul had dealt with, what the secrecy was about. Even folks like me and Sally, who were looking for a change in life, money, might have hesitated had they told us there was a danger of being killed by hairy creatures. The only thing I could hope at the time was that the beasts didn't get used to the idea of fire and I wouldn't end up like that horse.

The obvious thing was for me to head back to the steamboat, and though that wasn't a long distance away, it was enough of a distance in the dark that I wasn't willing to try it. I thought about another torch to use for making my way to the boat, but it might go out. And, unlike the huge roaring fire that was causing me to sweat like a church deacon caught with his dick in a cat's butt, a torch might not be enough to keep them at bay.

The night dragged on forever, but finally I heard the ramp on the steamboat come down and strike the shore. I saw two torches move in the darkness.

It was my replacement.

Suddenly there were other torches being lit, and they were tossed toward the shore. They were better torches than my flaming stick had been, and when they hit the ground they didn't go out.

I saw glimpses of the hairy things darting into the shadows. The two men carrying torches moved toward me. It was Preacher and Charlie.

Preacher fired a couple of shots into the night, maybe at something, or maybe to frighten whatever was out there, and then they were standing near me in the glow of my firelight.

"Where's the horse?" Preacher said.

"That's what you got to say to me? Where's the horse? They got it."

"Who got it?" Charlie said.

"Them," I said, pointing in the gloom. "Them. Big fucking hairy things with teeth like knives. They grabbed the horse and pulled it away, tore it open."

"Yeah," Preacher said. "They got the strength for that."

"I didn't see nothing," Charlie said.

"That doesn't surprise me," Preacher said.

"You knew about them all along," I said.

"I thought it better to take my time telling you," Preacher said.

"You sending me here could have got me killed."

"I was hoping the horse would get better. We can use another horse with all we got to do, and I figured right that you're a survivor."

"That's it? You could use another horse, so you sent me out here with those monsters."

"Monsters?" Charlie said, and he started looking around.

"They're getting bolder," Preacher said. "Usually, it's just one or two, and they aren't that aggressive. Easy to shoot at first, because they didn't know what a gun was when we first came. They do now. We taught them that."

"Tell that horse they aren't all that aggressive," I said. "He could answer, he might have a different story for you."

"All right, then," Preacher said. "Let's head back to the steamboat."

"With those things out there?" I said.

"Those torches are still burning. They hate fire the way a duck hates the desert. Come on."

I gathered up my goods, and with the shotgun clutched tight in my hands, we started back to the boat.

I kept looking over my shoulder as we went, trying to stay near the light of the torches on the ground. Now and again I could hear and smell those creatures out there in the dark.

By the time we got to the boat, lanterns had been lit all over it, and it was bright as a little city. Everyone who had been left behind was on deck. The ramp got cranked up and we stood at the railing looking out at the night. We didn't see anything but the big fire.

There were chairs on the deck now. Some of the barrels had been moved off the deck while I was on shore, tucked away inside the steamboat somewhere, though a few remained.

We all sat in the chairs that were arranged in a wide circle. All of us had our guns with us. Sally sat near to me. Possum was to my right, and the coat he was wearing was starting to smell as bad as the creatures. Or maybe that was Possum himself. Preacher was directly across from me, Paul to his left, Charlie and Jonah on the other side of him.

"Okay," I said. "We need some real explanation now."

"Rabbit, go over and pop the lid on the barrel on the far end," Preacher said.

I was angry enough to feel bold. "You pop the goddamn lid."

"You're working for me, Rabbit."

"I said you pop it. You sent me out there knowing full well those things were out there, and didn't tell me. Didn't send anyone with me. Idea was you might save a horse, and if you didn't, I was no loss."

"It wasn't like that," Preacher said.

"You don't need to explain yourself to him," Paul said.

"Like I said, you want that lid popped, you pop it," I said.

"All right, Rabbit," he said. "You're right. I owe you some explanation, but the best explanation is the barrel."

Preacher walked over there. After a moment, we all followed.

"This is one of them from the woods," Preacher said. "I want you to look."

The pry bar was lying by the barrel. He picked it up and used it to lift the lid. There was a lantern on the railing next to the barrel, and it filled the barrel with light.

Preacher scooped the salt until we could see the head of one of the creatures. One eye was open and packed with salt, the other was closed. Its lips were curled back and I could see its many, sharp teeth, gritted with salt. There were enough teeth there for two human mouths. Still, up close, it looked less like and animal and more like a human.

Preacher dropped the bar on the deck. The sound of it clattering made me jump. He studied me for a moment, said, "Those surgeons pay for corpses to cut up? What do you think a body like this would be worth? What do you think taking a few of these ugly bastards on a carnival tour would be worth? The money they'd make? No telling what Ole Salty here is worth?

"Most of these barrels are full of salt, a few are stuffed with dead steamboaters. But we get the rest of them filled with those hairy things, they would be worth a fortune. In the long run, maybe worth more than all that gold. Hell, we could pour the steamboat crew out, now that we know about these creatures. We keep this place secret, we could come back and pot a few from time to time. We also need to build a cage and bring out a couple alive."

"Yeah," Charlie said, "but that gold, it don't have no teeth."

"Ever observant," Paul said. "But you're thinking short. You got to see the big picture there, Charlie."

"Blackfeet have legends about hairy beasts that live in this valley," Sally said. "I thought they meant bears."

"Tomorrow, come day break, we're going to start harvesting them and filling these barrels."

"Don't know I like this idea," I said.

"You are in, or you are out, Rabbit," Possum said. "You either work for us, or you can eat a bullet, maybe get sold to the surgeons, we don't decide to go one hundred percent critters. Your choice. True for all of you."

"Yep," Possum said, and Paul nodded. They had their hands on their pistols.

We were in. What choice did we have?

Possum and Charlie roused the fire in the furnace and chugged us away from the shore and dropped anchor, then we all turned in.

I tried to sleep on the deck of the boat. All the others had gone inside and picked rooms. I lay there and looked up at the sky, which had gray cloud cover with moonlight shining through it. I lay there on my bedroll and thought about sneaking away, but to do that, I had to cross through where the creatures were, and at night. And I didn't want to leave Sally.

I stripped off and slipped over the side and swam around the steamboat, and finally climbed back up by means of the rope ladder, and redressed. The swim had made me feel cleaner. I shook off like a dog and put my clothes back on. I lay down on my bedroll and pulled a blanket over me.

The cloud cover began to blow away. The partial moon was shiny as if polished with a rag, and the stars were popping. And then I was asleep.

Come daylight, I awoke to Possum giving me a sharp kick in the ribs. It made me grab at my shotgun.

"Put it down, Rabbit Shit," he said. "Time to get up and kill monsters."

I got up and put my boots on. The others were on deck now. Sally looked solemn as stone. She had her shotgun cradled in her arms.

I went over to her.

"You okay?" I asked her.

"What do you think? I waited for Possum to stick his head in the room where I was trying to sleep with one eye open. I was going to blow his ugly head off. Anyone stuck their head in there, it was going to get blown off. You?"

"I think we got ourselves in a bad way."

"I got nothing against them hairy things. This is their place, same as the Indians. Always someone got to find something to shit on."

"Do we have a choice?"

"I plan to only kill one if I have to. If it comes after me. Otherwise, I plan to miss."

"I'll do the same."

"We have to stay sharp, Rabbit, look for a way to get out of this mess. I'm not interested in money or adventure anymore."

"I'd still like a few of those gold bars," I said.

"That would be nice, I admit, but I don't want to get raped and murdered for it."

I thought we might ride the horses on this hunt, but that wasn't in the plan. They were fed and watered and Charlie was left behind to shovel horse shit and spoiled hay off the floor, put it in a wheel barrow, bring it up, dump it over the side.

We had been here a little over a day, and so far we had managed to dump horse shit and dead bodies into the lake.

"They like to nest during the day," Preacher said. "Sometimes in trees. They've learned some lessons. They know what we're about now, and they have the strength, and now the urge, to tear our asses up. Stay alert."

We came upon the poor horse from last night. It was little more than some skin and bones. Those things had made short, hungry work of it. The fire had burned down and was now just a big pile of gray ash.

Possum got out his dick and peed in the ash, turned and shook his johnson at Sally.

"How you like that?" he said.

"Like what?" she said.

Possum made a face like he had bitten into an unripe persimmon.

"Put that damn thing up," Paul said, "before I shoot it off."

"Look here," Preacher said. "Drops of blood. We must have hit one last night."

"Seems that way," Jonah said.

"Here's what we're going to do," Preacher said. "We're going to stick together, but when we get farther up this trail, we're going to spread out some, but stay in yelling distance. That way, find something, others can come running. Rabbit. When we fan out, you and Bleedhead go together."

"Why can't me and Bleedhead go together," Possum said.

"Because I hate you and will kill you first chance I get," Sally said.

"Valid reason," Preacher said.

Possum stewed, but said nothing.

"Me and you, Possum, we'll go together. Paul, you and Jonah."

When we came to the split in the trail, Sally and I went up into the shadows of some great trees. The trees intertwined overhead. Sunlight came through, but it wasn't overly bright, and it was only in patches. It was cool under the soft shadows.

We wound our way up a slight slope. Finally, we came to a place where we could see large footprints, for the trees broke open above us and the sunlight filled the tracks. The light in the prints looked like thin honey.

The tracks climbed upwards. Sally bent down and put her hand in one and said, "This is too big for the creatures we saw last night. I think maybe those were young ones. This one is huge. Bigger than a grizzly bear track."

"You're saying this is a papa monster?"

"Maybe a mama monster. Listen, Rabbit. We could find the trail and get out of here, just go away and leave them."

"Without horses?"

"We could make it. I could lead us out."

That's when greed caught me by the shirt tail. "I still like the idea of a couple of gold bars. One bar apiece and we're rich enough for all our ages."

"They kill us, we're dead for a lot of ages as well. If I took off, would you come with me?"

"I'd like to, Sally. Really, I would. But I came with these killers not to be a killer, but to take some of their loot."

"It's stolen."

"I've considered that, and decided I could live with taking a gold bar, just enough to start a business. It may not be just, but I tell you, I have dreamed of it."

"I'll stick for now, Rabbit. I shouldn't, but I will."

There wasn't any hunting done on our part. We found a stream and sat by that in the sunlight and ate some jerky. It tasted especially good out there in the clear morning air with the stream bubbling clear and cold at our feet. We drank from it, and the water was sweet and satisfying.

We pushed our feet together. It was silly, but when we touched it was like I had been set on fire, and when we kissed, I felt as if I were all burnt up.

It could have gone farther, but knowing where we were and that the creatures were out there, we didn't think it wise, though this was an unspoken decision between us.

The morning rolled on and the sun became warmer. We heard shots in the distance, a screech. We heard Possum yelling from somewhere not too far away. Yelling for us to come back and join up.

We got ourselves together and started back, agreeing not to mention that we had seen the tracks. When we caught up with the others, they had three of the hairy corpses at their feet, and a fourth, what could only be considered a child, was dead and strung up on a tree limb, and Possum was skinning it, grinning as he did.

"What the hell?" Sally said.

Sixty-Eight Barrels on Treasure Lake

"One of them cut through my coat with its claws," Possum said. "Figured I'd patch it up with one of their hides, and this little one will make good patchwork."

As Possum skinned, the body turned on the rope, and I saw its little face, its mouth open slightly, its eyes wide and glazed in death, a trail of snot running out of its nose and back over its face and along its forehead. Blood dripped from the corpse as Possum peeled its skin off and left its furless body hanging there. I felt the same way I would have if I had encountered Possum skinning a human baby. In fact, without its skin, it looked even more like a human child.

Jonah said, "I shot one of them, killed him first shot. Right through the heart. It didn't tear up the body much."

"It was a good shot," Preacher said.

"Damn right," Jonah said.

"Preacher and Paul got one apiece, and Possum beat this one down with his gun stock," Jonah said. "It was clinging to one of them thing's leg. These are all female. Look between their legs, under the fur you can see their slits."

"I'll take your word for it," I said.

We helped them carry the bodies back to the steamboat, because we had no choice. We had to make travois to manage it. I offered to bury the child, but Possum said we ought to leave it as a lesson to them, to fear us. We left the child hanging.

Back at the boat, we helped empty out part of the salt, bend the bodies and stuff them in the barrels. We put the salt back in with them. It turned strawberry in color.

When we finished, we looked out at the shore. It was covered in the creatures, clustered there like berries on vines, but not too close to us. They were making a noise that made me wince, swaying back and forth.

"What's that goddamn racket they're making?" Possum said.

"They're mourning," Sally said.

"Sad when you think about it," Paul said, "so I don't think about it. I think about that money they're going to bring us. I learned a long time ago, you can't think on something being right or wrong, only if it's profitable."

The hairy ones began to throw rocks at the boat. They clattered on the deck, and one hit Possum in the shoulder. It wasn't a solid hit, but it made him mad as a wet hen.

"Goddamn it," he said. "We can pot a few and load them up when the pack scrambles."

And sure enough, Possum brought a rifle to the railing and shot at them, bringing a couple down not so much due to good shooting, but due to them being clustered together like black birds on a limb. The rest of the creatures scrambled back toward the woods. Paul and Preacher shot several before they all escaped, and this time Jonah missed, but not from want of trying. I shot over their heads with my pistol, as did Sally.

"That's why you worked in a saloon and you shaved logs," Possum said. "Neither of you could hit a boar hog tied to a tree right in front of you."

Preacher and Paul gave us a look that said they might think we weren't as bad a shot as Possum thought. Those looks made me nervous, but now pretty much everything did.

We went out to get their bodies. One was still alive. Possum beat its head in with the stock of the rifle. He said we ought to save bullets. Preacher complained that he may have ruined a prime specimen.

Minutes later, Preacher said, "Several of these critters are ruined. Head's all messed up. We got to do this better."

"We should shoot for the heart," Paul said. "But maybe the surgeons would want the heart."

"It's guess work, brother," Preacher said.

"I'll tell you one thing," Possum said. "There's enough of them we ought to make an example of a few."

With that he drew his Bowie and began hacking at the necks of the ones Preacher had said were ruined. He hacked with that razor-sharp knife until their heads came off. When he finished, he said to Charlie, "Go get the fire axe, half-wit."

Sixty-Eight Barrels on Treasure Lake

Charlie did that, and he was put to work cutting down some saplings, trimming the limbs, and then me and Sally, and Jonah were given the job of sticking the heads on the posts. There were four of them.

Charlie, watching, bent his head and vomited.

Raising the posts up, me and Sally, Jonah and Charlie, we pushed the sharp ends into the ground so that the heads were raised high, dripping gore.

"That ought to show them who's boss," Possum said.

We put the bodies, except for the headless ones, in barrels and salted them down. Paul was right about one thing. If you stopped too long to think about it, it made you sick, made you feel like something less than human, made the critters seem like something a hell of a lot better than human.

As night fell, rocks began to be thrown from shore onto the boat, missing me by inches in one case. Paul and Possum had me and Sally feed the steamboat's boiler. We worked it up until there was steam, and then Charlie, who had figured out the steamboat damn quick, took it out a good way from shore. Charlie looked happy at the wheel, like he had been born to it.

The hairy ones, the steamboat, that shiny lake, that valley. I tell you, the whole thing didn't seem real. It was like some mad bastard's dream.

Everyone went to bed in the steamboat, but I lay on my pallet on the deck by myself again, felt like hammered dog shit with a cat turd on the side.

The moon's glow, behind a dark rain cloud, was fuzzy and dim, the color of my soul. I had the memory of that child of the fuzzy things in my head, being ripped free of its skin like a squirrel for dinner, shining cold and white and blood-flecked.

At some point, Sally came to me, silent as a soft wind, and we lay together, and things were so much better for a while.

Shortly before light, Sally dressed, kissed my lips, and went away, like pollen on the wind. I felt very fine. I had done it before with prostitutes in the saloon, but I had never made love, I realized.

It was a wonderful feeling and it clung to me as the sky lightened and the moon eased down and the sun eased up. It was a feeling that carried beyond day break, all the way until we were on the hunt again.

"Tell you what," Preacher said, "since you and Sally didn't kill anything yesterday, I'm going to separate the two of you. I have a feeling you might have been contemplating something other than the hunt. Today, you go with me, Sally."

"You're not my boss," she said.

"Yeah, I am," Preacher said. And he had that look again, the one that made you realize that under his good looks and nice presentation, there was something far more beastly than the animals we were hunting and stuffing in barrels.

I ended up with Possum. Being with him was like someone had nailed my dick to a burning building. I wanted to be as far away from that crazy bastard as I could be, and now he was my partner.

"You smell like pussy, boy. You get some of that girl?"

"Shut up, Possum."

"Watch who you talk to, Rabbit. I might skin you like a critter, make a patch out of you to go on the ass of my pants."

We didn't find anything right away, but as mid-day came, and we sat to eat our jerky and drink from canteens, I saw a large beast perched between a split in some high rocks. He sat there making a shadow across the face of the rocks. I was facing in his direction, and Possum was facing in the other, which was a position we tried to take if we stopped, so nothing sneaked up on us.

I had my shotgun, but it was too far away to assure a shot, and then again, I didn't want to take the shot had I been carrying a Winchester.

The beast was enormous, squatted down on its haunches, and there was a lot of gray in its fur. It seemed quite content to be out in the sunlight, not a night creature at all. Its eyes were narrowed, its face taut in what I assumed was anger, but the truth is I was guessing. I was far enough away I couldn't be sure. He may have just needed to shit.

The creature moved and there was a snorting sound as he moved, and then out of the woods that surrounded us, and climbing down out of the rocks, were dozens of the creatures, a few large ones, but most of them smaller, their dark fur glossy in the sun.

I stood up then.

Possum had seen them now. He stood up too. He started firing right away, and having good aim about him that morning, he killed two or three.

I didn't fire a shot. Perhaps I should have, but I couldn't make myself do it. They were too human, and I think seeing them in mass like that, clearly in the daylight, drove that home.

Among the group was a small female clutching a child to her breast. She held back, not coming any closer. Possum pointed his rifle, picked her to shoot as the others closed in.

I don't know exactly why I did it, but I slugged Possum, caught him one on the side of the jaw. He went down and then they swarmed us. I heard Possum scream something, then I was hit in the back of the head with what I think was a stick, because my last memory before I passed out and ate dirt was of dust and bark flying past me on one side of my head like a flight of gnats, and then it was night-night in broad daylight.

I was surprised we hadn't been ripped apart and eaten. I was more surprised to see that all my other companions were there, except Charlie who we had left on the steamboat with the horses. We were in a rough pen of twisted sticks and briars. It was of some size. It took more than a little thought and skill to make something like that. It was like being inside a giant, prickly tumbleweed.

Through the gaps in the sticks and briars, we could see them moving about, large and small, young and old. Our weapons were stacked in a pile like firewood. I could see my shotgun and pistol. I remembered then that I had the two-shoot derringer in my coat pocket. I slipped my hand in to make sure. It was still there.

Sally took my arm. There were blood stains under her nose and her lip was busted. "They surprised us."

"They surprised us all," I said.

Possum had been beat hard. He was sitting on the ground. His face looked like a spotted pup. His lip was busted and his teeth were in bad shape. They hadn't been a gift from the gods before, but now they were a jagged, bloody mess. They had spent special time with him, and I assumed it was because of the child he had skinned. His possum coat had been removed. His ragged shirt was ripped more than before. His bowler was gone. His scalped patch was flame red.

Preacher and Paul were next to each other, close to the wall of sticks and briars, looking out. Paul had a cut on his forehead and his nose was pushed to one side. Preacher was banged up as well.

Jonah, limping, came over and stood next to them and looked out as well.

"They planned against us," Jonah said. "The hairy bastards. Bitches too."

"Of course, they did," Preacher said. "We plotted against them, and they returned the favor."

"Got to admire them for that," Paul said.

Me and Sally went over to where Preacher and Paul and Jonah were, leaving Possum sitting on his ass.

"They're pretty impressive," Paul said, leaning his big frame against the wicker pen, grabbing it and tugging at it. "Doesn't look like much, but it's tightly woven."

"Good of you to appreciate their craft," Preacher said.

"Give due where it's due."

Preacher laughed. "They're going to kill us, you know?"

"Of course, I do, brother. Isn't that what we'd do?"

"Damn straight," Preacher said. "Damn, if we could have got some of those big ones, now there would have been some money."

"What the hell are they doing with those trees?" Jonah asked.

There were so many of them out there, moving around, they were what you might call a horde. I studied what they were doing, and though I didn't have it figured, I had a feeling it wasn't going to be good for us.

They had Possum's coat on the ground and they were starting to make a noise, a kind of rumbling that sounded painful, like mourning. In front of them was Possum's coat, patched with the hide of the hairy child. They had laid it out, respectfully, before them.

There were two trees that were tall and strong but skinny and supple. Many creatures were climbing up on them, thick as ants on blades of grass. There were so many of them, when they clamored near the top, the trees began to bend. They were forcing the peaks of the trees to the ground. The two trees they were swarming were close together, and when then bent, they crossed against one another. The creatures that were on the trees stayed there, turned their heads toward our cage.

Three who were free of the trees came to our cage, twisted some vines and opened it. They came in and went straight for Possum.

He tried to fight them, but they had taken his gun and his knife, having learned by observation and experience what they were about. All he had left was a struggle and bad language. They dragged him from the cage, yelling and screaming. We did nothing, because there was nothing to do.

They went out, and two of them carried Possum away while one wound the door of the cage closed with vines. It was a quick, tight weave. They were certainly more than wild animals.

Possum was carried to the bent over trees, the tips still held to the ground by the hairy ones. He was near his coat, and he suddenly stomped a foot on the patch made from the child. "Diddle all of you big squirrels," he said.

A great hooting sound went up from the creatures, and they quickly tore off Possum's clothes, bound his arms and legs to the two trees, stretching him a bit, one arm tied to one tree, one arm to the other, same with his legs.

It was then I realized what was about to happen.

A great noise of hooting and screeching and hopping on the limbs began, and it went on for some time, and then the great beast I had seen in the rocks with the silver in its fur, the biggest of all of them, came forward, swinging his long arms. He was wearing Possum's bowler. He raised an arm and faced Possum.

"You can go poke yourself in the ass with a sharp stick," Possum said.

No matter what I thought about him, he was brave.

The hairy ones leapt off the trees and the trees snapped upright, and when they did, they ripped off Possum's arms and legs and tore open his sides. Blood splashed and made the air red, guts strung out of him like red and blue ropes. When the trees were upright, they shook for a moment, then regained their original position. The hairy ones delighted in the blood that had sprinkled on them. They pulled on the guts that had fallen on the ground and had become coated in dirt and leaves. They ate the guts quickly, leaves, dirt and all. The creatures quarreled over morsels, including a heart and liver.

Up the trees they climbed again, moving as quickly as squirrels. One after another they reached the tops, and more came after them, causing them to bend.

There were hundreds of the animals, more coming out of the woods and the rocks all the time, word seeming to have been sent throughout the valley by an invisible method of communication.

The entire tribe turned and looked at the cage, at us. Those in the trees and those on the ground. It was time for another.

I placed my hand in my coat pocket and cocked the derringer. There was no use trying to fight them. They'd win, and I only had two shots.

One for Sally.

One for me.

Sixty-Eight Barrels on Treasure Lake

The brothers and Jonah were on their own.

I thought about Charlie. At some point, even his slow brain might realize we were gone. If it did, and he came ashore, he wouldn't last long either.

My head was spinning. Nothing seemed real. I found I was looking as if down a tunnel. My vision on either side of my face seemed to see nothing. There was only what was in front of me. I turned so I could see Sally. I thought I wouldn't say anything to her, just shoot her.

The same three as before came to the cage. I could tell immediately from the way they looked at me, that they had picked me. They came in quick, and even as I tried to pull the gun from my pocket, they jumped on me. My hand and the derringer hung up in my coat. I tugged, but it wouldn't come free, the gun's barrel had snagged on some stray strand of worn pocket thread.

My plans to kill Sally and myself were gone. I was going to be tied to the trunks of those trees and torn asunder with a whip of those saplings, my innards consumed.

Sally jumped in the middle of them like a panther, but there were too many. They flung her into one of the cage walls. She bounced off the wicker weave and laded smack down on her face in the dirt. Her hands clawed at the ground as she tried to pull herself up.

Dragging me from the cage, they began to yank at my clothes, but before they could be ripped from me, a female of the tribe came screeching and hooting and slapping at the others, trying to knock them back. Her small child was slung over one shoulder, both of its fists grasping her fur and hanging to her like part of her body.

The others fought back. But it was brief, for out of nowhere came the big silver one wearing the derby. He came swinging and yelling and slinging the others aside like they were leaves.

The creatures hurried out of his way, gathered near the bent trees. The big silver one beat at his chest with both fists and growled so ferociously the mountains picked up the sounds and echoed them back to us.

The others quit chattering and grunting and hooting and such, and then I understood.

The female that had tried to help me was the one who I had saved from Possum's gun. I guessed then that she was the silver one's mate, the little one their child, and that the big guy wearing Possum's bowler was the boss.

The silver one called to the others in a howling voice, and three members of the tribe ran to the cage, opened it, rushed inside and dragged out Sally. I tried to get to her, as I was no longer held, but the silver one brought out his great hand and rested it on my chest. Sally was brought to me and dropped. She rose slowly to her feet, stood beside me, shaking, as was I.

The silver one gave off a little hoot, and the three went back in the cage and grabbed Jonah. The trees had already been bent by the mass of beasts, and two of them stood with vines to secure him.

Jonah turned toward us, his face white as a cold, winter moon. "For the love of god, help me," he said.

God wasn't there that day, or any day, I figured.

They fastened Jonah to the blood-stained trees.

I glanced back at Preacher and Paul, they both smiled at me, like it had all been a big joke. I saw then that my derringer had in fact come out of my pocket, and was lying in the center of the cage.

"There lies your freedom," I said to Paul and Preacher. "Two shots. Use them wisely."

They looked and saw the gun.

The silver one, as I began to think of him, was pushing us away from the others, perhaps to get us moving while their blood lust was on Jonah, who had begun to bawl like a baby.

We took the silver one's hint, and began to go quickly away from the tribe. I looked back at the big beast as we went, standing there, head held to one side, the bowler resting on it like it was made to be there. Then I turned my full attention to the skedaddle. When we were around a bend of shadowy trees that bordered the narrow trail, we broke for it and ran.

Sixty-Eight Barrels on Treasure Lake

We heard the great hooting sound of the crowd start up again, and then, even though we had already covered some distance, we heard the whipping of the trees, and splats of blood and innards landed in the limbs above us and some of it dripped down and speckled our faces.

On we ran, Sally in the lead, trying to reach the lake.

Behind us, I heard the derringer pop once, followed by a short delay, and then one more shot.

I expected the hairy ones to defy silver fur and come after us, but they did not.

We came out of the woods and down a rise, and there was the lake, and out in the lake was the steamboat, anchored and waiting.

Without discussing it, we grabbed one of the canoes, pushed it into the water, and paddled toward the steamboat.

As we sailed across the smooth blue water, Sally said, "Why did they save us?"

I told her about the mother and the child.

"But why me?"

"Because you tried to save me. They saw what we meant to each other."

"That strikes me as terribly human," she said.

We spent a week or so on the water, living off the food on the ship. There were lots of potatoes and onions and tins of water, and there were a few rotting squashes and the like. We even used the rotting squash by dropping it in hot water and boiling it with some beef jerky to make soup.

We helped Charlie shovel out the horseshit and feed and water the horses, who were beginning to look rough from lack of exercise.

One night me, Sally, and Charlie sat on the deck and looked toward shore. At night, the creatures gathered in great numbers and tossed rocks at the water, even though we were nowhere near them. Eventually, they came in the day, and they had the guns that had been taken from us. They pulled triggers and accidently shot one another, and then managed to fire out at the water, the shotgun pellets falling well short of the boat, but a few shots from rifles whizzed by us or struck the boat, took out some windows.

"Damn," Sally said. "They really are becoming us."

"Well, it was us who stirred them," I said.

They hauled their accidental dead away, and then one morning and one full night, none of the beasts were visible. We decided to investigate, cranked up the steamboat, and Charlie steered it toward shore.

No sooner had we arrived, then the hairy ones came out of the woods and down to the shore. A younger, smaller creature was now wearing the bowler, and the silver hide of the one who had helped us was crusted with blood and draped over the younger one's shoulders like a cape. The hide had been skinned off Silver One's skull, and it was flapping against the young buck's back.

The creatures had a new king. And the new king carried Possum's rifle as well as wore his hat.

The rifle was pointed at us and it was cocked and the young buck worked it quite well, probably due to watching Possum handle it. Fortunately, it only had a couple bullets in it, and once they were fired the rifle was no longer a danger.

Angered, the beast beat the rifle on the ground until it came asunder.

We steamed back out to the middle of the lake.

As our food became low, we fished, and sometimes at night we took the canoe in and foraged along the shore for roots, fruit and nuts from nearby trees.

In time, we noticed that the creatures were no longer coming to shore, that we had not heard hide nor hair of them in quite some time. We decided to roll those barrels that contained the bodies of their kind out on the shore. We popped the lids and left them.

The barrels sat there for a few days before one morning we woke up, looked out, and saw they were gone. They had taken them, bodies, salt, and all.

We watched that shore line for quite some time after that, but they didn't show. We decided they just might have lost interest in us. Or maybe they were merely lying in wait, as before.

One day, I said to Sally and Charlie, "I think if you're up for it, we can chance going out."

"I don't want to go," Charlie said. "I can fish, and I can manage to cut lumber on the far side for firewood."

The far side was pretty much a straight rock wall, but there were trees not far into the narrow shore, and as best as we could tell, none of the creatures lived there. But there was no way over that rock wall, and no way for even those climbing beasts to come down it. The trees didn't grow near that high.

We found we could take the horses and mules out there, and we could let them forage just off the shore where the grass grew high before it came to the slick rock wall. We could even ride them about, galloping them along the shore and into the trees, until we came up against the wall. The shore line on either end of where we rode the horses split and there was wide, deep water in the splits, so none of the creatures could come around and show up on our private shore line. We sometimes went there to build a fire and cook outside, as we hadn't even put a dent in the food supply on the steamboat, and there were fish to catch and fruit and nuts and wild vegetables to eat in abundance. Charlie played his guitar and sang during those cookouts. He was quite good. That place of ours on the far shore was nice and safe, but it was limited.

And that was why Sally and I decided we had to leave. It was all too confining.

"Seems like a big chance sticking around, Charlie," I said.

We were out on the deck of the steamboat and the sun was going down.

"I never been happy until I came here," he said. "I ain't so stupid here. I can work this boat, and I can survive. I don't need much."

"You aren't stupid, Charlie," Sally said. "You just aren't complex."

I could certainly see Charlie's point about staying where we were. When the sun set on the mountain and the last of its fire fell into the lake, and then the milky moon and stars came out made the water silver, it was a mighty pretty place.

"You could stay," Charlie said.

"I think me and Rabbit have to leave," Sally said.

We decided to swim my mule and her horse in. We saddled them up, brought an axe with us, and Sally brought a solid stick of firewood. Those were our weapons. There were a few guns and some ammunition on board, but we left that for Charlie, except for a ragged, .44 converted Colt with a small sack of shells. Sally carried that in the pocket of her overalls.

"Glad you're taking those critters," Charlie said. "That'll leave me with some stock to ride and sport, but I'll have less to fool with. One of them dies, I'll eat it."

"Practical," I said.

"Got dynamite on board too, some they had left. I want to leave, might can dynamite the lake where the river is blocked off from it. I could go out that way. I watched Paul do what he did, and I been around miners. I could do it I wanted to."

"I don't doubt it," I said.

"What I'm thinking, though, is I wish the way we come in was blocked up too. This is like the Garden of Eden I was told about, though I ain't got no Eve."

He looked at Sally.

"Nope," she said.

We lowered the gangway, and locked it with the chains just before it hit the water. I climbed on Clarence, and Sally mounted her horse. We bid Charlie good bye, and sporting our axe and stick of firewood, we leapt the horses off the gangway plank and into the water.

Sixty-Eight Barrels On Treasure Lake

The animals had a hard time of the lake, them being pretty much confined for so long, having only a bit of exercise from time to time on the far shore. But they swam and made it, leaving our legs drenched and dripping lake water.

We eased them onto the trail, looked up where the mountains split due to Paul's dynamite. I stopped by the hollow in the tree and took out the sticks of fused dynamite I had put aside. I put them in my saddle bag, and on we rode.

Moonlight rested on the split in the mountain, and the way it hit the shiny rock floor, where it tilted up, it was like we were riding a path to heaven. Several times, I heard movement in the trees, and I smelled the creatures, but we didn't see any and none came after us. Maybe they saw which way we were going and were proud to see us leave. Whatever the case, we continued without interference.

When we got through the trail, and on the other side, there was a burst of birds. The near fleshless heads of Preacher, Paul, Possum, and Jonah were mounted on the same sticks we had used to stick the heads of the hairy ones on.

The beast had truly learned from us, and none of it was good.

I looked at how risky the opening was, way the rocks were hanging after Paul blew the path open.

"Go on a stretch and wait," I said.

"Why?"

"You'll hear why," I said.

Sally took the reins to Clarence and rode out a piece on her horse, leading my mule behind her. I climbed up one side of the rocks with the dynamite. I put all the sticks in one spot, where the rocks looked to be hanging in a half ass way, and then I lit the fuses and scuttled down.

They dynamite went off before I made it to the ground.

I woke up with my ears ringing, and Sally cradling my head in her lap.

"You idiot," she said.

I raised up. It was hard, like maybe I had a rock on my chest, though I didn't. But I was damn sure bruised.

The path was closed. Someone really wanted over it, they could do it, but not with a horse. They'd have to want to climb.

"Why, Rabbit?"

"It's what Charlie wanted. He's got his own kind of paradise down there."

"That's a fact," she said.

We mounted up and rode on out.

I'll tell all of you, right now, there's no use in asking where that valley and that lake are. I won't tell it. I'm not sure I could find it anyway, and Sally hasn't tracked so much as a pig in a pen in the last few years. And we got the young one on the way. It's going to be a girl, says the midwife, but how she thinks she knows, I can't figure.

I do wonder now and again if Charlie is still there with that boat load of gold, and how the creatures are doing. Have they gone back to their simple ways, or did they change forever? Are they split amongst themselves and making war, having learned what killing was all about from us? Is one of them still wearing Possum's bowler like a king's crown?

One other thing I ought to mention. Before we left out of there, I put a gold bar in each of our saddle bags. That's how we came to own this saloon we got. That's how Sally bought a saw mill and hired the folks that work there. That's why this town is named Sally Rabbit.

Me, these days, I go by Mr. Rabbit.

Drink up.

Copyright Information

"Fishing for Stories" Copyright © 2020 By Bizarre Hands, LLC.

"What Joe Lansdale Means To Me" Copyright © 2020 by Robin Hobb.

Black Hat Jack Copyright © 2014 By Bizarre Hands, LLC.

"On Lost Worlds" Copyright © 2020 by Poppy Z. Brite.

"Fishing for Dinosaurs" Copyright © 2014 By Bizarre Hands, LLC. First appeared in *Limbus, Inc.: Book II*, edited by Brett J. Talley.

"I Should've Known Better" Copyright © 2020 by Richard Chizmar.

The Ape Man's Brother Copyright © 2012 By Bizarre Hands, LLC.

"The Yarning" Copyright © 2020 by David J. Schow.

Prisoner 489 Copyright © 2014 By Bizarre Hands, LLC.

"Harryhausen, Houdini, and Hisownself" Copyright © 2020 by Norman Patridge.

Sixty-Eight Barrels on Treasure Lake Copyright © 2020 By Bizarre Hands, LLC.